Earth & Evermore

The
Lighted Blade

John Consalvo

EARTH & EVERMORE: THE LIGHTED BLADE
Copyright © John Consalvo, 2015
All rights reserved

ISBN: 978-1-62217-481-2

To understand this story, it is imperative to embrace this one belief: the following events have already transpired in the past and in the future, while still remaining firmly planted in the present.

Contents

Introduction

I wanted to end it all. Indeed, I did. And yes, it is I, the author, speaking. I can vividly remember that Saturday afternoon before Memorial Day when I cried out to the King of the Universe, "Lord, in all of your perfection, I clearly must be the blemish on your record! Looking back on my years, I cannot fathom any usefulness or purpose for my existence. Why create me at all? I despise being played like some pawn in a foolish contest. It wasn't like I had a choice to be born!"

What happened next was quite amazing. I heard a still, small voice within my own heart speaking this question through a flutter of goose bumps:

"Are you sure?"

That was it. It wasn't an answer. But it was this question alone that opened my mind toward the endless possibilities I never could have imagined before that day. It was there when Gardenia was known to me (and that long before my existence here on Earth) that I, yes, even I, could have walked and talked with this mighty King of all Galaxies, the Creator of the heavens. Thoughts I had often pondered as a child were clearly coming back to me. The purposes of my days were slowly being revealed and my understanding of good and evil was gaining clarity. Most importantly, it was love that I had been introduced to — true love, which, if anything, is inconvenient and unknown to many of us.

John Consalvo

2014

CHAPTER 1

Establishing Soul Mates

G ardenia, one of the largest and most influential planets
in Elevemada, the Galaxy of Souls, was considered one
of the ten great worlds. Its surface was of pure beauty,
boasting mammoth double-arched trees, deep green grass,
abundant sparkling water, vibrant florae, and great cliffs with
shimmering edges of white stone. A uniquely delightful array
of souls, animals, and other life forms lived on and in its lands,
skies, and seas. Neither heat nor cold punished Gardenia; its
only seasons were spring and fall, similar to those seasons in the
temperate regions of Earth.

Each of the great worlds in the galaxy had its own
distinction. Alpha was famous for its knowledge keepers;
Omega, for its impressive lightning; Seocia, for the mermaids
that populated its deep oceans; Neumbessa, for its gentle souls,

the most sensitive and peace-loving in the galaxy; Fricto, for its vast ice caverns, never mapped by any, save for its reclusive, thick-furred inhabitants; Cymblali for music that even the most sorrowful could joyously dance to; Zae, where life was a festivity and the very air made one drunk with laughter; Remnas, never the same season from one day to the next; the desert planet of Banth, for its dancing moons protected by the mighty blue elephant of Dar, and especially its exquisite, diamond-shaped moon, Etherna, which revolved around the planet in the opposite direction from its sisters. Gardenia's loveliness, however, was known throughout the galaxy and considered by most to be unparalleled.

Soaring through the air like dragonflies, Jovan and Bethany raced each other around the planet's circumference as usual.

"Told you I was still faster," taunted Jovan. "You haven't come close to touching me in a thousand cycles. Come on! Keep up!"

"You're barely winning, Jovan. I'm getting closer and closer each time," Bethany snapped as she attempted not to feed into Jovan's ego. "Your favor is bound to run out sometime. Don't be surprised when I pass you next cycle. I don't want to hear you cry about it to the rest of the Blade when it happens."

"Beth, did you feel that?" Jovan shouted while maintaining his lead. "I think Jaesu is watching!"

"Wha-where? How d'ya know?" Bethany answered, trying to keep up while looking around.

"My soul feels goose bumps; he's got to be here. Now I definitely have to win."

"Yes! I feel them, too. Wait...Jovan!" Bethany tried to keep up, but with a final burst of energy, Jovan had all but secured his victory.

A huge pink cloud of stardust was up ahead: their finish line.
Jovan, always confident that he would win whenever they raced,
began to taunt Bethany some more.

"Look, I can even close my eyes and still win."

"You're unbelievable sometimes, you know that?"

"And here it is! Yes, shockingly, another victory for Jovan.
And the choruses of angels go wild!" Jovan said jokingly as he
crossed the finish line.

Jovan and Bethany were the dearest of friends. They were
both part of a closely-knit unit called the Lighted Blade. Their
days were spent racing each other, laughing, joking and having
fun as if they were children. Although they could be brash at
times, both were very well-liked throughout Gardenia.

This duo was made up of the two fastest flyers on the planet.
They were souls who didn't need spacecrafts, broomsticks, or any
tangible devices to travel. The souls of Gardenia looked identical
to humans but could fly and were free of flesh, bone, and
gravity's restrictions. They didn't need to eat or sleep, yet often
did so for pleasure. Souls lived in houses or aeries or clearings in
the woods—wherever they wished. All of their housekeeping was
a kind of play, expressing their personalities. Some found one
place and went back to it regularly; others liked to keep on the
move.

Jovan and Bethany had been living for thousands of
cycles—what those on Earth would call years—yet their
appearances mirrored those of fifteen-year-old human beings.
This was common on Gardenia. A soul's appearance matched its
personality. A wise soul could appear older while a fun-loving
soul could appear younger, with variations of everything in
between. Souls were wiser than human beings in many ways but

also far more innocent. Jovan and Bethany both were five-and-a-half feet tall—average size for a soul.

"There you two are. Been lookin' everywhere! Gettin' squabbly again?" bellowed a medium-sized brown-and-yellow eagle owl flying toward them. "I wonder what it could be about ...*hmm*, let me guess, *ummm* ...maybe, same thing it always is? Bethany losin' again, Jo?"

"MALVIN!" yelled Bethany in a pouty voice. "That's not nice. And for your information, I am getting faster and faster. Right, Jovan?"

"If you say so," said Jovan. "Malvin, she might just beat Brutus, the snail, on Neumbessa."

"You're hilarious," Bethany responded, rolling aqua blue eyes and swinging her light brown hair around the owl's face in one motion.

"Well, Bethany, at least you be gettin' fasta," Malvin quipped in his noticeable owl dialect, pushing Bethany's hair off his beak. "I don't suppose I'll be growin' any tallah."

"Come on, Malvin, not that again," said Jovan. "If Bethany can convince herself that she is getting faster, then I don't think it's half bad of you to believe that you will one day rival Punru in size. What do you think, Beth?"

"Malvin, don't listen to him," Bethany chimed in. "You're perfect the way you are. We are made differently to show our beauty in all sizes, colors, and shapes. Otherwise, we'd be the same, and that would be boring, especially if we were like Jovan over here."

"I not think so. They always select Punru to rule over the Owls and Seraphs tournament. He be a great-in-stature, wise, and fair owl. But I would liken a chance, too," responded Malvin.

"Ah, useless I am," he sighed.

"Has King Sardonia of Seocia decided who will rule the game this time around?" asked Bethany.

"Actually," Jovan replied, tightening his lips as if he did not want to give bad news, "I'm pretty sure it's Punru, guys. You know how it is."

Owls and Seraphs was the greatest sporting event throughout the Galaxy of Souls. The event had many moving parts, so to outsiders, it was difficult to follow and often viewed as utter chaos. But for those from the planets within the Elevemada, it was a most exciting time. One wise owl was chosen to officiate the tournament as the Ruler of Games, which was considered one of the greatest honors that could be bestowed upon an owl. It was usually bestowed upon Punru, an extremely wise, quick, witty, knowledgeable, strong, and large owl. Punru was eight feet tall and four feet wide, but legend had it that during these games he could stretch out to eight hundred feet. His feathers were colored dark blue, his claws made of pure gold. Nothing escaped his gaze during the games.

"Which reminds me... *um*...yes, that's a-why I was a-lookin'," Malvin added. "Aren't you both s'pose to be somewhere?"

Bethany looked at the owl, puzzled. "Be somewhere? I don't think...oh, no, Jo!"

"Yeah, we're in trouble," Jovan answered as he realized the time. "Gotta move quick, Beth!"

Bethany grabbed Jovan by the hand, and the duo flew speedily toward the surface of Gardenia.

"Wait! Slow d-down!" yelled Malvin, trying his very best to keep up.

"Qualifying match, Mal. If we are late again, Dara will let us have it for sure."

*   *   *

They descended quickly, landing upon the planet's surface near the brilliant river, Triumphant Waters, which was in their home city of Leafy Lantern. Jovan and Bethany were to meet the five remaining members of their unit, Lighted Blade, but none were there.

"Dara and the others must have left without us," Jovan said.

"Yeah, well, considering that we were to start at the second sunrise, the contest might be over by now," Bethany added.

They maneuvered themselves through the city quickly, looking for their teammates, and finally came to Scepter Mountain, which was located in the heart of the city. Like everything else in Gardenia, it was a sight to behold. The lower level was a carpet of leaves encompassing numerous colors. Dark red, green, yellow, orange, and sky blue were stitched into an ever-changing mosaic. The trees themselves, which began on the second level, were made of leaves that peeled off and fluttered down, only to return to their tree of origin over and over, shortly after caressing the ground.

Even in the midst of so much dazzling, moving color, Bethany was able to notice a pink sparkly figure reflecting off of one of the streams coming down the mountainside.

"Jo," she whispered, "I think that's Crystalline over there."

"The lioness?!" he yelled. Bethany admonished him to keep his voice down. "Aren't we going against them? And Scepter?"

"*Um*, yeah," Bethany responded. "Which is why I am questioning our walking through their mountain."

"Yeah. Not sure what I was thinking."

"You know," Malvin, who'd finally caught up and was out of breath, interjected, "for two beings who are literally the fastest in the world, you are both late an awful lot. And p-pretty slow in thought, at least, from an owl's perspective."

The pink shadow came upon them swiftly.

"Jovan! Bethany! Are you guys finished?" It wasn't the lioness; it was Dara. "We do have a qualifying tournament match today. Where have you both been?" she asked demandingly.

"Sorry," Bethany replied with her head lowered. "We got caught up in racing."

"Of course, you did. And did you win, Beth? *Um...*wait. Don't bother answering that. Either way, if we are to have any chance of advancing, we're going to need that speed from both of you," Dara answered while measuring the length of her long, pink, spiked hair in the reflection of a nearby fountain.

Dara, as leader of Lighted Blade, kept them together. Many knew her as gentle, fun, and caring, but no one would dare mess with her. She commanded respect from her unit and they, in turn, adored her.

"Does that mean it's not too late?" Bethany asked excitedly.

Dara sighed in response. "Well, if you mean 'is it acceptable to not be on time?' Then in that case, it is too late."

"Sorry, Dara. It's really my fau—"

"I know it is, Jovan," Dara retorted with a quick wave of her hand toward his face. "Let's get you up to speed. Oh, and by the way, Punru couldn't make the local contest. Malvin would have finally had his chance had he not needed to look for you. The teams settled on Foax instead."

Jovan and Bethany looked at each other and felt unsettled because they had let their friend down.

9

"Foax? She is so...*aagh*! That red, self-absorbed—"

"Bethany!" Dara shouted. "Quite unlike you. And now is not the time. This is a perfect example of how our choices have consequences—not just on us, but others as well. You could have altered Malvin's destiny just now. He could be fulfilling a lifelong dream, but no, he had to find you. Start thinking of those things the next time you both decide to gallivant around on game day."

"Well, Miss Dara, if I may—"

"No, you may not, Malvin. I am well aware of your feelings toward the red owlet. But each second is crucial here, so if you don't mind, my team needs to get going," Dara answered back as she lifted her head up. "Oh, and Malvin? Thank you for finding them." She blew a kiss his way in appreciation.

Malvin blushed and glided away to allow Dara the needed time to strategize with her two latecomers.

"Look, guys, don't think I am being hard on you without purpose. I am just as hard on myself. The only reason I bumped into you here was because I was searching for clues as to where Black could be. I admit complete fault, because while the seven lionesses we're up against seem to have a thorough plan, we don't. And that's on me. I'd just as soon take it on myself and wing it. But that kind of a plan can only go so far. I am sorry," Dara said humbly.

"Now that we are all happy and sorry, how are we going to win?" Bethany asked.

"Well, Dawn may be the smallest of us, but I'd wager she has heard every word we've said, no matter how far away or into the game she is."

"Unless she is being chased by one of Scepter," Jovan added.

"Wait. The game is already happening? I—"

"Yes, aren't you focused on what Dara is saying?" Jovan said mockingly with a wink.

"Back to the topic, guys. Come on! Remember, the new rules state that the captain must be captured by the opposing captain in order to win. This is where we could have used Dawn the most. That is where I didn't strategize. What that means is only I can capture Black, and only she can capture me. I need to know where to find her and keep her from finding me. That's where you both come in."

"Well, Jacen can see miles and miles and even more miles ahead. He would sure be useful in this strategy or whatever it is that we are doing," Bethany mentioned.

"Yeah, and if there's a way that he could relate what we are seeing to Dawn and—"

"See? Jovan, that is brilliant. And a perfect example of how that brilliance could have been used had you been here on time!" Dara admonished, but more playfully this time. "Okay, look. I will find Jacen. I think he was camped out near the Tree of Wonders, where the owlet is perched. Something tells me he's going to want the same vantage point as the gamekeeper. Once there, I will tell him to speak what he sees, so that Dawn, no matter where she is, can hear him—"

"Wait! We are forgetting something important here," Bethany interrupted. "What about Tree? That's the lioness with supersonic hearing. Whatever Jacen says, she will pick up, won't she? If she hasn't heard us already."

"I am well aware, Beth. I can handle Tree," said Dara as she marked the length of her nose with blue fruit paint while staring at the slightly taller Bethany.

"Stealth mode it is then, I guess," Jovan chimed in.

"I think you're right, Jo. Hopefully, Dawn is making arrangements as we speak," Dara answered.

"No one is more brilliantly minded than Marcus, and, of course, Glynn would be able to—"

"We've said enough already, Jovan," Dara answered as her hand covered his mouth. She had detected a lioness prowling. "I'm going to rely on you two from this point on to figure it out. It won't be long before Black senses me lurking around her mountain. Time to go."

With that, Dara darted out toward the Tree of Wonders in Gardenia's capital city, Elleb.

"Wow! We just got pretty thrashed there," Jovan said, shaking his head, disappointed.

"Hey! Cheer up! We can't afford to have you getting all mopey. Where are we going to go next?" Bethany asked, floating her hand through his brown hair.

Jovan paused for a moment as he gathered his thoughts together. "The mansion, of course."

"The mansion? Like Millennia Mansion? The library?"

"Absolutely. I am sure Marcus is there, and knowing our brother, he is reading some piece of literature for apparently no reason whatsoever."

"Well, how is that going to help us? And shouldn't he be scouting for Dara as well?"

"Let's get there first and see what happens."

Jovan wrapped his arms around Bethany and, at light speed, at which they could travel for short distances, the duo vanished.

* * *

Black had reasoned with her team that chasing after any opponents, besides the captain, would be a waste of time. She did, however, expect her fellow lionesses to keep the area scouted well and report back to her if Dara was spotted. Of course, Black needed to be sure that she wasn't being tracked by the opposing team either.

The Royal Gardens, where she was headed, started outside the palace walls and continued on for several miles into an area surrounded by a phalanx of tall trees. As Black neared her destination, she did not see anyone from either unit. What she did see was a garden forest dotted with plants and flowers of various species and sizes, split in two by the path of silver mist she had been lurking on. The surrounding elements had formed the mist beneath her paws as there was no solid walkway within the garden. Black couldn't help but smile as several delphiniums greeted her with a wave of their palatinate petals and a humble bow. Some of the flowers she had passed were almost three feet high, while others were significantly smaller. Yet they all provided an equal sense of life and laughter and made great company for anyone enjoying the garden.

As the lioness walked, her deep yellow eyes and silver whiskers shone brightly and were quite noticeable. Not only did the flowers greet her warmly, but even the trees gave welcoming shakes of their branches.

Aside from being a competitive lead cat, Black was the magnificent Queen Amana's most trusted advisor and had a love for all things within Gardenia. As she continued to walk and receive peaceful greetings, in turn and humbly, Black lowered her head toward the flowers and trees in respect.

The cat walked deeper into the shadowy parts of the garden, where the trees became more numerous and the stature of the flowers increased considerably. She heard footsteps. Quickly, she jumped behind one of the mammoth oaks. The sound became louder and louder until Black was able to see the silhouettes of figures around a nearby tree.

"Crystalline? Pastel?" called Black, annoyed that the noises weren't coming from Marcus. "I'm surprised to see you both so soon. Have you encountered Dara already?"

"Yes, my lady," Crystalline responded. "It was exactly as you said. And we did exactly as you commanded."

"She was cunning enough to sense us, but obviously not to capture us," said Pastel.

"Cunning?" Black answered back. "I am not sure I would agree. She noticed you at our den, did she not? What will happen when she is on foreign terrain, when she doesn't know her way as well? Remember, they have to be ready for what's out there!" Black ended her discourse with a sigh. "Where is she now?"

At that moment, Daffodil, another lioness, joined the gathering. "She ran back to retrace her steps. It's not what I would have done, but as much as I love her, she's quite difficult to understand at times."

"Very well," purred the lead cat. "Well, girls, I know Marcus is around here. It's time to break this up. But keep your hiding limited to this area. Waves is by the sea and Clouds is roaming the high points of the cities. So we should be all set there. With that said, Pastel, it's probably wise for you to take the reins. Seek out Clouds and Waves and find out what they have seen. I've kept Tree rather stationary for the time being to... listen in on any distractions. Once we nab Marcus, then we will be able to quickly end this."

"How so?" asked Pastel. "You still will have Dara to catch, which might not be easy. Actually, aren't we supposed to be helping them win?"

"And what good would that do? They would get routed in the real tournament. Not to mention, you know that I despise losing," Black replied. "Besides, we have quickly identified some of Dara's deficiencies. And I know Marcus; information flows out of him with every breath. Without him even knowing it, I'll bet he'll reveal a bit of his personal strategy to me when I find him. The guy boasts of his own knowledge so much, he should have been born on Alpha. Marcus's input will give us the insight we need to capture Dara, end the game, and get back to helping the queen secure the kingdom. Using Marcus is the smart choice. He knows his leader's mind, and he is brilliant; there is no shame in tapping into that resource."

*   *   *

Dara reached the Tree of Wonders. She saw Jacen, the tallest of her group, positioning himself off a section of jagged-edged rocks behind where Foax was hovering. The owlet was completely focused, using her vision and wisdom to govern the game.

Dara swiftly moved toward Jacen, but he shook his head and placed his hand over his mouth, as if to tell her to be mindful of her words. His eyes went up toward the tree in front of him. Dara turned to follow his gaze. Naturally camouflaged in the high branches was Tree, the lioness who had been ordered to remain stationary. Dara immediately charged toward the tree in an attempt to shake the cat out. Tree jumped down, noticeably annoyed to be removed from her space. She sarcastically hissed at Dara before strolling off to find another place to spy from.

"You chased her away; I hoped you would have allowed her to remain unnoticed," said Jacen.

"Be still," Dara responded, peering into his white eyes. "She can still hear us. Tell me what your super eyes have seen. I know you saw something. You must have. Tell me."

"You know me well! Indeed, I looked into Black's eyes early on to get an idea of her strategy. I think she noticed something, but I'm not sure she picked up on what it was. I would have whispered it so that Dawn could hear me, but Tree was skulking. I needed to be careful. These cats know what they're doing."

"We'll need to be careful of what we say to one another," said the captain. "Look in my eyes and into my thoughts and tell me if we have a chance."

Jacen looked through Dara's eyes and deep into her thoughts. He saw Dara's planning conversations with Jovan and Bethany. He chuckled and then shook his head with a smirk. "You are crazy, you know that?" he said. "It's a risk, so be sure to bring a book."

"A book?" Dara questioned. "*Hmm...*that sure sounds like Marcus." She lightheartedly kissed the top of Jacen's silver and white-colored head as a "thank you" before taking off toward the mansion.

* * *

Black entered Millennia Mansion. It was an extraordinary place full of knowledge—books, holograms, dreams, learned histories, and prophetic futures. Although it was never considered in the same category as the great libraries on Alpha, it still was quite impressive and a landmark for planet natives. There were several columns throughout the halls and rooms made of marble with leaves spiraling up and down the walls. The leaves changed colors to reflect the moods and emotions of the readers in the room. If most were reading something sad, the leaves would turn to shades of dark blue. If they were reading adventure stories or battle tales, the leaves turned hot red. And if the subject matter was joyous or comical, the leaves displayed bright yellows, pale blues, rosy pinks, or the green of spring buds. Under extremely rare circumstances, when the topic was death-related, the leaves would darken to midnight black. This was rare because death was mostly unknown in Gardenia and throughout the Galaxy of Souls, as a whole. The vast majority of beings had lived for thousands of cycles and expected to live for millions more. Death was a mere rumor, something that happened in other galaxies, but not here.

Black walked into a room lit with different shades of blue where she saw Marcus in plain sight. He was sitting on a giant green leaf pad, reading a book.

"Soaking in sadness, are we?" asked Black. "Finding you in a library certainly is not surprising, but I didn't expect to find you not hiding at all."

"Once again, you rely on what you see, great cat," Marcus responded in a deep, untroubled voice; his gaze never leaving his book. "And no, I'm not reading anything melancholy. The leaves recommended that I read *The Blossoming of One Lavender Plant*, as they consider it quite joyful. However, I am unmoved by it, and thus they think I am sad because I don't share their joy."

Marcus combed his hand through his thick black and gold hair and lifted his eyes to the leaves. "Look," he said to them, "don't be unhappy. I'm not usually emotionally touched by such things. That's how I am made. I appreciate you sharing with me this story of yours. But I read for the knowledge; you should know this. Take no offense."

"Well, mighty teacher, would you tell me the story?" asked Black jestingly. "Too bad the new rules don't allow me to capture you now, seeing that you wouldn't resist anyway. Yet it really doesn't matter as your Dara is no closer to finding me than she was when she and I first parted."

"Ah, yes…the game. I had almost forgotten," Marcus said in an uninterested tone as if the game were child's play. "Well, the book doesn't offer the adventures of Scepter or the mighty battles of Orion or even the Blue Elephant of Dar, but there is some… *uh*, well, it's pitifully shameful. The premise of the book is that, unlike most plants, this lavender plant is barely able to survive on sunlight and water. No one bothers to figure out why or what to do; the plant's guardians are far more interested in their own lives and take the plant completely for granted. So the plant struggles to breathe, longing for any life or company, even for those dreadful flies and bees and gnats bantering about in Seocia, to land upon it and begin the nurturing process."

"That's it?" said Black. "Well, that's a total bore."

The leaves within the library hall responded to her words by turning a very dark blue, and some even turned fiery orange in annoyance.

"*Um*…what I meant was…yeah," she muttered, trying not to hurt their feelings. "What I meant was, surely there must be some additional details Marcus is leaving out of this fascinating story."

This seemed to pacify the leaves; lighter colors of blue threaded through their curves.

"Well, I would be happy to read the entire story to you, if you like," chuckled Marcus.

"Exactly what I was hoping for," Black responded, in a noticeably sarcastic tone. "I knew I should have let you be," she whispered.

"'Chapter One,'" he began quickly in a robust voice. "'The Origin of Seed Law.'"

Black could not contain herself. Sitting there was maddening. She had a match to win, so she lept across the room toward Marcus in order to shake his rhythm and get him to speak of something useful.

The leaves, however, saw this as a sign of disrespect to their most sacred story. Two of the largest leaves shot out and clapped over her face while she was in midair, exhaling a chemical that happened to put several creatures, including big cats, into a short-term sleep.

"That put her out for sure," said Marcus. "I know it's a legendary story to you, but there was no way she was going to get through it. I can always count on your wisdom," he said to the leaves. A couple of the larger ones that he was using for armrests slapped his palms in a display of mutual congratulation.

*　*　*

Jovan and Bethany were hidden in the rafters. It had been Jovan's plan to have Marcus hide in plain sight, although he did not reveal this to Dara. Marcus, with his gift for drawing out a conversation, would provide an excellent distraction, long enough for Dara to catch up. Although Dara was the leader of the group and Marcus thought to be the most knowledgeable, Jovan had a knack for putting together quick-witted strategies that seemed to work out. Aside from his great speed, this was a gift he carried with him called favor. It wasn't tangible; he never knew when it could be harnessed, but when it occurred, it was easy for those around him to see it.

The two speedsters leaped down in front of Marcus. "Nice work!" Jovan said to Marcus. "I wasn't sure she'd buy it."

"Thanks, Jo," Marcus replied. "Now, let's hope Dara put the pieces together and turns her attention to here rather than to chasing around clues."

"What if she doesn't?" Bethany asked. "Shouldn't we come up with a contingency plan, just in case?"

"No faith in your leader, I see," Dara said as she unexpectedly entered the room. "I must say, team...quite impressive. Looking at the three of you and seeing her asleep... well, I'm not even going to ask. Not sure how this could play out if we ever made it to the finals, but hey, a win is a win, right? Let's get this over with. She is going to be one cranky kitty when she wakes up a loser." Dara briskly walked over to secure Black's capture and win the game.

Quick as lightning, Black jumped up and wrapped her paws securely around Dara, to the amazement of all. As was customary in the games, the keepers were attentive to whatever was happening within their playing boundaries.

Before anyone could speak, Foax flew in, batting her eyelashes and fanning herself. "Black has captured Dara! Scepter wins! Game agreed." She then flew away nonchalantly.

Malvin saw this and was annoyed, realizing that Foax seemed to disrespect the library, where soft speech or whispers were required. "Oh...um, sorry," he said to those who were reading. "Her first big match. She doesn't know," he whispered.

"Marcus, you swindler, I had a feeling you'd pull something tricky. Nice touch," Black said. "And, leaves, I'm quite surprised at you. However, Dara, I am pleased at the evolution of your thought process throughout the contest, you could have won this. And that Jacen, seeing into my thoughts...well, you all performed better than I expected."

Dara, uncharacteristically annoyed with herself, responded, "Thanks, Black, really. But it doesn't matter. We lost. I really, really thought...I mean, really hoped we had a shot at this one. I'm not even sure why the queen picked us to challenge you guys."

"I bet I know why," said a familiar male voice.

Immediately, all the leaves changed to purple and white and bent toward the ground in reverence. The pillars, books, vines—everything in the mansion—bowed. The beings in the room also immediately bowed. The brown-haired, bearded man before them wore a royal gown made of threads of white gold. His face shone with beneficence. This was the beloved Lord Jaesu, who ruled over the entire universe.

Lord Jaesu was one of the three creators. The other two were the Blue Spirit of Fire and the Great Father of Evermore. They were equal, but Jaesu was the one who mingled with the souls, befriended them, and responded to their pleas for help. "Rise, rise, my friends," he said joyously. "Dara, the queen was wise to choose you and the Lighted Blade. It is evident that you care deeply for one another and have strong soul connections. Soul bonds are uncommon throughout the galaxy. This bond you have makes you soul mates. And such bonds are eternal. A bond to another soul could mean the difference between unfulfilled potential and whether you can overcome the greatest of obstacles."

Everyone in the room rose and ran to embrace Lord Jaesu. He smiled and laughed again as he returned their embraces.

Always thrilled and excited to see Jaesu, Dara asked, "But can our connections to one another help us in such a game?"

"Dara, your team came within a hair of defeating the most instinctive defenders in the entire universe. And dare I say, you may have succeeded had you built a team scheme beforehand, instead of going into the contest thinking that you had to cover everything on your own," Lord Jaesu replied.

"You watched, Lord?" Dara asked in astonishment.

Jaesu responded with a smile, "Did you think I would miss such a match? Of course, I watched. Besides, Jovan wouldn't have let me hear the end of it had I found a reason not to. Am I right, Jo?"

"Well, that's because I was sure we'd get 'em," Jovan responded.

"Jovan? You knew he was watching?" Dara asked in a bothered tone. "Like, Lord Jaesu? Um...King of the Universe? And you didn't feel the need to tell me?"

"Apparently Jovan doesn't feel the need to tell you a lot of things," Marcus chimed in.

"Like what, may I ask?"

"The point is, Dara, think of how different the outcome would have been if you had planned with your team and used all of your team's talents from the beginning, as you did during the game when you met up with Bethany and Jovan in the mountain," Jaesu interjected to get the conversation on track. As he sensed Dara was about to jump in, he quickly continued, "You don't have to defend your actions. You are blessed with a great cast of friends and have bonds that most in the galaxy, or even the universe, would give anything for. Accept this gift with gratitude."

Dara bowed her head in thought.

"Surely, my dear, whenever the queen allows, I can assist you in such matters," Black added. The cat's attention was slightly diverted as she spoke. She had noticed that Jaesu had not come empty-handed. He had brought a book, certainly from another part of the library. "Lord, what is that you are carrying?"

"You are observant and inquisitive, O cat," Jaesu said in a friendly tone. "Always amazed I am at how curious cats are. Whether it is here, in the Elevemada, or Earth, it's a trait I certainly admire. Anyway, I have selected a tale that may help the queen in the coming days."

"See? I knew he wasn't coming just to see us!" Dara said jokingly.

"I am with you first, am I not? The queen doesn't even know I've arrived yet. So enjoy our time together and stop complaining." Jaesu's words were both friendly and gently teasing.

"He got you there, D!" Bethany said to Dara.

"*Humph*...I suppose," Dara responded in a bratty tone.

"What is that book about, anyway? It looks kinda creepy."

"Well," said Jaesu. "It is called *Medusa's Secret of the Deep*. The book is a historical depiction of battles with the asudem of Algolithar and the origin of their ruler, the Red Knight, Khrimson."

Everyone in the room shuddered for a moment, as if they had been told a scary late night thriller; however, their response was not one of fear, but one of interest.

"Aren't the asudem a waste of time? I mean, doesn't Orion neatly dispose of them whenever they are near?" Bethany asked.

"Bethany, listen closely," Jaesu said in a concerned tone. "All of you: never disrespect your enemy. Khrimson is powerful, and although you should not fear him, indulging yourself with pride and vanity will only give him greater power.

"The asudem are vicious soul hunters, destroyers who prey on the weak and celebrate hurting the lonely. As the queen's seraph, Orion does marvelous work protecting Gardenia. But do not believe it is an easy task! Despite his power, stellar dagger skills, and enormous size, even he is not impervious to battle wounds and is not immortal.

"He is different than we are. We are souls. The seraphs, even the mighty, only have a spirit and a body but no soul. That means he can live forever, only if he is never killed, whereas we will live forever no matter what we do. It's a matter of where we spend our eternity. It can be here, in the Galaxy of Souls, or for those who have made the harsh choice, the trials of Earth and then either the horror of Hadnessa or eternity in the most wondrous creation of the heavens, Evermore."

"Lord, why would anyone choose to live in a place called the horror of Hadnessa?" asked Marcus. "That doesn't sound like eternal magnificence to me."

"Marcus," Jaesu answered, "it can be difficult to understand for one who has never been flesh and bone. There are some truths you simply must accept. What makes life on Earth a trial, for now, is flesh and bone itself, combined with a sickness known only as legend within your planet, which is the urge to do evil — both to others and even to oneself. Right now, as bodies of souls and spirits in a beautifully harmonious world, it's difficult for you to even imagine the weight of flesh. It carries with it many joys, pains, feelings, risks, and rewards. Tens of thousands make the choice to journey to Earth daily. It is not something I would force on any one of you, nor would I keep you from it. I would prepare you, guide you, and protect you as much as possible."

"But why would anyone make that choice? It makes no sense to me," said Marcus.

"Who are you protecting us from?" asked Dara.

"Okay, okay. One at a time," Jaesu responded. "For many, this experience is the only way to know their strengths, their worth, and their true destiny. Without it, a soul can feel empty and a longing for more. It is also the only way one can get into Evermore. There are three doors one must pass through, and all three are on Earth. The door of life allows one to enter into Earth. The door of death causes one to leave Earth. It's the third door that is the greatest mystery. That is the door of Remembrance."

"Remembrance?" one of the plants asked.

"Yes. The weight of the flesh will fight the soul in a constant war to keep from remembering where it came from, thus making it difficult to ever find the door. It is this that makes the choice mysterious, fearsome, and ultimately rewarding."

"Doesn't sound rewarding when you put it that way," said one of the plants.

"Lord, my question, please. Hello!" Dara shouted. Though souls revered their Lord, they also felt very relaxed around him. They knew he loved their verve and differences.

"Yes, I am getting there," Jaesu responded. "Dara, although many battles with the asudem are fought throughout the heavens, Khrimson and his fellow henchmen are on Earth by the millions, roaming throughout its lands to tempt, taunt, and even torment all who abide in it."

"Millions? On a single planet?" asked Jovan.

"Indeed, Jovan. And when a soul is in flesh, because of the weight of that flesh—its gravitational pull, actually—time moves slowly in difficult moments and quickly in happier periods. Sometimes a single day can feel like a lifetime because, in truth, it is. Time moves more quickly when one is enjoying life. An entire revolution around a star can feel like mere seconds. Keep in mind that the universe was intended for all to live harmoniously as one, much like here on Gardenia, but pain and trouble came under Khrimson's rule. When one experiences such turmoil, time can become extremely heavy and burdensome."

"Lord!" shouted Dara. "Everyone knows you have the keys to all kingdoms in the universe. I haven't even seen Evermore. Who knows if I ever will after hearing this. Couldn't you show me where the doors are so that I could go through the Evermore entryway, avoiding the earthly trials?"

"If it were only that simple, Dara," said Lord Jaesu. "Ultimately, whether you end up in Evermore or Hadnessa must be a choice you make during your earthly trials. It is only through the earthly trials that you, for yourself, will find where you truly desire to belong. Although I will help you hold on to as many memories of this place and the three doors as possible, the flesh is a mechanism that helps to dilute and block any recollection of this dwelling. Some cry out to me from Earth, not even knowing that we have walked together in these worlds for millions of cycles. And when times are hard, some even wish they had never been born. They forget they made the choice, the choice to be born. It is not something to be taken lightly.

"As for Evermore, let me put it this way. You all have great, unique, and wonderful qualities. What if each of you were king or queen of your own world and reigned in a universe

26

more amazing than you could possibly conceive? Ponder that for a moment. Once that idea has taken hold, try to understand that I could combine all of your thoughts and imaginations and beautiful designs and concepts, and yet not even scratch the surface of how dazzling and miraculous Evermore truly is. Even if I did the same with every soul ever to exist, with every wonderful thought, hope, and dream ever dreamed, it would not match the beauty of one single grain of sand in Evermore."

"I still don't quite understand, Lord," Marcus said. "How is it possible that all of the imaginations ever created combined could not fathom the beauty of one place?"

"Let me answer this way," Jaesu answered back. "Marcus, what is four plus four?"

"Eight, of course."

"What if it isn't?" responded Jaesu. "It might be eight and a half."

"No, it isn't; now you are just being silly."

"And if I am not, how would you truly know? As brilliant as you are, even your mind does not have infinite understanding. Thus, it can only grasp so much."

"Hold up," said Bethany. "What you said before—we would get to be kings and queens? Like Queen Amana? Whoa! That is blade."

"Bethany, even greater than she," the Lord said, smiling. "Out of all of the majestic kings and queens throughout Elevemada, I consider Queen Amana to be the greatest, due to her selflessness and her love for the planet and, most of all, for her people. There isn't anything she wouldn't give for the safety of everyone and everything on Gardenia. With that said, kings and queens of Evermore are far greater than any others in the universe."

"What about Khrimson, Lord?" interrupted Jovan. "Isn't he King of Algolithar? Has he always been?"

"Khrimson." Jaesu paused and sighed somewhat sadly. "Yes, indeed, he is the ruler of Algolithar and was once a good friend…a long time ago." Noticeably shaken by the memory, he continued, "They all were. It was very different then. Khrimson went by a different name. He was the greatest of the seraphs. Even the mighty, with whom you are familiar—like Orion and Dar's Blue Elephant—were unable to compare. He was full of light, with a physical body chiseled from amoretto stones and a silver-tipped tail that could lasso an entire star. He was brilliant, charismatic, and musically gifted; his every movement made a sound of praise and celebration. He was one of the most popular seraphs. War and battles were never even a thought in the universe in those days, only unimaginable peace. Evermore was an eternity of harmony and unquenchable joy. He was truly one of our greatest creations. Then—" Jaesu looked down and paused again.

"Lord, what is it?" asked Jovan.

"The amoretto stones were amazing because they breathed with life, like many of the stones on this world," said Jaesu. "Khrimson went to the Great Father and asked if, instead of keeping him to reign in the Kingdom of Evermore, the Great Father would create for Khrimson his own world—a planet formed from the amoretto stone that he loved so much. He said he wanted the chance to enjoy a beauty of his own.

"The Great Father, always abundantly generous and loving, did as Khrimson asked. The planet was called Amore, after its origin of stone. The planet was a magnificent sight. The clear red river of Axzeon, with its banks and riverbed fashioned from millions of rubies, made this an enchanted kingdom. Khrimson had the power to alter small parts of the planet, to design palaces from the stone and gardens from the greenery and to change the paths of the small streams.

"As time passed, when Khrimson came back to Evermore, he seemed more and more distant from us. However, many of the seraphs whom he had befriended over the cycles went with him to Amore, so they could bask in its beauty. He then told a lie—a small lie at first. He told many of his fellow seraphs that he had actually created the planet of Amore. Gradually, he convinced them that he was equal to the Great Father. Khrimson promised that he could create worlds for each of them and help them be equal to the creator as well.

"Many seraphs did not believe such a notion, of course, yet millions did and followed him. I told you he was charismatic—a quality he had only used for good in the beginning.

"Then, as the Great Father finished constructing the Milky Way Galaxy—he loves to create and is forever building—Khrimson came into the throne room, ready to destroy him.

"Within seconds, the Spirit of Blue Fire caused a storm to fall upon him and his loyal seraphs, forcing them out of Evermore. The Spirit unleashed the powerful seraph Michaelio to defend Evermore. The battle waged on for one million cycles. Michaelio eventually prevailed, with the deaths of many seraphs on both sides.

"That was the day the universe shook. Many of Khrimson's followers fled back to Amore, but Khrimson himself continued to battle. At the battle's turning point, Michaelio used all of his strength to thrust Khrimson down toward the completed Milky Way, causing him to smash into Earth, splitting the planet in three. Earth was devastated, and Khrimson, greatly wounded, fell into a deep sleep.

"The smaller portion of the Earth's surface that had broken off the Great Father formed into Earth's moon, and the much larger portion he moved into a nearby empty space, and it is now known as Mars.

"Phan, another once-great seraph and Khrimson's second in command, sent legions to Earth to find Khrimson and bring him back to Amore.

"Upon his return, Khrimson was able to regain his strength, and the Amoretto planet was no longer called Amore, but Algolithar.

"Khrimson spent many cycles equipping his seraphs for war. He changed the names and forms of these seraphs, who are now called asudem. The capital of their world is Greystone. This is a cruel place, completely devoid of any of the beauty it once held. Evil destroys beauty over time. Beauty is too much a rebuke to those who cannot love.

"To this day, Khrimson and his legions roam back and forth from Algolithar to Earth, trying to destroy each and every soul they find because souls are also beautiful. It is far easier for them to succeed with the beings of flesh on Earth than in this galaxy, but nonetheless, they should never be underestimated."

The others were quiet for a moment, trying to fathom what evil was and why any being would choose it. It made no sense to them. If Jaesu had not looked so sad, they might have questioned him more. As it was, they felt as if the faintest shadow had been cast over them and they shivered.

Finally, Bethany asked, "So, back to the book. How will this book help our queen?"

"I wonder if telling you this will help," Jaesu responded slowly, "but I believe another battle is coming, and I would like to prepare her. And now it is time for me to do so. If she finds me here before I have seen her, then, well …I don't want to find out what would happen," he said with a smile. Then he put his arms out to embrace everyone before they began to depart. "Black, would you and Jovan accompany me on my journey to see the queen?" the Lord asked.

Black, speaking for both, responded, "Of course, Lord."

They began to walk away from the others. Jaesu could tell that the history lesson was weighing heavily on Jovan's mind and sought to give him courage. "My friend," he said, "you and I have walked through many centuries together. You know more about the universe than most. Still, you seem distressed."

"I am. It's hard to imagine what Earth is like. I hate to think of the souls there, not remembering, battling Khrimson alone."

"Jovan, when you were playing Owls and Seraphs, you worked with Marcus and Jacen on a plan to protect Dara, just in case it was needed, did you not?" Jaesu asked.

"Yes."

"How much more do you think I would plan for all of Gardenia? What I did not reveal to your friends is that each soul who makes the choice to go to Earth brings a seraph with them. Furthermore, the Spirit of Blue Fire oversees all happenings on Earth. Once a person finds the third door, then I am with that person always. I'm sure you have many questions, you whom I call my closest friend, but for now I ask that you be at peace and trust me."

"You know I do, Jaesu," said Jovan. "I will leave you and Black to continue onward. I'm sure I will see you shortly." After he ran his hand over the velvety fur on Black's head, he prepared to fly away.

"Jovan, wait!" called Lord Jaesu. He hovered with him, slightly above the ground and whispered something in his ear, admonishing him to keep it to himself for now.

Jovan's eyes widened in surprise as the Lord and the great cat continued their departure. He looked after them in awe, completely shaken by what he had heard.

He began to drift away from the planet and toward its moons. There was a small silvery beach he liked to lie on when he needed to think. The cool waves and gentle winds helped settle him, while the songs of seabirds contained inspiration he could understand when he was alone.

"There's more to tell, isn't there, Lord?" asked Black as Jovan disappeared into the distance.

"Yes, Black," answered Jaesu. "It's coming. It's time. The greatest war in both the Galaxy of Souls and on Earth will be upon us soon. We must be ready."

CHAPTER 2

Seeds of Destruction

Deep within the coldest part of the universe lay the
core of all evil, hidden inside the Uqwih Galaxy was
Khrimson's lair: Algolithar.

Algolithar was the home of death, pain, suffering,
treacherous desires, sickness, and despair: all the doing of the
fierce legions of the asudem. Seraphs protected souls, but asudem
hunted and obliterated them. They detested every soul on every
planet and world, but they especially enjoyed feeding on the
darkness they sowed when they enticed souls with flattery and
empty promises, slowly persuading them to turn from their
dreams and hopes. They used lies, trickery, half-truths, and the
difficulties of the flesh—whatever it took to turn souls from
the light. Some asudem preferred to play on greed and lust or
the bitterness of loss. Others specialized in turning generosity
into profligacy, joy into self-indulgence, and responsibility into

domination. Corruption was achieved once a soul had outlived its purpose to the asudem. Then, it was given over to damnation in Hadnessa—the deadly world of fire and ice, eternal terror, and loneliness.

In a distorted form, some of Amore's former splendors, such as the red stream and amoretto rocks, still remained. Now they spoke more of power and display than of beauty, but Khrimson could not see the difference. He maintained them to flaunt his insolence toward the Great Father, not realizing that all but the corrupt could see that true beauty had long since fled.

Khrimson's ability to bring torment upon any being in his power was unmatched. Betrayal, even when inflicted on him from others if it were possible, was something he admired. Inflicting punishment was a pleasure he not only enjoyed, but craved. The lust for the throne of Evermore, which he had been denied, became a hunger that was never sated. No amount of power or cruelty could sate him, not even for an instant, yet all he thought about was the satisfaction he would one day feel when utter and eternal power was his.

Khrimson was called the Red Knight, and he was feared and worshipped throughout Algolithar. His ambition was to destroy the destiny of every soul ever created. Because he had never gained access to the Elevemada, he could not corrupt souls before they entered flesh. Therefore, his focus had been on Earth for many millennia. However, his desire for access to the Galaxy of Souls never waned.

* * *

Khrimson's throne was made of obsidian, shot through with streaks of blood, blood gathered from those he had tormented on

Earth. Extending from the throne was also an obsidian walkway that stretched for miles between two rivers of lava. The edges of the walkway were adorned with the skulls of men and women from Earth who had succumbed to his influence during their earthly lives. The skulls of the vile Adolf Hitler, the manipulative Queen Jezebel, and the deranged Roman emperor Nero were among the plethora decorating his hideous estate, representing Khrimson's greatest accomplishments throughout history. He did not revere them, appreciate them, or praise their loyalty; instead, he enjoyed mocking their naiveté in foolishly allowing themselves to be deceived.

These souls—famous on Earth as the most evil of the evil—had once been pure, leaping into the Carriage Stream to test themselves and win Evermore. Khrimson had manipulated them and changed their destinies. Keeping their skulls reaffirmed his own greatness.

Khrimson spent most of his days on Earth, leading ongoing battles for souls. But he often returned to Algolithar for strategic assembly with his chief general and second in command, Phan.

"LEGIONS! Rejoice, for your lord and master has returned!" the evil lord bellowed from his walkway, causing massive shouts and chants from the asudem as he walked toward his throne. He appraised the skulls on each side of his walkway, both new and old. "*Ah*, I have made additions to my collection. Yet I never tire of this classic: oh, Saddam, you fell for everything. And to watch you crawl out of that rat-invested hole in humiliation ...*ah*, little could give me more pleasure. You were loyal to me all the way, and I hated you all the time. Wonderfully tragic, wouldn't you say, Phan?"

"At all times, my lord." Phan nodded. "The East-West clash is coming along nicely. Though, I must say, the child soldiers in Africa were also quite brilliant. Watching children kill their parents! What could be more delectable? Are you sure you want to attempt another attack on Gardenia? Orion overwhelms our legions with great ease for they are virtually powerless in the Elevemada. May I recommend a continued and stronger assault on Earth? With the population increasing, there are so many more opportunities for conflict."

Seething anger filled Khrimson's face as he grabbed Phan by the throat. "Listen to me, you fool! I am not the lord of revenge, horror, and violence because I heed advice from pathetic excuses for generals, such as you. I—and I alone—am the brilliance; I am the beauty; I am the lord at ALL times, as you said. Remember it!"

Khrimson had a terrifying power called *Harrow Plasm*. This allowed him to take hold of anything in spirit form and cause it to temporarily be cast into flesh, which he would then destroy piece by piece, causing excruciating pain. At the end, the spirit was as it had been in the beginning, nothing left of its experience but the memory of agony. All of Algolithar heard Phan's screams as Khrimson unleashed this power. Each of them had felt this horror in times past and knew they would feel it again. This was how he kept his legions in line.

"Now, remove yourself from my presence and prepare to take the legions to battle Orion as I have commanded." When he finished speaking, Khrimson flung Phan away from the throne.

After Khrimson, none was more powerful than Phan, but even he felt uneasy at the prospect of battling in the Elevemada, regardless of how many legions were with him. Nonetheless, he had no choice but to quickly prepare himself for war, knowing this war might well be his last. On neutral ground, there was no foe he feared, but in Elevemada, the seraphs had power that Phan's armies were unable to match.

As part of his combat ritual, Phan chained a pet slave to his belt. Phan had a special talent as well: he was able to deflect any pain levied upon him onto the slave, leaving himself untouched. The slave he chose for this battle was called Pity—once known by a different name, one never to be uttered in Algolithar.

Pity had been loyal to the asudem for many cycles, but over time she had begun to regret her decision to join Khrimson in the Pillar Purge against the Great Father and Evermore. It was very rare for any in the asudem to openly express such doubts. All feared Khrimson, but most were so entrenched in evil, that any sensitivity or moral qualm had been seared away long ago. There was only one way— Khrimson's way. Pity was an extraordinary case. She had stopped attempting to hurt others in battle. When on Earth, instead of tempting humans with powerful seductions and deceptions, she had begun to silently encourage them to overcome the intentionally weak charms she was using. Shajcell, an evil enchantress and loyal servant of Phan, recognized Pity's betrayal and revealed it to Phan.

Shajcell was uniquely powerful. It had been said that if a man ever spoke her name on Earth, she would grant him the woman of his desire, even if it was not that woman's choice. Only women under the protection of Jaesu himself were immune to this enchantment. All other women, when entranced by Shajcell, would become overwhelmed with passion and what they thought was love for the men who desired them.

Many of the men who called upon Shajcell were vile and wicked, but at times good men had been known to call upon her in desperation to gain the heart of the woman they adored. Shajcell relished those opportunities. The good men, under her influence, also would become wicked. Even more insidiously, they never saw that they had changed. Just like the twisted men before them, they treated the women she charmed for them as trinkets or playthings rather than as living beings deserving of true love. They abused their women in every malicious way possible, all the while thinking that they were still good men, that if anyone was at fault, it was the women.

What gave Shajcell the greatest pleasure was watching the women choose to stay with these men, despite being beaten and spat on over and over again. Shajcell's great deception was making women feel that they were still, somehow, loved by their men, while the men felt that they had been tricked—given love that wasn't really love, which made them bitter and angry. Very, very few ever considered that the desire to make a woman love them rather than try to earn that love and accept whatever happened was the key to their downfall.

The payment Shajcell extracted from the men who called upon her was twofold: they had to have her name tattooed on their bodies as a physical confirmation of their allegiance to her, and they had to call her name upon their deathbeds.

Shajcell was very attractive to the human eye, and she had a way of holding men's gazes. She had long reddish black hair and a haunting glide to her steps. She studied her clientele—their likes, dislikes, and attractions—and matched her appearance and behavior to each man's desires. This gave her an enormous advantage in seducing her prey.

She was no ally of the men she seduced. Upon their deaths, she would take their souls for her own and would multiply the torment they each had inflicted on earthly women a thousand fold before finally sending them to Hadnessa to remain in a conscious state of torment for all eternity.

Shajcell had a passionate hatred for men because they resembled Jaesu; she despised women because they reminded her of the kind of seraph she once had been. Seeing Pity's concern for these humans had both sickened and angered her.

Once Phan heard of Pity's treachery, he cursed her, shrinking her goddess-like form to a pitiful creature no more than two feet tall. Then he had beaten and chained her to the Harrower.

A shiny black hexagram in the chamber hall, the Harrower wasn't much to look at, but its power caused immense pain. It was a horrific machine that mirrored Khrimson's ability to manifest flesh upon a spirit in order to inflict severe anguish. This cruel device caused a soul or spirit to feel flesh burning and tearing, only for that flesh to grow back again as the process to be repeated over and over.

"*Ah*, there you are, slave," said Phan to Pity, who had been chained to a wall outside of Greystone. "I have a special delight for you."

Pity, so weakened by endless cycles of torture that she struggled to stand, looked at him blankly.

"You will be accompanying me into battle!" said Phan with a sinister sneer.

"You mean as a slave shield? But, Master, I..."

"SILENCE!" Phan shouted. "Do you not know that I can bring upon you your greatest fears and horrors?"

Pity softly responded, "And you do ...always."

Phan had no patience for any trace of defiance, so he formed a hot wind to fire her into the Harrower as a means of punishment.

Pity immediately began to scream and beg for the agony to end.

"It would be so easy to end your agony, if only you would renounce your devotion to Evermore and show loyal worship toward our great master once again," said Phan, who was playfully stroking his chin. He then sighed. "Yet you will probably never learn, and I will have the pleasure of torturing you forever."

"Please, I beg you!" Pity shrieked in pain. "I can't ..."

"Now, why should I release a traitor such as you?" Phan mocked.

Pity could no longer respond. She was in shock. No matter how many times she had been put through this device—and there had been many—the torment was always fresh, and always unbearable. Pity also knew that, no matter what Phan said, mercy would never be an option. Even if she repented for the sin of showing pity on souls, he would continue to torture her for pure entertainment for eternity.

"Very well, little deceiver," Phan said sinisterly. "I need you in prime condition to be my shield when we go into battle." He motioned with his hand, and the Harrower released her. He then abandoned her temporarily to continue preparations for battle.

Pity crawled to her corner, feeling as if she bore a thousand wounds. That she had no flesh to soothe or heal only made it worse.

Near the end of her time on Earth, Pity had hated watching humans suffer as a result of battle or disease. She thought there could be nothing worse than being chained to flesh that bled, suppurated, and grew hungry and thirsty. Yet now she knew what was worse: to feel all those pains without the natural limits of flesh, without even the small mercy of a glass of cold water.

* * *

Khrimson was holding a meeting with his generals before his return to Earth. Phan had called them to assemble at Vulture Mountain, a massive volcano whose highest crater housed a nest of Goliath Vultures. At this gathering, Khrimson intended to discuss a new aggressive war strategy he had devised over thousands of cycles.

The asudem present were of many classes—class being determined by ability. Draken Knights were the most revered as they most closely resembled Khrimson, the Red Knight, in appearance. None had his beauty, his amoretto eyes or his silver tail, but they had black diamond-shaped beards and whipping tails that were flexible yet as hard as granite. Draken Knights ruled the night and were princes of the skies on Earth. Their ability to pave the way for death by creating sickness and disease on Earth was a power that even many seraphs could not combat.

Phan was a Draken Knight. His metallic face intimidated even the asudem. There was no beauty in him. His look was as vicious as his intentions. Wherever he walked, a long onyx- and iron-studded cape trailed behind him, emanating vast amounts of fear.

Among the other classes of asudem were the Caultresses, a group of female enchantresses, seductresses, and duchesses of the supernatural. Their ability to mask and deceive was unparalleled. These were the beings that led priests into mortal sin, thinking they had found the secret to divine love. These were also the ones who coaxed women into murdering their infants by whispering that the babes were possessed by devils. Shajcell was the ruler of all Caultresses.

Lurkas were creeping arachnoid beings, who, from their many hiding places, breathed a chill breath of fear. On Earth, a Lurka could use fear to manipulate a human's choices—not a terrorizing fear, but the more subtle fear that begins with doubt.

The Polarstones were huge beings that were mighty in space battle. Made of ice and stone, they could transform into ice comets anywhere in the universe. When on Earth, they could absorb nearby waters and rain, causing droughts and turning fertile land to desert.

Sandcastlers promised great wealth and could manipulate beings into trading their souls for riches. They lacked fierceness in battle but were powerful in scheming. Belshazzar, an asudem who had Khrimson's ear, was one of these.

The final class was composed of the Goliath Vultures. They were vast in size and well-respected in warfare, bringing horror wherever they went. By far, they were the most intimidating of the asudem to behold—five hundred feet long by two hundred feet wide, with the faces of ravens and the bodies and claws of vultures. Goliath Vultures were great warriors with a penchant for feasting on dying souls. Once a soul had given up on finding the door to Evermore, these great beastly birds would begin to gnaw the soul into utter destruction.

These were the classes of Khrimson's asudem. Each of them had internal ranks as well. Just as the Gardenians had Orion, they, too, had a protector—but she was no seraph. The Dragon Knightress, Medusa, the mighty serpent in the sky, watched over all of Uqwih, especially Algolithar. More horrifying than any other creation, she was very rarely seen by even the asudem, as Algolithar had never been attacked since its formation. This caused many, including seraphs, to believe the planet was invincible. Varying legends of Medusa's origin had been spread throughout the galaxies. Indeed, she once was beautiful with a majestic name, but after the purge, her hideousness was so great that even she would not look upon her own reflection. In disgust she went by the name Medusa, which in the tongues of spirit and men was the backwards spelling of asudem. This was done as part of a secret covenant with Khrimson for reasons unknown to either seraphs or asudem.

"Legions of darkness, deception and despair: we have come to it!" Khrimson shouted to the assembled throng. "In this age, our long-awaited and destined conquest of the universe begins at last. We have won and lost many battles, and we are still here. Those wondering if the powers of the Great Father and Jaesu are limitless need wonder no more. You are so wretched in their eyes that they would have destroyed you long ago if they could. But they cannot because they have a weakness."

A murmur of shock went through the crowd at this statement. "It's true, my friends!" Khrimson cried. "Think for a moment. Think of Jaesu's precious souls within the Elevemada: those who are sent to Earth, those he claims to love. Outside of some squabbles with seraphs and our own miscalculations, we have gone unchecked to and fro in the lives of these souls. Look at the walkway of the Greystone palace! Behold the thousands and thousands of skulls representing a sample of the lives we have eradicated throughout time. If the Great Father and Evermore had the power to defeat us, oh, yes—trust me, my friends—they would have done so.

"The final battle will not be easy to win, but we will win nonetheless," he continued. "On Earth, we have controlled many politicians, kings, queens, and rulers of all cultures in all lands. The religious factions have such beautiful, vigorous hate toward one another that it pleases me to see them volunteer for battle. We have helped humans, in the name of science, create atomic technology, and revealed their nakedness to them in so many ways that they have become desensitized to their flaws and mesmerized by our powers.

"All of the years of destroying families, infiltrating their systems of education, and replacing the natural purity of creation with physical, emotional, and spiritual pollution will finally begin to make sense to each of you. I have kept my plan secret for many cycles, but now it is time to unleash our hatred."

Khrimson's followers were in awe with their attention completely fixed on him. He climbed onto his own protector, Mynogor, a colossal Goliath Vulture who often ferried him throughout the universe and was a feared warrior in battle. As the vulture lifted off the mountain, Khrimson closed his speech from midair.

"Generals! Phan will reveal to you your orders. Phan! Assemble the Legions. Lead the charge into Elevemada and shake Gardenia to rubble. Orion has defeated us many times before, but this time we will destroy him and those pathetic souls on Gardenia. Don't fail me! Soon, we will reveal ourselves on Earth and crush the insignificance of their creation. Rise and stand! You are the dawn—you are the morning star—YOU are the kings and queens of the universe! And I am lord of ALL!"

Thunderous applause erupted throughout Algolithar, such that the ground shook. "Now, Mynogor," Khrimson said to the mighty vulture, "Show the Earth a sign of my coming—and of their destruction!"

Obediently, the giant vulture breathed a huge ball of gas and fire that rushed fiercely into space and turned into an explosion of light and gas several million miles away from Algolithar. Its light was visible throughout the Milky Way. Those on Earth saw it as a comet surrounded by varying colors of red, one that had never been seen by the astronomers whose telescopes were always trained on that sector of space. Both astronomers and citizens on the Earth stood in amazement at the supposed comet's beauty.

Khrimson flew away from Algolithar to begin his mission.

"Lord," Shajcell said to Phan, walking swiftly and confidently toward him, attired in her effervescent, long alizarin gown, "where is the master going?"

Phan's expression gave her the impression that he was keeping that detail hidden for a reason. "I need something from you, Shajcell," Phan said, instead of answering. "I need your talents and charm on Alpha."

Surprised, Shajcell responded, "Alpha is in the Galaxy of Souls."

"I'm quite aware of where it is. But it is a key to our strategic initiative."

Confused, Shajcell retorted, "But my lord, the master has assigned me to continue my assault on the women of Earth."

"Yes, yes, I know," replied Phan. "Then there must be some protégé you trust, no? I need one who can physically transform into whatever attracts a specific soul most, much like you."

"Well, there is only one: me. Many men on the Earth call me the goddess of love, did you not know?" responded Shajcell, shimmering with vanity as her long, straight dark hair attempted to mask her exceptionally striking light brown face.

Phan desired her and hated her at the same time, which did not seem like a conflict to him. "And they call you much worse after you take them from the Earth, I'm sure," he said impatiently.

"Alina," Shajcell suggested. "Take Alina. She is nearly my equal in every way, except for my skill for torture. She will see your task done."

"I thought you would say as much. Very well then," Phan agreed. "Have her take the path toward the sixth moon. There she will find a pool of water behind the Falls of Madness where she will transform into vapor and begin her invisible journey to the Elevemada system. Have her take this small locket. Within it is a powerful mirror that will reveal her target upon reaching Alpha."

"This is really it?" whispered Shajcell. "The great battle."

"All of Evermore will tremble when we are through. We will unleash dreadfulness upon them," snickered Phan. "All will beg to serve us …but in due time, princess of pain. Now I must get my slave ready for the first leg of this war."

Shajcell bowed to Phan and went on her way.

"Ambiandis!" Phan called out. "Are you prepared to sow the seeds of destruction throughout mankind?"

A grim shadow appeared, gave a simple nod in reply, and vanished. Ambiandis was a mystery to both seraphs and asudem. He was powerless away from Algolithar or Earth, where he thrived on the lusts of the flesh — the more lust he could ignite in others, the more he multiplied into clones of himself. His shadow could break apart and enter the beings on Earth who had given into the lust of the eyes and flesh. Over the years, he had built a strong foundation on Earth with the help of other demonic forces. His part in this invasion would be one of great significance.

If all went according to plan, this war would never be forgotten and the asudem would rule over the universe forever.

CHAPTER 3

Faces of Royalty

O n the outskirts of Gardenia's Royal Garden rested a
fascinating couple. Euwyn, a white buck, and Jasmine,
a red doe, had a love for each other that was so intense
that it was rare, even on this world of love. They spent their days
walking endlessly throughout the fields and woodlands of the
planet. As a tribute to their love, the trees and bushes where they
resided would often display pink leaves: the hue of their two
colors blended. The couple's close friend, Roslyn, who assisted
the trees in decorating their part of the planet, was also a unique
soul. Standing about five feet tall with long scarlet-tipped brown
hair, she loved the moods of nature and kept to herself, except
when spending time in the woods with Euwyn and Jasmine.

"Good morning!" said Roslyn to the forest. The trees and

bushes rustled their leaves as a way of returning the greeting. "Have Euwyn and Jasmine gone for their morning stroll?"

"No, they haven't," said the large white buck walking out from among the leaves.

"Euwyn!" Roslyn said exuberantly. "You surprised me. I was about to go through my routine and decorate for you both."

"I told Jasmine to sleep in this morning as we have planned a special journey to Diamonda."

"The underwater mountain? How beautiful! Never gets old, does it? You both must have many cycles of memories there."

"It's our place. You know? But as beautiful and amazing as the Diamonda is, it's nothing compared to my dear Jasmine," Euwyn said with humility. "However, there is another reason I am encouraging her to take an extended rest. I need your help with this." Euwyn showed Roslyn a shawl that he had been working on. Stitched from the pink leaves Jasmine loved so much, it glistened with threads of white gold. "As you know, she has a stunning blend of dark red and black freckles. I haven't been able to find a red to match her, and this is supposed to be a surprise for today."

"That is fantastic, Euwyn. She is going to leap like none other!" Roslyn shouted. Euwyn motioned to her to keep the volume down as he didn't want to ruin the surprise.

Euwyn looked at the tips of Roslyn's hair and noticed how similar they were to Jasmine's coloring. Roslyn calmly took a small piece of her hair and held it over the shawl. Immediately, the hair and leaves responded to each other. The hair grew to outline all seventy-seven leaves so that the shawl was outlined with Jasmine's red complexion and Euwyn's white, both embracing their joint color.

"Does that help?" Roslyn asked with a smile.

Euwyn stood in awe. The shawl was now more magnificent than he could have imagined. He couldn't find the words. "I don't know what to say. Roslyn, thank you. Jasmine will look radiant."

"You did the work. I just built on your imagination to provide the final piece," responded Roslyn. "If she's still resting, now might be the best time to put it on her. I know I, for one, love waking up to surprises."

"I had thought of that but then decided on something a bit more momentous. You see, there is a line of trees that go all the way toward Diamonda… Well, let's say I have a different surprise in mind."

"Gotta say, you truly are the romantic of the woods," said Roslyn, smiling.

"Euwyn, Euwyn, where have you gone off to now?" Jasmine's voice was heard from inside the deer den.

"*Oops*…well, I better get in there," Euwyn said to Roslyn quickly. "I am in your debt."

"No, you're not! Go spoil her. Hurry!" said Roslyn as the buck started walking back. She resumed her practice of putting leaves together gracefully for the pair. Adorning the woods was something Roslyn enjoyed immensely. She couldn't help but imagine the look on Jasmine's face once she saw the gift that Euwyn had fashioned for her.

"That was wonderful of you to do for them, Roslyn," said the beautiful and legendary Queen Amana of Gardenia.

Embarrassed to be caught off guard, Roslyn immediately bowed to one knee. "Forgive me, Your Majesty."

With a glowing smile, Amana gently clasped Roslyn's hand

and raised her up. "Friend of the forest, there is nothing to pardon between us. I was merely taking in the love that you have for our planet. I am always honored by those who cherish Gardenia as much as I do."

Like Roslyn, the queen was no more than five feet tall, but that was where the similarities in their appearance ended. Amana had long blond hair, ivory skin that shone like starlight, and deep sapphire eyes. She wore a pale blue royal gown with a graceful diadem outlined with green emeralds and red rubies.

"It is quite beautiful, my queen," said Roslyn. "The forest, I mean. Your every step brings more beauty to it, they say."

"They do?" laughed Amana. "Who is this 'they' you speak of?"

"Well, I overhear Marcus, Dawn, and the rest of the Lighted Blade sometimes, all of the townsfolk and even the trees and flowers say so."

"Well, it is true," said the queen. "But it's no more magnificent than what you did for Euwyn and Jasmine. That is the true beauty and wonder of our world. And although I am called 'queen,' it is all of us that share rule of Gardenia."

"Yes! I feel exactly the same way—well, except for the queen part. I don't... but you know what I mean."

The queen smiled in response. "Would you mind walking with me, Roslyn? I don't want to intrude on your day but was hoping for some company on my way back to the palace."

"*Um*...me? Company? You sure I'm the kind of company you are looking for? I mean, most folks think me peculiar, you know, with my leaf-decorating habits."

Amana nodded in affirmation and, with a smile, walked over a plain-looking wooden bridge. Roslyn followed her quickly to keep up. A series of double-trunked trees created an arch over the bridge, and waterfalls flowed out from the sides of each trunk into the Paragon River. It made for a beautiful sight. Many who passed through felt abundant tranquility.

"No, you misunderstand, Roslyn. I appreciate your love for such things, actually. Even as queen, I frequently wonder if many think me bizarre for spending much of my time with creatures and nature." The queen looked upward and admired the double-trunked trees. "They are something, aren't they?"

"They are indeed, Your Majesty. I am often riveted by the trunks and how they are completely separate from one another at first. Then the trunks meet and as the trees grow higher, the branches of the trees intertwine, seeming to take hold of one another to become almost one tree. It's like one hundred trees become one tree—beautiful and mysterious."

"So you think me mysterious, then?" the queen asked.

"Wait, what …*um*, no …I was referring to the trees and the falls, and—"

"It's quite all right, Roslyn." Amana laughed, seeing the apprehension in her walking companion. "Can a planet not take on the characteristics of its queen?"

"I didn't mean that in a bad way, you know."

"I know you didn't. I am well aware that with the throne comes an element of mystery."

"Is that a drawback?"

"Sometimes, yes; however, in many cases, it's a comfort. Don't get me wrong. I miss the days of being amazingly close to a soul or two, but with the challenges that being queen presents, an added layer of mystery can certainly be an asset."

"Has anyone ever gone beyond your veil of concealment?"

"Well, it's not entirely like that—and, yes, there was one," Amana said. She then allowed her mind to drift off to many cycles earlier, long before Jaesu had crowned her queen. Her thoughts returned to a moment when she had been wandering the fields and talking with the flowers. Even then, she'd felt different from everyone else, as Roslyn had. Only Jovan had ever taken the time to sit with her and inquire about what brought her joy. She'd never made much mention of it, but his visits made her happy—it was what she'd looked forward to most. They would walk, fly, and lie out in the fields, discussing the stars, creatures, seas and mountains. Although she wasn't a part of the Lighted Blade, she'd formed a strong friendship with Jovan and, among all the Gardenians, felt closest to him. Because of Jovan, she looked up to Lighted Blade and their abilities. None of them had any idea of her admiration—at least, to her knowledge.

Plenty had changed after she'd replaced Queen Cha, who'd been eager to take the challenge of becoming human on Earth. But for Amana, this planet with its marvelous, abundant life was the greatest place she could imagine. She cared for everything within Gardenia with all of her being. Once she'd become queen, Amana came into her power through Jaesu's teachings. Amana's slightest touch brought life; everywhere she walked, a secret path of joy was folded into the planet. Wherever her foot trod, living things reached their greatest potential. Plants became greener, water bluer and trees taller; it was even assumed that if dreaded death ever came to Gardenia, Amana's love would be enough to turn it back. But for all of her power and authority, she often longed for the talks with Jovan that she used to have. Still, she wouldn't change a thing. She loved to love, and to reign as queen in a place she was utterly in love with meant more to her than all else.

"Your Majesty?" Roslyn asked, trying to get the queen's attention.

"Oh, I'm sorry, Roslyn," Amana responded with embarrassment. "It was long before I was queen."

"That *was* a long time ago. Do you remember how things were then? I wasn't fully created yet, so I don't really know—just some things which I was taught and read."

They came to a field of pristine green grass which went on for miles. There were mountains in the background, but something in the middle of the grassy field had caught Roslyn's attention. It was a blue blade of grass surrounded by a fiery light.

"You've never been this close, have you?" Amana asked.

"Close? To the grass?"

"No, to what is in the grass."

"Are you referring to that light?"

"Yes. The one that has caught your gaze. No need to be coy with me, Roslyn."

"It draws me in, like it has some sort of power."

"Let us go a little closer, then."

The queen and Roslyn easily floated their way through the tall grass which came up to their midriffs. Halfway toward the blue blade, they were no longer effortlessly gliding toward the light but forcefully pushing the grass out of their way. This was new for Roslyn, as physical struggle was not known to many Gardenians or to souls in general. Roslyn could tell that this was an exercise Amana had participated in before.

"You sure we should be doing this, Your Majesty? The grass doesn't seem to want us getting any closer."

"Just a little bit further! Keep pressing forward."

When they finally got to the mysterious light, it was still only a blue blade of grass. But the fact that it was so different from the others made the unique grass especially interesting.

"I'm not sure I understand, Your Majesty," Roslyn said. She was nervous that Amana was taking her into her confidence. *What if Amana thinks I am smarter than I really am?*

"This, Roslyn, is the Lighted Blade."

"The Lighted Blade? Like Dara and Glynn and Jovan? *That* Lighted Blade?"

"Yes!" the queen answered. "It is after this they are named."

Roslyn stayed silent for a moment as she examined the blue blade of grass.

"It is our life force, Roslyn," Amana said. "Our planet could not survive without it."

"But I thought the queen—"

"Yes, but the queen's power works together with the Lighted Blade. The purpose of the queen is to give love to Gardenia and the purpose of the Blade is to provide peace to all life attached to Gardenia. Together, we form an unbreakable bond of life."

"I don't have any words for this!"

"Think back, a few minutes ago, to how much attention you gave to one strand of grass, even from a distance, due to its uniqueness. And you fought to get to it. You are much like that grass, my dear Roslyn—different, distinct from others, and important in so many ways. Many admire you from a distance, but a time will come when they will fight to get closer to you."

"Why me? I don't understand."

"You will soon enough."

Roslyn still looked confused.

"Earlier," Amana continued, "you asked about the mystery of my role being a comfort. Much like the grass surrounding the Blade becomes harder to pass through and to penetrate, that shield of mystery works in the same way."

"Yes! I can see that. I understand. It is much clearer now."

"So in time, you will understand what I meant in comparing the Blade to you, as well," the queen said. "But for now, let us continue to walk. I feel Jaesu's presence somewhere near."

"Should I go? I mean being in the presence of a queen is extraordinary enough. One can only imagine the importance of conversations between you and the King of the Universe," Roslyn interjected.

"I would completely understand it if you chose to go about your day. However, I would be remiss if I didn't mention to you how much I would appreciate your remaining just a little while longer."

As they turned a corner toward the palace, Amana could see Black, her most trusted advisor, with Jaesu.

"Your Majesty!" said Jaesu, with a head bow and a smile. "And Lady Roslyn, very nice of you to join us."

Amana and Roslyn immediately fell to the ground, reverently bowing toward the Lord. The trees and creatures behind her did the same. The rocks crackled as one in thunderous applause.

Upon rising, Amana responded, "Well, it would have been nice to know that you were coming."

"Then it would not have been a surprise."

"Normally, I would let that one slide, but I must admit to finding it utterly convenient that your visit occurs during the qualifying round of the Owls and Seraphs tournament between the cats and Blade."

"Oh, yes, quite convenient indeed," responded Jaesu.

"And? Is that all?"

Jaesu responded with a smile, "Roslyn, how very nice to see you. Has the queen been this inquisitive all afternoon?"

"With all due respect, you are Lord of all Galaxies, but she is still Queen of Gardenia, so it is best for me to practice wisdom and stay out of this," said Roslyn.

"Indeed, you are wise, young one. I cannot fault your choice there," Jaesu said, laughing.

"Are you finished?" Amana asked. "I mean, if you truly only came to watch the match, then I suppose getting your thoughts on the matter couldn't hurt."

"You should be proud of both teams. Gardenia will be well represented. Black and Scepter emerged victorious, but I was impressed with how quickly the Lighted Blade adjusted to Scepter's style and strategy throughout. You may just have a champion in that team someday."

"I, too, was impressed, Your Majesty," Black joined the conversation. "And you know that I don't impress easily."

"That is for certain, Black. I know that firsthand. And, Lord, you mean an actual winning team, a championship team, from Gardenia?" the queen asked.

Jaesu and Black nodded their heads simultaneously.

"That is striking. Very good. The match went well! Will you be leaving at once?" Amana continued.

"Trying to get rid of me so soon, Your Majesty?"

"To the contrary, my lord," Amana answered. "Actually, I'll confess to hoping you would stay longer as I can't help but enjoy my time with you."

"I will never grow tired of hearing that. And yes, I plan on staying a little longer. Actually, I've asked Orion to join us for a briefing."

"Briefing?" The surprise in her voice was difficult to mask.

"Yes, in the event an attack may come on Gardenia. We should look at some precautions, just in case."

"Orion's prowess has never been breached," the queen responded sharply. "Thousands and thousands of asudem have fallen by his hand over the cycles."

"You know I wouldn't mention it if it weren't worth discussing," Jaesu answered modestly.

Roslyn was beginning to feel a little more awkward as this kind of conversation seemed way out of her depth, and was probably something she shouldn't be hearing. But she felt even more uncomfortable at the idea of interrupting these two titans during such a conversation. She listened attentively, assuming she would soon be dismissed.

Amana could feel Roslyn's confidence in being around such company begin to diminish and knew Jaesu could as well. "Actually, Roslyn, if you wouldn't mind, I may have need of your services even more than I originally anticipated. Would you object to continuing with us?"

"*Um*, of course not, Y-Your Majesty," Roslyn answered, startled. "However long you need me, I'll be here."

"Thank you, Roslyn. I know this isn't normal for you, so I appreciate your feelings in this matter."

Three of the four entered the queen's palace. For a moment, Roslyn stood in awe outside the palace. She hadn't been this close before. Its entrance was guarded by four large pearl-colored bucks on one side. A colossal pale-blue bear was on the other. There were many different rooftops, spanning the width of the palace made of massive rosebuds arrayed like that of the queen.

Roslyn joined the other three inside. The huge front door led into the foyer, where two more pale-blue bears were always on watch. The foyer itself was remarkable. The floor was made exclusively of aquamarine stone. On the left wall was a waterfall that flowed into a pool that took up a third of the room. The wall on the right-hand side was a vertical garden of long-stemmed dark red roses standing completely straight. Roslyn took special notice of those. Their color was identical to the edges of her hair.

The domed ceiling displayed a live motion visual of the ten great worlds of Elevemada. The scene was always changing from planet to planet, with the focus forever on space shots of the planets and their moons. This made the foyer stand out even more because the room was lit beautifully by the thousands of stars playing upon the inner surface of the dome.

Hidden in the domed ceiling's dark skies were black owls who always kept watch. Their eyes matched the stars so closely that even Amana could not tell the difference with her naked eye.

The walkers entered into the Ferrous Conference Hall, soundproofed by enormous shark and dolphin pools made of thick crystal and glass covering the length and width of each wall in the room. The doors that opened to the conference hall were made of iron. As in the foyer, the Ferrous Conference Hall's ceiling displayed live visuals of outer space.

The outer perimeter of Gardenia was where Orion patrolled. Orion was a mammoth presence, roughly two hundred feet tall and about half as wide with muscle like stone. He had bright, merry black eyes, cherry-red lips and straight, medium-length black hair. His bellowing laugh could be heard for miles, especially during battle. Although he had always been known as a mighty warrior, Orion was gentle in spirit and loved the people of Gardenia. He also took his responsibility as Queen Amana's personal seraph and protector seriously. He wore a golden band around his head and a belt around his waist. The belt held three jewels. The jewels were boomerang daggers. Orion preferred peace and talking with his fellow seraphs and friends on Gardenia, but he also made sure any asudem heard him loud and clear as he was defeating them in battle.

"Orion, are you there?" Amana asked, peering at him in the hall's ceiling.

Upon seeing the group of four through a beamed hologram, Orion bowed his head in reverence toward Amana and Jaesu. "I am here, my queen. Great power and might be upon you, Lord Jaesu, King of the Universe!"

"It is good to see you so jubilant, my friend," Jaesu responded. "Not due to the lack of battles, I hope."

"I would prefer it this way. No battles, just peace and rest. At least, until the Owls and Seraphs tournament begins," said Orion. "I rather dislike distractions from the championship rounds."

"Well said. I couldn't agree more," replied Jaesu. "Sadly, I expect that you should be a little more on your guard than usual."

"Oh? I assumed the asudem had given up all attacks on Elevemada. They are powerless here."

"Not according to the foretelling *Mysteries of the Deep*," Jaesu responded, lifting up the book he had referenced and handing it to Amana. "It looks like we should be expecting days of great battles and even worse to unfold."

Queen Amana looked at knowledge as a gift and knew it wise to heed Jaesu's words. She called for a quick pause in the meeting, so she could review the passages marked by Jaesu. She removed herself from the hall and went into her own personal sanctuary off the main hall. She sat at the marble desk in the middle of the room and began to read.

One of the marvelous things about Gardenia was that none of the furniture or homes or palaces had to be built. Instead, minerals and plants responded to the thoughts of souls by transforming and reforming into whatever was needed. In this case, knowing that the queen was looking to read, particles in the room arranged themselves into a marble desk and chair, while the walls reformed into vertical gardens—because the queen preferred gardens during times of trial. The ceiling in the sanctuary mirrored her emotions, in this case becoming as cloudy as an approaching storm. She sat down and continued to read further into the book of prophecies. Gardenia had seen battles before, but this felt different to her, especially with Jaesu himself delivering such a solemn warning.

Jaesu, Black, Orion, and Roslyn continued to discuss the matter while the queen studied privately.

"Roslyn, I barely noticed you. Forgive me. I wouldn't normally expect the renowned Lady of the Woods to be in the palace discussing war operations," said Orion.

"Neither did she expect to be here, Orion," replied Black.

"While it's true that I can't quite see how my presence here is needed, I've quickly learned to trust her majesty's requests," answered Roslyn. "And what do you mean by *renowned?*"

"The deer talk," said Orion. "You are very well loved and respected by all of them. They call you 'Lady of the Woods.' Did you not know?"

"Cute, real cute," Roslyn replied. "I was certainly unaware of such a moniker."

"It suits you, Roslyn," Jaesu interjected. "On the topic of your presence here; it is both good and wise that you honor and trust, especially during times when it isn't justified by your own understanding."

"Roslyn's purpose here will be unveiled in due time. If there's one thing I know about the queen, it's that she always has a plan, even if it's beyond my own logic," Black said. "But we have somewhat of a crisis on our paws, I would say. Lord, are you able to share with us some of what concerns you?"

Queen Amana came back into the room, talking as she walked toward the group. "War is like a set of twins, equal in look and result but defined by integral differences: one, to achieve power and two, to defend the innocence of life and love. The most magnificent of us never lose sight of either; we never give up on the latter or give in to the former, no matter how enticing the former may seem," she said.

Roslyn, feeling as if she were growing by the minute, was still astonished that a commoner like herself was in this sort of company. *What purpose could I ever have in battle? I'm a deer herder, a woodslady.*

"Orion, according to the prophetic mysteries, we have much to prepare for," the queen continued. "Waves of asudem attacks, strategically coordinated by their chief general, whom I interpret to be Phan, will hit the Elevemada soon and, more specifically, Gardenia. We are talking about millions of asudem."

"Phan? *Hmm...* Well, I can take 'em, Your Majesty!" bellowed Orion. "His power is great, but in the Elevemada, he can be defeated. They won't know what hit them! I will have them cowering back to Algolithar faster than a cardinal wing fold."

Jaesu, Black, and Roslyn looked at Amana. "That's just it," Amana replied. "They've never defeated you, no matter how many they send into battle. Yet they are going to bring out their legions in masses along with Phan, whom they haven't sent into battle here since the purge. There's something off. It's too easy. It must be a diversion of sorts."

"A diversion?" asked Black, as she tossed a peach pit from her mouth toward the queen.

"But from what?" Orion asked.

"Earth. It must have something to do with Earth," the queen replied, reforming a peach from its pit and tossing it back to Black. Peaches were the great cat's snack of choice. The cats and other animals on Gardenia, unlike souls, had to eat, but they didn't eat the flesh of other animals. Fruit, nuts, and other foodstuffs sustained them well.

"Perhaps we are giving them too much credit here?" asked Orion. "Couldn't we assume that they are coming in large numbers to fight, the same as always? I mean they haven't come close to defeating us yet. It's like they never learn."

"Careful, my friend," cautioned the queen. "Always respect your enemy. If they choose to disrespect us, then fine, but we should not make that mistake."

Orion quickly conceded with a nod that Amana was correct. "What else could it be? Why Earth?"

Roslyn had a point she wanted to raise but felt it was better if she stayed silent. Jaesu noticed her thought and glanced at her and then at the queen.

The queen picked up on it. "Roz, what do you think?"

A bit nervous and shy that she was being called out, Roslyn timidly spoke her mind, "I wonder if they are trying to interfere with the Carriage Stream?"

The Carriage Stream, often called Endostream or Carriage,

was the tubular path souls took through the galaxy upon making the choice to embrace the challenges of becoming human on Earth. If the Carriage was blocked or destroyed, it would impede any soul from getting through into the lifeway, which they had to enter in order to be conceived. Roslyn continued, "I mean, if they are planning a simultaneous attack on both, wouldn't taking out the Carriage enable them to maximize their resources effectively on Earth?"

"But the Carriages come from all ten planets, not just Gardenia. They would have to defeat us all in order to be successful. They haven't yet defeated even one of our worlds … ever," Black replied.

"Still," said Amana, "if they could block the Carriage, it would cause an enormous current shift between both of our galaxies and minimize future resistance on Earth. It doesn't seem logical that they could win perhaps, but in this case, they still win by losing. We must be on our guard in either situation. I have summoned an emergency meeting with all ten kings and queens of the Elevemada. We'll meet on Alpha. I fear the Elevemada, not just Gardenia, will be in great danger if we do not plan well. My Lord, we will need you with us."

An emergency meeting among such rulers was very rare. Amana had never called for, nor participated, in one before. It had been many cycles before her reign when the last emergency session had taken place.

"I am with you and will journey with you to Alpha," Jaesu responded. "I agree. A conference among the leaders is needed, but do you think it wise to abandon the throne of Gardenia, even for a short time, knowing what we know?"

"The throne will not be abandoned. Roslyn will lead in my stead until we return, which shouldn't be long."

Shocked at the queen's decision, Roslyn jumped in. "What!? Your Majesty, with all due respect, I don't think that's—"

"Careful, young one," the queen responded gently. "If Lord Jaesu is indeed King of the Universe, which I believe he is, and if Lord Jaesu trusts my judgment, which I believe he does, then I ask that you continue to trust me as well. Besides, Black and Orion will be your right and left hands. There aren't many who love Gardenia with the fervor and passion you do. Right now, your planet needs you. Your queen needs you."

"Nothing to worry about, Roz; it will be like taking a peach from a tree," Black responded, though she was also surprised that the queen had planned for this.

"Of course, I trust you, my queen, but I don't feel ready," Roslyn said.

"Sometimes events choose us," Jaesu said, as he placed his hand on her shoulder to calm her.

"I can show you how to use the queen's mystic window while she's gone, so you can see the look on Jasmine's face when she gets the shawl," Orion said deviously.

"ORION!" the queen admonished. "Isn't that supposed to be a private moment?"

"I was trying to reassure Roslyn and put her at ease, Your Majesty."

"Like you aren't the least bit curious?" asked Amana archly.

"Well ...*umm*..." Orion tried to form a response.

"I thought as much," said the queen with a brow-raising nod toward Roslyn. "It is paramount that I share this knowledge with my fellow kings and queens. Before you know it, your hands will be decorating with those beautiful pink leaves once again."

"Although unworthy, I am honored to guard your throne, my queen." Roslyn bowed, knowing the queen must leave quickly.

"Then we must go now, Your Majesty," Jaesu said. "The sovereigns will be at Alpha by the third sunset."

"You're right, Lord," said Amana. "Roz, walk with Jaesu and me for a moment." They began to walk toward the foyer of the palace.

"I want you to remember two things: those who greatly desire power are unworthy of it, and everything that happens, no matter how great or small, happens for a reason. Nothing in our lives is random or trivial."

"Yes, my queen. I will be mindful."

"Let us go," Amana said to Jaesu. Jaesu took off his cloak and covered them both. They were gone instantly.

"Wait …where'd they go?" Roslyn asked.

"Remember, Lord Jaesu is in many places at once," Black said in response. "He can portal to a million different planets in a split second with a million others as he did with the queen. Don't try to figure it out. It's another one of those things our minds will forever be unable to comprehend."

"How long will it take for them to get there?" Roslyn asked.

"I would imagine that they are there already," Black replied.

"Let us review palace security dealings and protocol to get you up to speed."

* * *

"Welcome to Alpha, Queen Amana!" shouted King Handel of Alpha from his perch across from the Water Tower. The Water Tower was a powerful skyscraper spring of water reaching from the ground to the clouds. It had many landing platforms and beautiful walkways, all made of water forever in motion. The platforms never lost their shapes, just as a river flows yet keeps its shape within its banks. Springs within the tower could move upward or downward as needed. Across from the tower was a mountainous glacier which fed melted ice to the tower through a stream at its lower level. In turn, the tower recycled water from an opposing stream, which became part of the glacier.

Inside the glacier was a secret place known only to kings and queens called Sickle of the Sovereign. This was where Amana was transported. She was confused when only Handel welcomed her, and not Jaesu. The room was quickly filling up with other kings and queens. Handel, noticing that the Gardenian Queen was taken aback, went over and gently whispered in her ear, "Remember, our great king is in many places at once. I was meeting with him as he was transporting you. It's all right. I don't think I'll ever get used to it either."

This put the queen at ease. "I appreciate that," she whispered in return. "I have not been in this room before. It's quite an interesting place for this kind of gathering."

"Thank you, great queen," Handel replied. "With the magnificent cities we have, no one would think to find us in a glacier."

Amana nodded in agreement. She made her way around the room to exchange brief pleasantries with her peers. Time was short, so lengthy conversations would have to wait. She was a little sad about this, as the whole event was awe-inspiring.

"Magnificent rulers!" called out Handel. "I welcome you here to Alpha for this most important conference. Our King Jaesu has joined us today to discuss a possible threat to the Elevemada. Lord Jaesu?" Handel handed the podium over to Jaesu.

"Thank you, King Handel, and also thank you, great kings

and queens, for understanding the urgency regarding this matter. We are entering troubled and confusing times, unlike what many of you have been used to. Before I turn the remainder of this short conference over to Queen Amana, I must say this: no matter what happens, keep your faith in our Great Father and know that you have been chosen to lead at just this moment. Be encouraged and of good cheer. I am with you always," Jaesu concluded.

All bowed in unison, glorifying him.

As Queen Amana took the platform, all attention was on her. "Fellow monarchs," she said, before pausing. "Knowledge is to an Alphan as breath is to a human. I am sure the mighty King Handel could instruct us on the prophecies written in *Mysteries of the Deep*. Many of these prophecies foretell battles and trials. I believe the time the prophecies speak of is at hand, and a surge of massive, simultaneous attacks on Gardenia and Earth will soon occur. Other parts of the Elevemada may be at risk as well."

"Another attack on Gardenia? A big one?" asked Queen Tamika of Zae. "Haven't they seen enough of their asudem destroyed at the hands of Orion? Besides, if this is the battle spoken of in the *Book of Mysteries*, then Phan, their chief prince, would have to lead them. I find that highly unlikely."

"I was thinking the same thing, Tamika," said King Francois of Fricto. "Logically, it is foolish that they would send waves of their legions to both Gardenia and Earth. Why not focus on Earth alone, as they have done through most of the ages? It is where they are most powerful."

"Yes, yes, we thought exactly the same thing," Amana responded. "But what if they are looking to attack the Carriage somehow? What if they use Gardenia as a diversion? Asudem could then fortify their attack on Earth with fewer souls to contend with, while the Carriage is blockaded."

"They would need to blockade ten of the Carriages, and not just Gardenia," said King Handel. "That's a tall order. Perhaps we are getting ahead of ourselves."

"Yes, we understand that," said Queen Amana, discouraged by how the debate was starting. "I am not asking for a battle plan or a decision on an attack. What I am saying is: be on guard. Inform your seraphs. Let's commit to one another to keep the lines of communication open. If any of us sees anything off, we'll inform the others. And if an attack happens on Gardenia, then you will know to be prepared. Most importantly, my friends, let us remember that our Lord Jaesu has warned us that troubling times are ahead. No matter what comes, as his chosen leaders, we can resist any attack or bombardment, if we keep our faith in our leadership and bonds with one another."

All agreed. Not everyone believed that war was coming (none had seen the signs in their worlds), but they agreed to keep communication a high priority, just in case. There was some discussion of past battles, of the various weaknesses of the asudem, and they reviewed security and communications arrangements, altering the latter slightly to make them more efficient. Then the meeting was formally brought to an end. Immediately the room filled with social chatter, talk of Owls and Seraphs and mentions of amazing new music from Cymblali. The smiles and laughter of the gathering were disconcerting to Amana.

Before leaving, King Francois of Fricto drew her aside and said, "Gardenian Queen, these meetings are for real emergencies and not children's tales. I know you meant well, but apparently you are a novice when it comes to the realm of battle, with all due respect." The tall, bald king put a hand on her back.

He was many cycles older than she, and she felt his amusement at her expense, his condescension toward this young queen who thought she understood battle.

Amana, even more dejected, went over to Jaesu as she bowed in the direction of her fellow kings and queens. "Are you ready, Amana? Do not be alarmed, but when you return to Gardenia, I will not be there. You will see me shortly. I must go to the Great Father on an important matter," said Jaesu.

"I am, my Lord. Thank you. Understood. I probably won't ever get used to the quantum leap. I'd much rather be relaxing under the trees and simplexes of my world," she said with a slight smile. The meeting was not what she'd expected—how could the other sovereigns not take Jaesu's warning seriously? She wanted to be home. She took hold of his robe.

*   *   *

They arrived safely on Gardenia, though not in the palace. Amana found herself in Millennia Mansion. All of the leaves were black, and the air was full of the sound of desperate weeping. She saw Bethany and Jovan bent over in excruciating pain—something she had never experienced or seen, but recognized as if it had always been a part of her life.

Orion was unable to protect himself. The queen felt completely powerless and paralyzed. She heard a peal of sinister laughter and watched as a fire blazed up throughout the library, burning the leaves. Being after being was slaughtered, the animals' blood running red over the cold marble floors. The throne from the palace had been moved to the literature hall and was being protected by two female souls. She, then, saw a shadow of an asudem standing over Orion, about to slay him. Before that could happen, a brilliant light filled the room, annihilating the asudem.

"Amana! Your Majesty!" said Roslyn frantically, as she had been trying to get the queen's attention for several moments. "Are you okay? Can you hear me?"

The queen looked around. She was back in her throne room in the palace with Black and Roslyn by her side. She was unsure as to what had just happened, but she knew she had to make her way to the mansion to find out. She was shaken and needed answers.

Jaesu was no longer on Gardenia. She must have had a vision. It had felt incredibly real and terrifying, particularly because Amana had never before experienced a vision herself.

"The meeting went …wait… where is Orion?" the queen said. "Black, we must be ready!"

"Your Majesty?" Orion said. "I am right here. You froze for a few minutes. Are you well?"

"I don't know. I just don't know. There is something very wrong. Roslyn, stay with the throne. I am going to Millennia to meditate," the queen said.

Black, Orion, and Roslyn looked at her and one another with great apprehension and confusion as she left the palace. Something had clearly happened to the queen. They felt it.

"Perhaps dangerous times are truly upon us," Orion whispered.

CHAPTER 4

The Opening

The Owls and Seraphs tournament was played on a different planet each cycle. Each of the ten worlds hosted in turn. Now it was held on the oceanic planet of Seocia. The planet consisted mostly of mountains of various sizes, narrow valleys, and mighty oceans. Thousands of different sea creatures inhabited its large seas. Massive sea turtles, leviathans, giant squid, sea horses large and small, flying fish, swordfish, deep ocean fish with pebbly eyes, whiskered catfish, and mermaids with glittering tails were among the remarkable residents of Seocia.

Walkways of sand and stone several miles long acted as bridges connecting the mountains to one another. The capital of Seocia was the floating city of Xaree. The city looked like an inverted mountain, floating in the sky with huge oysters dangling from its sides. Each oyster contained pearls so big and bright they could be seen from a great distance. Seocia's sunsets were famous throughout the galaxy because of how the light from the pearls mingled with the light from the setting suns.

Many had come to this lavish world for the annual sporting event. There were several weeks yet before the games were to begin. However, most of the teams selected to play had already arrived in order to train and get familiar with both the terrain and their opponents.

The Lighted Blade had been given spacious guest quarters in one of the many royal buildings made of pearlescent shells and carpeted with springy seaweed. Each member of the team had his or her own room with furniture and plants anticipating individual preferences. Jovan's room, for instance, had windows on three sides so he could watch everything going on around him, with plants drawing his attention when anything new was going on. Bethany's room was full of sweet fruits and candies; it was a hobby of hers to experience new tastes. She immediately began thinking about what she'd bring back to the cats.

Along with great speed, Bethany had a powerful gift called *magnetize*. This allowed her to call any solid object to her at will from great distances. As soon as she saw the fruits and candies, she immediately called them; her hair from excitement transformed from light brown to fiery red as she couldn't contain herself. But after a moment, she came to her senses and figured it would be best to leave them for the time being.

After they had settled in, Bethany and Jovan wandered around the city. "This is amazing, Jovan. I have never seen anything like it," said Bethany. "The water palaces and sea dragons … everything is so magical!"

"For certain, and the teams appear to be a lot more than we are used to dealing with. Take a look." Jovan pointed toward another team practicing what seemed to be basic exercises. They still came across as far more organized than the Lighted Blade had ever been when prepping.

"*Whoa!* Who are they? They all look super good."

"Well, Beth, it IS the biggest sporting event in the galaxy. Not sure any of the planets want to send their amateurs, ya know?"

"Except ours. I wonder if Dara has seen the other teams?"

"I don't know. But what I do know is that we are going to need to get a plan together, a real plan. We can't wing it; we will be stardust in moments if we try that here."

The pair continued to walk through many of the pre-tournament festivities and galas. There were small musical groups, acrobatic displays, and friendly meetings of old competitors—those who had passed beyond active play but not yet gone to Earth. The Lighted Blade had been well-known throughout Gardenia, but none of them, save for Dara, had ever been off-world before. With the possibility of an attack on the horizon, Queen Amana had required Scepter to stay behind on Gardenia to help with security. To their surprise, the Lighted Blade members had been chosen to represent the planet. They were unaware of the rumors of battle. Amana kept such things confined to her inner circle, which now included Roslyn.

"Jovan, I think there are more teams over there by those small mountains," said Bethany.

"Great. A little scouting couldn't hurt, at least until we meet up with the others."

Bethany quickly grabbed Jovan's arm and dragged him over to one of the large sea turtles. On Seocia, sea turtles were one of the splendid tourist attractions; they provided enjoyable ferry rides to and from the mountains.

"Come on, Jo. Please, we may never get back here again!"

Jovan rolled his eyes. "Okay, Bethany, don't forget why we are here," he said, although secretly he liked the idea of riding on the turtles.

They climbed onto a giant green turtle with a black-and-gray shell. He began to swim toward the practice area.

"Hey! How do you know where we want to go?" asked Bethany.

"I'm a sea turtle, little soul. I always know where I am going. And the name is Hal, not Hey."

"Oh, I'm sorry …wow, now I am embarrassed! Very nice to meet you, Hal. I am Bethany, and this is Jovan."

"Greetings, Hal," Jovan said. "How did you know where we were headed? I know you said you are a sea turtle and all, but—"

"Young master, we sea turtles have longitude and latitude lines built into our very cores. We always know the direction we are meant to head. From what I understand, we are like this in any world we inhabit," Hal responded.

"That is blade! Any world?" asked Bethany.

"Blade? I don't know him," said Hal. "But, yes, even on outer system planets like Earth, our relatives are the same. Knowing the right path is instinct for us."

"Don't mind her, Hal," said Jovan. "'Blade' is just a lingo we use when something is top notch."

"Top notch? *Mmm*…I see. Perhaps we should part ways with the vernacular."

"Have you taken anyone else to the practices?" asked Bethany.

"Why, yes, several," Hal replied. "The captain of the Alpha team—Phyllis, I believe her name is—and that captain of the Gardenian team, Dara. They were on the last trip."

"Dara and Phyllis? They were together?" asked Jovan.

"It is quite common for captains to get together and discuss the events and the like," said Hal. "First time for the two of you?"

"For what?" asked Bethany.

"OWLS AND SERAPHS, child, of course!" snapped Hal. "You certain that you are playing?" he asked sarcastically.

"Yes, she is playing, Hal. She may be slow-witted, but believe me, that's about the only thing she is slow in. Once she gets out into the open, you will see that she's among the fastest in the galaxy," Jovan answered.

Bethany was surprised and appreciative that Jovan stuck up for her. While they were close, he usually joked around regarding her, especially in public. The sudden change comforted her, even if it was only temporary. "Yes, well, Jovan is the fastest ever, so I still have some work to do."

"Fastest ever?" questioned Hal. "Well …big words from a rookie. I have heard from several patrons that Anton from Alpha is a megastar—that the Alphans have all but secured another title. Perhaps I could start passing your names around. It might help sort the odds out a bit when it comes to the wagers."

"Anton?" asked Jovan. "Guess I shouldn't be disappointed then. To be the best, ya gotta beat the best. He'll get his chance."

"You might want to humble up, boy," Hal said.

Jovan was confident in his speed. He looked forward to great challenges. Deep down, he knew that he could be outmatched by those from other worlds, but that didn't shake his poise in the least.

"Is that the entrance?" interrupted Bethany.

"Sure is, little one," Hal responded. "Just fly through that tunnel there, and the practice waters are on the other side of the mountains. You will notice that the mountains surround the waters in order for you to have, at least, some privacy. I will be watching out for you both to provide a return voyage."

Jovan and Bethany thanked the turtle and took off for the practice area before hearing a familiar voice.

"Where have you been?" asked Jacen. "Can you believe this place? It's utterly different from Gardenia. Water everywhere! Did you ride one of those leviathan beasts over?"

"*Um*...no ...a turtle," said Jovan.

"But a big turtle named Hal, and he was very nice!" added Bethany.

"Oh, me, too," said Jacen. "I was wondering if anyone had tried to jump the dragon."

"Got a feeling we aren't supposed to try," said Jovan.

"*Um*, yeah ...good point."

"Hal, the turtle, said he'd ferried Dara here with the captain of the Alphans," Bethany said.

"That would be correct. They are right over there," Jacen said, while pointing.

Dara was continuing a conversation started on the turtle ferry with Phyllis. The Alphans were the favorites to win the event every cycle, and more often than not, they did. The combination of Phyllis's stature, which was considerably taller than any female from Gardenia, beautiful long shiny black hair, flawless white-as-snow complexion, and fame throughout the galaxy somewhat intimidated Dara.

"So how does this team you have now differ from teams you have won with in the past?" Dara asked. "Is it possible to differentiate one level of success from another, especially when you have won several championships?"

"I think the team that we have now might be the best of them all. Anton is our most dominant player and my heir apparent, at least, if I have anything to say about it."

"Heir apparent?"

"*Ah*, I think I have said too much." Phyllis smiled. "My team doesn't even know yet. I have been talking with Jaesu about making the choice. You know, to take on the trials on Earth."

"Whoa ..." said Dara, surprised. "I don't understand. You have everything. You are from a great planet and captain of a great team. You have everything."

"Hardly, Dara," Phyllis responded, shaking her head as her thumb caressed the bottom of her own orange-red lips. "Alphans naturally learn and experience so much of life that one can actually become bored with not being challenged."

"Challenged?" asked Dara. "Shouldn't life be joyful?"

"Joyful is in the eye of the beholder, agree?" Phyllis replied. "My idea of joyful is learning something new, preferably many somethings new. When I was a young soul, I soaked up knowledge speedily, as most Alphans do. Now that there is little left for me to soak up—here, anyway—I feel worthless. I want to take things to another level."

"Worthless?" said an astonished Dara. "I can't imagine—"

"You are from Gardenia; I wouldn't expect you to."

"I'm not sure what you mean by that," Dara answered defensively.

"It's nothing, really, Dara. Gardenia, from what I understand, is a peace-loving, lively planet. Jaesu creates souls to suit their respective worlds. Alpha is a non-stop, large-city world of beings competing for knowledge and skill. Your queen probably selected your team for Owls and Seraphs or perhaps offered you a qualifying round. Alpha has huge tournaments with many teams, all great teams, to determine who moves on. I often think that is what keeps us sharp and gives us our edge."

"Iron sharpens iron. Isn't that the old saying?"

"Yes, indeed. I see you have gained some knowledge as well."

"Well, we aren't completely dull-witted on other worlds."

"I wasn't suggesting—"

"It's okay. I understand. Besides, if you make the journey to Earth this cycle, then I won't have to worry about facing both you and Anton in future tournaments. That is, if he is as good as you say." Dara clearly was annoyed with Phyllis; she knew quite well how good Anton was. She had been scouting him for several cycles on her own.

"It's his reaction time that makes him superior," answered Phyllis. "And it's more than muscle speed; he can anticipate actions from an adversary like no soul I have ever seen. That's really what makes him the fastest soul in the galaxy."

"Second fastest," Dara shot back. "Don't think anyone could take down Jovan in a chase."

"*Ha-ha-ha,*" Phyllis laughed. "Gardenians are so adorable. This is the big time now, sweetie. I did some scouting, and I have heard some respectable things about your team, but let's be honest: Your types have never played in a real tournament game. Do you even have a stratagem yet? Don't get me wrong; I'm not being insulting, just adjusting your expectations a little."

"Well, the games aren't for a while yet. Why don't we give the dignitaries and visitors some entertainment? For fun, you know? Think about it—the great Anton from Alpha versus Jovan the Gardenian. We are playing in the first round anyway. It would be a great introduction to the tournament, and quite unexpected."

"My dear!" said Phyllis, shocked. "Do you think that Anton, the greatest player in the Elevemada, would really grant a request to race someone from Gardenia? We have nothing to gain. I think not."

"Your team is full of champions. And my team may not have the trophies or the titles, but they are champions to me. I know how competitive they are. If your team even has a minuscule amount of the heart mine has, I would be stunned, to say the least. I don't care how many awards you've won," Dara said in a spirited tone.

"I see you are no fool, yet I fear you will still be disillusioned," admonished Phyllis. "Nevertheless, you may be on to something. Kings and queens should be arriving shortly to mingle with one another. With all of the visitors here, a contest to keep them from getting bored may be just the thing, even if such a contest is destined to be one-sided."

"Very well, then. I'm sure Jovan would be delighted to enter into a sprint against *his majesty*," said Dara, attempting to get on Phyllis's nerves by mocking Anton's prowess.

"We'll be waiting," said Phyllis. "In the meantime, I'll tell the mermaid council about the exhibition. That will get the word out quickly. I'm sure the attractions and the cities will empty as audiences flock to see Anton flash his brilliance."

Phyllis told the mermaids and sea turtles, persuading them to spread the word. She knew King Handel and his entourage had already arrived at the practice field. Handel could not wait to greet his great captain. He relished the Alpha team's dynasty of winners in Owls and Seraphs.

Phyllis could see him in the distance. His rich red robe lined with white silk over a tall, slender build and medium-length blond hair made him stand out. He was a popular king. Like many on Alpha, he trusted in knowledge much more than in emotions, feelings, or relationships.

"How is my favorite captain?" said the king as he embraced Phyllis. "Are you ready to bring us another trophy?"

Phyllis bowed. "But, of course, Your Majesty. Have the others arrived?"

"You mean the monarchs from the other worlds?" Handel asked. "Yes, many are entering in now, as a matter of fact. We will be overseeing the events from up there." He pointed to a long, spacious room cut out of the mountain. It was a royal suite, offering complete privacy, as well as a spectacular view of the games.

"I have a surprise for you, my king," said Phyllis. "You may be happy to know that we have set up an opening act and have put Anton in the competition. The news is being spread as we speak."

"Anton?" said the king with raised eyebrows. "Who would dare race him with the whole galaxy watching?"

"Some peasant from Gardenia named Jovan."

"A Gardenian? Battling Anton?" laughed Handel. "That is preposterous. *Ah*, very well. Queen Amana will take the embarrassment like a good sport, I'm sure. She has a good appreciation of history and knows her place."

Phyllis could see Dara coming toward her. "Your Majesty, here comes the Gardenian captain. I would hate to be rude." Phyllis winked and curtsied to her king.

"Very well. This is going to be amusing. Either way, a race to start things off is a grand gesture to those waiting."

Phyllis called out to Anton who was close by. She introduced him to Dara and the Blade team. Anton stood six feet tall with a muscular build that seemed carved out of stone. His eyes were black with dark blue pupils that dilated most when he was in a competitive mood. His hair was also black and long, shoulder-length with dark blue accents. Though extremely handsome, his face was stamped with a faint arrogance. The crowd watched his every movement. He was considered the top player in the Elevemada, and such arrogance was considered normal for an Alphan.

"Dara, my dear," Phyllis said. "This is Anton."

Anton bowed to Dara respectfully. "Pleasure to meet you, Dara. We look forward to a great contest with your team once the games begin."

"Thank you, Anton, and we the same," responded Dara. "Phyllis, Anton … here are Jovan, Bethany, and Jacen."

As they all bowed to one another, Anton noticed Bethany and asked, "Are you the Bethany of Gardenia with magnetizing ability?"

Bethany, trying to hide her delight that she was known to an Alphan, replied, "Why, yes. That would be me."

"I understand you have great speed as well?" Anton asked.

"I'd like to think so, but haven't quite figured out how to beat Jovan here," Bethany answered as she playfully elbowed Jovan.

"Well, keep your eyes fixed on me, and you will figure out how to beat him," Anton said with a smirk as he backed away to get ready for the race, turning his gaze to Jovan.

Punru, the great owl who had been chosen to moderate the Owls and Seraphs matchups, would also preside over this race. The captains each met with their respective player. Kings and queens were filling up the royal viewing room and were exchanging salutations while eagerly awaiting the action. Word had spread very quickly. People from many worlds were cramming into the practice area to watch this exhibition. Although most on Gardenia celebrated Jovan and believed him to be the fastest in the galaxy, none of the other worlds knew much of him.

"Jovan," said Dara, "just be you. Don't let him rattle your nerves. Even if you don't win, you deserve this chance to go against the best."

"I go against the best each morning in Bethany—don't ever tell her I said that," replied Jovan. "I'm not looking for fame, but I'm gonna win this." He turned from Dara and waited to hear instructions from Punru.

Phyllis offered last-minute guidance to Anton and brought the coaching to a close with, "And remember, Anton, no matter what, you are an Alphan. You are better than they are. You are, by far, the most gifted player anyone has ever seen. This race might as well be over already. Now put your greatness on display."

Sitting atop one of the massive boulders way above the racecourse was Glynn. His brown color and tan robe mixed in well with the rocks where the other souls and animals couldn't notice him. He preferred to feel the conversations from the audience and observe rather than participate directly.

"Something feels off," he said to himself.

Both racers went to the starting circle. Punru had begun his introduction to the race and relayed directives.

"Now, contestants, I shall be watching the race to ensure fairness and fun. Once you both shoot out from this practice area, there will be three mountains that you must target, each one higher than the one before. Your mission is to race each other to the top of each. When you reach the highest point of the third mountain, you race back and grab this scroll from my talon. Now, mind you, the third mountain is very high, and with Seocia being a water planet, that's important to remember. Are we ready?"

Jovan and Anton looked at each other and nodded their heads as if to say, "Let's get this going already!"

"Ready!" shouted Punru. "Begin!"

Anton shot off the line with all speed into the tunnel separating the practice area from the surrounding oceans and toward the three mountains. Jovan, a notoriously slow starter, already trailed Anton by a great distance. He exited the tunnel and calculated the distance to the mountains. They looked several miles away. Jovan had a habit during his races of talking with Jaesu. Although Jaesu wasn't racing with him now, Jovan always felt his presence. "Lord, it looks like we are behind again. I know, without your favor, I'm never as fast as I am with it. Grant me great wisdom, so I can win this thing, O mighty King," Jovan prayed.

The crowds filled the coliseum in the practice area and thronged the railways and balconies of the surrounding mountains. Dara was nervous but still proud of Jovan. She looked over to the grounds far below the royal suite. Just outside of the tunnel, Jaesu was watching the race. Trying not to stir up the crowd or get in anyone's way, she slowly made her way out to him.

"I thought I'd find you here. Shouldn't you be with the other kings and queens? Being that, I don't know …you are the highest king ever?" Dara asked Jaesu.

"I wasn't invited." He smiled in response. "Besides, I enjoy watching from here."

"Not invited?" questioned Dara indignantly. "Who are they not to invite you?"

"Dara," Jaesu responded gently. "They are kings and queens. I gave them authority, and even I must respect their choices. If I forced them to do my will, then there would be no need for kings and queens, true?"

She knew he was right, but didn't like it. She didn't need to be forced to show respect, and neither did Queen Amana. "So who are you rooting for, Anton or Jovan?"

Jaesu let out a subtle laugh. "I root for them both to do well, and I am proud of each of them."

"Avoiding the question, I see."

"I'll say this. I prefer to help those who ask for help," Jaesu said.

"Well, I don't think any of them needs any help with …wait a minute…."

Jaesu already knew where she was going and softly said, "*Shhh…*," as he placed his index finger over his lips. "Let's see what happens."

Anton soared through the skies and passed the first mountain with ease. *I am surprised this race isn't closer,* he thought to himself. Jovan was still a long way behind. He saw the second mountain closing in and the third mountain beyond. It was going to be quite the climb, even when flying.

"Can't you be at many places at once? Are you flying out there now?" Dara asked Jaesu.

"I certainly can, but in this case, I am just here, next to you, enjoying the race as a fan, both of the sport and your company."

Jovan finally passed the first mountain, still not gaining any ground.

The second mountain was a huge beast in size. Its top reached well into the clouds. As Anton approached the summit, he knew he was still well ahead of Jovan. *This is the best they have? We're going to bury them in round one. I hope he is learning something for next cycle.*

Jovan looked up to see that Anton had conquered the second mountain. He also noticed there were diagonal tunnels which allowed light to pass through. He could see the movement of water at the mountain's surface. On Gardenia, when a tunnel of any kind was close to water, wind passed through it. *A mountain this size on top of a massive body of water just has to invite a strong wind blowing up from the bottom.* Jovan continued to pray, yet he gave up his position and dropped low toward the sea, risking falling further behind. He dropped lower and lower. The crowd was surprised at the move and started to mock him openly. Some even thought he had given up.

"What is he doing?!" Dara asked Jaesu.

Jaesu remained silent. Dara could tell he was concentrating on the race.

As Jovan had hoped, a massive gust of wind acted as a slingshot, sending him through the air fast. The tailwind's force catapulted him over the mountain's peak fading just as he closed behind Anton. There was a huge gasp and applause throughout the audience. They had never thought to see something so surprising and exciting.

"You knew that was going to happen, didn't you?" Dara shook her head toward Jaesu playfully.

"Who? Me? What would ever make you contemplate such a thing?"

Anton looked at Jovan in disbelief. No one had ever caught up from so far behind. His confidence was shaken. The two souls were neck and neck, facing the planet and couldn't help but glance at one another as rivals. Anton wondered if he had finally met his match, as both racers had passed the middle of the third mountain and were speeding toward its highest point.

"You cheated! You had to have," Anton yelled toward Jovan.

Jovan laughed in return. "I did no such thing. And besides, I'm just a Gardenian. We're not knowledgeable enough to cheat," he said in a smart-aleck way.

The competitive spirits were gaining steam, closing in on their target. Each reminded himself that he must touch the top before racing back.

Suddenly, as the peak was within range, the two young souls saw an unexpected sight: a female with tumbling red hair, smooth, light-blue features and mesmerizing eyes. Neither had ever beheld such a beauty. She was crouched on the peak, awaiting them both. As they reached the top, she spoke, "Well done, boys! Now catch *me* ...if you dare."

She then darted like lightning toward the finish line. Anton and Jovan were both completely caught off guard racing back, no longer thinking about each other or the contest. This being intrigued them. She was faster than any spirit.

Anton lost his focus. It wasn't about being faster than Jovan, but being the fastest in the galaxy. And right now, this being was leaving them both in the dust.

Both contestants increased their speed; the crowd watched in awe. Incredible speed and this new, beautiful being had captivated all spectators. Anton and Jovan were solely fixated on catching and passing her. The finish line was in sight.

"Who is she?" Dara asked Jaesu. "Did you place her there to distract Anton?"

Jaesu looked on curiously. "No, Dara, not at all." He was being more serious this time; she could tell he wasn't playing around.

Anton and Jovan each closed the gap, but she was still poised to finish first. Suddenly she pulled up and stopped, turning her attention toward the two competing souls. Stunned at her halt, neither had time to react. They both sped through the finish line and grabbed the scroll at once.

"TIE!" yelled Punru.

The crowd erupted in applause. Even though there was no winner, they had been quite entertained. Anticipation for round one was at an all-time high now. A legitimate rivalry had been established between Alpha and Gardenia, not to mention the question on everyone's minds: Who was that being, and where did she come from?

Both racers, annoyed with themselves for not attaining victory, nodded in respect to one another, still very distracted. They descended to the practice area along with the mysterious being.

"Well, flyers of modest speed," the female being said, "I hope I wasn't a distraction." She laughed before soaking in some applause.

The rivals raised their eyebrows and shook their heads. Oddly, they felt comfortable around her, as well as subtly excited. It was a different feeling than either had experienced before.

"My manners!" she said. "I am Eleanora." She looked up and down at them. "And I already know who you are. No hard feelings, I hope, but being this was an exhibition to unofficially decide who the fastest soul in the galaxy is, I felt slighted not to be included."

"Eleanora?" Anton asked. "I'm sorry; I have no idea who you are."

"I'm from Banth. Well, one of its moons anyway—and no, not Dar, but Eliix, the dust moon. Most people from my world don't even know who I am. Don't feel surprised."

"I've never met anyone from Eliix," said Jovan. Before he could stop himself, he continued, "Is everyone as beautiful as you?" He was immediately embarrassed and confused. He'd never reacted to beauty with such a sense of …well, he didn't know what.

"You are a sweet one, Jovan," she replied. "I couldn't really tell you for sure. There aren't many of us on Eliix. We are scattered."

"How did you find out about the tournament on Seocia then?" asked Anton.

"Well …" she said, sliding her lovely hand down his cheek. "I'm not hidden under a rock, if that's what you're asking. I'm pretty smart for a girl from a desert moon. Whatever literature I can get my hands on, I study. Although, I'm sure it doesn't compare to the libraries and literature found on Alpha."

"Study?" said the boisterous King Handel of Alpha. "Did I overhear correctly that you are from Banth?"

"I am, Your Majesty." Eleanora bowed. "I pride myself on being quite the student in mysteries and prophecies, even more so than on my speed and agility. Racing is more of a hobby."

"Well, Banthan," said Handel. "I find that most extraordinary." He also could not help but be captivated by her beauty. "Perhaps you'd like a pass to study within the halls on Alpha?"

"I think the Millennia Mansion on Gardenia would suit you as well," Jovan blurted out.

Eleanora shined a smile toward them. "Thank you both. To have such an opportunity would be magnificent in either place."

Bethany watched from a distance. For some reason, she was becoming quite agitated with the looks Eleanora was giving Jovan. She'd never seen anyone look at another soul quite that way. She flew over and grabbed her counterpart's arm. "Jovan, we gotta go!" she said.

"Wait! What, *huh?* Relax!" Jovan said to Bethany.

"Who is this little creature, Jovan?" asked Eleanora. "Is she your maker that she gets to give you commands?"

Bethany shot back a look that she hadn't ever given to anyone; with it came an emotion she didn't recognize and didn't like either, but couldn't resist. She found herself blaming Eleanora for this feeling and this, too, was uncomfortable. "Jovan, Lord Jaesu wants to see you now! We gotta go."

With that, he acknowledged the request. "Very well." He regretfully departed with Bethany toward the tunnel.

"What was that?" Bethany asked.

"What?" Jovan replied.

"Don't give me, *what,*" she responded. "That thing. Who was she? And why was she looking at you like that?"

"Her name is Eleanora. She wanted in on the race or something," answered Jovan. "I didn't see her looking at me strangely. I have no idea what you are talking about."

"Well," Bethany said, in clear annoyance. "I did, and for some reason, I didn't like it very much."

"I'll be sure to tell her that the next time I see her," Jovan said. He felt guilty, though he didn't know what he had to feel guilty about. He shook his head to clear it of this nonsense.

"No, I will tell her myself. Thank you very much," snapped Bethany. "Where is she from, anyway?"

"She said Banth, on Eliix. Didn't even know anyone lived on that moon. Oh, well, there's a lot I don't know, I guess."

"Yes, that's for sure …plenty," Bethany agreed as she slanted her head and tightened her lips.

"Aren't you going to congratulate me on a good race?"

"What for? You didn't win," Bethany said. Even though she wanted to hug him and tell him how proud she was, her nerves were seething. "And if Miss Superstar hadn't shown up, you would have won, but you allowed that thing to distract you."

They were at the edge of the tunnel where Jaesu was. Jovan began his response, "I was—"

"She's right, you know," said Jaesu. "You would have won had you remained focused. But nonetheless, I am proud of you; you hung in there and did well."

"You're always proud of Jovan," Bethany said sarcastically.

"I am always proud of all of you," Jaesu responded. "You know what I love the most? I am excited to be around you all partly because you are happy and enjoy being around me as well. It touches my heart that you all make such an effort to find me and cherish whatever time you have with me. In turn, I feel the same way. Although I love everyone equally, those that call upon me and enjoy me allow me to enjoy them, too, and that is quite special."

"In other words, Jovan," Dara interjected, "he was rooting for you the whole time."

All four broke out in laughter. The bad feelings diminished.

King Handel and Anton continued their conversation with Eleanora. Both were fascinated by her knowledge and beauty and were truly amazed that someone hidden away on a remote moon surrounding Banth, of all places, could have such a great understanding of the universe and such appeal.

"Tell me, Eleanora. What is it about the mysteries and prophecies that intrigue you?" asked Handel. "What are you studying now?"

"Everything about them, Your Majesty," she replied. "I love the many riddles and the great wisdom that follows from solving one of the riddles. Sometimes it reveals things that I am not too comfortable with, however."

"Yes, sometimes that is true," said the king as they began to walk toward the royal suite. "Is there anything in particular which troubles you now?"

"Well, yes. Can I tell you?" Eleanora asked. The king nodded. "Well, it is my understanding that the asudem of Algolithar will attack my home world of Banth."

"Banth?" The king laughed aloud. "I think you may be mistaken, young one. Even the Red Knight himself wouldn't attack Banth. You, yourself, have to have seen that majestic blue elephant roaming the skies throughout Dar. No, if there is an attack, and that's a big if, it would happen to Gardenia first and then Omega and eventually Alpha."

Eleanora looked down with an air of sadness. "Forgive me, Your Majesty." She gazed at him with a look of desperation. "I wish you were right. I do not think our great elephant can withstand what is to come. According to my studies, in the book *Shadwon of Sand*, the interpretation that the great battle starts at Gardenia is a miscalculation."

King Handel was stunned, not only because someone was disagreeing with him, but because she had mentioned a book he had never read. As king of the knowledge center of the galaxy, he prided himself on having read every piece of literature in the galaxy. "Well, I am sure you know this passage from *The Prophetic Beyond* which states: 'The Merciful will fail to shine; in that day far from divine; death and war before unseen; will eat the dust and burn what's green.' We interpret that 'green' as Gardenia, by far the greenest world within our galaxy," Handel explained.

"Yes, I understand your logic, great king," replied Eleanora. "There are two pieces that many overlook, though. First, 'eat the dust' could only symbolize Banth, being that it is home to mostly sand and dust moons. I know many interpret the 'dust' to symbolize the human flesh on Earth, but as is explained in *Shadwon of Sand*, that perception is misguided. There is an additional passage attached to what you just shared: 'For when the green is burned by flame, and the moons of dust engulfed with pain, the worlds will hide beyond their shore, and the Earth itself will be no more.' Now this added event is not predetermined, as it only comes to pass if the asudem who attack Banth are not pushed back to Algolithar. This is why most scholars do not recognize it."

King Handel felt quite uneasy having heard all this. Oddly enough, he truly trusted this being, even though he didn't know her. She carried herself with profound poise and humility—to an extent that touched him soul to soul.

They reached the royal suite. Eleanora and Anton could go no further. The room beyond was for kings, queens, and their advisors only. "I have enjoyed meeting you, Eleanora," said the king. "Perhaps Anton can show you around on Alpha."

"Thank you, Your Majesty. I look forward to that, at the conclusion of the games, of course." Eleanora smiled.

Anton and Eleanora began to walk down toward the practice area. Her attention was devoted to the legendary Owls and Seraphs performer. "What is your favorite part of the games?" Eleanora asked.

"All of it," said Anton. "I enjoy the challenge of figuring out someone else's next move. I feel like it's me against the entire galaxy and, for whatever reason, I feel right at home."

"I know exactly what you mean, Anton," she said in response. "I would like to spend more time with you throughout the tournament and hopefully on Alpha, as the king mentioned, but only if it wouldn't serve as a distraction. After all, I was rooting for you to win." She subtly tossed red hair toward his face.

"I think we could work that out," Anton said nervously.

*   *   *

In the royal suite, the kings and queens were talking about the race, possible battles in the future, and comings and goings on their worlds.

King Sardonia, ruler of Seocia, was always a very welcoming host and a favorite among them. He was gentle, loved to listen and as such heard many points of view. He was honored to host the games. Sardonia had short white hair with a black Mohawk and a sleeveless robe showing off teal arms, which matched many of the sea creatures of his world.

Queen Tamika of Zae was in a beautiful pale gold gown adorned with emeralds and tourmalines. Her skin was a deep brown with a long waterfall of silky hair a few shades darker. She carried with her a rod of rubies to signify the love and power of her people.

King Francois of Fricto was seven feet tall. He was bald with dark blue skin and very light green, almond-shaped eyes. He walked with an ice staff that never melted as long as he held it.

Queen Eva of Omega was considered a rare beauty. With her fine black hair in a cloud around her face, she could command a room with a gentle smile. She wore a simple white gown; her trailing scarf was made of flashing lightning.

King Cicero of Neumbessa had thick brown hair and a full, curly beard. He wore a large golden crown wherever he went. He was known for the never-empty chalice of wine always by his side and a carefree grin.

King Solrac of Cymblali had wavy black hair, long-lashed black eyes and wore a robe of many colors. He didn't talk much, but smiled often and allowed music, which always accompanied his steps, to speak for him.

Queen Delya of Remnas was noticeably shorter than the others; she wasn't more than four and a half feet tall. She had reddish-brown hair, an open, honest face and a cloak that changed from silk to wool to cotton to feathers, in honor of her always-changing world.

King Efraim of Banth had sunshine-colored features, long straight blond hair and blue eyes. He carried a staff that could act as his dancing partner, which made for very humorous and entertaining gatherings at times.

Overall, these giants of royalty respected one another and felt safe in one another's company.

King Handel used a hologram to call back to his home world of Alpha. He had to speak to a knowledgeable servant squirrel to ask a troubling question. "Winnow," said the king discreetly.

"Your Majesty, this is a surprise." Winnow bowed.

"Winnow—quickly—are you familiar with a book titled *Shadwon of Sand?*"

"I'm embarrassed to say, Your Majesty, I am not. I do long for additional knowledge and cannot believe that any book is beyond my knowledge."

"That makes two of us," whispered the king. "Make this your highest priority. Go and look to see if this book exists; if so, read it and get back to me immediately. If it does not exist, also get back to me right away."

"On it, my king!" Winnow said as the hologram closed.

King Handel, so impressed with the Banthan he had just met, went over to King Efraim to inquire of her.

*   *   *

Black had been mingling with dignitaries for the queen throughout the day because Amana was still not feeling well after her vision. "My queen, you should take some time with the others. It will help you, I think."

"Oh, Black, I wish I could. Something has changed in me. Something is off. I trust you know me well enough to know I am not myself."

"Indeed, Your Majesty, indeed," Black replied.

Amana looked around at her colleagues and noticed one important figure was missing. "Where is Jaesu? We need him here. I need him here," she said to Black. "The others already think I'm irrational for sounding the battle alarm at the last meeting."

"I am right here, Your Majesty," said Jaesu.

"Oh! Where have you been?" Amana asked. "Forgive me, my Lord," she added quickly as she straightened up and bowed.

"I have been with the Lighted Blade today," Jaesu answered.

"Why haven't you come here sooner?" Amana questioned.

"Why is this the first time anyone has asked for me?" Jaesu asked. "I try to avoid places where I'm not wanted." He smiled. "Political gatherings don't like me too much."

"Lord, I am concerned. I am having visions and can't understand them. Please help," the queen pleaded.

"In due time, Amana. Because you have trusted me, I trust you to see great mysteries. Your heart is close to mine. Follow it and it will follow me. Know this: many will mean well but fail because they try to take it on themselves and not follow me. I am the answer to the mysteries, but even the great kings and queens need to decide for themselves if they will choose my answers over their own."

"But Lord—" Amana attempted to reply.

"CAN I HAVE EVERYONE'S ATTENTION? URGENT I TELL YOU!" came from King Sardonia. "I have received disturbing word that the great blue elephant of Dar has fought off several asudem in a surprise attack against Banth. Before he disposed of them, one of them claimed that this was only the beginning and millions more were coming. This coordinated attack coincides with us all being on Seocia for the games and cannot be accidental. As host, I call for a temporary postponement of the upcoming games. I encourage you to get back to your home worlds and prepare your defenses. Then we must communicate on what to do in order to protect Banth!"

The monarchs did not panic but were obviously disturbed. King Handel raised his eyebrows and thought, *If Eleanora was correct in her interpretation, I could have saved an entire world—had I acted soon enough.* Winnow, who always worked very quickly, opened communication.

"Your Majesty," he said. "The book is indeed here on Alpha. I feel even more embarrassed knowing that. It predicts that the battle of all battles will take place in Banth. That is the first I have heard of such things."

"Winnow, you've done well," said Handel. "Fortify our defenses. I am coming home."

Amana grabbed Black among the commotion and looked at Jaesu and said, "My Lord, can you get us home safely and get Dara and the team out of here?"

"They are already home, Your Majesty," said Jaesu. "Take my robe, both of you."

Black and Amana took hold of the robe and headed back to Gardenia. They landed inside the Millennia Mansion. Amana looked around when they arrived. Then, all of a sudden she was somewhere else. She was on a cold moon of ice, water, and stone without Black or Jaesu. It was night and the full moon lit the entrance to a cave just ahead of her. She saw a slim woman with long black hair standing over a pool of water, arms and hands gleaming in the silver light. Amana felt both terribly afraid and strangely attracted to the woman's actions. She tried to call out, but as soon as her lips parted, the woman vanished.

Amana awoke from this vision back in the mansion with Black. Some great power was at work; she just didn't know what. She pulled Black close to her. "Stand with me always, even if I get ridiculous."

"You are ridiculous," said Black gently, as she patted the queen's face with her paw. "Even so, you can always count on me, Your Majesty."

"Thank you, dear friend. I don't know what is going to happen to us."

"Do not fear, my queen."

"I do fear, Black."

The lioness licked a paw and cleaned her wise face with the back of it. It was a sight Amana knew well—one that always amused her.

"Yes, well, you're not the only one," said Black. "We will be triumphant."

The queen nodded, then went into a leafy corner of the hall to meditate. Black sent a message to the rest of Scepter to join her and began researching battles and defenses. She had a feeling things would never be the same. Soon the big cats were in the hall, conferring and lashing their tails in resentment. It comforted Amana to have them so close. She prayed for the beings on Banth.

CHAPTER 5

Deception

"General." Commander Aijsas knelt before Phan. "Our scouts were captured and dismantled by the elephant as expected. Will we still be as successful with the element of surprise no longer on our side?"

"Well done, Commander," replied Phan, "And yes, even more so. They have always known we are coming."

Commander Aijsas looked confused for a moment. "My Lord?"

"What they haven't always known is fear. Just the anticipation of fear weakens them. Fear, deception, jealousy, and even idle distractions are unseen weapons in war that allow the enemy to tear themselves apart from the inside. I have designed many great wars over time, many through covert operations and even many more in the brazen you-know-we-are-coming-and-you-can't-stop-us manner. But the one constant to achieving victory is to allow the unseen weapons to take hold first and to let the enemy tear themselves apart from within. Once that is done, then it is essential to allow time for confusion to set in. Soon, the enemy is begging to be conquered.

"We have built and refined this battle plan for ages: the greater the enemy, the greater the preparations. The Father, Jaesu, and the Blue Fire Spirit are worthy adversaries in battle, but this time we shall destroy all that they hold dear and rule over Evermore and the universe with them as our servants and slaves."

"Yes, my Lord," said the commander, nodding. "If I may ask, sir, where will our great Lord Khrimson be during the battles?"

"It is of no concern!" replied Phan angrily, firing several stones toward Aijsas's head. "Just ensure your troops hold their ground and await their next orders from high command."

"My Lord," Aijsas bowed and slowly retreated from the battle platform outside of Algolithar. He could see a million asudem soldiers in formation. Phan was leading the battle in person with a slave chained to his side as a shield. Even the commander saw that this battle strategy was quite different than in times past.

*   *   *

On Alpha, battle measures were beginning as well. King Handel, after studying the Shadwon of Sand with his alarmed advisors, began to instruct other worlds to send their seraphs to Banth and its dancing moons. Handel had already pledged his personal protector, Heda, the four-headed leopard, to Banth. Under normal circumstances, teaming such a seraph with Basheere, the mighty giant blue elephant, would be far more than necessary for the legions of asudem. In this case, however, most agreed that it might take many powerful seraphs to defeat the coming enemy.

As promised, Anton began taking Alpha's most famous visitor, Eleanora, throughout the magnificent city world. Alpha was not green like Gardenia, engulfed with sand like Banth or watery like Seocia. This world consisted of thousands of unique cities. Most citizens of the planet took great pride in their culture and history. Since Alpha was the first planet created in the galaxy, it was easy for Alphans to believe they had been chosen for something great, and that belief was endemic among them. They were very sophisticated and very opinionated, fond of trying to catch each other in errors of fact or logic. Yet the people were good natured and truly loved knowledge above all things. Their core belief was whoever acquires the most knowledge has truly achieved the meaning of their lives as ordained by their creator.

Anton had been instructed to make sure he brought Eleanora to the Fortress of Lords. This was one of the great centerpieces of Alpha's culture.

"I am quite honored you would show me around the way you have, Anton," said Eleanora. "After all, you are among the most famous souls on Alpha, not to mention the Elevemada. And you're kinda good at Owls and Seraphs," she playfully mocked.

Giving a tour was not something that Anton would normally do, but he was mesmerized by Eleanora. He'd never met anyone like her. *Maybe everyone on Banth has such charm.* To believe that made his very personal feelings less worrisome: he wasn't used to caring so much about someone else's opinion of him.

"The honor belongs to me," replied Anton. "For cycles and cycles, we on Alpha believed ourselves to be the fastest and most knowledgeable souls in the universe, and then you show up from the far reaches of space and shatter that perception in mere seconds."

"Don't be so hard on yourself," said Eleanora as she gently put her arm in his. "After all, there is not a lot a girl can do on a desolate moon; I've had many cycles of practice—sadly, alone. The fact that you demonstrate greatness in front of many makes you even mightier."

The words soothed Anton and made the worrisome quality of his feelings diminish. She was spectacular, speaking of the same greatness Phyllis often insisted on. "Eleanora, I have to say, you're rather wonderful," gushed Anton—a sentiment completely out of character for him. "I feel like I have known you throughout the cycles. Every minute, I feel I can trust you more and more. Even our king trusts you! That is quite a remarkable feat for anyone, I might add."

"Well, I am not sure how to respond to that except for this, upon passing you and Jovan on Seocia, I sensed a connection between you and me which I couldn't explain. I have never felt anything like this before. So yes, I must confess, I knew you were truly extraordinary from that instant."

They entered the fortress. Covering the walls from the floor to the cathedral ceilings were innumerable and varied paintings and other artistic masterpieces. "Have you ever seen anything like this before?" asked Anton as he noticed Eleanora's mouth drop in awe.

"No. This is unbelievable." Eleanora continued to gaze around in delight at first, but more and more as if there was something specific she had been hoping to see.

"What is it?" asked Anton. "Is there something I can help you find?"

"Nevermind. It's senseless and I probably shouldn't even mention it in such a majestic hall," she answered, looking down.

"No, it's not senseless. You can tell me…anything!" He was flushed with an eagerness he couldn't understand. Her company felt thrilling to him, and at that moment, he knew there would be no greater priority than her happiness.

"Okay, but don't mock," she responded. "These are all astonishing pieces of art and decidedly beyond compare. But…I guess…I was hoping to see some of the prominent works from Banth. I recognize many of the other worlds represented on these walls. I discern from this that we are perceived as a lowly world, but—well, there was this one piece on my home moon called the Red River Stone, and it always brought such joy to me and my people. They took it and put it in one of the great museums. I don't know, I hoped for a moment…"

"Not senseless at all. I totally understand," said Anton. "If it is as magnificent as you say, I am quite certain that it will find its way here."

"I suppose," Eleanora responded as she subtly pressed her hands down her satin gown. "You are probably right. And maybe it isn't even that magnificent. Perhaps it's my meek perspective."

Anton suddenly felt sympathy for her, an emotion that had been unfamiliar to him before. He felt less inside himself, and yet like he was a bigger person than he had previously been. This drew him closer to Eleanora in a dazzle of tender feelings and gratitude. He wanted to do something exceptional for her, something that would make her blissful, that she'd never forget. But what could he do for someone who seemed to know everything about everything? Anton continued to ponder this thought as they toured the fortress.

*   *   *

On Gardenia, Queen Amana had been sparring in conference with King Handel. Handel's request for the other planets to send their seraphs to Banth for protection did not sit well with her. Although Amana agreed to send aid to the distant moon, she felt it unwise to send her seraph so far from home, thus leaving Gardenia unprotected. "I don't see why all of the seraphs from each world need to go," the queen said in a hologram conversation with Handel.

"Why should they suffer due to disagreements among monarchs?" Handel questioned. "Sending the seraphs there would resolve this battle swiftly and ensure the asudem never return."

"Handel, are you able to guarantee such victory? Because anything short of absolute certainty won't do it for me, I'm afraid."

"Amana, I understand your caution; you are a young queen. But you are being unreasonable," Handel continued. "You know full well no one can make that assurance. But I think this would go a long way to securing our peace. We will rid our galaxy of those that mean to harm it—or at the very least, reduce their numbers considerably. You know we are not aggressors, but we can be fierce defenders. Why not get clear of these traitors now?"

"Speaking of long ways, it's a very long way from Gardenia to Banth," said the queen. "As for your argument—it is not that I disagree in theory, but what does Lord Jaesu think? Have you talked with him?"

"Your Majesty, please," Handel replied confidently while placing the Alphan crown on his head. "Our King Jaesu is wise and good; we know this. But a man of battle, he isn't. He talks of eternal things; his canvas is vast. He has placed us in charge as rulers for the here and now. Read up, young queen. Even during the purge at Evermore, it was not Jaesu who battled Khrimson, but Michaelio, the chief seraph of Evermore. Don't get me wrong; Lord Jaesu is brilliant and farseeing, no doubt, but he has not proven to be one of action during such crises."

Queen Amana felt very differently. She placed complete trust in Jaesu for all matters. To not do so was completely foreign to her. She loved Jaesu. It would always be judicious to consult with the one who ordained her as queen in the first place—who, with the Great Father and the Blue Fire Spirit, had created her and Handel and everyone else. Maybe it was because she truly didn't believe she had the answers and was more collaborative than most, but either way, she couldn't imagine making such rash decisions without Jaesu, especially with him so readily available. What would it cost to consult him?

King Handel was making a mistake, and though she wouldn't say this to him—it would not be respectful—she wouldn't change her mind. "My dear friend, Handel, I will gladly support efforts to assist on Banth, but I do not think it is wise to abandon Gardenia altogether. Therefore, I will be instructing Orion to maintain defense of Gardenia. Of course, I will reach out personally to the Banthan leadership to explain my actions so that they understand my thinking," she concluded.

"Amana, I am sure you have sound reasons for your decision; however, our partners within the galaxy vehemently disagree with you at this time. I hope the chosen course does not prove unwise and cause the planet of Banth to suffer. I know you have the best of intentions and will also assist in explaining your position to the others," King Handel responded, his tone formal and courteous, his expression disappointed. The conference ended shortly thereafter.

"Black, I must go to the Temple of the King," Amana said. "I need to pray, think, meditate on this decision and trust that I am certainly making the correct choice."

"Yes, Your Majesty."

Black, as an important and loyal advisor, would usually stay close to the queen to offer guidance in many areas of governance and battle strategy. However, at certain times, it was important for the queen to be alone with her thoughts. Black understood this, but didn't like the queen being alone now. She worried about what lay ahead and about Amana's emotional state. Yet Black knew better than to contradict the queen, so she stayed behind with her cats.

"I need that rat of an asudem, Khrimson, to sharpen my claws on," Black muttered.

*　　*　　*

The Temple of the King was in between the palace and Millennia Mansion. It sat on top of Blue Jay Hill, facing the palace. Columns made of silver and white gold supported the temple. Marble stairs led up to its entrance. Swarms of blue jays passed over it all day long, singing beautiful songs they invented as they flew. The door was a seven-leafed clover: green with silver accents. It would open and close with the energy of a thought. Inside, there were four golden cherubs, one in each corner of the ceiling; each holding dual-edged torches. Blue fire sprang from these, one across the other to form an "X" on the ceiling. Altars appeared anyplace where a soul desired to pray. There were no set pews or railings. The temple was a peaceful place, especially with the sounds of blue jays singing outside of it.

Amana entered, faced the wall on the right-hand side so as
not to stand out, and began to meditate. "O, Great Father," prayed
the queen. "I try to do what I perceive as your will. If you can
see us, you know that we are in trying times. Such times often
pass us by here on Gardenia and in the Elevemada, but not now.
Please guide me and show me if I have made the right decision in
keeping Orion here. It is not out of selfishness, and I humbly beg
that you keep those on Banth safe, should evil befall them. I feel
strongly that trouble is coming to us as well …yet I don't wish to
be divisive within the group of royals. Please grant me wisdom."
She then bowed at her altar as the blue fire slowly surrounded
and embraced her, not burning but warming, giving her a peace
she had not had before. She walked out of the temple and, to her
surprise, Lord Jaesu was awaiting her.

"Are you at peace, O great queen?" asked Jaesu.

"Am I making the right choice? Or should I send Orion to
Banth?"

"Amana, you are a brave and wise queen," he answered.
"There are times when patience is called for from a leader
and other times when immediate action is needed. But in both
circumstances, seeking and applying sound wisdom will raise a
victory flag more often than being careless. And I sense none of
that carelessness in you."

"Do you still think war will come?" asked Amana.

"Yes," replied Jaesu. "But do not let that frighten you. Be
prepared and ready to answer the challenges yet before you.
They will grow as you get stronger. One usually cannot happen
without the other."

"But what about Handel and the others who are sending their
seraphs? Are they making the right decision?"

"Much like you, queen, those that seek me out will receive guidance on these matters. Trust in the steps that you must take in faith and watch how events unfold."

As they both continued walking toward the palace, Malvin flew up in a panic. "Lord Jaesu! Queen Amana!" He had to take a few breaths before he could continue. "My queen, King Efraim of Banth has just been notifyin' the kings and queens that they be spottin' many legions headin' to Banth. Most of the seraphs haven't gotten to Banth yet, and it looks to be too late for any additional resources to arrive."

Amana looked at Jaesu. He could sense she was very concerned about her decision and placed his hand on her shoulder to reassure. "Your Majesty, why don't we go back to the palace and observe the situation?"

"Yes ...yes, Lord, you are right," the queen responded, shaken up.

"Thank you, Malvin," Jaesu said to the owl. "Advise Black that the queen will be there shortly and to monitor events."

Malvin flew back toward the palace as Amana continued struggling with her intense fear of war alongside the curious sense of peace within her. She was glad that Jaesu was with her as she didn't know what her reaction would have been in that moment without him.

* * *

On Banth, both Basheere and Heda were awaiting the legions of asudem to arrive. The other seraphs were leaving their home worlds but would never arrive in time. Heda had four heads and each of the heads had its own voice and personality. They were named after the letters that made up their name.

"H," A said. "I only see a couple of thousand asudem! I hope there's more, because I will feel deprived if those all aren't for me."

"Yeah, H," E chimed in. "Basheere has been known to take on ten thousand or so with just a whisk of his trunk. I am going to be one cranky leopard-head."

"Pipe down," H commanded. "You both are getting spotty on me. If there's only a few thousand, then great; we will help the big galoot and move along."

"But that doesn't sound or look like the millions and millions of asudem King Handel was warning us about, does it, boss?" D asked H.

"What it looks and sounds like are several thousand cold-spirited, power-wielding, slave-mongering asudem heading this way. Don't get lost in the numbers, soldier. Just one can be enough to wipe us out!" H exclaimed.

Basheere never said much, especially during battle preparation. But even he expressed surprise that only several thousand had shown up. Perhaps the asudem had underestimated him? *Highly unlikely,* he thought. But none of that mattered. If they had underestimated him, then he would ensure that they would not make the same mistake again.

Several legions of asudem entered the Banth system and were positioned to target the planet's surface. Basheere let out a huge scream as only this blue elephant could. All of Banth and her moons heard the battle cry. He leaped off of Dar, the diamond moon, and into outer space with both his tusks shooting fire. Within minutes, two full legions were destroyed. He then coiled his trunk so tightly that it created a powerful wind that pulled the remaining legions closer. When the great elephant released his trunk, the legions were smacked with deadly force and scattered into retreat.

"Ya know, boss," A said to H, "I could get used to fighting these kinds of battles, considering that WE DIDN'T GET TO DO ANYTHING!"

"*Hmm...* I don't like it, gents," H said, concerned. "The intelligence must be off."

"Maybe they are coming back?" D asked.

"No," Basheere responded in his customary deep sounding tone. "I can sense them from great distances. They have already retreated a long way from this system. However, I will remain on guard. You are free to stay, of course. But I would contact King Handel if I were you."

Just then, the rest of the seraphs sent by the group of royals arrived at Banth.

"We're late?" asked Juuma, the powerful werewolf seraph of Zae.

"You are!" said Basheere. "The battle is over."

"Over?" Juuma asked. "We were told this could last a cycle— that it would be the battle of battles."

"For you guys maybe!" laughed E mockingly. "But not for the big guy over here."

"Quiet, heads!" H ordered. "What my lack of common sense-having fellow leopard-head means is the battle was quite short in time and in numbers. Basheere could have taken on twice as many legions by himself without even breaking a sweat. There doesn't seem to be a great need for us to be here and, as Basheere said, they aren't coming back. I am contacting my king now. There must be something we are missing."

Deception

The seraphs were confused. Could it be that they truly didn't know their own abilities and that the battle of battles was going to be this simple for them? Yet Phan had been known to wipe out several powerful seraphs in his day. Would he be chased away so easily? Had he even been here?

*   *   *

Back on Gardenia, Queen Amana and Lord Jaesu had arrived at the palace. Black was waiting with an update. "Your Majesty, King Handel has an urgent request out that you speak to him at once."

Amana wasn't sure if she wanted to contact Handel since she had apparently been wrong in not sending Orion to Banth. Taking a deep breath, she initiated the holo-conference. "Handel! I am here."

"I bring interesting word from Banth," Handel said in a joyous tone. "The battle is over."

"What? Over?" Amana said nervously. "Did any seraphs survive?"

"Survive?" He laughed. "They were no match for Basheere alone, much less any of the other seraphs. Basheere wiped out thousands in minutes. And he has advised that they will not be returning any time soon; they are in retreat. Perhaps we overestimated our enemy? Well, in either case, I figured you would want to be at ease knowing that Orion remaining at Gardenia didn't cost us. I have advised the remaining seraphs to head back to their worlds."

"Doesn't that sound strange to you, Handel?" asked Amana curiously. "Wouldn't there have been more of them? Was Phan with them?"

"I'm not entirely sure. Heda asked the same question regarding the numbers. *Hmm…* well, it looks like we are out of the woods either way," Handel replied.

"Excuse me, Your Majesty! Quick! There is an urgent warning from Orion!" Black interrupted.

"My queen!" Orion blurted, obviously alarmed through the hologram. "Asudem have entered our system. I don't know how many there are, but from this viewpoint, it looks like quite a lot."

"WHAT!" shouted Amana. "Handel! Are you hearing this?"

"Yes …this…" he stammered while ruffling through his thoughts. "Unexpected, this is."

"Orion, is it something you can fight off?" the queen asked.

"There's no end to them; they are still pouring in and getting closer. Hundreds of thousands, it might even be millions of them," Orion responded.

Amana had no time to feel vindicated that she hadn't sent Orion to Banth. She was grateful he was still there but even more concerned that he was on his own. Gardenia did not have armies. She was protected from any onslaught by the Queen's Seraph—in this case, Orion. He had never come close to being defeated in battle before, but handling thousands of powerful asudem was task enough. Going against millions was not something she wanted to chance.

"Handel, are there any other seraphs to send?" Amana asked.

"You are asking for help from seraphs now? How ironic," Handel replied.

"This is no time for politics! We may be under attack!"

"Yes, well," Handel thought aloud. "Basheere is probably too far at this point, and the other seraphs have begun traveling back to their home worlds. I could try to have them aid you, but I fear it will be too late."

"Send any help you can gather!" Amana said, bringing the conference to a close. "Please!"

As the conference closed, Amana accessed her screen port, which could show Orion and everything surrounding him. If a battle was to take place, she would be watching it up close in order to best prepare the planet. Gardenia knew nothing of war. She could now see Orion and his viewpoint. She also had the ability to monitor anything entering or leaving the planet's atmosphere. The asudem were now visible on screen. As Orion said, their numbers were great.

"Lord Jaesu," Amana said as she looked over at him. "What are we to do? I fear for Orion. I know he has always won his battles, but I don't know if he can handle this many opponents. I don't want to put him in harm's way anymore than the planet."

"Sacrifice is a part of love and life, Amana," Jaesu responded. "Orion knows what he is doing. You also know that there isn't any boundary he wouldn't cross to protect Gardenia and his queen."

Amana's gaze was fixed on what was happening. As the asudem got closer to Orion, the great multitude was slowing down. Upon closer look, the queen's worst fears were realized. This gathering didn't look to be a random attack. A decorated general was at the front of the many legions, armored in silver and black. She knew from her studies over the cycles that this was the legendary Phan. His army now stopped as he floated toward Orion.

"Well, well," snickered Phan. "My old friend, the mighty Orion, Lord of the Sky. How powerful you would have been had you joined us. We may have already conquered Evermore with you. But, of course, like so many others, your weakness dissolved your strength. You have allowed yourself to become pathetic and useless. I believe you are impeding our path. So I must ask you to move aside now."

"Phan!" shouted Orion. "I see you are still licking Khrimson's footsteps. You are no more free or powerful than that which you have chained as your shield. All of you are slaves to Khrimson's lies. You have come to Gardenia to face me and thus your doom."

"Enough!" Phan responded. "Hand this traitor his spirit by severing his head—now! It is pointless to resist defeat, Orion," Phan said as he slipped back behind two legions.

As a legion immediately moved into attack position, the great seraph quickly pulled two diamond daggers from his belt and boomeranged them through several legions, cutting them in half. Phan wasn't shocked at the ease with which Orion disposed of the first two units, nor did he seem concerned. He knew there were thousands more awaiting their chance at this seraph. Phan's strategy was simple. He knew Orion was not immortal. Although it could take a while, he would wear him down with sheer numbers.

Several more legions began their assault. Orion initially made quick work of them. His trademark was letting the enemy know he was having a good time at it as well. He was yelling out comments such as, "I hope you have a million more of these," and, "I am embarrassed to be seen handling such disproportioned competition," and even, "Why don't you run back to Mommy Medusa so she can teach you the art of battle?"

The reality, however, was that Phan's strategy was starting to pay off. Orion was getting weaker and weaker the more legions he took on. Mostly it was fatigue, but he also suffered a number of small wounds, the kind that don't kill or cause permanent damage, but sap energy. One or two legions were enough to tame the average seraph. Orion did not fit into that category, but even he had his limits. Although the limits were not approached yet, Orion knew there was no way he could defeat the millions of remaining asudem. But he would never give in or show his concern.

* * *

On Gardenia, the members of the Lighted Blade were gathering together in the plains, having returned from Seocia. With their naked eyes, they could tell there was a battle in the sky, but couldn't make out the details.

Jacen used his long-distance vision to view the craziness. "It's a battle alright, and a pretty big one. From the looks of things, Orion is getting wiped out. He is holding his own, but there are far too many of them."

"No! Can't be!" responded Dara. "Orion is invincible!"

"You know what is weird?" Jacen asked as he continued to survey the battle. "Remember what Jaesu was talking about? You know the fallen angels; the ones that were once seraphs that turned into asudem, but have regretted their choice?"

"Yes!" Bethany replied. "They get cursed or something and turned into slaves. Lord Jaesu mentioned something about them being chained to their masters or something."

"Well, whoever the leader is up there has one chained to him and is using it as a shield to deflect Orion's diamond daggers," Jacen informed them.

"If Orion is in trouble, then Gardenia is in trouble!" Jovan exclaimed. "We have to do something!"

"JOVAN!" shouted Dara. "We are not soldiers. We are not prepared for battle."

"*Hmm ...*well, technically," remarked Marcus, "Orion won't be prepared for battle either, once he is destroyed by the remaining asudem."

"You know what I mean," said Dara. "Going up there against warmongering asudem would be absolute madness. The queen would kill us herself before we could ever get up there, she'd be so annoyed."

"But Orion is our friend. We need him," said Glynn.

"And he needs us now!" Dawn chimed in.

"Dara, trust me!" Jovan jumped back in. "I have an idea, but you need to trust me. It's a bit off the edge. If worse comes to worst, just grab onto Bethany or me. Even many of the asudem wouldn't waste time chasing us."

"I don't like this!" Dara said nervously. "What is your plan?"

"Leave it to us," Jovan retorted. "However, once we get into space, the rest of you stop and keep your distance from the battle. Bethany and I will draw closer to the battle."

"*Um ...*we will?" asked Bethany.

"Yes! I will explain once we are up there," Jovan responded. He was confident that he wouldn't have to, Bethany could typically pick up on the thoughts of her friends, especially during intense moments.

"Jovan, this is crazy and risky," Dara said. "It's my responsibility as your leader to stop you. But ya know what? Let's do it. It will be good preparation for my next challenge."

"Challenge?" Jovan asked. "What challenge?"

Dara stuck her tongue out sarcastically and said, "I will explain later!"

"Listen!" Jacen interrupted. "If we are gonna help Orion, then we have to go now! He is going to be ash if we wait any longer!"

In the palace, the queen was still monitoring the battle alongside Jaesu and Black. "My Lord, Orion is about to get killed out there. Lord, please help him! I know war and violence is not your way, but please, for the sake of our defense and for Orion. You know he isn't immortal. Please!"

Jaesu bowed his head and closed his eyes and remained silent. Amana was concerned that he wasn't saying anything. She was about to contact the other kings and queens to see if any backup seraphs could, by some miracle, get to Gardenia in time. Then, she saw something shoot out from Gardenia toward the battle.

"Oh! What is that?" Amana asked in astonishment. "Is that the Lighted Blade flying into battle? What are they doing there?" she yelled. The queen continued to look at Jaesu and Black; neither offered a response.

"Lord Jaesu! Please answer me!" Amana pleaded. "Jovan and the rest will be annihilated out there. Phan can inflict great horror upon them! Please! Have mercy."

Jaesu continued to keep his head bowed and eyes closed, seemingly oblivious to her words. Neither Black nor the queen could figure out if he was meditating or in disbelief that his friends, including Jovan, who many considered to be his closest ally, were about to face great danger. Amana was frightened and frustrated. Black was pacing, her claws clicking on the marble floor, tail whipping the air. Her place was here, but she, too, wished she could be up there helping Orion. The great seraph was not only Gardenia's protector; he was her dear friend. It wasn't right for one being to have to face so many opponents.

The Blade had reached the outer atmosphere of Gardenia. Now all of them had a vivid view of the battle. Orion was hurt, silver ichor running from many wounds and noticeably tired. There was no end in sight as more and more asudem kept coming in to battle him.

Jovan signaled to the team to stop and wait. They were about fifty miles from the battle. Jovan instructed the rest of the Blade to await his and Bethany's return. If they did not return, he charged them to flee back toward Gardenia. The team didn't understand everything as he kept some pieces of the plan hidden, a typical Jovan trick. He looked at Bethany to ensure she knew what he was thinking. Her eyes opened very wide. She slowly nodded in agreement. The duo took off from the stationary team and flew toward Orion.

Orion saw them as he was feverishly fighting off asudem. He couldn't believe his eyes. "Jovan, what are you doing? Get out of here!" he screamed as he continued to fight ferociously, knocking out more and more soldiers of Phan's army. Jovan and Bethany were the size of squirrels in comparison to Orion and, in most cases, half the size of the smallest asudem.

"Orion! We can't let you take this on alone. You are our friend!" Jovan said. "We both know you aren't going to be able to hold out much longer. I'm gonna need you to trust me!"

"Sure, like I have time to decide who I can and can't trust right now!" Orion screamed in frustration as he continued to strike at the enemy.

"Do you see it, Bethany?" Jovan yelled.

"Yes!" she yelled back. "And we are out of our minds!"

Jovan was remembering something Jaesu said to him in secret during a walk outside of Millennia Mansion. He believed that the members of the Blade were meant for something greater than Owls and Seraphs and enjoying life. There was some meaning to his life, and he was going for it. Dara was watching from the distance—a nervous wreck—while the others tried to keep her calm. Jovan moved toward Orion's ear.

"Shield your eyes and get ready to absorb and comet!" Jovan said to the mighty warrior.

"Absorb and comet? You're crazy," Orion responded. "I'd have to stop fighting for a moment to recharge, I can't spare a second."

"Shield your eyes now and be ready for it," Jovan said.

"Be ready for what?" Orion yelled.

"You'll know when you'll know," Jovan said. Most souls couldn't stand that about Jovan. He seemed to always be working on something and leaving details out; it drove them all mad.

"Bethany! You need to close your eyes. Just trust me; I'll make sure nothing happens to you," Jovan said. "When I tell you to open them, then do your thing."

Bethany trusted Jovan with her whole being, but she thought this plan was complete madness. Her bond with him was far stronger than her doubts, though.

"I'm going in!" Jovan flew into the midst of the battle, far enough in to be noticed by the asudem. Several were confused as to why a soul would be out there. He made eye contact with Phan, who was incensed that a minor soul had the audacity to look upon him. He saw it as a sign of disrespect. He ordered several legions after Jovan. Jovan was obviously very fast, but he was not moving or leading them on a chase. Walls of asudem closed around him and several started toward Bethany to capture her as well. All the while, Orion was fighting with his last ounce of energy. Then Jovan did something completely unbecoming. He screamed as loud as he could with every ounce of his being.

"BY THE POWER OF JAESU ...LET THERE BE LIGHT!!!"

Immediately, a flash of light beamed through the entire galaxy. The asudem were temporarily blinded by the light flash and paralyzed by fear. It would not last long, but this was it.

"Bethany, now!" he yelled.

She opened her eyes and located her target: Phan. No, his shield, his slave. She put her hands out and screamed, "MAGNETIZE!"

At that moment, Pity was broken off of Phan and drawn irresistibly to Bethany. Bethany's magnetic pull was unstoppable; she used the chains around the slave as her target. Bethany caught Pity; Jovan nodded at Orion, smiled in triumph and turned back toward Gardenia. Jovan and Bethany flew to the remaining members of the Blade. Orion then used his power to absorb the stunned asudem, pulling every last one of them toward him. He followed that by using his massive hands to create a ball of his captives. He turned it faster and faster until every one of them was stuck inside. Orion fired it as hard as he could, forming a comet. He threw it toward Algolithar with great power. The comet raced through the universe, increasing in size and speed until it reached Algolithar and crashed, causing a huge explosion. The damage was incredible and many of the asudem perished in the crash. A massive crater punctured the side of the planet. Although Phan survived the crash, many of his legions were turned to ash.

Queen Amana breathed a sigh of relief, even though she was still shuddering and faint from everything that had transpired. *Let there be light?*

She said to Jaesu sharply, "I thought only you, the Great Father, or Blue Spirit could use that! You gave Jovan—your friend, of course—that ability, didn't you?" she charged.

Jaesu expected that reaction. "Perhaps Jovan stumbled upon a thing or two. Would that be so bad?" Jaesu asked, chuckling.

The queen looked at him and replied, "Of course not, but I was so worried, you could have, at least, told me. I am queen of this world …well …even though you are King of the Galaxy … oh, never mind."

"You asked me for help and guidance, Your Majesty. Sometimes it comes in forms you don't expect," Jaesu said.

"Well, I suppose you're right… but, oh, I'm gonna get that Jovan. He had me so worried!" Amana said.

The Lighted Blade members had already begun their descent as the queen waved Black and Jaesu to follow her down to greet the unlikely heroes.

Amana had been through a lot recently, from the visions and the disagreements with Handel over whether or not to send Orion to Banth to the harrowing sight of Orion almost killed in battle. She'd been worried that her world would be conquered. Then she'd been frightened the Blade might be captured. She hadn't even stopped to realize that a massive war was over— against all odds—and Gardenia was safe.

She saw the Blade team. Her first inclination was to scold them for being reckless and then thank them, but by the time she got to them, she grabbed Jovan and hugged him tightly. She reached out her left arm to grab Bethany and hug her tightly as well, as she cried profusely. No one had seen the queen this way before, but everyone understood her emotion. Black wanted to cry, too, but being a mighty cat, never would show that side in public. Jaesu looked at Amana and was proud of how she had handled the most difficult task the young queen ever faced.

Pity was covered in ash and chains. Bethany released her. Pity slowly crawl-walked toward Jaesu. "My Lord, Jaesu, forgive me! I was a part of the purge so many cycles ago and was deceived. I knew it was wrong; I have regretted it since. Please do not send me from your sight." Her voice was crackled with emotion.

"Little one," Jaesu responded. "They call you Pity, do they not?"

She nodded.

"You may not remember, but that was never your name. When I created you, and I remember the day, I called you Grace, and therefore I give you grace. I have longed to be reunited with you, my friend."

Her eyes opened and filled with tears, allowing emotions she had suppressed for millions of cycles to surface. Ash covered, she still attempted to crawl to Jaesu to grab onto him and thank him. Queen Amana looked upon her with grace, not pity, and touched her face. The ash melted away, dissolving into the air. The former asudem began to grow to her normal size, and her youth was returned to her, as if she had never left Evermore. Her thin, silver hair was replaced by tiger lily orange with ponytails on each side of her head and one on top. Her eyes were green like the most pristine grass, and all trace of the suffering she had endured was gone, except for the deep compassion in her smile.

Grace looked at herself in the still surface of a nearby pool and was in complete awe. She was not the same naïve being she had once been—nor did she want that ignorance back—but she was profoundly grateful to see the youthfulness that reminded her of Evermore. She immediately fell at Amana's feet.

"Your Majesty!" she said. "Thank you!"

"Rise, Grace!" the queen said as she pulled her up. "None could ever imagine what one such as yourself has gone through to get to this point. I am blessed that you are here. I would even be more honored if you chose to make this your home world."

Grace looked at Amana with happiness, then looked to Jaesu. She bowed to one knee before him and asked, "Lord, would that be permissible? I know I am unworthy of such goodness."

"Grace, you are worthy; it's up to you whether to accept that," Jaesu responded kindly. "And besides," he continued with a smile, "I don't make it a habit to disagree with Queen Amana."

Black mumbled quietly, "That's why he is king; he always chooses the wisest path," and everyone laughed and embraced.

A great battle had been fought, and Phan's armies had been conquered thanks to Orion, the Lighted Blade, Queen Amana and Lord Jaesu. Yet, there were plenty of unanswered questions. Queen Amana asked Grace to join them at the palace. But before they left, Amana asked Bethany and Jovan if they would escort her up into Orion's realm. They each grabbed her arm and, with blazing speed, flew her to Orion. She knew he would need to rest after the battle, but wanted to thank him first. His heroics went a long way toward saving Gardenia. Without Orion, nothing Jovan or anything that anyone else did would have been enough.

Orion saw the three of them coming. He was at a loss for words, rare for him. When Amana alighted on the upper atmosphere, she removed her crown and bowed to him in gratitude. Bethany and Jovan did the same. Orion was the most humble of beings. For his queen, whom he served and protected, to have performed this gesture touched him greatly. She removed an emerald stone from her crown and pulled and smoothed it into a ring. The emerald circle floated toward his right hand. The emerald represented both life and peace. As the cool circlet slid onto Orion's finger, peace stole upon him and carried him into a temporary slumber. The enemy was defeated; he could rest. Amana put her crown back on her head and kissed him on his forehead, whispering, "Be at peace, kind warrior."

Bethany had tears in her eyes. She still couldn't believe what they had done, what dangers had faced them. She slid her fingers through Jovan's, and he squeezed gently.

The three returned to the others. Amana began walking with Grace and Black as Jaesu walked with the Lighted Blade just behind, knowing Dara had news to share with the team.

"Queen Amana," Grace said humbly, "your beauty and power is known even among Algolithar, yet it doesn't do you justice."

"Thank you, Grace," said the queen. "I trust that we will have lots to learn from one another. I am grateful that you are here on Gardenia."

"Freedom is a gift," said Grace. "To be free from freedom is to be a slave. I know that now. I won't ever take Jaesu's mercy, your kindness, or Gardenia's magnificence for granted. I've been through far too much."

"I would love to know more about Evermore and Algolithar," said Amana, "when you are ready to share, of course. I know some things may be difficult to talk about, so I won't pressure you."

"It will take time, but there is one thing that I know for certain."

"What's that, Grace?" the queen asked.

"This war is not over," she answered. "I believe that it has only started. I know this doesn't make sense, so many of the asudem have perished, but neither Khrimson nor Phan will accept defeat."

"Sadly, Grace," said Amana, "I believe that you are right." Amana noticed that even though Grace was healed, she still had a scar on her left shoulder. She didn't have the heart to ask her yet where it came from, but it was hard not to look at. As she continued to gaze at it, she was transported to a massive library hall. It went up and up, and on and on, as far as the eye could see.

There was an old man with a long, white beard looking through thousands of books who said in a loud voice, "What was once here is still here, and what was once not here is also here; who will help me find it?" From behind she saw a girl, like the one in the last vision, with long black hair. She was laughing quietly and ignoring the old man's plea for help. Amana was sure that this girl was the same one who had been in the other vision, though neither time did she see the girl's face. The laughter became louder and louder and then, Amana was back on Gardenia.

"Your Majesty!" Both Black and Grace were yelling, trying to get her attention.

"I'm sorry …I just …" the queen said, shaken up, as she always was by her visions.

"You saw her, didn't you?" Grace asked.

"Saw who?" Amana said in a frightened voice.

"The girl… the girl with black hair," Grace responded.

"Yes!" the queen answered, terrified. "Who is she? How do you know what I saw?"

CHAPTER 6

Walking with Death

More than a million asudem had perished at Orion's hands. Algolithar was pierced and scarred like never before. Upon impact from the asudem-filled comet, the planet shook with a mighty quake. Lava-laced tsunamis doused several of its kingdoms while fire devoured a third of the surface. However, the capital city of Greystone remained unblemished. Among the small group of surviving asudem was an angry and venomous Phan. He had convinced himself of certain victory. Now, not only was he defeated, but he was also stripped of his slave, which he considered an even greater embarrassment, especially because it had been done by a band of souls.

Phan looked around in wrath at the sudden destruction in many of Algolithar's cities, including the capital city of his home kingdom of Phanthoma. His palace was there—nearly as fine as Khrimson's—along with the residences of his most trusted lieutenants.

Phan detested being humiliated or disrespected. There was nothing that could enrage him more. Even losing a battle didn't affect him as badly as having his reputation slighted. Being the butt of tales and scornful whispers made him seethe like nothing else.

But Phan was always clever. He would use this humiliation as a way of goading his troops to redeem the loss—as soon as he finished assessing the damage and mastering his own rage.

As Phan approached Greystone, thinking about this and trying not to show the personal side of his anger, he was greeted by a visitor dragging behind him a long black and purple cape. Phan was not facing the black being, but could feel the presence of Belshezzar, Khrimson's most trusted messenger and among Phan's own chief rivals.

"My dear brother, Phan," Belshezzar purred, using charm in his voice and the ten fingers on each hand to outline the chinless area of his face, "I am honored to be in your presence, as always."

Belshezzar was not truly respected among the fellow asudem. Khrimson often excused him from battle and never chastised him publicly. It was hard to imagine Khrimson caring for anyone, but Belshezzar seemed to be an exception. The useless being was pampered and untouchable. The asudem resented his privileges and didn't feel he could be trusted. Many talked among themselves speculating that Belshezzar would betray them to Jaesu for any promised power or authority over them. Belshazzar was disdainful toward other asudem, openly parading his freedom from work and his status—higher than them all, save Phan, who was considered his equal.

"Your presence does not honor me, forked tongue lizard-possum," snarled Phan. "What is your business?"

"Oh, now, now …you shouldn't feel vexed with me. I'm sure you know that I have our great master's ear. How I phrase my report to him will have shape in how he deals with you, particularly after such a pathetic battle."

"Battle, *brother,* is something you know nothing about. Your opinion is less than worthless to any warrior. Whatever your message is, hurry it up and leave me be," Phan snarled in a low, angry voice.

"Well, since you are being so uncouth, I will tell you that the master would like an update." Belshezzar laughed wickedly. "But from the looks of things, I don't think it will be a long audience. One word will do. *Failure.* He will be most dissatisfied, I'm sure. And wouldn't that be a pity." He looked around curiously as he continued, "Speaking of which, where is your slave? Have you lost her as well?" he asked with a mocking frown.

Phan was overcome by rage. He thrust his left hand back behind him toward the throne room and instantly a surge of massive power filled him. He then took his right hand and grabbed Belshezzar by the face, screaming, "I AM YOUR LORD AND MASTER! BEG ME TO LET YOU LIVE!"

Many of the surviving asudem watched in awe; none would ever dare lay a hand on Belshezzar themselves. Belshezzar's countenance changed. The smugness, vanity, and arrogance, which usually clothed him, evaporated. Never in his wildest thoughts had he seen this moment coming. He was sheltered, protected by Khrimson. His general cowardice, growing worse by cycles and cycles of soft living, made it impossible for him to imagine anyone defying the master. But it was happening, and

Khrimson was a long way from Algolithar. Only he and Phan knew where Khrimson was, and it was too far to expect help.

Belshezzar tried to speak, to remind Phan of how viciously he would be punished, but the firm grip Phan had upon his face kept him from making a sound. As seconds passed, Phan continued to slowly crush the face of his peer and antagonist. Belshezzar struggled, but his strength was no match for Phan's.

The thought of how angry Khrimson would be with Phan and the torment he would unleash upon him certainly crossed Phan's mind. But it didn't matter. Anger and hate were in control now. He was unstoppable. It was as if he were beginning to crave the torment. He whispered to Belshezzar, "Bye, brother," crushing face and neck into dust and burning the rest of the quivering body alive.

For a moment, a deafening silence filled the air; the asudem were struck dumb in amazement. Then they began to roar and chant in unison: "Phan, Phan, Phan, Phan!"

The roar became louder and louder until all the remaining asudem on the planet chimed in. They had suffered a huge defeat at the hands of the Gardenians, but witnessing Phan's fatal attack on Belshezzar buoyed their spirits. As they chanted, however, they knew Phan's doom was sealed. Khrimson would destroy him for this act of rebellion. They didn't feel sorry for him, but they did feel admiration. Some flicker of an idea of nobility and independence passed through their spirits, though they would have denied it to their last breaths.

"I will go admit my action to the great Lord. But do not let our defeat dismay you!" Phan charged. "A greater plan will be revealed to you. Algolithar shall be victorious once more, and the asudem shall rule the universe!" he shouted to raucous applause.

At that moment, a great black horse with fiery yellow eyes and powerful wings appeared from the ruins of Phanthoma. It was Phan's horse, Sardis. Sardis swept down and landed beside Phan, nickering in greeting. General Phan leaped on the horse's back. They ascended toward the sky to have a face to face with Khrimson as the crowds of asudem continued to roar.

*   *   *

Khrimson was touring the planet Saturn. He went there often, in secret from even many of the asudem, to strategize attacks on Earth. He loved Saturn's rings; they made him feel like royalty. He also loved the irony of doing all his planning in the shadow of Jupiter, the planet of the kings. He believed this to be a slap in the face to Jaesu. But Khrimson's appearance on Saturn was not for meditation this time. He had a very important meeting with an extremely important guest, the master of death himself: the Grim Reaper, Rizhanaite.

The Reaper was arrayed in a dark gray cloak with a hood that concealed his face. Pure white eyes, ghostly and cold, were all anyone ever saw of his visage. The pitch and tone of his voice changed with each conversation. He carried a pickax, basically for effect, as no one had ever fought him in battle.

Khrimson always hated meeting with Rizhanaite. Rizhanaite was beyond his reach and understanding, forever playing by his own rules. Rizhanaite presided over death and, in most cases, even the Great Father would not interfere. Khrimson knew he was wise to fear such a being whose loyalty was only to death itself; a being who had no known weakness to exploit. Rizhanaite's strength was in proportion to the number of beings who died and worked in the death prisons as dark energy, always seeking the ultimate death of the universe by pushing galaxies further and further apart from one another. Power to kill was given to him over all life, save for that of souls, unless they were embodied in the flesh.

"Why do you always request to meet in this desolate waste of space, Khrimson?" Rizhanaite remarked as he glided toward the dark lord.

Khrimson, extremely nervous when around Rizhanaite, responded by ignoring the question and pushing forward with his own plan. "An offer to make you, Master of Doom."

"Your flattery never works with me, vain spirit. Remember, I was created to be impartial and to obey none. Even in the instances when some escape my grasp, it is because the Great Father takes them himself. But beyond that, the ability to release any from the death prisons or to kill and capture for the prisons is fully within my power and purview. None dare oppose me, and there is no appeal. So what is your proposal, foul spirit?"

"The release of every asudem killed from the dawn of creation. *Every* asudem," demanded Khrimson.

"You will make no such demands of me, spirit of arrogance and envy!" Rizhanaite charged.

"Of course, my friend, I actually wish to propose a *deal*."

"A deal? *Hmm*...well, whatever you ask for will be expensive. You know the rate."

"Ten human souls for every one asudem, still the same?" asked Khrimson.

"It is. Payment must be made up front, and I do not want children, the unborn or souls who claim Jaesu as their Lord; none of those who will go immediately to Evermore or its provinces."

"Very well, so let's agree for every ten qualifying human souls, you will release one asudem?" Khrimson verified.

"You needn't ask me twice. I know nothing of dishonesty or lies. When I send cancer to kill a man on Earth, there is nothing dishonest about the shakes the man goes through or the pain and struggle to survive. You, however, are the father of lies and deception." Rizhanaite paused for a moment. "What is that?" he asked, pointing toward a shadowy figure descending from the sky.

"I believe that is Phan, my chief general," answered Khrimson.

"A visitor! Another reason why it's a disgrace to commune with you on this world. We should have met on Mercury, my home world," Rizhanaite said under his breath. He knew Khrimson was petrified of both him and of Mercury's iron core. The planet was very hot on one side and frozen on the other. Khrimson preferred lukewarm temperatures. Extreme temperatures made him uneasy, yet it was the magnetic field on Mercury which chilled Khrimson most. A part of him often feared that he would never leave that place if ever he landed there.

Phan and Sardis descended through majestic rings, landing on the surface. Sardis stayed behind as Phan approached Khrimson. Phan was tense, knowing it would be suicide to explain to his Lord he had killed Belshezzar.

Khrimson was unusually calm. Perhaps it was because of Rizhanaite's presence, but who could tell with Khrimson? Maybe he enjoyed the anticipation of destroying Phan. The general strode forward, determined not to show fear.

"Welcome, my trusted servant. What news of the battle do you have for me?" Khrimson asked. "Where is your pet? And why are you here? Do I not have a trusted messenger expressly charged with bringing me this news?"

Phan glanced at Rizhanaite and then gazed deeply into Khrimson's eyes. He saw no glimpse of what his Lord was thinking. "We had the great Orion defeated until a band of souls interfered and distracted us long enough to be annihilated. Two souls stole my slave, and Belshezzar is dead!" he said angrily.

This kind of news piqued even Rizhanaite's interest. He was quite curious how this was going to pan out.

"What do you mean, dead?"

Phan could see Khrimson wasn't concerned about the battle—just Belshezzar. "My Lord, I know you trusted Belshezzar for many tasks, but his incessant mocking of me and the rest of the asudem over millions of cycles built up a smoldering hatred within me. His face and very presence became repulsive to us. In my great disappointment over the battle, still carrying the blood rage a warrior is made of, I could not resist. I smote him. I knew the torment I would receive at your hands, and I am here to face it. I made myself his lord and master and ultimately his destroyer. I am not ashamed to say that he begged for his life like a coward in the end," said Phan in a stern voice, not mentioning that Belshazzar, in fact, had not been able to speak while dying.

Khrimson looked at Phan. His face flooded with color, cycling between a bloody red and thundering black. "So I am clear: you made yourself his lord, you stole my most prized asudem from me, you killed him, you rebelled against me, you were envious of his title and favor with me, you broke your word to me that you would never harm him; for a moment, you made yourself greater than even me …is that correct?" Khrimson asked.

"Yes, my Lord," Phan answered, looking at him steadily.

Then a huge echoing laughter could be heard throughout Saturn. It was Khrimson. He continued to laugh for several minutes before he stopped. He then looked at Rizhanaite. "Finally."

Both Phan and Rizhanaite were confused.

"Finally," Khrimson said again. "Phan, Belshezzar was a test for you these great many cycles. In order to be a true king and ruler of Algolithar, one must rule with hate, malice, jealous rages, cruelty, manipulation, death (he winked at the Reaper), deceitfulness, ruthlessness, and the will to disregard all for the pure enjoyment of self-gratification. You finally have discovered it!" He grinned deviously. "Now we are ready for the next set of attacks."

Phan looked even more confused.

"Your defeat in battle was by my design," stated Khrimson. "Your pet was taken from you by a soul named Jovan. He is part of a formidable enemy group on Gardenia called the Lighted Blade. They have by now freed your slave and restored her power, youth, and beauty with that nauseating mercy of theirs. They embarrassed you, Lord Phan. I watched it all unfold long before you entered into the system."

This enraged Phan. But he still remained silent.

"What is the matter, powerful prince?" mocked Khrimson. "Are you torn between envy, hatred, and loyalty to me?"

"No, my Lord," Phan said grudgingly. "My loyalty is always to you."

Khrimson remained silent for a moment and shouted "FOOL!" As he spoke, red and silver lightning arced from his hands, engulfing Phan. In less than an instant, Phan was dead.

"Ensure that he is taken to the death prison and that he is made the least of all peasants. Let him wallow in shame and humiliation. When you release him, he will be filled with such rage that my enemies will be consumed by his fury," Khrimson declared to Rizhanaite.

"It will be interesting to see how you tie this plan of yours together. I will be watching," said the Reaper. "When is my payment going to arrive?"

"Trust me. You'll know when you'll know. Just guarantee me the immediate release of my asudem once I deliver payment," Khrimson answered.

"Trust you? Must you make me laugh more? You, the ancestor of deceits? But I suppose I do trust your will to dominate. Your guarantee is sealed with me. I will be waiting." The Grim Reaper vanished.

*　　*　　*

On Alpha, Eleanora and Anton continued their adventure of learning about one another. By now, Anton was completely captivated by Eleanora, to the point where common sense was overwhelmed by her mere presence. "Eleanora, would you ever consider living with me here forever on Alpha?" Anton asked. "Over time I imagine I could become king, and we could rule the greatest planet together."

"Anton, you honor me," Eleanora replied. "And I'm sure that would be a wonderful life. But Alpha is far from the greatest planet."

"You mean to say that Banth is?" asked Anton, trying to be careful not to offend.

"Oh, gosh, no!" Eleanora laughed in response. "Banth is a dust hole compared to the great worlds."

"I am confused," said Anton. "Is it Seocia? Omega?"

"None of those, Anton," Eleanora replied. "The greatest planets by far are the ones that Jaesu and the Great Father bless us with once we reach Evermore. The ones they give to each of us to create and rule over. Oh, Anton, I have seen them in many visions and dreams. They are far more beautiful, more abundant and richer in knowledge and magnificence than any Elevemada world will ever be."

"Evermore? But wouldn't we have to make the choice to face the judgments on Earth?" asked Anton.

"Of course, silly!" laughed Eleanora. "You mean to say that you aren't making the choice? With your talents and abilities?" She looked down. "You know, we could be together forever if you made it. You could rule over an entire world and be completely separate from everyone else, except me. It would just be us." The way she said those words sent a shiver down his being. He wasn't sure why he would want to be separate from everyone else, but in her voice, he heard a promise that it would, in fact, be a most exquisite destiny.

Still, he was concerned. "Are you suggesting that we go the Khrimson way and ask for a world away from Evermore?"

"No, no, of course not. How could you think that of me?" Eleanora replied. "Our lords are powerful and majestic. We should learn as much as we can from them. We can be alone together in Evermore. That is one of its greatest features. Whatever you most desire, you find there."

This conversation wasn't one Anton had hoped to have any time soon. He didn't think he was ready for the trials. But he didn't want to let Eleanora down. On the contrary, he wanted to impress her more than he had ever wanted anything. "Come with me," he said to her. Anton grabbed her by the hand, and they flew together toward the king's palace. He took her into the hall outside the throne room. She had already seen so many of Alpha's wonders that the hall, although beautiful, didn't cause her to gasp as much as some of the other places. "Look around!" Anton said.

"What am I supposed to be looking for, Anton?" Eleanora asked. He remained silent. She saw the busts of great kings, the many Owls and Seraphs trophies, a walkway of water leading to the throne room and several other unique attractions. But she still didn't know what he wanted her to find.

Then she saw the entryway to the throne room. Above its doorway was a painting. Not just any painting; her favorite from Banth, *The Red River Stone*. She leaped with glee and threw her arms around Anton. "How did you find it? Was it always here? Oh, my Anton, you are amazing!" she proclaimed.

"Once we received word that Basheere and Orion defeated the asudem in battle, I sent a small squad to Banth in order to retrieve it for you and the rest of the galaxy," Anton said as he began to brush Eleanora's hair away from her face. "Such beauty, such treasure should not be hidden away in a place you so eloquently call a dust hole."

"Oh, Anton!" She grabbed him and nestled her head against his chest. "I do want us to live together forever. We can do this in Evermore. I know you are nervous, but we can do it together, and after a few cycles, we can join as one on the other side and have our own kingdom. I would only desire to serve you throughout eternity." She looked him in the eyes, her own eyes soft and full of adoration sheened with tears. "Anton, let us then take the Carriage ride to Earth together like Phyllis did. And soon after, the universe will belong to us, and you will be mine forever!"

Her pitch was too much for Anton to resist. "You and I forever? You can make that promise?" Anton asked.

Eleanora nodded and then bowed her head shyly. "I look forward to seeing you crowned as king—as *my* king!"

"Would you not rather be queen of your own planet?" Anton asked.

"I would refuse such an offer in order to be with you!" she answered. "No longer do I walk the sands and dusts of the waste, wandering throughout the emptiness, questioning my origin and my hopes and dreams. For in this short time that I have grown to know you, I have learned that it is you whom I am bound to from flight-to-flight here, and breath-to-breath there. I never expected companionship like this. I didn't know it was possible. But, Anton, you have changed my understanding of what Lord Jaesu wants from us souls. You are the one I have seen in my visions, standing by my side. I never wanted to tell you this ...maybe you don't feel the same ...but I can't imagine a sweeter destiny than being queen to your king."

Eleanora was aware that she had to be careful. Anton was not a man, with a man's desires. He was a soul, still close to the light of Jaesu. Yet he could be touched by devotion, flattery, and hints of what those on Earth called passion. If she succeeded in getting it just right, Anton would be swept away.

"What if I did make the choice? Would you truly make it with me?" Anton asked hypothetically.

"I would follow *His Majesty's* lead of course," she said taking his hand, simultaneously influencing their direction toward the Carriage Endostream. "But let me ask you something first."

"Anything!"

"Do you love me? I mean *really* love me? With all of your being? With a love that could rock the foundations of the universe?"

"I have already told you. These feelings that I have are unknown to me. You have captivated my very soul, which is my very being."

"What if I wasn't as beautiful as I am now? What if I looked wretched?"

"I can't imagine that. It's impossible for me to fathom."

"Okay, well, what if I wasn't of the Elevemada."

"Well, of course, you are."

"Just play along. What if I wasn't?" she asked as they came upon the steps where the stream entrance was housed.

Anton was so entranced by her and the conversation they were having he did not realize where they were headed. "If you weren't from the Elevemada, it wouldn't make any difference to me. Now that I have had this small time with you, I couldn't imagine spending any more time without you. I would run to the far reaches of the universe to find you if I had to. That's how strong my feelings have already grown."

"Wow," she answered with a slight blush, putting her head down. "And if I were a sorceress?"

"A sorceress? Is that not forbidden in the Elevemada?"

"Play along, Anton. Haven't we established that I wouldn't be from the Elevemada?"

"Yeah, but a sorceress? That would make you, in this case, from Algolithar."

"Still within the far reaches of the universe, am I right? Are you saying that your love for me has limits? I mean, if so, then maybe we shouldn't make the choice for Earth. The trials there will be great. If something as simple as a home world can deter you from your feelings, then—"

"Who said deter? I was thinking of an answer to your question."

Anton could see that Eleanora was shaken by the thought of him not loving her now. He couldn't bear it. He would do anything to put her at ease.

"Don't think, Anton, feel," she whispered seductively in his ear. "What does your heart tell you?"

He paused and looked at her and around all of Alpha before finally noticing the stream. "It tells me that you, and you alone, are my destiny."

"Then let me share with you my one secret." She put her hands out and formed a frame of moving pictures from the air as if it were one of the great paintings in Alpha's literature halls. "Tell me what you see, my love."

Anton looked and was amazed that she could create such a view within the air. "How did you—"

"Just tell me what you see. Combine your brilliance and your heart. If you truly love me, this will prove it."

Anton beheld a woman with long black hair. She danced around a strange, unfamiliar pool. He didn't know her, yet he was drawn to her.

"Well?" Eleanora asked impatiently.

"I see a woman. One who doesn't look like you, but who reminds me of you—of the feelings I have for you. She is dancing."

"That is what you see. What is it that you feel?"

Anton was unsure how to answer because his feelings for the woman in the vision rivaled his feelings for Eleanora.

"I want to be near her, close to her. It's like some sort of magnet. Much like what I feel for you and the feeling quickly morphs into a greater feeling within me. Wait! I see something else now. She is saddened. I cannot understand why, but she is crying. This indeed is a strong sadness. I can't bear to watch much more."

Anton closed his eyes and turned his head. The quick vision had brought him both great joy and great pain. Much like many of the feelings he felt around Eleanora, these were again new experiences.

"What is it, Anton?"

"That sadness, even for a moment, was suffocating. I wanted so badly to take it from her. And I felt utterly powerless. In that instant upon seeing the first tear, there was nothing I wouldn't have done within my power to remove the cause."

"So a being you do not know dances and brings you joy, then cries and brings you sadness?" Eleanora asked.

Anton wasn't sure again how to respond. "Yes, it would seem."

"What is her name?"

"Her name? How do I—" Anton kept hearing a specific name he had never heard before, over and over in his mind. It was *Alina.* "I'm not completely sure of myself here. But I keep hearing Alina."

"Anton, you have proven your love to me."

Anton was very confused by the statement. "I don't entirely understand."

"You see, that is my last secret. The woman you saw is me. The enchantress, the sorceress, the magnificent power formed from the stones of Algolithar. Yes, I am she. I am Alina. She is on a quest for her true love, Anton. And indeed, she has found it. What you saw was the inner depths of my heart. And only my true love, with such a heart of knowledge, could have seen into my heart."

Anton trembled. His insides shook with both fear and excitement. He felt a part of him pleading within to run to Jaesu, and yet another part of him wanted to be even closer to this beautiful being before him. That she had deceived him wasn't even a concern. He was trapped within her web. What he did not know was that the vision she had shared with him wasn't a doorway into her heart but a spell and curse upon his eyes. She had subtly been manipulating him with curses since Seocia. Now he was under her trance.

"Would you choose me over anything?" Alina asked.

"I think, yes. I know I shouldn't, but I am overcome with this feeling. It leads me beyond my fears."

"Then let us make the choice—together. We will find the third door into Evermore and reign in seclusion forever. I will be yours for always." Alina then pulled Anton close to her and kissed his lips. Anton had never kissed another, nor had he even seen it done. Yet it was natural to him, and he was locked on to her embrace. Alina passed on the remainder of her curse in that first kiss.

"Alina," Anton said, gasping for air for an unknown reason after breaking the kiss. "I think I am ready to make the choice."

"It is beautiful to hear you say my name. But wait—shouldn't we tell Lord Jaesu or King Handel? They will want to see you off." Alina knew that Anton would feel shame and a sense of rebellion toward them based on the curse she had planted within him. But she wanted him to confirm it.

"No, it is only you and me now. Let us go meet our destiny together."

Alina quickly shielded Anton's eyes and flung him into the stream to immediately begin the morphing process toward Earth. However, she did not follow as she had promised. She turned away and laughed at her conquest.

"If only they knew what awaited them," she said to herself.

CHAPTER 7

Choices

"I have seen her before," said Grace to Amana. "I saw her on Algolithar. She is a loyal servant to Shajcell, a goddess of Algolithar, who is the great seductress of men."

"Still, I don't understand. How could you know she is the one I saw? Or that I was having a vision?" asked the queen.

"You were motionless, and your eyes became fixed on something. So it was simple to tell that you weren't fully here and that your mind was otherwise occupied. I could not see who you saw exactly, but I felt it. I felt her presence as if she were here— the cold and the damp and the confusion which you sensed. On Earth, many blind men have greater vision than those who have sight because they have mastered their other senses and aren't distracted by what is in front of them. I guess it's like that."

Amana, while troubled by the visions, had already thought to herself that having Grace on Gardenia could benefit her from a strategic standpoint. Grace's ability to feel what she was feeling in trance was unexpected, although certainly welcome. "What other surprises do you have to share, Grace?" Amana asked.

"Oh, well…It may not look it, but I maneuver quite well in flight, and I was once a great huntress. With her majesty's permission, I believe that while I am small in stature, I could stand on the shoulders of Orion and combine with him in battle."

"Thank you, Grace, but the truth is, Orion is a mighty warrior and has never been defeated. I have not seen you in battle and am honestly not sure I would want to put you into harm's way."

"Never been defeated? Orion?" Grace asked. "Are you sure? *Hmm…* Perhaps, we should ask him."

"Why? Do you know something?"

Grace pranced around with her hands behind her back, whistling as if she was having fun knowing something the queen didn't. "Let's say that Orion might have a small blemish on his record. But we should have him tell us. Come on! It will be fun!"

"I don't know why I am entertaining this, but fine, let's go," replied Amana as the two took off toward Orion.

* * *

Meanwhile, the Lighted Blade had gathered with Jaesu.

"Dara, I think it's time that you share with the rest of the Blade," Jaesu said in front of the Lighted Blade members. Dara had left the team in suspense, regarding the challenge she had mentioned before the fight with the asudem.

"There's no easy way to say this," she began, looking around in an attempt to avoid eye contact with the team. "I have decided to take that next step, fill the void, and prepare myself for the ordeals awaiting me on Earth, to become flesh and make an impact for mankind and to eventually see the glorious gates of Evermore."

The team fell silent. They didn't know what to say. This was their leader and, more importantly, their friend for over a thousand cycles. Dara was the founder of the Lighted Blade and her ability to keep them together was not something any in the unit took for granted. Her choice, surprising as it was, started them thinking about themselves. Some began to wonder if they could ever take the same road.

"Well, don't just stand there, guys. Talk to me. I'm here," Dara said nervously. She wasn't afraid of Earth, but she was afraid of letting her teammates down.

"We don't want you to go, of course, but ..." Dawn started off. "Speaking for the team, we all know it's time. You have taught us so much by your example and caring for us. You will make Earth a better place and most assuredly dance through the gates of Evermore."

"Yes!" said Bethany. "You will see your dreams come true before you know it."

"You are a mighty blessing and will continue to be so," said Glynn.

"Not possible to be forgotten or replaced. Thank you for everything," said Jacen. "Even when you were mad at me, I knew that you always cared."

"Like everything else we have done, you have always taken that first step to give us confidence. I imagine that this will be no different. I have a feeling that it won't be long for the rest of us to follow your lead once more and make that choice ourselves," said Marcus.

"Does this mean I am the leader?" Jovan said jokingly.

"Jovan!" Bethany huffed. "Can you ever be serious? I mean, seriously?"

The team erupted in laughter. "In all solemnity," Jovan interjected, looking at Bethany first before moving back to Dara. "As blessed as we have been to have you lead us, you will be an even greater blessing going forward. May greatness follow you throughout eternity."

"Amen," Jaesu added.

The team united once more to join hands and point to the sky in order to form the Lighted Blade as a unit.

Souls, although immortal, experienced an innate desire to get to Evermore. That desire grew daily within them, becoming a mammoth void over time, giving a soul the feeling that it was being consumed. Once souls reached that point, they made the choice to take the next step toward Earth in order to get to Evermore. Upon making that choice, most souls talked with Jaesu first to ensure they were prepared for the trials and had the inner strength to overcome them.

Sadly, many didn't have this strength. They decided not to take the third door and moved on to other pathways, which mostly led to the horrors of Hadnessa. This was never what Jaesu wanted. It was his will and hope that all who decided to go to Earth made it to the riches, glory, and permanent peace of Evermore.

Evermore was more beautiful than any living being could possibly imagine. There were stories of streets of gold and souls becoming kings and queens of greater planets and living waters, but mostly that Evermore was tailored to each being's core desires. Those desires were formed long before the being ever reached Earth. It was in the Elevemada where they were formed, all uniquely.

Dara's next step was to walk to the platform and jump into the Carriage Stream. The stream was connected to Earth like a silver thread. This connection did not end in space or when entering into the Earth's atmosphere; instead, it was linked directly to an egg as it was fertilized within a human mother. While a soul raced down the stream, they transformed into a seed that would find its way into a womb. There were many elements to this mechanism that none understood. Once the child was born on Earth, the parents would name their newborn. A most mysterious law was that the name the parents decided on was the name given to their child upon creation at the Elevemada many years and cycles before. This mechanism of the spirit was unknown and impossible for a soul or human to comprehend, even on worlds such as Alpha.

Dara made her choice because she knew that she had been created to help others. The same was true for the rest of the Blade. There was something in her that felt the eternal purposes of Earth and Evermore far outweighed what she and her comrades had been doing on Gardenia.

"I am going to miss you all," Dara said. "Marcus, continue to be brilliant. I hope you are right about the Blade joining me, because I am going to need someone to teach me braininess on Earth.

"Jacen, may your vision provide a path for those you encounter, both souls and mankind.

"Glynn, always use your discernment wisely. Your feelings are a gift. Don't ever be ashamed of them.

"Bethany, be resilient, spirited one, for the attacks are countless. May your purest heart overcome every doubt and let no one take your crown.

"Dawn, you are smallest among us, but far from the least. May your keen hearing always find the steps of your enemies, no matter how they try to hide, and also find the steps of your destiny upon your greatest journey.

"And Jovan, in many ways, yes, you have always been our leader. Perhaps not in title, but in heart and mind. We look up to you. What a mighty talent you are. I am so grateful for your friendship and courage. May your favor do wondrous things for Jaesu before the end."

With that she looked at Jaesu as if to say she was ready to get going.

"Aren't you forgetting something?" she heard from the side. It was Daffodil, her close friend from Scepter, followed by the remaining cats. "If you need me, I'll find you," she said to Dara as they embraced.

"Do not forget what we discussed at the mansion. The secret to Owls and Seraphs unlocks many of the secrets to life on Earth and thus is its major purpose. Be wise and love all unconditionally," added Black before placing her heavy paw on Dara's shoulder. "Remember, the cats on earth know more than people think."

"There are cats on Earth?" asked Bethany.

"Earth is full of animals," said Black. "They, too, are weaker there. How you treat them is a mark of how well you are following your path. Is it not true, Lord Jaesu?"

"I would not contradict you on that, Black," he said. "There is not a being on Earth or in the Elevemada whom I don't love and cherish."

Dara wept. She was going to miss everyone and everything, but she had thought this over for some time. She knew she was making the right choice. She grasped Jaesu by the arm and abruptly started walking up the mountain toward the Carriage Stream. He walked with her, sharing one final journey—as he often would unless the soul had no interest. This was the moment when Jaesu would share intimate details of life, consciousness, and good and evil. This was usually a special time for both Jaesu and the soul making the choice. It was a face-to-face conversation, and it was the last and best time to gain the understanding needed to battle the flesh and the walkways of Earth.

Before they went to Earth, souls knew very little of temptation and suffering. But at this moment, they could sense what was coming, as well as remember clearly the brightness and glory that was the Elevemada. Often times, Jaesu would share visions of a being's future for them to cling to. It would remain within their hearts, though they wouldn't remember how it got there. Dara looked back toward the Blade once more and then continued with Jaesu toward her next journey.

* * *

Amana and Grace were awaking Orion from his slumber. "I can't wait until he sees me," said Grace. "It's been forever!"

"You have met before?" asked the queen.

"Yes! Of course, long before the purge, he and I …well … let's say, I think he will remember me." Grace, tired of waiting for him to awaken, reared back and flew toward him rather forcefully, with the idea to bounce off of his back. "Wake up!"

Orion jumped up as if he had been attacked. He looked around and realized it was a false alarm. He saw the queen and immediately bowed his head. "Your Majesty! I must have overslept."

Amana laughed. "No, not at all, Orion. We have a guest whom I think you might be interested in."

Orion looked and saw the tiny girl next to Amana. He thought it was Grace, but it couldn't be. He had watched her become seduced by Khrimson's charismatic ways. He had battled against legions that had included her. It wasn't possible. "I'm not sure I entirely understand," he said to the queen.

"*Ahem*," interjected Grace. "Can you confirm to our great queen that there used to be one person who always got the better of you when it came to strategy battles before the purge?" she said feistily.

"It is you! GRACE!" Orion said excitedly. He didn't feel the presence of an asudem, but the presence of one who had been his friend for many cycles before the purge. Long before the wars, there had been no difference between seraphs and asudem. They were one and the same. Everyone was considered an angel, as they were then called. But once the battles ensued, the angels were separated into seraphs who protected Evermore and asudem who served Khrimson. Many relationships were severed due to the purge. "I don't understand."

"I am just putting the pieces together myself, believe it or not," Amana answered. "While Jovan was showing off his skills, Bethany found Grace chained to Phan as a repentant slave shield. She used her magnetic skills to force Grace's release. Jaesu restored her place, and she is with us now. I'm sure you would have noticed had you not been battling thousands of asudem yourself."

"Yeah," Grace added jokingly. "I guess you've lost a step since I've been gone."

"Well, for the record, I don't recall anyone beating me in any old strategy sessions," Orion said.

"What?" pouted Grace. "How many times did you ask me to teach you evasive maneuvers, how to think ahead, how to play chess—long before I passed it to humans?"

Orion bellowed in laughter and responded, "I must admit, it is crazy how that game has flourished on Earth. I can't actually put into words how shocked and happy I am to see you. Did I hear the queen correctly? Are you staying on Gardenia?"

"Well," Grace replied as she glanced over at the queen.

"In talking with Grace and in light of recent events, I think it would be wise and comforting for you to have a sidekick," Amana said.

"Sidekick?" Orion said, surprised and slighted. "Was I not fast enough in this most recent battle? Is it because of Jovan's help? I really haven't lost a step, Your Majesty. I would die for—"

"Orion!" Amana stopped him mid-sentence. "You are the greatest warrior in the entire galaxy. I am always honored by your courage, loyalty, and love. However, I fear greater battles will be coming. For you to have someone with whom you are comfortable and care for will only make you stronger and happier in my view. That is all. Don't think of it as anything more than that!"

"Yeah, besides," added Grace, "I wouldn't want to be stuck down there while you have fun up here."

"In any event, I would be glad to share the stage with Grace," Orion said. "There is great power in little people, I am told." He smirked at Grace.

Grace's size was insignificant in comparison to Orion, who was massive. She fit perfectly on his shoulder. "Be careful. We little people have a way of BEING HEARD!" she yelled in his ear.

Amana laughed at them both, certain now that this was a good idea. "Well, I think my work here is done."

"Wait! Your Majesty," Grace said seriously. "Your visions about Alina—what will you do?"

"Meditate and wait for the next one, I suppose," Amana replied.

"Before the purge, on Omega, there used to be a place where one could walk into their dreams," Grace continued. "The dreams would become more vivid. It was said that the Blue Fire Spirit would appear to those pure in heart to unlock great mysteries."

"*Ahh...* yes, the Eve of Illumination," Orion said. "That's a cavern; I don't imagine that has been in use for many cycles."

"Not in use?" Amana replied. "Why? What is Eve of Illumination?"

"Eve of Illumination is said to be named after Eve, a great princess of Omega from long ago who was among the first to take the journey to Earth," Grace said. "Before making the choice to come to Earth, she used to go into a special cavern to try to understand the dreams she was having, which ultimately led her to make her choice. Her story is much larger, I believe, but it's sealed away in mystery as the cavern has not been opened since she journeyed to Earth."

"She was quite revered among the Omegans, but to ensure she did not become some sort of deity among them, the kings and queens that came after kept her cavern hidden from those looking to misuse it. Its name is based on revelations she received from the Blue Fire Spirit," added Orion.

"It is far from the major cities. Over many cycles of disuse it became buried and removed from common knowledge and conversation," said Grace. "However, if you travel toward the highest mountain and follow the moonlight over its great canyons, between the shores you will see a crevice, edged in pale blue stone like none other on the planet. Fly inside of it and look for a blue lamp. It's deep down in the shadows. Legend has it that if the blue lamp is lit, then the Eve of Illumination will be there."

"Thank you both. I'm not sure what it is that I should do, but for certain, these premonitions aren't going away, and the warnings are getting stronger," the queen said.

* * *

Bethany and Jovan were strolling through the Royal Garden. They had been discussing Dara's choice. Although they both were happy for her, they were going to miss her. "How do you think she will do?" Bethany asked Jovan.

"Are you kidding? She'll be great. I mean, we are told they struggle far more than we do here, but her perseverance, caring, and willingness to bring others together are strong qualities no matter where deployed. At least, that's what I think."

"I'm going to miss how she would take me under her wing and laugh with me. She was the authority—I never forgot that—but in a soft way. I loved her off-the-cuff, last-minute panic strategies. I don't think I did at the time, but looking back now, I see some method to her madness."

"Have you thought about it? You know, making the choice?"

"Yes …but I would never do it without you."

"Really? Is that a good thing?"

"Of course, it is," Bethany replied. "We have been the closest of friends for so long. We know what each other thinks and feels and, yes, we are super close with the rest of the Blade—like Dara,

Jacen, and all—but as strong as those bonds are, soul mates as we all are, my connection with you runs far deeper."

"I know exactly how you feel. But I have to wonder if there is a purpose for us out there. You know, like Dara was talking about. I have walked with Jaesu so many times over the cycles, and there is something so pure about him. He has a peace and love and joy that I have never felt in any other being. I sense no void in him. Not like us. So I have to wonder if the connection that you and I feel is a precursor, a prelude to something greater. I can't explain it."

"That's just it. With us, you never have to explain. It's like I'll always know what you're thinking. I'm nervous that, once on Earth, we might lose that."

"Not necessarily!" Jaesu entered into the conversation.

"Lord Jaesu!" Bethany responded, caught totally off guard. "Did you hear that? I thought you were with Dara."

"She is long gone and, believe it or not, has started to live her life on the Earth. Besides, like you have the gift of magnetic pulse, I have been blessed with the ability of being at several places at once," Jaesu answered with a smile. "I am also with Jacen, Glynn, and Marcus right now, in deep conversation."

"I'll never understand that part," Bethany said, shaking her head.

"I asked him to come and walk with us, Bethany," Jovan said. "I had a feeling there were questions we would want to ask, being that Dara just became an earthling."

"*Hmm*," said Bethany "Well, warn me next time, Jovan!"

"I thought you always knew what he was thinking," Jaesu chuckled.

"Very funny," Bethany answered, folding her arms.

"Lord, I asked you here because …well, you know why," said Jovan. "I think making the choice has been on our minds for a while. With Dara taking that first step, it feels almost like a confirmation of sorts. What can you tell us? Is this feeling normal, or am I missing something?"

"Yes and YES," Jaesu answered. "Your thoughts are normal, and there is yet a lot that you are missing. But let's talk about some of the things Bethany mentioned. On Earth, there are occasions—very rare, but they do happen—where you might meet someone whom you feel like you've known for centuries, even though this is the first time you've laid eyes on each other. And sometimes you meet someone that you are immediately unsure about or suspicious of—and, of course, there are many shades in between. The reason is simple. Everything you experience here has an impact on your being and feeling and personality on the Earth. Those you are close to here, you will naturally be close to there. You will hear a term used on Earth… *kindred spirits*, which refers to people who are very much alike or deeply bonded with one another. There are other people whom you will instantly fear or feel uncomfortable around, no matter how hard you try to get along. This can be because of a rivalry you had with that soul here or, more commonly, because your personal seraph is battling an asudem spirit attached to the other person."

"You mean we get our own personal Orion?" Jovan asked. "Whoa! That is totally blade!"

"Well, in Orion's case, he is bound to Queen Amana—but yes, most times souls are granted seraphs," responded Jaesu.

"Most times?" asked Bethany.

"Yes," answered Jaesu, looking sad for a moment. "There are those who place their faith in themselves alone and underestimate how hard the trials of Earth are. They sometimes believe that a seraph protector—the earthly term is guardian angel—is a sign of weakness. I tell you both: it is a sign of strength. It shows wisdom and prudence. Should you make the choice, I implore you both to be wise and select a seraph protector because it is very difficult to make it back to Evermore without one."

"Wow! I guess I always knew about the seraphs, but they really weren't factoring into my decision," said Bethany. "What will they do on the Earth?"

"This is especially interesting, because your human eyes will not see your seraph—or anyone's seraph or asudem—but a person can often feel them. You can feel peace in times of trouble, which usually means that your protector is attempting to calm you. Or you can feel trouble in time of peace, which can mean that your protector is trying to warn you of upcoming trouble. Even though your flesh may weigh you down and iron out your memories somewhat, your conscience will serve as a guide. There are times when things will feel familiar, yet you have never experienced them before. On Earth, they call this *déjà vu*. But the reality is, it's something you have seen or done here in preparation for your life there," Jaesu answered.

"That sounds like an awful lot, Jay," Jovan added.

"I'm not going to tell you anything that isn't true," responded Jaesu. "It's not an easy road. But without question, it is a road that both of you are ready for and were meant to take. As souls, your callings far exceed the wonders that you have experienced here and the tribulations awaiting you on Earth. If I could show you or explain it to you, I would, but it is impossible for even me to explain Evermore in a way that gives it justice."

"Is there anything you can tell us about it?" Bethany asked.

"*Hmmm* ..." Jaesu pondered. "You have heard of golden streets and living waters, of course. But let me phrase it this way. Bethany, what are your deepest—in the very core of your being—deepest desires?"

"Well, that's easy," Bethany chimed in. "It's ...no, I think it's ...it has to be, of course, that I would get to beat Jovan racing around the planet once."

"But why?" Jaesu asked. "What drives that competitive spirit and edge that you have?"

"I have no idea; I just feel it."

"Evermore is made up of such feelings and desires. The ones you can't interpret now but drive you to become who you are. Once you get to Evermore, there's no figuring out anything. Evermore is customized for every unique being that has ever been created," Jaesu continued. "You are all created individually and uniquely. When you get to Earth, you will have things called *fingerprints*. Every single one that has ever been created is different from the next. There are no templates in life. Just like the hair you have now. Every being has a different number of hairs on his or her head. Could you tell me how many there are without counting?"

"Of course not. That's impossible," Jovan said.

"Impossible only for your eyes and understanding. Evermore is a place where you will know the answers to every question upon taking your first steps. Think of it this way: on Gardenia, when you want to sit down, the stones and trees create seats for you, and you sit in unison with them and commune as one. On

Earth, they kill the trees, chop up the stones and create furniture that is temporarily there."

"What? How barbaric!" Bethany shouted.

"And outdated. Hello? Aren't they current?" Jovan interjected.

"For them, yes, they are, Jovan," Jaesu answered. "But their version of becoming the creator through the lens which they call technology hasn't even caught up to Gardenia, much less Evermore, the let-there-be-light tactic, which you pulled against the armies of Phan? Earthlings are several thousand cycles away from knowing how to do that. As far as barbaric goes, Bethany, they make do with what they have. Their faith, generally speaking, is in knowledge and technology more than love or kindness or peace. Don't get me wrong. I love the arts and sciences. Knowledge is beautiful, but it can become a waste if treated as a deity. Life is simple at its core. The desire to love and to be loved is at the heart of it all, and no amount of knowledge or riches can ever take love's place."

"Lord, that certainly makes sense and all, but on Seocia, the Alphans were really high on knowledge, and they looked like they were doing quite well in their own way," Bethany said, with Jovan nodding agreement.

"Again, Bethany, knowledge is not the enemy," Jaesu replied. "But let me tell you a story about a girl I know from Earth. Her name is Tamara. By Evermore's standards, she is very beautiful. By man's standards, as well. She was blessed with a wonderful family and multitudes of riches. On top of that, she had accumulated more knowledge and education than anyone in her circle. And what a heart she possessed! Tamara was incredibly generous toward any that needed help. Without question, this was a woman who was both a blessing and blessed. She became one with a man, Carlos. They were the closest of friends, much like you and Jovan are now. They were together for a long time. They made a covenant with one another to be together forever. Well, forever only lasted a moment as Carlos broke the promise to be with someone else and forgot Tamara."

"Oh, my goodness!" Bethany said, beginning to cry. "I cannot imagine."

"Would you believe," Jaesu continued, "this young woman cried to me every day and in no way could any of the riches, knowledge, power and glory that she had accumulated rescue her from her sorrows or dry her tears? It was heartbreaking. I helped her through it, and she eventually met a new friend, Paolo. He was quite pure in heart and spirit. He had little wealth, and his knowledge was of a different kind, not so easily flaunted. But he knew love, and his love knew no boundaries. Where the rest of the world saw mediocrity, Tamara saw a city of bright jewels."

"What did you do with Carlos, Lord?" asked Bethany.

"I eagerly wait for him to come to me, so I can help him turn his life around," Jaesu said.

"You would help him? He seems so mean and horrible," said Bethany.

"Believe it or not, Bethany, on Earth you both will have the capability to be as horrible. Should I love you any less?" Jaesu replied.

Both of them kept silent as they continued to walk with their Lord. The three of them passed the Golden River. Its water was transparent, like all water, but when, at least, two of the suns were in the sky, it shone like gold. Bethany and Jovan swam in these waters together for cycles and cycles. They had never thought of loss or treachery. Jaesu could see and feel their struggles.

"Both of you are the apples of my eye," Jaesu said. "My love for you is everlasting, and I will stand with you always, even during your hardest struggles. Should you make the choice to go, may those words be permanently sealed within your heart."

"Lord?" Bethany inquired. "I can't imagine Jovan and I being that far apart from one another. You know, like Tamara and Carlos? Is there any way I could remember him as we are now?"

"Sadly, no," Jaesu answered. "The flesh will wipe your memory almost completely. But I promise, should you ever meet, you will both feel a connection like no other."

"Could you like, write his name on my flesh, maybe over here?" she asked, pointing to the spot just above where her heart would be if she were human.

"Well…" Jaesu laughed. "You could do that yourself on Earth. They call that a tattoo. I could draw his name as a birthmark, but I think your parents, whoever they may be, would be confused and think it a sign to name YOU Jovan."

"*Ewww*, gross!" Bethany said, grimacing.

"Hey!" Jovan chimed in. "I happen to be fond of Jovan. I am quite blade, ya know."

"And I am quite bored of you saying that you are quite blade," Bethany shot back.

"That's it! We are ready!" Jovan asserted.

Bethany's eyes widened in shock. Her spirit agreed with him, but she still couldn't believe it. A part of her felt it was rushed but another part of her believed it to be perfectly timed. "We are?" she questioned.

"Yes, we are." Jovan looked at her. "I feel it within your very depths, as I feel it within mine. It's time for us to make our mark on history for our Lord, our purpose, and to be rid of this void."

Bethany looked at Jaesu and nodded her head in agreement. "Will we tell Marcus and the team? They might not understand with Dara leaving so recently."

"This time that I have been talking to you has taken nearly an entire cycle," Jaesu added. "Yet to us it felt like seconds. And during that time, I have also been with Marcus and Glynn and Jacen. All of them have been inspired, as you are, by Dara's choice."

"They are making the choice, too?" Jovan asked.

"Yes! They already have," Jaesu answered firmly.

"What about Dawn?" asked Bethany in a demanding voice.

"She has not shown any desire as of yet," responded Jaesu.

"She is smaller than the rest of us and far quieter," Bethany said.

"I'm not sure those things have anything to do with it, Bethany. Dawn is often precise and although quiet, she listens better than any, and thus would be a tremendous addition to any challenge," Jovan said.

"Wow, you really have been listening during our talks," Bethany joked.

"Yeah," Jovan laughed. "Hold on… Aren't we forgetting something? We can't leave without telling Aman …I mean, Queen Amana."

Bethany shot Jovan a look, annoyed that he almost said Amana without using her title. "Jovan is probably right, Lord. We should wait for our queen."

"Queen Amana has taken a journey which will delay her," Jaesu replied. "However, I have words from the great queen for you."

At that moment a recorded hologram of Queen Amana appeared before them:

Bethany and Jovan,

I dare not call you mere citizens of Gardenia, but the closest of friends to me. I am proud of you both for coming to such a decision. I have wept knowing this day would soon come.

Jovan, thank you for standing in the breach for me long before I was queen, befriending me, walking with me and totaling the stars with me. Do not think for one single moment that I have ever forgotten even a flash of what we have shared. It is with a heavy heart that I congratulate you on your choice. I know you will be mighty upon your return from Earth in Evermore.

Bethany, although we have been closer at some times more than others, I have always admired your heart and willingness to fight and compete. Such traits will provide you strength and courage on Earth when you least expect it.

My love is with you both always. I give you the blessing of life from Gardenia. May it serve you well and keep you strong. Hold on to Jaesu, no matter what you are told as you both grow. Choose your seraphs wisely. I look forward to hearing about your adventures upon your entrance into the unimaginable beauty—Evermore.

I wish dearly that I could be there with you now, but trust that I am doing our Lord's will and preparing for the shaking of the heavens. I miss you both already.

With all my heart and love, I bow to you now for the king and queen you both shall be.

Amana

Bethany and Jovan remained silent. Jovan teared up, remembering the closeness he and Amana had shared before she became queen. Bethany, although touched, did not quite understand Jovan's emotional attachment to the queen.

"Is it now time for seraphs, my Lord?" Bethany asked.

"If you both are ready, then yes," Jaesu responded. "I have assembled your choice of seraphs on the maroon moon."

"That is relatively close by," Jovan replied.

"Yes," Jaesu answered. "But there is one condition regarding how we get there."

"OK?" Bethany said curiously.

"Both of you," Jaesu said, "race me there!" He showed a joyous smile as he took off, with the other two flying fiercely close behind, trying to catch up. Jaesu could not be outraced by any being, and though he was not competitive against souls, even though he loved to pretend to be competitive with them—especially Jovan—this race had a special meaning for all of them. They had raced for many cycles, and much like Bethany always lost to Jovan by a split second, Jovan always lost to Jaesu by the same amount. It was their last jubilant time together before the choice. Jaesu had known that a strong Gardenian era was coming to a close and the Lighted Blade would take that next step toward its destiny.

CHAPTER 8

Tales of Vision

O n Alpha, King Handel was in the throne room finishing up a conference with many of the other kings, queens, and advisors. He had a scheduled visitor awaiting an audience with him once the meeting was completed. "Ah, Eleanora. Very good to see you. I trust your presence here brings word that you have decided to stay with us a while longer?"

Alina went down on one knee with her head lowered. "O great King Handel, mightiest ruler throughout the galaxy, I am both humbled and honored to be in your presence. Since nothing escapes your eye, I am sure you know by now that our great friend Anton has decided to make the journey to Earth and has been conceived safely."

Handel, very surprised by this turn of events, tried exceedingly hard not to show it. The news crushed him. Anton's celebrity and importance to Alpha as its Owls and Seraphs champion was not to be underestimated. How would the souls react once word got out? They would have wanted to send off their hero themselves, much as they had with Phyllis. "Well, of course, I am always aware of such matters," he said hurriedly. "Does his departure impact your decision regarding Alpha and Banth?" the king asked.

"Well, Your Majesty," Alina began her response, remembering to keep her eyes low, "I was hoping to get your thoughts on transferring my citizenship to Alpha. I am very talented when it comes to the games and believe that my abilities, which you may have witnessed on Seocia, can bring further greatness to his majesty's kingdom. Alpha's birthright is to always be the champion among the stars, and I desire to represent Anton and his home world in that march toward greatness."

The king, very pleased with her response, became puffed up regarding his own abilities and proud of himself for ruling such a benevolent world. "Alpha would embrace your service to her kingdom, Eleanora. Indeed, I have witnessed the powerful talents you possess. With Phyllis and Anton no longer on Alpha, I am in need of a mighty player—a standout and a team captain. Perhaps a new kind of leadership could prove useful. Eleanora, would you take on the honor of being Alpha's captain on our Owls and Seraphs team?" Handel asked.

"Oh, I couldn't, Your Majesty," she said, feigning humility. "With so many incredible souls of knowledge and wonder here on Alpha, being a part of the team would be more than enough. I couldn't possibly assume the role of their leader."

"Nonsense!" the king said loudly. "It is your humility that shows your leadership qualities. I believe you will lead us to many victories. It is settled."

"In that case, great king, for as long as you reign, I will never take the journey to Earth. Your faith and trust in me deserves the same in kind. Thank you, mighty one."

"I foresee many great things ahead for the both of us," said the king. "Here is something that, as the new captain, you may find intriguing. The Owls and Seraphs tournament, as you know, has been postponed, but once confirmation arises that our battles are completely over, we will reconvene on Seocia and, as slated before, our first round opponent will be Gardenia. What will interest you most is that the Lighted Blade, our previous opponents have mostly taken the course for Earth as well. It should be an easy task for you to disrupt and eliminate whatever team they bring into the mix."

The new captain smiled wickedly. "Very well, my Lord, I look forward to adding another trophy to your throne."

*   *   *

On Gardenia, Roslyn was following her normal routine as Euwyn and Jasmine continued their long walk toward the Diamond. It often took them nearly an entire cycle, but that long time away was the biggest joy. The many days alone together, soaking in the experiences with each other were special. Roslyn, even with them gone, enjoyed spending her days with the forest, chatting with the trees, the birds, the moss, and the stones. She understood them as no one else did.

"I thought I'd find you here," said Black to Roslyn. "Perhaps that's why the queen likes you."

"Because I'm easy to find?" she laughed.

"Yes. There's a certain reliability implied by that."

"Is that your way of saying she left for a while and would like me to handle things?"

"And I guess that's the other reason she likes you," Black sighed. "You are perceptive."

"I'm not sure that I am cut out for such an important role. I was pretty much terrified last time."

"Precisely why I think she calls on you for such tasks. She won't be gone long."

"Then take a walk with me. I want to see something. Considering that I'm in charge now." She winked at Black as the lioness shook her head.

The two walked and talked about leadership and strategy, nature and love, and how they reflect each other. Black explained to Roslyn her philosophy of government, which she drew on as an advisor to the queen. Roslyn, in turn, shared with Black her affinity for the life on Gardenia. "I don't really see any difference between me and that clump of moss," she concluded.

"Well, that's what I'm for, I guess, to tell you this, there is a difference."

"*Shh.* There they are," Roslyn said as she pointed toward the end of the bridge.

"Who?" asked Black.

"Euwyn and Jasmine. You don't see them?" Roslyn responded. "He's about to give her the shawl."

"Shawl? What's a shawl? Like a snack?" Black asked.

"No! It's romantic. Euwyn made her this beautiful shawl to cover herself with as a symbol of his love for her. I think it's amazing."

"So, it's …a …covering thingy," sighed Black. "Like I said, it would have been better off being a snack. Do you happen to know where the purple peaches grow?"

"Okay, settle down, I want to hear," whispered Roslyn.

*   *   *

The buck and doe couple were across the ledge and completely oblivious to Roslyn and Black. They were enjoying their view under the very tall trees and watching the falls within the Diamond. The water seemed to be made up of shining bits of light, the lacy white froth, both exuberant and tranquil.

"All these cycles, and you grow more beautiful by the day," Euwyn said.

"All these cycles, Euwyn, and you always know exactly what to say at exactly the right time."

"Well, you wound up with the perfect buck."

"No, but almost," Jasmine smiled, and she placed her head on his neck.

As Jasmine closed her eyes, Euwyn looked up at the tree directly over them. He had set up an elaborate plan for her to receive the surprise gift. Several cardinals had flown to the Diamonda, following Euwyn and Jasmine. Each cardinal gently maintained a hold on the shawl and guided it toward the doe. Euwyn nuzzled Jasmine's neck and moved away from her softly. Jasmine opened her eyes, and before she could utter a word, the shawl fell beautifully over her entire body. She looked stunning.

"Wow, that was some trick by the cardinals," said Black.

"Black! *Shh* …" whispered Roslyn. "That was timing and creating the perfect moment …you know? Romance?" She shook her head at the cat in disbelief. "Trick." She rolled her eyes.

"Euwyn? What is this?" Jasmine said in shock.

"It is a small token of my love, expressing how beautiful you are to me," Euwyn replied.

Blushing, with eyes full of joyous and grateful tears, Jasmine said, "Did I really say *almost?*" She rubbed the side of her face into Euwyn's neck.

"Okay, we can let them be now," Black said.

"No, wait, this will be the best part," whispered Roslyn.

"*Um,* I may not be quite the romantic, but, child, I know when it is time to go. Hear what I'm sayin'?" retorted Black.

"You're right. Let's be off. After all, I have a kingdom to direct," sighed Roslyn. She petted Black on her head and neck, which only Queen Amana dared to do. Black noticed something strange happening. When Roslyn petted her hair, the ends of her beautiful black fur became dark red like wine. The color faded after a minute, but Black had been startled and felt a new and powerful connection with Roslyn. This was a source of wonder to Black because until now she had only felt bonds with Amana and her fellow cats.

*　*　*

On Algolithar, Khrimson had returned from Saturn to rally the asudem once more. He walked the long path toward his throne, admiring the skulls, proud that the walkway became longer daily, and never bothering to try to remember whom the skulls had belonged to. Three asudem were awaiting Khrimson at the edge of his throne room. The three were on one knee and were shaking with fear.

"Anaihiss, you have some news for me, I presume?" asked Khrimson. "For your sake, it better be worth interrupting my enjoyment of the latest members of my collection."

"My lord," Anaihiss replied, still on his knee and still bowing, "I have received word from our great treacherous sister Alina that members of a group called the Lighted Blade have recently chosen to take the Carriage Stream to Earth. She said it was urgent and a matter that would be important to you. So we waited here until you returned."

Khrimson silently clenched his fists in anger. This was unexpected. *This weakens Gardenia, yes, but could strengthen Earth.* He considered what he already knew. If Earth was going to be taken, then he needed to be present on the planet soon to lead the battles there. He still desired to take Gardenia as a part of the sequence, but trusted only Phan to orchestrate his strategy and lead the attack.

He turned to Anaihiss. "I see you have brought me crucial information. My only question to you, O demon of the coldest star, is what have you done to stop them from infiltrating Earth? Have you introduced a disease to afflict the mothers? Have you caused miscarriages? Have you whispered in their ears that they are unfit to be mothers, unworthy to carry children? Have you convinced them to abort? Have you attacked the Carriage Streams to keep the Gardenians from getting to earthly conception healthily—at the very least causing their senses to be damaged at birth? Which of these have you accomplished to show your great worth to your lord and master?"

Trembling even more, Anaihiss and his two cohorts responded, stammering, "M-My lord ...m-my master, we-we... brought you word, s-so that you could do what is wisest. As...n-none are ...w-wiser ...than you." The asudem were hunched over even more now.

"Why did I include such brainless and worthless fools into my purge and kingdom? What if the Gardenians were coming here to attack? Would you still be kneeling? Or would you fight? Don't even defame me with an answer," Khrimson said viciously. He then screamed for the highest-ranking asudem remaining. "SHAJCELL!"

Within seconds she appeared.

"Ruler and lord over all." She bowed as she appeared in the throne room.

"Where have you been, princess?" hissed Khrimson.

"My Lord, I was on Earth clouding the mind of the U.S. president. You know it is a favorite game of mine. Terrorists blow up their barracks and consulates overseas while he has affairs. And this time, with me," she replied.

"Were you playing the intern role again?" asked Khrimson.

"Actually, I was a bit more nostalgic. I was looking for something more from the days of the Roman Empire. So the president is currently having a covert affair with his cousin," she answered.

"So much mightier than your brothers you are, princess. You deceive, manipulate, and can travel from Earth to Algolithar in nanoseconds upon hearing my voice. I have a pressing charge for you," said Khrimson. With that, he smote the three asudem trembling before him. "Take these three to the Reaper on Mercury. Exchange them for three other asudem. Tell him one must be Phan and the others can be of Phan's choosing. Advise the Reaper that I will be collecting Phan on Saturn at the small crater where Sardis waits. Soon, Phan can claim his revenge."

"My lord," Shajcell answered curiously, "what has happened to Phan?"

"Let's say he needed a reminder to prepare himself to be the ruthless ruler he was fashioned to be," Khrimson said, laughing. "Now, my dear, off with you. I have yet another journey to make."

With that, Shajcell took the three asudem and left for Mercury. Although the Reaper's price for prisoners was ten human souls for one asudem, one dead asudem could be exchanged for another. This happened rarely, but as Khrimson and the Reaper were currently on speaking terms, he was sure the Reaper would oblige and release Phan.

*   *   *

Flying in between the crevices of Omega was Queen Amana. She knew if there was any hope of unlocking the riddles and visions she was faced with, she needed to get to the Eve of Illumination cavern. She had already flown so deep into the crevice that all around her was darkness. Amana had managed to avoid the powerful lightning, which happened on Omega quite frequently. Although the spears of light energy couldn't kill a soul, the lightning could certainly cause some delay.

She continued to fly downward as the darkness deepened and the air grew chill. Not a hint of moonlight was within her gaze, she could feel the crevice getting narrower and narrower. The Gardenian queen knew that, if Eve's cavern no longer existed, it would take several cycles to find the way back out.

Amana flew with great speed and perseverance further and further down, but she was starting to get nervous. She could hear and feel the wind, but could not tell if it was due to her haste or if there was an outlet of some sort. She asked Jaesu for guidance, hoping he could hear her even from these depths.

Shortly thereafter, she saw a faint blue dot, miles further south, but the dot was easily visible given the amount of time her eyes had been adjusting to the darkness. At first, Amana feared her mind was playing tricks on her, but she followed the light nonetheless. As she got closer, the dot appeared to keep moving forward. It was as if the dot was leading her down a precise path. She began to hear whispers and see the translucent forms of ghosts. These kinds of ghosts were unfamiliar to her. She had always assumed they were only memories or dreams, not as real as she was. But now the ghost of an older woman approached, wearing a dark cloak around her head, her hands knotted, face full of anguish. The ghost drifted closer. When she was almost on top of Amana, her withered mouth opened, and in a surprisingly loud voice, she screamed, "GO AWAY! TURN AROUND NOW!"

Amana was startled and more than a little frightened, but she persisted. Other ghosts made their way toward her—men, women, children, a mix of human ghosts, a few dressed richly, many in rags, all with eyes that seemed to look straight into her heart. Some reached for her with cold fingers, though their fingers never touched her; others shouted with mouths wide open, so she could see the endless darkness inside them. Still others muttered a litany of fears, trying to find the one that would weaken her.

Amana had fear, but she would not oblige them by turning back. "Lord Jaesu has not given you dominion over me. Show me what I seek," she said, not to any ghost in particular, but to all of them and to herself.

As she fought off the distracting ghosts, Amana observed that the dot had come to a halt. She moved closer to it, and the light began to expand. It had come to rest on a ledge in front of a cave. Amana could hear voices that sounded like children laughing in secret. Eventually, she descended onto the ledge and saw that this blue light was now in the form of a being. She could not tell if it was male or female, but it became more powerful by the second.

"Who are you?" she asked.

The blue being's laughter was a bouquet of children's voices darting swiftly through the cave. The being was light blue outlined by darker blue. It began to pick up speed; Amana had to give it her all just to keep up. She followed the being through a complicated maze. Corners came quickly and were turned quickly.

The maze ended abruptly, but Amana's speed carried her past the endpoint. She noticed there was no ground beneath her feet. For the first time in her existence, she was unable to float as souls do. She fell and screamed, unable to catch her balance as she tumbled faster and faster. She trembled uncontrollably.

Amana turned so that her eyes faced the direction that she was falling and, when she did so, noticed the ground was getting closer and closer, and then …her fall ceased about five inches before she would have hit. The being stood over her and gently lifted her by the hand. Amana was much shaken and afraid.

"Do not fear, Your Majesty," said the being. "I am Estelle, the Lamp of the Cavern. Welcome to the Eve of Illumination."

Amana looked around. She was in a uniquely designed cave. It had plant life and libraries, water streams separated by little hills, and a host of other features. She noticed that the design of the cave incorporated a small piece of each world in the Elevemada. As she walked further, she saw a patch of dirt, a substance she didn't recognize. Dirt was foreign to her, as plant life on Gardenia grew without soil. She approached it and said to Estelle, "What is this?"

"Why, it is Earth, Your Majesty," she responded. "Have you not seen this before?"

"No, I don't think so," the queen answered. Amana then saw two padlocked doors made of steel and stone. She could hear sounds coming from behind them. From the door on her left she heard the sounds of choirs singing. From the right, she heard the sounds of people screaming and chains smashing and grinding against one another. It was a horrible sound; it made her quiver. "What is behind those two doors?" she asked.

"That is not something that you need to know at this time," Estelle responded sternly. "I must leave you now. Wait here. Do not move from the Earth."

Estelle disappeared. Amana stood as instructed, not moving from the patch of dirt that represented Earth. She looked around and marveled at how beautifully crafted the cave was, wondering why she had been asked to stay on what she considered to be the least attractive area. She shifted her balance and noticed that something was holding her to the ground. She didn't know how strong it was because she had no intention of disobeying Estelle, but she began to get nervous once more. *I should have never left Gardenia.* Nevertheless, she was here in this strange place, doing what she had been asked to do.

Amana waited for a very long and quiet time. She sighed, leaned, wriggled her body, and did anything she could do to keep from moving off the patch of dirt.

The plants at the front of the cave started to wilt. She watched as the water between the hills turned to sand and the libraries floated high up and whirled in a circle, the colors of their books glowing brighter and brighter until she saw they were no longer books but the jewels in a crown. The dirt at her feet formed into chains around her, now she was definitely locked into place.

She did not like this.

More cries pierced the air, not just from the door on the right, but from every direction. Then, from out of the door on the left emerged a man who looked like a great warrior. He wore a white cape on his back and a dark red medallion around his neck. From the same door emerged a white tiger, roaring loudly. The tiger had eyes that were as blue as mountain ice and long, saber-like teeth. As she watched it pace in front of the door, it wavered, its body splitting in two with tremendous speed. Twin tigers now roared at her, completely separate from each other. As soon as she accepted that this impossible thing had happened, the two merged back into one. Then both the warrior and the tiger ran toward her. She was stuck. The chains beneath her held firm. The warrior reached for what she assumed was a weapon, and the tiger leaped toward Amana's head, mouth open wide.

"Stop!" a calm voice was heard. "Be still, child."

Amana was terrified. She had closed her eyes at the last second and could not see who had spoken. She wondered if she was still alive and in the cave. She slowly opened her eyes. A female being stood in front of her. She had long black hair set off with dark blue lowlights. She was outlined in blue, like the previous being, and was incredibly beautiful. The ferocious white tiger curled at her feet, purring like a kitten. The warrior fell to one knee and remained motionless. Everything in the cave stopped.

"Queen Amana of Gardenia," said the woman, "great power exudes from you. Your reputation precedes you, or perhaps I should say follows you, traveling even to us in the past."

"I ...I don't understand. What is happening? The past? What's going on here?!" she shouted out of fear and frustration.

"Relax, young queen," said the woman.

"I am thousands of cycles old. I don't think 'young' is the best word to use to categorize me," Amana said with irritation.

"Your Majesty," the woman said, "as I speak to you, it is two million cycles before your creation. When you see this, I will be one hundred billion cycles old. So yes, 'young queen' will suffice. I have seen this moment. Although I know your actions, your questions, fears, and doubts, you are not speaking to me as I will be in your day; you are speaking to me as I am now, in my time."

"So are you saying that I went back in time somehow?"

"No, of course not, silly girl," the woman said with a laugh. "You are where you are when you are. And the same goes for me; I am where I'll be."

This did not resolve the queen's confusion. She cocked her head, sighing.

"Just know you need to trust me."

"Trust you?" Amana asked. "I am in a frightening cave with ferocious and crazy animals, following dots, talking to an unreal woman from the unimaginable past ...and you want me to trust you? I don't even know you."

"Yes, you do," said the woman. "You didn't do those things you mentioned by accident. You are searching for something...or someone..."

"How would you know?" said Amana, clearly annoyed.

"Two million cycles ago, I built the place where you stand right now," said the woman. "It was then when I made the decision to be the first from my world, of my kind, to make the choice for Earth. From that moment on, none have ever been able to enter the passageway through here, except for you. And it is because of you that the cave remains lit in the Crevices of Omega."

"Eve?" questioned Amana in a surprised tone. "I—I'm so sor—I don't know what to say. Please forgive me."

Of course, this is Eve. How could I have missed it? But the chains and the tiger and the time travel had seemed more like something from Hadnessa, not Evermore. And she was not yet recovered from the shock of falling, the taunts of the ghosts, and the great darkness.

"I would have reacted the very same way," Eve responded. "Actually, to be truthful, I was far worse."

Amana noticed that the tiger had disappeared—as had the two doors and the plants and seas and hills that represented the planets—the cave had become completely void of everything, except for Eve, the queen, and the chains.

"Reacted? Didn't you say that you built this place?" asked Amana.

"Yes," replied Eve. "But not in the way that you are thinking. This place is powerful with the Blue Fire Spirit. So communing with him in deep meditation allowed me to see and experience things I could not have imagined or understood. The longer you searched for this place with a pure heart, the more in tune with that very same meditation you became. The warrior you saw is named Davin. He is the seraph whom Bethany has chosen to protect her during her stay on Earth. The tigress you saw is named Dmna. She is two and yet one, as you saw. Dmna is the seraph who will be guiding Jovan while on Earth."

"So they have indeed gone already?" Amana asked. "I knew they would, but—"

"Yes, they have," Eve interrupted. "Do not let that diminish your reason for being here. The answers you seek have their importance and are crucial to each second that passes in both of our entangled times."

"So where should I go from here?" Amana asked. "Do you have the answers that I pursue? I'm not even sure that I know the right questions."

"It is here where you will find what you are looking for," Eve responded. "But be on your guard. What you will see is a mixture of the past, the present, and future that may or may not happen. You will not be able to decipher which one is which. And as you have already found out, the power of this chamber is such that you will not only see the visions but will feel the pain, cold, love, heat, rain, and sun. You will fight harder and become stronger than you ever have been before.

"You are mighty, Your Majesty, and blessed in all ways. Do not be startled or afraid. The chains surrounding your energy are so that you understand the weight of the flesh and the feeling of being trapped in it. Do not allow this weight to tame you.

"When I leave, this room will take you to whatever is in your mind, to the questions that you have had recently, especially those based on your visions. I must tell you that you may not remember everything, only what you bring with you."

"Who decides that?" asked Amana.

"You do," Eve answered. "You will not understand it if I explain it, so I will not. What is best for you now is that I depart and allow you to take on this important challenge."

"W-wait, don't go!" shouted Amana. "I have one more question."

"One," nodded Eve.

"Why is Omega considered *the end* on Earth but yet is the second planet created within the Elevemada?" the queen asked.

"Very curious but wise question," replied Eve. "Omega is the symbol of the end on Earth, but since then, millions of planets have been created, thus symbolizing the brightness of futures in all of Evermore. A human lifespan on Earth isn't a drop of water in comparison to the oceans within our galaxies combined. Many on Earth believe that their several decades of life are all that exist, and that they exist for no purpose. As you know, I was there. And I was face to face with Jaesu there. Even during my lifespan, I thought such things, but enough for now. I must say farewell."

"But what about the fruit?" Amana asked, trying to get Eve to stay a little longer. "It was Adam's fault, not yours—Am I right? Answer me that!"

Eve smiled. "Farewell, great queen."

With that, she disappeared. The cave was completely dark now save for a candle seven yards in front of Amana.

Amana looked down and saw space and stars below her feet and all around her. She saw three beings that had just finished racing. They were Jaesu, Jovan, and Bethany. She watched as they selected their seraphs. Then she saw her own past before she was queen. Amana was reliving her friendship with Jovan on Gardenia, walking around with him, counting the stars.

She felt a cold breeze suddenly. Snow started to fall, gathering thickly on her hair and shoulders. She was in an unknown land. The skies were gray, and the buildings thick and ugly. Creatures roared by in a straight line with a horrible stink of oil and smoke.

She was still walking with Jovan, yet this was not the Jovan she knew. He looked beaten. He had a scrape on his cheek, his clothes were old and patched, and he was crying. The pain she felt was indescribable. She not only didn't know why he was crying, but she couldn't even name the feelings he had. That didn't stop her from experiencing the pain; it pierced her to the marrow and seemed endless.

Then that scene disappeared, and she was with Jovan as a child. He was bruised and bloodied, dressed only in a pair of too-short pants, curled in a ball, and shaking in the corner of an empty room. Weak sunlight struggled in through the dust on a small window. She knew what this feeling was, though her experience of it was merely the tiniest fraction of Jovan's. Loneliness.

These are the trials of Earth? How brave souls are!

She reached out to touch Jovan and heard him scream, "DON'T TOUCH ME! I'M FILTHY." This horrified Amana and brought her great sorrow. She reached out again, and Jovan ran away from her screaming again like a frantic child, "I SAID DON'T TOUCH ME!"

Amana heard thunder. She was in an elegant, high-ceilinged room with an expansive view of a strange city, being pelted by rain. The buildings were immensely tall but all gray, brown, or black and rectangular, hardly any softened with adornment or curves. Someone was laughing—Bethany. She was adorned in jewels with false colors on her face. She looked raggedy in comparison to how she had looked on Gardenia.

Bethany was surrounded by a crowd of people similarly dressed in finery and yet dull, who spoke to her as if she were a person of great importance. Everyone in the crowd was in a festive mood, except Bethany. Amana could see her heart and how deeply it had been damaged. She didn't know why or how, only that it had been.

The queen tried to go to Bethany and put her arm around her, but Bethany didn't even notice she was there. "I just want to die," she whispered, which was a shock to the queen. "Won't you let me die and go away?" she said, finally looking at Amana. The queen heard a sinister laugh but could not see what being or person was laughing.

Her thoughts were pulled to Gardenia where she saw Alina, the woman with the black hair, holding Roslyn's throat with one hand and pointing toward Jovan and Bethany.

Alina spoke to Amana. "Try to save them, and I will destroy her." She watched in horror as Alina slit Roslyn's throat. Alina said, "I will devour them and ultimately bring great pain to that which you hold dear." Then Alina pointed toward Jaesu. He was weeping, watching Jovan and Bethany choose to spend their eternal lives in the home of Hadnessa. This was the ultimate torment and horror for any being. And it was eternal. Jaesu wept and wept, calling out for them, especially Jovan, his closest friend.

Amana saw Jaesu and Jovan laughing on Gardenia. They raced and joked, and she even saw and heard Jaesu's whisper to Jovan, "Don't forget the asudem who repent. The *light* can set them free, if you know where it comes from." She saw Jovan call upon the flash of light at a great battle.

Then everything stopped and became quiet. She heard a slight crack but couldn't decipher what it was. The noise grew louder. All around stone was being crushed and dirty sand swirled in a low, threatening sky. Once again, it was a place foreign to her. She noticed an enormous prison in the background, thousands of stories high, the walls transparent but she somehow knew, unbreakable.

There were millions of people in this prison, each in a cage, the cages crowded on top of one another. There was a second prison adjacent to the first. That one held tens of millions. She pondered the difference between the prisoners. They looked the same and were crowded in identical cages.

In the middle of the floor, in clear view of both prisons, was a man. He was being beaten. Amana realized that the cracks she was hearing were the whips used to pummel this man. She saw several men who looked like warriors enjoying lashing the man. He cried for help as the leather straps raked over his back. The queen noticed that the tens of millions in the second prison were cheering loudly with each stroke across the prisoner's back. Those in the other prison remained silent and in awe. Then one of the warriors replaced the whip with chains comprising razor-sharp spikes and started to whip the man with greater force.

The pain was excruciating. Amana grimaced with each lash because it felt as if it were happening to her. She'd never imagined such pain could exist.

The warrior wielding the whip was different from the others. While they wore only gold-plated helmets, basic chest plates, and tin kilts, this warrior was fully armored. He had a tail that was silver and black at the tip. The only being that Amana knew of who had such a tail was Khrimson. She had never seen his face before, but then she heard a scream.

"Khrimson!" the man shouted.

Smiling and giving the whipping a rest, Khrimson responded. "Yes? Are you ready to entreat for clemency yet?"

"What will it take for you to let these people go?" the man asked.

"Let them go? *Hahahahaha*," he laughed wickedly. "They are prisoners, sinners—are they not? They are evildoers. So by law, I own them all!"

"What will it take?" the man asked again as he received another lash, causing blood to spurt, even onto the queen.

"Take? None of these people are worth freeing. But, I suppose, the million who are silently rooting for you, I will free. One for every hundred years of whipping you accept," Khrimson said.

"Do it!" said the man. "And what about the ten million?"

"Are you mad?" Khrimson replied. "These are the ones who cheer your torment and root for me. How could you ever think of those people?"

Frustrated, Khrimson wrapped his tail around the man's neck and then tossed him toward the cell with the ten million. Those within reach kicked dirt on the man, spat on him, and even attempted to urinate on him. They clamored harshly for more punishment.

"You see?" Khrimson said. "They are animals, far beyond saving."

"What will it take?" the man said, even more eagerly.

Khrimson became angry. "It would take your chastisement and death to get the keys of both of these prisons from my hand."

The man wiped the blood from his brow. Amana saw something she could not believe. The man was Jaesu, her lord, king, friend, and most importantly, mentor. She never could have imagined him in this helpless position.

"You win this round, Khrimson," Jaesu said. "If you agree to release the keys, then I will do as you ask. I will die for them all."

Curiously jealous and angry, Khrimson began to choke Jaesu with the whip. "You who are a king, a king of gods, come down to Earth as a man? You, of all people, made the choice? For them? These guilty, wretched hatemongers are deserving of such a sacrifice? I was right at the purge. You are weak." With that, he slammed an eight-inch spike through each of Jaesu's wrists. Jaesu screamed.

Amana could not bear to watch any longer, and yet her gaze was still fixated on what was before her. Khrimson used his tail to rip into the flesh of Jaesu's sides, and again blood sprayed everywhere. He drove the spikes into his feet as well so that there could be no escape.

"If you were truly a king, truly the son of the Great Father, then you would have been able to free yourself and defeat me," Khrimson said. "Whether it is now or later, you will soon admit that I am your lord and master."

Jaesu could barely lift his neck, and he was trying to speak as his spirit left his body. "J-Jovan. Please hear me." With difficulty, he cast his eyes toward the prison with the ten million. And there, hidden among those who enjoyed the torment, was Jovan. He was completely oblivious to what was happening and looked like he couldn't have cared less. Jaesu persisted.

"Jovan, this is for you …be strong, my friend. My love is with you always." With that, Jaesu died.

Amana screamed loudly as the prisoners, Jovan even, cheered Jaesu's death. The skies became dark, the clouds black as cinders, and the ground shook feverishly. The prison gates were opened, and the prisoners were free. The cell with the million emptied out quickly. The million were rejoicing and running far from the hideous place. They knew they were free. But the prison containing the ten million didn't change. The prisoners chose to stay inside.

Then Amana looked and saw Jovan, Bethany, Dara, Marcus, and Glynn walk out of the prison. For a moment, the queen sighed and thought that they had let go of their bonds. But they walked to where Jaesu's corpse lay and looked at the warriors. They each handed the warriors a whip and hunched over in order to take a beating. They were beaten to death in a most gruesome way, one after another. Amana had to watch as each one suffered and died. Then the ground shook even more than earlier and a white light broke through the ash-filled skies and shone on Jaesu's body. The spikes melted from within his hands and feet, and he rose up. The warriors cowered in terror as Jaesu was shown to be quite alive and well. All in the prison knelt out of a reverent fear. But then Jaesu looked around and saw the Lighted Blade members dead. He wailed and grabbed Jovan's head and held it to his chest. "Why? Jovan, Bethany… Why? Dara, Marcus, Glynn? Why?" Jaesu continued. "I took the punishment for you. Why did you still choose to take it on yourselves?"

The crying continued, and Amana wept along with him. But then the scene changed. She was facing Alina once more. Alina again held Roslyn with one hand and Bethany and Jovan in the other. "Who will you save, Your Majesty? These two or Roslyn?" Alina asked mockingly. "Know that there are consequences. Choose quickly."

Amana tried to leap and grab onto Bethany and Jovan. She knew something had to be done. Her hand successfully landed on

Bethany who fought against her quickly, shouting, "I THOUGHT I TOLD YOU TO LET ME DIE!" Bethany, in turn, grabbed onto Amana. "You want to see death, Your Majesty? For real?" Bethany whisked Amana away into a place full of fire, lava, and glowing coals. Agony seared through Amana as she struggled, involuntarily screaming. "This is going to be my home and yours now, too. You are a fool for coming here. It's over now."

Bethany had taken the chains and attempted to chain Amana to the floor of what the queen assumed was Hadnessa. Then Amana heard a familiar voice. "Great Queen!" It was Eve. "This will not be a part of the vision if you can fight your way out. You know what you must do. You must get out of those chains to escape this lair. Hurry!"

This alarmed the queen terribly. She pulled and pushed and tried to loosen the chains—to no avail. The pain was so intense that she could not think straight. She felt her goodness and life slipping away. Her one instinct, which she had always kept with her, was to call on Jaesu, which she did.

A black dragon flew next to her. "Jaesu is not here. He will never come here. He passed on through to Evermore. You are doomed."

Her eyes began to weaken, and her body grew limp from the pain. But then something the black dragon said made sense. Amana uttered, "Jaesu did this already. He died. He came back and said we didn't have to endure this!"

At once, everything stopped. The chains broke free and the two doors from the beginning reappeared. But this time, she was on the other side of the doors. She flew to the door that had been on her left earlier, and it opened automatically.

She was in the cave again. All around her, she heard explosions, and she knew she had to leave at once. She flew out of the cave. The door slammed behind her, and everything was dark.

Amana could feel that the cave, the Eve of Illumination, had been destroyed behind her. She felt her body as it floated but she could not see anything. Her eyes weakened again and she began to fall asleep. Once sleep took her, she dropped straight down into the darkness.

*   *   *

Flying down toward the Reaper's haven on the planet Mercury, Shajcell as Khrimson had demanded, carried the three asudem given to her to pay the Reaper's price. "To what do I owe this rare visit, witch?" asked Rizhanaite.

With a sarcastic grimace, she replied, "My lord Khrimson has asked for the release of his servant, Phan," said Shajcell. "And the other two asudem corpses are for any two additional asudem Phan wishes to bring with him."

"Very well," Rizhanaite said. "But tell your master this is the last time that we will do such sidebar tradeoffs. The next time he wants a side deal, he must come to Mercury himself."

"I don't think he'd ever do that," said Shajcell.

"Exactly. That is why I said *last*. Here is the key to Phan's chambers; you may free him. He will not be in a pleasant mood."

Shajcell took the key quickly and, with arrogance, went to unlock Phan's cell. Phan immediately choked her and flung her across the planet. He had no idea that it was Shajcell, he was reacting in rage and pain and frustration.

She flew right back in his face. "Phan, you fool! I freed you. Now choose two asudem from these halls to take with you to Saturn in order to face our master. Choose wisely. He is waiting for you there!"

Phan thought for a moment and saw that Shajcell was right. His anger was best directed at Khrimson. He wanted revenge. It didn't occur to him to wonder why he had been freed. He called upon Legatious and Denacta to join him, as they were both cunning and powerful. "Now we will see who the real master is!" Phan said as he and his cohorts made for Saturn.

Shajcell mocked a head bow toward the Reaper and took off for Earth.

"There's a chill in the air," Rizhanaite said aloud to himself. "And I like it."

CHAPTER 9

Rags

On Earth, in a place called Bensonhurst, located in Brooklyn, New York, lived a man by the name of Vanno Ciccere. He was a twenty-year-old hardware store clerk whose parents were considered off-the-boat folks from Naples, Italy. He didn't have much education and was the younger of two children.

Vanno spent most of his time with his older brother, Frank, and his friends at a local college pub called Marino's Sports Bar and Grill. They frequented this establishment because of the underground reputation it had for letting known underage locals who wouldn't rat them out drink as long as they were, at least, eighteen.

Vanno's size in many ways defined him. He was a slightly below average male. His height was five feet five inches, and he weighed about one hundred and thirty pounds. But as small as he was in stature, his backbone was significantly smaller as he was considered a pushover by those around him. His father had passed away when he was quite young, and Vanno's mother raised his brothers and him. Vanno had spent his whole life following after and idolizing Frank. Although Vanno was a hard worker, he had a reputation for showing little to no initiative in anything. He had to be told what to do in order to do it. This characteristic had dictated the course of his life.

As usual, he was in the bar with his brother and pals, just finishing up a round of pool. A very good friend of his ran into the bar, calling out his name: "Vanno! Vanno!"

Vanno looked at him. "Carter, you all right, brotha? What up, kid?"

"I've been trying to call you for an hour already!" Carter charged. "It's Dara! They rushed her into an ambulance. She's going into labor! Lyanne is with her and just told me that the doc thinks she havin' it tonight. We gotta get down there quick!"

"Oh, yeah?" Vanno said. "Then we best be goin' for sure. It's not every day a man gets to be a father for the first time."

"Whoa!" said Frank with a high-wattage smile, his arms outspread. "You can't get up and go outta here without a celebration! Carter, come on! We hafta toast my little brother. Great news!"

"Frank," Vanno jumped in. "I think Carter's right; we gotta get goin'."

"Vanno!" Frank put his arm around his brother's shoulders, "When did you grow some scales? I have two kids of my own, remember? I know what it's like. Don't let this moment pass you by without celebrating with your friends. Look, I get that you want to be with Dara. But this stuff, labor, it takes hours.

Sometimes days, ya know? She don't need you now; she's got her friend, and that's what a woman wants when she's going through this—another woman, just like you need to be with the guys. Look at me. I pretty much have two wives and two beautiful children. Trust me, Vanno. I know what's best. Come on, Carter. Pull up a chair, baby!"

Vanno and Carter gave in to Frank. He was their leader. People didn't always like Frank, but many admired him because he had such a dominant personality and was so sure of his own worth.

Frank had been a great high school quarterback. The guys he hung with didn't forget that, or forget how his confidence had made them feel gratified for his friendship when they were in school. Frank was six feet tall, one hundred eighty pounds, and full of bluster—sometimes interpreted as charm. It was said that he could sell anything and also that he would sell anyone anything.

"Iced tea for me, Frank," Carter said softly.

"ICED TEA?" Frank said obnoxiously. "Come on. Lay off this *I'm an alcoholic* stuff. That's your wife talking. Don't be a wuss. Joey, make Carter a Long Island." He looked over at Carter, shaking his head. "No twelve-step program is gonna ruin my brother's big day."

"Really, Frank," Vanno mumbled. "None of this is necessary." He was eager to get out of there and felt awkward putting Carter in this position. He knew what drinking did to him.

"You know what, Vanno?" Carter chimed in, his eyes on the bottles. "It's okay, boss. One won't kill me. Just don't tell Lyanne."

*   *   *

It had been twenty Earth years since Dara had made the choice to leave Gardenia. Time moved at a different pace in the Milky Way and the Elevemada. What seemed like merely days to those on Gardenia were years on Earth. This was another part of the law of life that souls had never been able to comprehend.

Later that day, at Staten Island University Hospital, Dara Ciccere gave birth to a strong and healthy baby boy. She had hoped that her husband would have been able to make it. Vanno told her he would take a day off work, so they could experience this together. But he was nowhere in sight. Neither was her brother, Carter. If it weren't for her closest friend, Dara would have delivered the baby alone. Her parents lived in Philadelphia and couldn't have made it to the hospital in time to see their young daughter give them a grandson.

After the hard labor, the doctors took the baby away to clean him up. Dara had seen him for a moment, and she was replaying that vision in her mind. She was weak but felt like a mother bear—she'd do anything for this beautiful, precious boy. She'd give him a good life if it killed her.

Lyanne hadn't left her side. Dara was sedated, but that didn't stop Lyanne from talking. "I am going to kill my husband when I see him! I bet he ran off to some bar or is at the track or something."

Dara placed her hand on Lyanne's forearm as a way to let her know that it was okay. They were both used to disappointments. "Thank you for being here," Dara whispered to Lyanne. Dara's gratitude made Lyanne even angrier with Carter and Vanno. She had seen her best friend being taken advantage of for far too long.

Lyanne watched as Dara fell asleep. They had been close friends for many years. Both of them had come from rough, alcoholic families and grown up in neighborhoods where various forms of child abuse were the norm. Somehow, they'd gotten an idea of what loyalty and kindness were and through many ups and downs, they had one another's back.

Lyanne sat on the edge of the hospital bed and silently prayed that somehow, some way, her friend could catch a break and get out of the nightmare she had been living.

*   *   *

In a room across the hall at the same hospital, a young woman whose name was Sarai Patric Crowmire had just given birth to a little girl. The nurses said this baby had forced herself out with great speed. Her mother named her Bethany. The baby had big, beautiful blue eyes, and there was no quit-point to her crying. Two men in suits were waiting outside of the room. They wore sunglasses and stood noticeably still. Sarai, whose husband also was not present, wasn't alone either. Her in-laws, Josephus and Phyllis Crowmire, were with her. Their son, Alcee, was traveling home from work. He was a corporate law and process consultant for some of the top companies in the world. He had a very polished reputation—and being a Crowmire didn't hurt. His father, Josephus, was a highly regarded senior senator representing New Jersey.

"She is beautiful, Sarai," said Phyllis. "I am hopeful that she will ultimately get your magnificent red locks."

"Thank you, Mom," Sarai replied. She always had a hard time calling Phyllis Mom because they weren't really close, but she didn't want to disrespect her either. She had only been dating Alcee a short while before she became pregnant. He had proposed to her, and they'd had a discreet wedding in order to not draw attention to themselves or the Crowmire family. Many folks thought of the Crowmires as the new Kennedys. They were wealthy but generous, good-looking, and athletic. Everything they touched seemed to turn to gold. Alcee was already being thought of as a presidential prospect due to his charisma, money, and family name.

"You have given us great joy, Sarai," Josephus said. "I am only sorry that Alcee didn't make it home in time to witness it. A truly remarkable little girl is before us."

"Thank you both," said Sarai. "You two have been so amazing for me—and now Bethany. I couldn't have asked for anything more. I truly feel honored and blessed to be a part of the Crowmire family."

"Excuse me, I don't mean to be a bother, but it's time for Mrs. Crowmire to get her rest," interrupted the nurse.

"Well, thank you, Millie. I think I can last a few more hours," joked Phyllis, realizing that the nurse was talking about Sarai.

"I WILL tell you that the lady across the hall waiting with her friend finds little Bethany quite the looker," the nurse replied.

"Oh, really? Very nice," said Phyllis. "I think I will go take a look at their baby as well."

"Must you, darling?" sighed Josephus.

"Of course I must," Phyllis replied. "Forgive him, ladies … he's not a lady."

The other women chuckled. Phyllis had a way about her. Being a senator's wife and a distinguished attorney didn't seem to insulate her from the common folk. She was very knowledgeable and loved to share; at times, she would even show off her understanding of others.

"Sarai, since Mrs. Crowmire is off to save the planet, I think I will step out for a few and allow you to relax as well," Josephus said.

"You know, she helps get you more votes by saving the world," said Sarai.

"I know it," laughed Josephus. "I sometimes wish she would take my seat as she can be far more persuasive than I."

Josephus walked out and asked the guards to keep watch over the room. There was another guard stationed at the end of the floor and in the lobby for their protection. Josephus noticed that Phyllis and the girl across the way were getting along quite well already, so he had time for a quick phone call.

"It's Lyanne with an e at the end," said Lyanne.

"I have a cousin with the same name, but he spells it Lyaneh with an e-h at the end," said Phyllis politely.

"He?" Lyanne asked, "I don't think I've ever met a guy with my name before."

"Oh, absolutely," Phyllis replied. "It's quite common."

"I guess that shows I don't get out much," Lyanne responded, looking down and feeling a bit awkward.

Phyllis peeked into the room at the sleeping patient. "Are you guys together?" she asked Lyanne.

"Dara has been my closest friend for years. My husband, Carter, is her brother and her husband, Vanno…Well, he wasn't even here to witness the birth of his son," Lyanne said, looking at her watch sadly and shaking her head. "They both should be here by now."

"Oh, dear," replied a concerned Phyllis. "I am sorry. I didn't mean to…"

"No, it's okay," Lyanne responded. "I just start getting the feeling like this is it for us, ya know? We grew up in struggling homes with hardly anything, both of us working full-time since we were fifteen or so and now are havin' to lug around husbands who apparently have no ambition. I have two children at home and I am petrified that they might turn out like their father or me." Lyanne looked down at Dara and took a breath. "And then there's Dara, who is special to me because she's always been good to everyone. Her husband takes her for granted and has no reason to, ya know? I wish she would get a break.

"Now with the baby ...I know for us ...I mean, I love my kids, but it hasn't done a thing to change my husband. I know he still drinks and gambles even though he says he stopped. I'm sorry ...I want better for her—even if it's too late for me.

"*Ugh*, I shouldn't even be telling you this. I just met you five minutes ago. I'm so sorry." Lyanne laughed slightly at herself. "Is it Phyllis with an F?"

They both laughed together some more.

"You know what, Lyanne?" replied Phyllis. "I like you already. All men can be unbearable ogres in their own way. But don't believe for a second that men can't be tamed." She smirked.

"That's the problem, I think. Everything seems to tame them too much. I wish they were more ambitious, out on the pavement, and more tame and loving at home," Lyanne responded.

"If you don't mind me asking, where are you currently staying?" Phyllis asked.

"Oh." Lyanne thought for a moment. "We are all from Bensonhurst originally, but Carter and I have recently moved out to the Port Richmond area."

"Port Richmond? *Hmm*... Can't say I'm too familiar with the place," said Phyllis.

Lyanne quickly glanced for a moment at Phyllis. She was wearing a gray fox fur jacket—not exactly spring attire—two diamond stud earrings in each ear, a silk scarf that had to be French or Italian, designer glasses and jeans and high-heeled patent leather boots. With her thick, black, perfectly coiffed hair and expert makeup, she looked stylish and beautiful and not a day into her thirties.

"I hope you don't take this the wrong way, because you seem all right," Lyanne said, "but I didn't expect you to know Port Richmond. It's not exactly a well-to-do area, and you look like you just walked off a movie screen."

"I appreciate your honesty, Lyanne," said Phyllis. "I could bore you with tales of how poor I grew up or the struggles in my home country and say that I understand where you are coming from. But the truth is I'm quite wealthy. I am not ashamed of it. I have been blessed, and I do what I feel is best. If you aren't wealthy, you shouldn't be ashamed either. You have two children whom you love, a dearest friend who is also now a mother, and, I'm sure, a lifetime of experiences worth sharing with others who are going through similar struggles. Lyanne, you can be anything you want to be. It may be a cliché, but it's true. Just take the blinders off your eyes and create your own path."

Lyanne was floored. She'd expected some phony *this ol' thing* remark, but instead found herself captivated by Phyllis's candor.

Lyanne was average height for a woman, and rather thin. She had dirty blond hair and hazel eyes. It was easy to see the lack of sleep and constant struggles on her face. She'd never known any rich folks, save for those who came into her workplace, and that was very few because the place where she waited tables wasn't fancy. "I don't quite know what to say. I appreciate that you're treating me like a real person."

"You are a real person, Lyanne," said Phyllis. "That in itself is the wealth of the world. It's the people. Not the processes or the red tape, or titles. It's the people. And in a couple of brief moments here, I have found you are quite remarkable."

"Wow …you talk differently than anything I am used to," said Lyanne.

Josephus made his way back to his wife. "Almost ready?"

"Josephus, don't be rude," Phyllis shot back. "This is Lyanne. Her dear friend Dara, resting over there, just had a baby boy. Dara's husband is …at work, much like our Alcee. Lyanne was telling me how much she's enjoyed transitioning from Brooklyn to Port Richmond." She named the towns as if she were saying Manhattan and Easthampton.

"Hello, Lyanne," smiled Josephus as he shook her hand. "First Brooklyn, now Port Richmond—Staten Island, am I right? I guess that means you aren't eligible to vote in New Jersey, *eh*?" He laughed.

"Josephus!" Phyllis jumped in firmly.

Lyanne laughed at them, obviously enjoying their company. "It's okay, Phyllis—all men are ogres, right? Josephus, it's very nice to meet you, sir."

"I see you have her spewing your feminist doctrine," Josephus snickered.

"Oh, darling, you know I'm no feminist, just a Phyllisist. It's my way or no way," Phyllis winked at Lyanne.

"Oh, don't I know that all too well," Josephus laughed. "I spoke with Alcee. He will be here shortly, and the car is waiting to take us to the fundraiser."

"Politics, my dear Lyanne," Phyllis said. "Here we are dressed like this, going to a fundraiser in a stretch limo."

"It's okay," Lyanne smiled. "I attend fundraisers weekly. The bottom of my purse or the cushions in the back seat of our car provides funds for me whenever I'm desperate."

"Well," Phyllis said, rummaging through her designer purse. "This is my card. Now I mean this. Please call me if you need anything. I mean it now. You're one of my favorites already."

"You're a lawyer?" asked Lyanne. "*Whoa!*"

"I'd much rather you call me to talk, but if something arises where you need legal counsel, I'll be more than happy to point you in the right direction," said Phyllis. "Sadly, the ogre is growing impatient, so it's best we get going. But feel free to visit Sarai, just across the hall. I believe you girls will get along famously."

"Thank you. Thank you both. I don't have a card." Lyanne blushed. Phyllis gave her a quick hug and Josephus nodded toward her as they rushed off.

"You gave her your card like she was some sort of transaction, Phyllis," Josephus said sarcastically in a low tone.

"That's exactly what she is. Trust me. She'll see us on TV and tell her friends in Staten Island who have friends in North Jersey about us, and she'll be perfect to show off to the cameras. We'll get lots of wows for mingling with the commoners. So predictable," Phyllis said, she then stopped, and turned around quickly, and jogged back to Lyanne's room. "Oh, Lyanne!"

"Yes?"

"The baby's name, dear.... What's his name?" Phyllis asked.

"Jovan. With a J," Lyanne answered with a smile.

"Jovan? Interesting," Phyllis said. "Ta-ta." She gave Lyanne a quick wave good-bye as the elevators doors closed.

* * *

Phan was enroute to Khrimson's lair on Saturn. As he and his two fellow asudem made their descent, they torched the particles that made up the surrounding rings. Normally, Phan would never do anything to desecrate Khrimson's favorite planet, but he was in a seething rage and his anger caused tremors for miles. He had always longed for the throne of Algolithar and now knew that being Khrimson's loyal servant would never land him there. Khrimson's ploy to demote him into the torcher prisons was the final nail in their relationship. Phan knew that, if he could deliver a mighty blow against his lord, the asudem would revere him, and he would rule Algolithar as an even greater leader than Khrimson had been.

The two asudem with him were enforcers. Legatious and Denacta, both loyal to him throughout the ages, were mighty warriors and respected by seraphs and asudem alike.

They landed on the planet's surface next to Sardis. The enormous horse was patiently awaiting his master's return.

"I trust you despise this dreadful place, old friend, as much as I do," said Phan as he petted his horse. "It's time for us to face the master once and for all."

The horse responded with a quick head toss of acknowledgement and a bearing of yellow teeth. Phan vaulted on the animal, his two allies floating by his side as they made their way toward Khrimson's den.

The pathway was far different from the one to Khrimson's throne on Algolithar. The ground was covered in shifting sand; finding his lair would not be easy. Eventually, they would have to walk rather than float or ride, as the den was not visible to the eye.

It was a clear night. They could see millions of stars. The sands began to change colors from brown to red to white, eventually settling into a rusty tan. Sardis sensed something and jumped back, which alarmed Phan.

"What are you seeing?" he asked the horse.

"It's not what I'm seeing, my lord; it's what I'm feeling," Sardis responded. "The ground…it swells—"

At that moment, a whirlwind pushed up from the ground beneath their feet. The foursome started to fall through the sands as if they were in an hourglass. They landed on hills of crystals that turned to sand upon first touch. The crystals were gray and black and formed a pathway toward a black harp. Phan followed the trail and stopped before the harp. Again a whirlwind formed, but this time it became a sand cyclone. The cyclone lifted Phan off of Sardis. The sands blinded and held back the horse and the two asudem. Phan was unafraid; he had been expecting some kind of trap.

He continued to be lifted up by the sandstorm. The sand slowly stopped spinning, and the wind fell silent. Phan was still high above the planet's surface, but could feel himself standing on an invisible platform. He saw the ground beneath him shake and a massive quake ensued. The ground began to crack apart. He looked up and saw the same thing happening to the formed ground above him. He realized that he was in the planet's core and that this was indeed a trap. He was stuck in the middle.

Phan heard the familiar echoing voice of his master.

"Mighty Phan. Warrior God of icons, of the ages even, why are you so still?" asked Khrimson with a wicked laugh. "Your peasants beneath us cannot help you. Oh, it is now just you and me, Phan. You and me."

"Release me from this witchery, and you will see what I can do!" shouted Phan.

"Oh, but that is just it. I am unlike the Father or Jaesu. I won't give my adversary equal footing. If you are worthy of me, then release yourself. Save yourself. If you can and defeat me, then I will indeed kneel to you. But if you cannot release yourself, then how could you ever hope to destroy me?"

Khrimson was as invisible as the platform. Phan could feel him and hear him but could not see him. Phan tried to push himself off the platform, but he could not. He was sealed somehow.

"*Ahh,* the mighty Phan unable to release his poor self," laughed Khrimson. "You are worthless. To think that I even considered you for the throne of Algolithar ...*bah* ...I must find a new servant, one who is worthy of triumph."

Phan continued to fight with even more vigor and anger. He felt new strength coming into him, but he was still unable to pull himself from the platform.

"*Ah,* yes. The throne. You have longed for it. I know," snickered Khrimson. "You thought you might have hidden that from me. But you could not. I know your deepest desire. Do you not know that I, yes, Khrimson, can grant those desires? Did you not know that, I, Khrimson, am greater than our maker? Deep down, I know you have had doubts. You are a fool to doubt your master. Is there another worthy enough for my crown? Or is there still an asudem in you ready to bow to me?"

With that, Phan erupted with newfound power and broke the platform in two, thus releasing himself from its grip. "Come face me!" Phan shouted.

"*Hahahahaha* ...face you," Khrimson murmured. "Here I am!" He appeared for a split second. Phan went to grab him, but then he was gone. "No, I am over here!" He appeared again, and like the first attempt, he vanished before Phan could take hold of him. This continued for quite some time.

Phan's anger made him stronger, but his failure to secure a victory over Khrimson wore down his patience and self-control. "What is it you want, Khrimson? Why send me here if not for battle?"

"Oh, I have plenty of battles for you, mighty warrior," sneered Khrimson. "There is no need to battle me, when it is I who is willing to now ...grant you what you want."

Phan looked confused for a moment. "What do you mean? It is your throne which I desire most of all, as you have said."

"Indeed...oh, indeed. Complete this task for me and you shall have it. I will make my throne on Earth," said Khrimson. "But this task appointed to you will be crucial to your reign on Algolithar. Know this, mighty general: the plan from the beginning was for you, me, and Shajcell to rule the universe. And we shall."

"What is the task you speak of?" Phan asked begrudgingly.

"Do not sound so excited," Khrimson hissed emphatically. "You will enjoy this task. I give you free reign to decide how to go about it."

"Go on," Phan said with a little bit more spirit.

"The harp which you saw is a portal," Khrimson informed him. "When you play it, a transporting process will begin. This portal is tied to Alpha, but what I need is not on Alpha. What I desire is someone to destroy a relic, a strand of grass on Gardenia known as the Lighted Blade. It, along with the queen, gives life to Gardenia. I believe that Gardenia's and Earth's fates are intertwined. If we can destroy that blade, then we will be on our way to severely weakening Gardenia.

"Utilize all of your skills and strategies. This is why I have brought you here. Once you have removed the blade from Gardenia then the throne of Algolithar will be yours ...forever." Khrimson laughed uncontrollably.

Thinking it over, Phan realized the strength of the plan and started to devise his own strategy to achieve the task. He immediately descended upon the harp with Sardis and his fellow asudem. Phan stretched out his hand across the harp, playing a random melody. The sands rose up from the ground, spinning the four allies into a whirlwind until they vanished.

*   *   *

In a little Brooklyn apartment in Bensonhurst, with a dull carpet going bald in spots and mismatched thrift shop furniture, Frank and Vanno were sitting on the couch watching a Rangers vs. Islanders matchup. "I don't know, Frankie. It's been a couple of days, and I still ain't been to the hospital to see my boy. Dara is probably furious—or even worse, broken-hearted," Vanno said.

"Vanno, the most dangerous time in a marriage is when a woman has her first child," Frank replied. "They start to think maybe they don't need you so much, and they think they don't have to try anymore because you're not going to leave. That's the trap, right there. You won't abandon your kid, and your wife now gives what remains of her love to the baby. You have to remind her what a man is. I told you to do this in the beginning, but, of course, you didn't." He paused and Vanno flushed. He didn't know how to be a man in the way that Frank defined it. Even less did he know how he himself defined being a man. He just knew that he was lacking somewhere.

Vanno didn't know why Dara married him. He used to think she was too good for him, but since she apparently loved him, she probably wasn't. And now the pregnancy …he hated to admit it to himself, but in the last few months, he hadn't liked looking at her body. He hadn't touched her in weeks. He was excited about having a son, but also scared. How could he be a father? What if he screwed it up? As much as he thought Frank was wrong about him staying here, it was more comfortable to stay here listening to his brother whose self-assurance had always seemed so enviable.

"Like I told ya, Vanno, women need to learn from the beginning that, if there is a glass of water, they don't ask us to get it for them; rather, they ask us for permission and then go get it themselves. Their sole purpose in life is to serve us. It may seem like a jacked-up approach, but take my word for it. Once they know that you have a heart that beats to please them, then they will either abuse you or think you are weak, especially a knockout like Dara. If you ever expect to keep her loyal to you, then you best put her in her place."

Frank had touched on Vanno's deepest fear. Dara would leave him. He wasn't good enough. Surely the way to keep her was to treat her well. But he knew lots of guys who treated their wives or girlfriends well and still they left. Frank said it was because the guys acted weak, and he'd heard women say things that sounded the same.

The brothers both heard a car door slam. Dara had come home with the baby. Vanno knew she would be hurt to see him just sitting there in front of the TV. He got up and tried to straighten up the apartment. Why hadn't he done the dishes? Or taken out the trash? He saw through the window that Dara had a bundle—his son!—in her arms, while Lyanne had a baby bag and some groceries. He was going to meet them outside when—

"What are you doin'?" Frank shouted, brandishing his beer. "Rushing right out there shows any woman that you are whipped. Grow some backbone, sailor. Sit your behind on this couch and make her come to you. You are now the papa shango, the lion in his pride and the keeper of the order. She needs you now more than you know. Don't trust in top forty cheesy garbage. The honeymoon is long over. What you want now is loyalty and respect."

"But you aren't exactly loyal to your significant others, big bro," Vanno struck back, stopped in his tracks, looking out of the curtain nervously at Dara.

"Precisely why *they* are loyal to *me*. They want me with them and are willing to turn a blind eye from time to time," Frank responded, leaning back. Frank had a mellow tenor voice that sounded pure Brooklyn, but also something else. Their mother used to call it a radio announcer voice. Even when he was saying something Vanno knew was wrong, there was an intimacy and authority in that tone that had made him feel safe when he was four-years-old. It still made him feel safe today.

And why shouldn't it? He's my brother.

Hearing Dara at the door, Vanno's body jerked to go greet her, but then looked at Frank and sat down.

"What are you both doin' here?!" yelled Dara. "How dare you sit there while I gestated your child for nine months—and which, if it weren't for Lyanne, I would have delivered on my own? Vanno, do you have anything to say for yourself?"

"Well, I …" Vanno tried to explain.

"I thought not," she said as she put her hand up. "Any other man would be sprinting over here to see his son and wife but not you …you're just like a lazy bum, chillin' on the couch, watching the game as always. Hell! Any real man would have been in the hospital with his wife, excited to be a part of their child's birth."

"Dara's right, Vanno," Frankie said lazily to Vanno's great surprise. "I have no idea what you were thinking missing such a moment. Dara …honey …I tried to tell him, but you know Vanno. He loves his hockey."

Dara was no fool, and she despised Frank. "And sadly, he loves his brother more. Much more," she shot back. "I find it insulting but hardly surprising that, having convinced Vanno not to come to the hospital—because I have no doubt that was *your* idea—you now have the gall to pretend you are on my side. I still loathe you, Francis."

"Hey! HEY!" Frank shouted. "No one calls me Francis. Especially you, ya little skive."

"How dare you!" Dara shouted at Frank, before looking back at Vanno. "You gonna let your brother talk to me like that? Do you have any self-respect, any dignity at all?"

"Leave my little brother alone," Frank said in a condescending tone. "Besides, he has all of the dignity in the world, and he gets it from …me." He brushed hair softly out of her face as Lyanne walked in the door.

Dara calmly handed the infant to Lyanne. She slowly put on an apron and walked through the connecting door into the tiny kitchen. Vanno was nervous about what she was doing. Frank wasn't nervous at all.

"Look at that, Vanno. Your wife's gonna make us dinna!" Frank said. He looked over to Lyanne with a nod and a wink.

"How YOU doin', sweet cheeks?"

Lyanne, always repulsed by Frank, ignored him.

Dara was rattling pots and pans in the kitchen. She grimaced at the dishes and empty pizza boxes, then turned on the stove and pulled out a frying pan. Not finished with the conversation, she went back into the living room and held the pan in her right hand. Frank was chomping on some gum and smirking at them both. He loved that he could keep his little brother in his place.

"You know what? All this time arguing and I haven't even had a chance to see my boy yet," said Frank antagonistically, as he moved over toward Lyanne to look at baby Jovan. "Wow, if I didn't know any different, I'd say he's my son. Looks just like me."

As soon as the last word came out of his mouth, Dara reached back with her left hand and cracked Frank in the mouth with a frying pan as hard as she could. His right cheekbone swelled immediately. "Don't you ever, EVER come near my son again! Do you understand? Otherwise, by hook or by crook, they will find your face severed from that pea brain of yours. Now get out of my house before I call the cops for trespassing and endangering a minor! Remember—it's my name on the lease!" Dara shouted.

"You trollop!" Frank yelled. "You trying to kill me or something? Good luck with that, you ugly sow. Vanno! You gonna let this dame treat me like that? Be careful, boy; be careful how you answer." Frank was holding his face, noticeably embarrassed.

Vanno went to get up and say something to his brother. Dara took the pan in her right hand and made like she would hit him with it. "Don't you move, Vanno! I'm not done with you yet. You've had nineteen years to stand up to this scum of the Earth, and now it's my turn." She looked back at Frank and motioned her head toward the door, her chest heaving with rage. Frank could see that she meant business. Being essentially a coward, he backed out the screen door and went on his way. They could hear the tires on his 1977 orange Chevy Nova Coupe squeal as he drove off.

"Honey …" said Vanno. "I'm really—"

"Don't even," she said and then slowly took Jovan from Lyanne and showed him to Vanno. "You see, there is your beautiful baby boy—your son, Jovan Ciccere."

One glance and Vanno was speechless. The baby was the most striking thing he had ever seen. His eyes filled with tears which he quickly blinked back. "Wow …you are quite amazing, aren't you?" he whispered to the child. It seemed to him the baby looked straight into his eyes.

Dara quickly gave Jovan back to Lyanne. "Lyanne, could you take the baby into the bedroom for a moment?"

Lyanne didn't hesitate. She took the baby's bags and Jovan, whispering soft lullabies to him so that he wouldn't scream.

"You happy with the child I carried?" Dara asked Vanno angrily.

"Baby, you don't underst—" Vanno started to speak.

"Well, until you make some serious changes and get your act together, that is the very last time you will ever lay eyes on my son."

"Dara, honey, what are you talkin' about? I can explain everything. He's my son, too!" Vanno retorted.

"Oh …" Dara shook her head as a signal that she was about ready to go off on Vanno. "Your son? *Your* son? Was he your son while I was delivering him and you were taking shots with your brother at the bar? Oh, yeah, Carter told us everything. Was he your son when last month you said you were going out for the newspaper, of all things, and didn't come back for two days? Not even a phone call? Who does that?"

"Dara, that's not fair; I told you that I ran outta change," Vanno answered.

"Change? Really? You must think I am an idiot. And then when I found out that you and your brother had gone to Jersey for two days with Suzie Sleeparound, you have the nerve to tell me that Frank asked her to go?"

"But, baby, he did," Vanno said in a panic.

"I KNOW HE DID! I KNOW IT! I KNOW IT! That …" Dara sighed and shook her head. "I don't even know why I waste my time with you. Vanno, are you ever going to stand up to your loser brother? At this point, I am tired of having to fight this battle with you over and over again. I am tired, sore, and worn out. Most wives get pampered when they return from the maternity ward. Me? I gotta beat up some dude, take care of my newborn, and raise a child …you." Dara was trying to calm herself down. Something was happening to her, though. She was at a breaking point.

"Dara, listen. I have some shortcomings, true, but no one is perfect, baby. My brother is important to me; you know that. He had a big hand in raising me after my father and stepfather passed on. He means well, you know that …" Vanno explained.

"Vanno," Dara shook her head, laughing. "You are a sucker. I hate to tell you that, truly I do. But your brother doesn't care about you. He adores the way he can manipulate you and push

you around. He even tries flirting with me, your wife, in front
of you, knowing that you won't do a damn thing. Heck, he just
insinuated that your son looked like him. Have you any pride,
Vanno?"

Vanno kept quiet. He looked down and didn't have anything
to say. He knew she was right. He'd always known that. But
somehow he felt bound to his brother, like it was beyond his
control. Dara was strong; she didn't know what it was like.

"Look Van," Dara said, gently moving toward his face. "I
know somehow, somewhere, that you love me and maybe even
the baby. And Lord knows that I wouldn't have stuck it out with
you if I didn't love you so much. We've had some laughs. Some
good times. You can be a nice guy, you know that? But I can't
raise my son around you if you are going to continue to follow
your brother's lead instead of leading your own family."

"Wha-what are you saying, D?" Vanno asked with tears in
his eyes.

"I'm going to stay with Lyanne, Carter, and the kids for a
couple of weeks," Dara said. "They are going to help us out. This
will give you the time you need to decide if you want to make the
choice to stay with us and be a family. But it has to be without
your brother. Just us and our dreams."

"Dara, hold up," Vanno said. He couldn't believe this was
actually happening. But at the same time, he'd known she'd leave
him someday. Sure, she had reason to be angry about Frank, but
that wasn't the whole deal. It was like Frank said: she had a baby
now and she didn't need him.

"No, Vanno," Dara interrupted. "If this is going to work out
between us, then there are some ties that need to be broken.
He runs your entire life, and I won't allow my son to watch his
father be a slave to any man."

"I am a slave to no one," Vanno said with sudden anger.

"Good. Then you should have no problem proving it for the next couple of weeks. Once we come back, if you are ready to put your brother behind us, at least for now, then we will be so very happy with you. If not, then we will move on. It's that simple." Dara paused and gave Vanno a soft kiss on the cheek. "I married you because I love you, Vanno. Please don't let me down again." She picked up a couple of things and went in to get Lyanne and the baby. Vanno stood rooted to the spot until they left.

"Dara, I have no idea what comes over you sometimes. It's so amazing," Lyanne said.

Dara looked down as if she wondered the same thing. She was normally mild-mannered and generous, even to complete strangers. Dara was very family-oriented by nature and always felt it was important to keep everyone together. She couldn't understand why others weren't like this, too. But for all of her caring and sacrifice for others, whenever she felt put into a corner, something came out. It was almost as if she became a different person. The normally reserved young woman would attain the courage of a battalion general during a crucial battle. She never quite understood it, but it was well known to those around her.

As they were walking to Lyanne's car, a being unbeknownst to the girls began walking with them. It was Dmna, the white tiger. A smaller being, a seraph in the form of a robin, also unseen, appeared on Dara's shoulder.

"Dmna? Is that you?" the hyper robin asked excitedly.

"Oh, joy," Dmna responded with a hint of sarcasm. "This is going to be a long ride, I think."

"Well, not really, Dmna," the robin said. "I take this route quite often. If there's no traffic then—"

"Oh, Chaos, my favorite robin ...*um*, not." Dmna sighed, smiling. "Have these many cycles not dimmed your speed or slowed your mouth?"

"Very funny, Dim," Chaos responded. "I'll have you know that my ability to sing advice into Dara's ear makes her quite lethal."

"And your annoying qualities make me quite lethal as well," Dmna joked.

"Seriously, Dim, ya think they will ever be able to see us? You know. The humans?" asked Chaos.

"Yes. At judgment day," Dmna answered, rolling her eyes. "Just keep Dara from getting lethal on Jovan, and I think you and I will get along okay ...okay?"

Chaos looked at Dara and then at the big tiger and Jovan and thought that to be quite advantageous. "You have ...quite a point, Dim. Quite the point, indeed. I actually feel safer havin' you guys around. That Frank, he got rid of his protector and is working on Vanno's. Frank's been hanging with some asudem now for a bit. But with you around, now that Jovan is here, I think he will be less scary; at least, I hope so."

Lyanne and Dara strapped young Jovan in the back seat. Dara sat next to him as Lyanne got into the driver's side. "And we're off, kids," Lyanne said, driving toward her house in Staten Island.

*　　*　　*

Amana had been fighting her way through darkness since escaping Eve's cave. She was surprised that finding her way out took even longer than to get in. There was no blue dot to follow or wind to hear. Not even ghostly voices led her way. It was just her alone in the dark, as if she were in a room with no windows or doors or cracks anywhere for light to seep through.

Many thoughts were racing through her mind. *What is happening on Gardenia? Are Bethany and Jovan safe? Why didn't Jaesu tell me about the sacrifice he made on Earth?* There were so many questions.

She had flown for what seemed like days, the images from the cavern tumbling through her mind. But still there was no hint of light. Memories of joy and love seemed impossibly far away; a cold indifference enveloped her. She felt hopeless. "Jaesu, if you can hear me, please get me out of here. I don't like this place. It is not only lonely, but also purposeless and removed from all feeling and emotion. In here, I feel as if I had never been created. Please, Lord, help me."

She didn't feel the prayer the way she often did, but she knew it was what she could muster. She continued to fly with her hands outstretched. Then she felt a tug on her arm. Amana couldn't see anything. She started to feel something or someone pull her. The force picked up, pulling faster and faster. She had no idea how fast she was going because she was in complete darkness and couldn't even feel a breeze. She still knew, somehow, that she was going very fast.

The queen began to scream, and then the motion stopped. She looked around; she could still see nothing. There was something in her hand. It felt like a doorknob. She was relieved that there was something tangible at last. She turned the knob to the left and nothing happened. She tried again, same result. She then turned the knob to the right and felt a click. With a slight push, a door opened. She didn't care what she found—it would have to be better than what she had just experienced.

As she took her first glides through the doorway, she realized that it was a stone she was walking out of—a very large stone. What caught her eye was a huge and majestic tree laden with the most pristine fruit she had ever seen. The branches were sagging from the weight of so much fruit. Around the tree, on a carpet of green grass in the strong sunlight of a late spring morning, she saw every animal ever known to her on Gardenia and hundreds of others unknown to her, in perfect health, eyes and fur gleaming. She could hear the rustle of many more, further away. There was a sound that she realized was thousands of tiny breaths woven into one: foxes, bears, cats and wolves, sheep, birds, and antelope. It was a sound like the wind, but much sweeter. All of her sadness fell away. She felt an amazing peace, excitement, and love such as she had never known, even on Gardenia in the happy times. It was wonderful. This was everything she had imagined Evermore to be.

Then she noticed a man petting a fawn under the mammoth tree. Had he been here a moment ago? He must have been—he looked like he'd been here for ages. He was bald with very deep, dark eyes and was clothed in sackcloth. She didn't quite understand that part. This seemed to be a place for a king, not a peasant. Still, even though she was a queen, she felt unworthy to be in the presence of this man.

"Hello," she said.

The man stared at her and smiled but didn't say a word as he continued to pet the young animal.

"My name is Amana. I am Queen of Gardenia," she said. She didn't think Gardenia would matter to the man. This place was unlike any world she had ever been on.

The man still kept silent. He released the fawn, and it began walking toward Amana. In an eye blink, the fawn became a wolf. This startled the queen for a moment, although she thought she ought to be getting used to such things. "Do not be frightened, Your Majesty," the wolf said to her. "My name is Enoch. I am the keeper of this world until the appointed time."

"What world is this? Who is that man? And what are you keeping?" Amana asked.

"The stone from which you have entered is the forbidden stone. You are on the small moon that orbits the Kingdom of Evermore," Enoch replied. "You are on Eden. That is the Tree of Life, and this place is its garden."

Amana was overcome with awe. Everything that had been frightening and terrible about the Eve of Illumination cavern was now transformed into its opposite. "And the man, Enoch?" Amana asked curiously.

"Oh, forgive me, Your Majesty. That man is me," Enoch replied. "As one who has surveyed this moon for many hundreds of cycles, I have learned the way of the accord."

"The accord?"

"Yes. It means agreement. The many animals here can transform based on my thoughts and speak for me, as our minds and chemistry are in accord, so to speak," Enoch answered.

"This is so strange to me, Enoch. Please understand, that I have recently been through—" Amana stopped speaking and looked around. Enoch was gone, as was the wolf. All of the animals had vanished. She then heard a voice and hoof beats behind her.

"You were saying?" It was Jaesu. He was sitting on a beautifully winged white horse with mild blue eyes and delicate, flaring nostrils. "Forgive the intrusion," Jaesu said.

"Jaesu!" Amana ran and hugged him tightly. "How did you find me?"

"Find you?" Jaesu tilted his head with a funny frown. "You asked me to get you out of that place of emptiness, did you not?"

"Yes, but …I was alone …I wasn't sure—"

"If I was with you? Or if I heard you?" Jaesu interrupted. "Amana, I am with you always. Even during the darkest and hardest times. Sometimes trusting that intuition of yours is better than trusting your eyes."

Then a magical table appeared under the Tree of Life. It was covered with a silver cloth on which rested a magnificent array of fruits—different varieties of pears and plums, peaches and apples, melons, mangos and berries, all perfectly ripe and glowing with color. None had a blemish or was in any way less than perfect. There were also cakes and pastries of every kind, nuts, and flagons of wine and water.

"Will you join me?" Jaesu asked.

The queen smiled and ran to the table. She saw two chairs made from a rosy-colored gold. One chair had a raised design of flowers that grew on Gardenia. Amana knew that to be her chair. "Lord, this place is the most beautiful place I have ever imagined," she said. "Am I still in one of those visions?"

"It is quite perfect, Amana," Jaesu replied. "And no, you are not in one of those visions. This is as real as it gets."

She looked around and soaked it in. She could see the animals hiding behind the trees near the hills, giggling and hoping to get a glimpse of the speaker or to hear a few words of the conversation. She noticed that the horse was getting a bit impatient as well. "Who are you, my friend?" Amana asked.

The horse looked at her and bowed his head in respect. "I am Pegasus, Your Majesty. I am the seraph of the great Lord Jaesu. It is my honor to serve the everlasting King of the Universe."

"All right, all right," Jaesu laughed. "You can be real with her."

"In that case …throw me an apple, if you don't mind," Pegasus answered.

Jaesu shook his head while not losing his smile and chucked the apple to the horse. "Will that hold you?"

"Splendid. I could fly for a thousand cycles after having just one of these," Pegasus said happily.

"I have read that the mighty Pegasus is the greatest of the seraphs; is that true, great horse?" Amana asked.

"It is true, Amana," Jaesu answered for the horse. "He is far too humble to agree with such an assessment, but there is neither an asudem nor a seraph greater in any galaxy. I am truly blessed to have such an ally and friend."

Pegasus lifted his proud head and stood tall, honored by his lord. He was a legend, even though he spent most of his time in Evermore, where few could see him. It was said that his wing beats were strong enough to cause cyclones and hurricanes. There were stories that he could gallop from one star to the next. The greatest strength of the horse, however, was his loyalty. During the great purge, he'd joined Michaelio to secure Evermore and the outer galaxies.

Amana tried an unknown blue fruit. It gave her a strong energy jolt and caused her taste buds to dance. "What is this?" she asked.

Jaesu smiled and also took some fruit to eat. "These are very good, indeed. They are called blueberries."

"Blueberries? Well, I guess that would make sense," said the queen.

"Sometimes, the simple things in life are the greatest. These are very well known and loved on Earth as well," Jaesu replied.

At the mention of the word Earth, Amana had flashbacks of everything she had seen in her visions: the violence and suffering on Earth and what befallen Jovan, Bethany, and Jaesu. She grabbed her head and leaped from the table into the air. She could not shake the visions. Amana slammed herself into the tree again and again, trying to shake the pain of the visions.

Jaesu stood calmly and said in a soothing voice, "Be still, my dear."

The queen felt peace flow through her. She slowly slumped to the ground next to the tree, resting in a daze. Jaesu handed her a piece of pumpkin cake. "Amana, you must eat," he said.

Amana at first did not want to eat, but knew that Jaesu was always right. She trusted him even when she didn't quite understand what was happening. She took the cake and ate it. With her head resting against the tree, she began to feel rejuvenated. Pegasus walked over to her, concerned. Wanting to show support, he lowered his nose toward her and gently rubbed his velvety muzzle on her cheek.

"Lord?" the queen asked. "Why didn't you ever tell me about Earth? About the sacrifices you made? Not just for the earthlings, but eventually for all of us."

"Oh, Amana," Jaesu sighed. "I wanted you to know when you were ready. Even now, there are so many things that may be difficult for you to understand. Everyone gets a choice whether or not to face the trials on Earth and have a chance to get to Evermore. I made the choice to put myself on the line in order to give others the option of freedom."

"But, Lord?" Amana pleaded. "I saw—and felt—some of the pain you went through, the agony. I saw the pain many of my people and others had gone through and put you through. It was unbearable. I could never imagine having to do what you did."

"It will be worth it in the end, Amana," Jaesu answered. "I dare not say it was easy, but it certainly was well worth it."

"You know what was the worst, Lord?" the queen asked.

"What?" Jaesu replied.

"I saw Jovan, my dear friend, your closest friend, turn away from you. And I saw his pain. And even worse, I saw your pain. I watched you cry over him and so many others, but him in particular. You are the mightiest of kings, King of the entire Universe, and it was as if you were hurting over filthy rags."

Amana continued, "It was as if you didn't even want to go on. I could never imagine you hurting so badly. It was so unfamiliar to me. I speak of love and hear about love but truly did not understand love until I saw that. You died for so many, knowing that they hated you. I looked upon Bethany and Jovan—the Blade—they were nowhere near that third door to Evermore. Tell me this! What happens if they don't make it?" The queen was very distraught.

"Amana," Jaesu said soothingly.

"No!" she yelled. "Tell me! I was their queen and friend! I deserve to know!"

Jaesu teared up and bowed his head as his voice got low. "They would be forever in Hadnessa, separated from me, with no chance of ever returning."

It was the answer she had been expecting, but that didn't make her any happier. "What?! These are your friends, your servants, and my people. You can't sentence them to die forever!" she frantically shouted.

"You are a wise queen. Would you not do everything in your power, even against the odds, to spare the smallest creature?" Jaesu asked.

"Of course, I would," she responded.

"But what if that creature didn't appreciate it or care?" Jaesu asked again.

"It wouldn't matter, because it's about how much I care for them. It's unconditional," Amana answered.

"And what if they decided that living on Gardenia with you was something that they didn't want, if they went among those on another world, even Algolithar? What would you do? Would you force them to stay with you because you knew what was best?" he questioned.

"Well, if it is what I knew was best for them then, yeah. I think…I don't know." Then she was quiet, thinking. Those who made the choice to face the trials were also facing their true selves. If they chose to not be a part of Jaesu and Evermore, then he loved them enough to let them go, even after battling to help them find him at the third door for seemingly ages which she knew was far more painful than holding on.

"You see it now," Jaesu said softly.

"Yes," she said, looking down.

"Sit and let us continue this some more," Jaesu asked.

Amana paused for a moment. She looked around and tears began to flow from her eyes. "No," she answered. "Lord, there is something I must do."

With a concerned look, Jaesu asked, "What is it, O' queen?"

"I know Jovan and Bethany, especially Jovan. I know of his caring for you and of your caring for him. I cannot bear to see both of you separated from each other forever," Amana said.

"But Amana, you don't know what will happen," Jaesu replied.

"I know. But that's not good enough," Amana responded. "Lord, my walk with you is the greatest joy of my existence. And Jovan has also been a great friend of mine. I love the bond that you two have. It pains me so much that even with such a great friendship, you could be separated eternally. The pain that I feel is because that bond you have with Jovan, I have with you." She paused. The tears were flying down her face profusely. "I would do anything to keep you from feeling such agony. Anything! That is why I have decided …I am making the choice to go to Earth. I will find Jovan for you. And keep him strong for you."

"Amana!" Jaesu raised his voice. "You cannot save them or him. Only through the Blue Fire Spirit can such a thing occur. Ultimately, Jovan must make his own choice."

"I know him!" the queen responded. "I know that in the depths of his being he already has made his choice for you. He is bound to be lonely. I know I can't save him. But I can be a friend to him, as he has been to me… As you have been to me."

"You are willing to give up your throne for the chance of falling and spending eternity in Hadnessa, away from all you have ever loved, just to stand with your friend?" Jaesu asked.

"Without regret," Amana whispered.

"You are truly the greatest among the kings and queens in the galaxies beneath Evermore," Jaesu said. "You have demonstrated great love, truly. This was not taught to you; you have captured what the Blue Fire Spirit represents, and he has become a true part of you."

"There is one more thing, Lord," Amana said. "I know that Orion is bound to me as my protector—what the law of the universe calls 'an eternal link.' Even so, I ask that he remain the seraph protector of the new queen and of Gardenia."

"Amana, to go without your protector makes the journey nearly impossible," Jaesu said, concerned.

"I know, but I trust my bond with you. I trust you to find a way to not let me fall," Amana answered. "I am still a queen until I leave. Please allow me this request. I desire to keep my people safe long after I am gone. I love them more now than at any time before."

Jaesu looked at her with compassion. He knew how deep her love for life was, and especially Gardenians. "I will honor your request, great queen." He wiped the tears from his eyes as he spoke. "However, I ask a request from you."

"Anything, my Lord," she answered.

"I ask that you choose the new queen. I chose you as queen, and you have been a brilliant one. You have proven yourself in so many ways—none greater than the love and sacrifice you are willing to make for our friends. It is only fitting that you decide the fate of Gardenia," Jaesu said.

"Then I shall crown her personally?" she asked.

"Yes, of course," Jaesu replied.

"I will relinquish the throne to Roslyn, should she accept. I will go see her immediately and ask that you join us, Lord," the queen said. "She may not believe that she is ready, but I know that she is. For some reason, I trust no one else to put their hand to the wheel of Gardenia."

CHAPTER 10

The Coronation

As he rode his black horse, Phan, along with his fellow asudem, made their way through the portal. Everything became still once they were inside. The surroundings were similar to those of Saturn: a dark sky with stars visible. The main difference was a long red river with huge sandstones arching over it and a red, watery substance coming out of it. However, the river did not move. Whatever had come out of the sandstone arch was still as well.

They began to walk through the river, which felt more like thick sludge than water. Nothing moved in this portal. Sardis was noticeably annoyed with the surroundings. The powerful horse could normally breathe out black smoke through his nostrils, but in this place, nothing was coming out.

"Don't fret, Sardis," said Phan. "It is wiser for the unknown to fear us than for us to fear the unknown."

The horse was not afraid but certainly was uncomfortable not knowing what exactly they were walking into.

They were at the top of a small hill and had walked through this bloodlike river for longer than they would have prefered. Just then, something unusual appeared in the distance.

"Look, master!" Denacta pointed toward a distant object. "It looks like a small flame is shimmering at the end, up ahead. Can you see it?"

"That could be anything, Denacta," Legatious replied.

"No!" Phan interceded. "Denacta is exactly right. It looks like a window with a candle on the other side, or, at least, something resembling a candle. Either way, we must be close."

They continued to move toward the strange object. As they got closer, shadowy figures could be seen in the supposed candlelight. Phan was certain the journey through the portal was at an end. *Now where will it lead us?*

*   *   *

"Eleanora!" said King Handel from his throne on Alpha. "I have some stirring news to share with my favorite captain."

Eleanora walked closer to the king and went down to one knee, bowing deeply. "My lord, your servant eagerly awaits this news."

"I have just come from the gathering of royals, a meeting of importance between kings and queens only. Queen Amana of Gardenia has shocked us by making the choice to go to Earth," Handel answered.

"What?" Eleanora's eyes opened wide with fear before she caught herself. "Oh …it will be a tragedy to lose such a legendary queen, symbol of our galaxy's greatness. Has she started her journey?"

"*Ah* …indeed, you are correct regarding her legend," the king replied. "However, it is because of that that we, as her peers, have asked her to not leave until she has officially crowned her successor. We would like to be there, not only to celebrate the succession but also, as you have so eloquently stated, because of her legend. She has certainly been a truly good queen."

"When will this celebration of her majesty's honorable choice commence?" asked Eleanora.

"I am glad you asked," said Handel. "It will take place in short order. Each king and queen has been invited to bring with them any members of their court they desire. Thus, I thought it wise to bring you and introduce you to the home world of your Owls and Seraphs opponents."

Eleanora bowed before Handel. "I would be honored to accompany you, Your Majesty. I am appreciative to be in attendance at such an historic event."

Handel smiled in approval and slowly sighed, leaning his head back as he thought about Gardenia and the Elevemada. He wondered about a future without Amana. She had often been his political opponent, but there wasn't another king or queen whom he had greater admiration or respect for. He appreciated Gardenians and their love for life. He thought it foolhardy, however, that their love for life exceeded their joy for knowledge.

As he was in thought, he gazed upon the portrait placed high above, over the entryway of the throne room. "Eleanora?" he asked. "That picture, I recall Anton telling me, it is from your home world?"

"Why, yes," she said, glancing up at it for a quick second. "It is of the Red River Stone."

"I have fancied it several times now since he brought it into the throne room. I actually had it moved here. It is incredibly stunning, especially the illustration. It is as if I could reach into it myself." The king continued to admire the painting. "Your knowledge of such things still intrigues me, Eleanora. I have never seen a likeness take on traits of a changeling before."

"Changeling?" she asked.

"Of course. You don't have to pretend for my sake," he laughed. "I have seen this now hundreds of times as I've come in and out throughout each day. Don't tell me that you cannot see the moving horse in the painting."

Eleanora did a double take. She had not seen the horse moving before and was caught off guard. She didn't want to let the king know that, however. "*Um* ...well, Your Majesty, it's, *um*—"

"Wait!" he interrupted. "I want to watch this. This is quite remarkable."

They watched as the horse galloped to the forefront of the painting, carrying what looked like a warrior. There was an additional warrior on each side of the horse. They now were almost at the edge of the picture and had gotten larger with each step. It was as if the horse was walking toward the Alphan king. Handel was nervous, but also very curious. He knew he was witnessing something unknown to him and, as always, the thought of gaining even more knowledge pleased him more than any level of respect or adoration from others.

Then something incredible happened. The warrior dismounted and started to come out of the painting. A red light shone through the portrait and throughout the throne room.

Eleanora began to tremble. As she faced the light coming through the wall, she fell to one knee and bowed to the painting.

Handel looked at her with disgust and curiosity. "Get up! I say!" he shouted to Eleanora. "You only bow to your king and to none other! Understand me?" However, before Eleanora could respond, the massive-sized warrior had come out of the painting entirely and was standing in front of Handel.

The king could not believe his eyes. The warrior was the most incredible specimen Handel had ever seen. Only now did he begin to feel afraid. He thought to call in his guards or even the Alphan protector, the four-headed leopard who guarded the world. But the warrior was too fast for him. A strong hand held him by the throat, lifting him high above his throne.

"She *is* bowing to her king, you fool!" said the warrior. "Look upon me, King of Alpha. You who worship knowledge above all else, what do you see?"

The king was shaken and trembled deep within his core. He was utterly terrified and any desire to speak was dissipated by fear seeping through his entire being.

"Let me help you then!" said the warrior. "I am in many of your books—most of your forbidden literature. You've read so much about me that you have ceased to acknowledge my actual existence! It is I, Phan of Algolithar, the right hand of the great Lord Khrimson."

"But—"the king fought to push a word out. "Y …you are supposed to be a fairy tale… a metaphor, something that doesn't exist!" Handel cried out.

"Simple-minded sage!" Phan responded. "You pride yourself on knowledge and yet do not have an inkling of wisdom. None of your writings say that I do not exist. You have exalted yourself above them. Now you can spend all of eternity doing just that."

Phan started to tighten his grip on the king's throat.

Eleanora looked up and saw that Handel's likeness and greatness was being transferred to Phan. She then looked at Handel; his likeness was departing from him. He now resembled a feeble old earthling with a long white beard, a hunched back, and crinkled skin.

"What has happened to me?" Handel cried.

"Legatious! Denacta!" Phan called. The two warriors came out of the painting, answering their master. "There is a dungeon library beneath this chamber. It spirals downward seemingly forever and is full of knowledge. Take his majesty down and imprison him, so he can never escape. Let his thirst for knowledge save him." He then looked at Handel. "You will see that it won't, old man, as your predecessors found out during their earthly journey. This is how they ended up—like you are now." He grabbed him by the throat once more and forced a copy of Handel's mind into his own. Now, not only did Phan look exactly like King Handel, but he could speak and think like him. Every memory and strategy, plan and thought Handel had in his mind was now in Phan's.

The two asudem did as they were commanded. Handel tried to scream for help, but to no avail.

"You have done well, Alina," said Phan. "The disguise becomes you."

"My lord," she said, raising herself up from her bow. "I did not know you would come so soon, or even at all."

"The secrecy was necessary!" he responded abruptly. "The strategies we employ now must not fail …and they will not."

"It seems as if I'm not the only one living in disguises?" Alina snickered.

"My princess," Phan answered. "As I am now King of Alpha, you will be Queen of Gardenia. And we will destroy this pathetic little creation of a galaxy to begin our conquest of the universe."

"If I may," said Alina, "what of Amana's coronation? Will we still be attending?"

"Oh, yes, young huntress." Phan smiled. "This is where it comes to a halt. All of their love and joy and peace—we shall destroy it. More importantly, we must alert our Lord that Amana will be racing to Earth shortly. He will want to know and will certainly have something special planned for her."

Phan then motioned to Sardis, who was still in the portrait, to come close to the frame. "Yes, right there, Sardis. You will not like this, but I will need you to stay in there a while longer. Having someone of your power overseeing the throne room while we are gone will ensure nothing interrupts our plans."

Sardis was not happy and let out a grumble, but he obeyed his master. Sardis was a most loyal servant and knew that he was feared and respected by many. His eyes were very useful to Phan. Whenever he needed to communicate with Khrimson, Sardis could project Phan to wherever Khrimson was in the universe. He had overheard Alina and Phan's conversation regarding the need to warn Khrimson. He walked up to the edge of the frame and opened his projecting eyes, firing a hidden-spectrum beam toward the throne so that Phan could relay his message.

"Thank you, Sardis," Phan said, stepping into the beam, awaiting Khrimson. He only used this method in dire situations, and Khrimson always answered it.

"I am here, my friend," snarled Khrimson. "*Ah* ...I see you have indeed captured the throne of Alpha, and even better, you have used your skills to immerse yourself in the king's very essence. No one will be able to see through that disguise! Shrewd and wise, great Phan, you have something else to tell me?"

"Yes, my lord," Phan said, bowing. "We have just been informed that the Queen of Gardenia, Amana, has decided to make the choice to go to Earth to take on the tribulation."

Before Phan could continue, Khrimson let out a thundering shout, so loud that it shook the entire throne room. "Curses! You let her go without telling me? Do you know what that will do to our plans on Earth?"

"My lord, you don't understand," Phan interrupted. "She has not left as of yet. She will be crowning the new queen herself. Once she has done that, she will jump the Stream toward Earth."

Khrimson's countenance changed. He gently placed his hands together as if he were in thought. "*Hmm*...I see. Well, this is certainly a fortunate turn of events. We cannot have her roaming the Earth. She must be destroyed. You know this, don't you?"

"I do, great lord," Phan replied. "This is why we wished to commune with you. While on Gardenia, the queen is extremely powerful; it is said that only Jaesu can match her on her own world. However, once off Gardenia, she may not prove as powerful. And if memory serves me correctly, Gardenia will not be as potent without her either—at least until the new queen realizes her own strength, which should give us ample time."

"Well," Khrimson continued to think, "what about Orion? As her personal guardian, he surely must be accompanying her, no?"

"Not necessarily, my lord," Alina said, quickly walking into the beam.

"Alina, it is unwise to interrupt dark lords," Khrimson hissed.

"Great one," Phan added, "no matter how it works out, whether Orion joins her or not, we will win. Either she leaves herself unguarded and we destroy her and then take on Gardenia afterwards, or she remains guarded and leaves Gardenia unprotected. We can plan for both and take whichever victory offers itself first."

"I see your point, Lord Phan," Khrimson answered. "Under no circumstances can she survive, you hear me? If your warriors cannot kill her in the Stream, then send an enchantress to convince the mother to give up her child, or kill the mother, cause her to fall ill ...I don't care what it is we do. Just destroy her."

"But, my Lord, she's just a minor soul," Alina interjected.

In anger, Phan flung his arm toward Alina, tossing her across the room and smashing her head against the marble walls. As he hit her, she became flesh temporarily—long enough for her to feel the extremely painful effects. "Know your place!" Phan said angrily.

"Huntress," Khrimson said to Alina. "She is a mighty queen. Many forget who they are meant to be and are forever searching, but I fear this one will not be as easy to deceive as the others. I am counting on you both. Destroy her and take over the realm of Gardenia. Once we accomplish this task, the universe will be that much closer to being under our rule."

*   *   *

"She really is extraordinary, Sarai," Mrs. McTenneb said. "As you know, I have provided private instruction for many children—quite brilliant, some of them. Without question, your daughter is considerably gifted."

"Isn't she, though?" Sarai responded while quickly removing an emerald green scarf and maroon hair tie from her long red hair. "I certainly don't mean that arrogantly. But when I was two, I maybe could speak a few words and such. Bethany has picked up things so fast since she was a toddler. Even in areas where I struggled, she seems to excel. And of course, she's had a great instructor," Sarai said with a gracious looking smile.

Mrs. McTenneb, about thirty years her senior, put on her overcoat. "I appreciate that, Sarai. Thank you. Bethany, for certain, makes it quite enjoyable."

Sarai took a peek down the long hallway full of family photos to ensure that Bethany was nowhere in sight to overhear.

"Mrs. McTenneb, might I trouble you with a non-education related question?"

"Of course, dear," she said while adjusting a hat.

Sarai gathered a nearby jacket and quickly scampered down the hallway to see where seven-year-old Bethany was. She was reading a novel, nestled by the fireplace. "Bethany? Honey, you ok?"

"Yes, on chapter nine. This chick is ridiculous," Bethany answered, wrapped in an ivory knitted throw blanket, hot cocoa stationed on the nearby end table.

"I'm just going to walk Mrs. McT to the car. I'll be right back."

"Okay, Mommy," she responded, clearly more interested in her book.

Sarai opened the door for the tutor as the two of them exited the foyer, moving onto the front porch of the beautiful Victorian home. "How has she seemed to you lately? I mean, not so much with the school work, but with, I don't know, everything else."

With a puzzled look on her face, the tutor responded, "I'm not sure what you mean. We don't really talk much beyond the schoolwork."

"It's just that, I remember being her age, having fun and laughing, and yes, at times, I do see that in her. I want her to succeed, but I worry she may resent her life." Sarai abruptly paused to take a breath, concerned that she may have come off as overly nervous. "I'm sorry. I am rambling. This sounds absurd."

"Have you ever…" Mrs. McTenneb interjected while removing car keys from her plain brown purse. "What I mean to say is, and please don't be offended…with Bethany getting a private education at home, is she ever around other children? Does she have many friends? Or for that matter, did you at her age?"

"Please don't think I would be offended. I am the one reaching out to you here," Sarai answered, now halfway up the driveway next to the McTenneb's silver Buick sedan. "It's a good question. At her age, I had a few very close friends. Of course, none of them are in my life now, but yes."

"And Bethany?" the teacher asked as she started the car to warm it up.

"Well, she has Ireka, who lives next door to her grandparents. Probably her closest friend, but even that doesn't resemble what I remember my childhood being like. But then again, like I said, none of my friends stuck around. Perhaps, Bethany is doing something right."

"Perhaps, she is extraordinary," Mrs. McTenneb retrieved her eyeglasses from the glove box. "You know, for what it is worth, my childhood friends are still in my life. And their children and children's children."

"Really? After all this time?"

"Trying to say I am old, are we?"

"Oh, my goodness! Mrs. McT, I didn't mean—"

"Rubbish child. I know quite well how many years I have been on the Earth." She laughed it off.

"I'm just surprised at that amount of loyalty. I've never seen that before."

"Well, it's not something I would want to go through life without. One of those things one cannot put a price on. You know, if you want, we are all getting together tomorrow night for…" Mrs. McTenneb then caught herself and closed the car door. She rolled down the window and added, "Never mind. I'm sorry. I was rambling there. I'm sure Bethany will be just fine."

"Wait. You were saying something about tomorrow night?" Sarai asked with a confused look on her face.

Mrs. McTenneb was usually very polite, courteous, and yet straightforward. "It's nothing, dear, really."

"Hold on. Did I say something wrong? Please don't go yet. I want to hear more." Sarai clearly could see something had bothered the teacher, and she didn't want her to leave offended. Then she thought and realized what might have happened. "For Christmas Eve? Is that why you and your childhood friends are getting together?"

"Please, Mrs. Crowmire," she answered with her eyes quickly showing a glassed over look, ready to leak tears at any moment. "These people are my closest friends, my family. I wouldn't want anything to happen to them."

Sarai was caught off guard because Bethany's tutor always called her by her first name. "I don't understand." She then paused again and noticed the bare evergreen trees and the lightless roads in the winter air. "Oh, you mean—"

"Yes, the new law," Mrs. McTenneb snapped back.

"I—I'm sorry. I wasn't thinking. Truth be told, my in-laws' beliefs and aspirations have nothing to do with me."

"Don't they, though?" The teacher shifted her car from drive back into park. "I didn't see a tree or wreath or a manger or hear Christmas bells in your home."

"Well, sure, there is a public image I have to uphold because of my husband, of course. But I loved this time of year as a child. And even so, I still try to celebrate in my own way, subtle as it is."

"Yes, I saw the scarf and hair tie. Not quite two turtle doves and a pear tree. But one can only do what she can, I suppose."

"I could get into trouble for that you know," Sarai answered with half a smile.

"Hardly, if at all," Mrs. McTenneb responded in a serious tone.

"Okay, look, I've taken enough of your time already, really. Thank you for all you are doing with Bethany. And please don't worry; I won't say a word about your gathering. Besides, I don't even know where it is."

"You're twisting my arm here." The older woman sighed and, in turn, gave a half smile also. "I'll tell you what. You show up tomorrow late afternoon at my home with little Bethany, and I'll show you real friendship."

"Really?" Sarai jumped and clasped her hands quick as if she were still a child. "Bethany will be so excited." Sarai could hardly contain herself as she reached through the car window to give the teacher a hug out of appreciation.

Appearing fairly startled, Mrs. McTenneb responded, "Yes, and I should really be off. Reginald will worry if I'm not home soon."

"Well, you best get going. And thank you!"

Mrs. McTenneb smiled somewhat reluctantly, raised the window, and backed her Buick out from the driveway and drove off.

*   *   *

Seven years had passed since Dara had given Vanno her ultimatum. She worked two jobs to support Jovan, who was in kindergarten. One was as a part-time weekend cashier at a local supermarket and the other was as a Richmond County court stenographer. It had been a hard road for her those seven years. She had not forgotten the moment when she'd walked in her apartment to find Vanno missing and a note that read. "Dar … you were right. I'm nothing and definitely not worthy of a wife and son. I'll never stop loving you, but for now this is best. Sorry. Here is the money from my last paycheck. It's $200. I'll be at Frankie's if you need me. Much love, Vanno."

And that was it.

"Jovan! You've been sleeping all day. For the tenth time, please wake up!" said the long haired brunette woman. "Everyone will be here before you know it."

"Five more minutes!" he shouted back in a cranky tone.

"In five minutes, I'll let Ava chop some of that hair off in your sleep. I know you will just love that."

"Not cutting it!" he answered as he put his entire head under a pillow as if to ignore his mother's voice.

"Come on. Stop messing around, Jo. We really need to get a move on here." Dara then looked at her own long hair and said in a soft tone, "Actually, his hair is almost as long as mine. Perhaps we should cut it."

"*Ugh*! All right already! I'm up!" the boy yelled as he quickly sat up in bed.

"I knew that would do it," she said. "Ava, Mrs. Harrieta, and the Lansdales are in the other room. Oh, and Mrs. Harrieta made your favorite — cinnamon gingerbread cookies." Dara scurried about to check on the defrosting turkey and ensure the place was clean, which she had already done several times over.

Jovan sat up in somewhat of a daze, just coming out of a deep sleep. He could hear laughter coming from one of the other rooms, which let him know that some folks had already arrived. Although he was still half out of it, the sounds of "Christmas Time is Here" playing reminded him that it was, indeed, Christmas Eve. Christmas was a special time for Jovan. He, like many children, looked forward to the gifts, but he also enjoyed the festive nature of the day and time. The sounds of laugher and music, seeing people that he normally didn't see, and, of course, the food all helped make for a most memorable occasion. Although he was quite young, Jovan could tell that everyone seemed happier this time of year than at any other time. He didn't necessarily know why, but it didn't matter much.

"Are you still in here?" his mother yelled. "Jovan, please hurry it up and get ready before more people arrive."

"All right! All right!" Jovan rose up and stomped his way toward the bathroom, clearly in a grouchy mood. "Such a grump monster. Not hurting anyone by sleeping-whatever"

Dmna lifted up her head from her customary position of lying in an upper corner of any room where Jovan would sleep. "Jovan! You know that grouchiness needs to chill. It's Christmas Eve, dude." Dmna dropped from the ceiling to go watch the boy in her charge while he brushed his teeth. She petted his face, assuring him that it would be a great day.

Dara, although she could not hear or see Dmna, knew that the mood wouldn't last for long; after all, it was Christmas Eve, and that always brought out the best in both her and her son. She walked into the main room where the small amount of company was gathered. This was to be temporary, however, as many more guests were expected to arrive.

The Lansdales, Malachi and Monique, were removing decorations from a box. Monique had an amazing talent for beautifying any room, while Malachi would read the paper and sometimes peel potatoes, if needed.

Mrs. Harrieta, aside from her delectable baking abilities, also knitted for a hobby and was on the couch finishing up a Christmas blanket started the previous Christmas Eve.

Ava Carbone was one of Dara's closest friends and had come early to help out wherever she could, all while keeping Dara from pulling her hair out.

Everything was so positive. Regardless of any fears or pressures any of the group may had been going through, whenever they were together, especially during the holidays, the air of good vibes would always take over.

What none of them knew was that the more they and their seraphs were together, the stronger their seraphs would become in the process. When this happened, joy and laughter would be in their midst.

Khrimson and his allies hated when this happened, as this sort of fellowship seemed to provide souls with greater protection from his taunts and trances. Many of the asudem worked tirelessly to keep good friends and families apart. The more isolated they could make an individual, the weaker their seraph would become. This had been a key factor in many of Khrimson's great victories in the past.

"Are you guys ok with everything? Is there anything I can do?" Dara asked.

"Yeah, girl," Monique responded. "Take a breath. You been runnin' round like mad all day."

"Hear, hear!" Ava interjected.

"You know how I get. We don't have much time, and everyone is counting—"

"On us like last year and the year before," Monique cut her off. "D, have I ever let you down? In a few hours, this place is gonna be hoppin'. Mrs. Harrieta's cookies and whatnot never disappoint."

"I know, I know!" Dara answered. "I just want everything to be perfect."

"Perfect?" said Ava, sipping on some punch. "With this awful lime-green colored flattened carpet and those creepy looking radiators in the back room?"

"Hey! I happen to like those radiators," Malachi said as he lifted his eyes from the newspaper. "They don't make 'em like that anymore."

"Of course, you would say that," Monique retorted, "considering that you are the only one reading a newspaper nowadays."

"All in all, Dara, it's going to be perfect. It always is when we do Christmas here," Ava said, while getting more punch. "I'm just glad we only have to deal with this carpet once a year."

"With the new law in place, this worn out ol' carpet might be the least of our concerns soon enough," said Dara as she started to wipe down the table.

"The gall of some people. Are there any other states following suit?" Monique asked.

"Nope, just Jersey for now," Dara responded.

"I think it's been a long time coming, not just for Jerseyans but for everyone," Ava added. "On both Staten Island and Brooklyn, I've noticed less Christmas merchandise available, fewer plays at the schools ... and the music at the stores? Nothing Christmassy at all."

"They say it's to bring more harmony among the people," Mrs. Harrieta answered, "but a hefty fine and then jail time? For Christmas? I've seen it all."

"It's both Christmas and Chanukah actually...for now," Malachi interjected.

"You think they will do more, baby?" Monique added.

"Are you kidding? Whatever the government can do to minimize the freedoms of the people and increase the scope of their own power, they will do just that. So, yes, it would not surprise me if Ramadan or Kwanzaa and other holidays are next," Malachi replied noticeably concerned.

"As it is now, the law states that we may observe the holidays while in the state of New Jersey as long as it is in private. No public assemblies, churches, or even decorative lights on the lawns," said Dara.

"No wonder Jay mentioned that we might get a larger turnout than usual," Ava remarked. "Well, hello, stranger, get over here, and give your aunt Ava a hug."

Jovan had just come out dressed in a red and green striped collar shirt, long sleeved over red corduroy pants that Dara had picked out for him to wear. He ran to Ava and gave her a big hug as requested. Jovan loved Ava, who he fondly called his aunt. She was hip, could always make him laugh, and constantly encouraged him to be himself. This was one of the reasons he so proudly kept his hair longer than most boys his age.

"What happened to the music?" Jovan asked. "I heard music playing before."

Mrs. Harrieta leaned over toward the boy, so he could see strands of her orangey red hair coming out from her beret. "You know what, honey? You sure did. The grownups just got to talking, and when that happens, all the fun stops."

"Okay, problem solved," said Dara as she turned the music back on.

"'Silent Night'? Really?" Monique asked in a derisive manner. "You got nothin' more fun than that? They might be trying to damage our spirit, but they can never rob our joy. I'm going to need something more upbeat if you want me to make this baby sparkle."

"Thought you said you'd never let me down," Dara added sarcastically.

"How is a girl to adorn a room to greatness if she is sleepin'?"

"Fair enough. You got it," Dara responded as she switched out the vinyl record on the phonograph.

"All right! 'Jingle Bell Rock'! Now I can get behind that," Monique said excitedly. "That's our cue everyone. Get the reindeer in gear, and let's get to sleddin'. Time to work!"

"Reindeer? Where?" Jovan asked excitedly.

"Right over here," Ava answered as she lightheartedly placed a red nose over Jovan's. She went to follow Dara through the white saloon swinging doors into the kitchen.

"Hey!" Jovan said, pulling the nose off.

"Pay her no mind, scout," said Malachi. "Here, take this can of snow and get ready to spray the tree down when I say we're ready. Cool?"

Jovan nodded enthusiastically. He loved to use the spray cans of snow on the Christmas tree.

Once behind the kitchen doors, Dara checked to ensure no one was around, and while opening the oven, she whispered to Ava, "Does he seem okay to you?"

"Seem okay? Who?"

"*Duh*! Jovan!" Dara responded softly but with clear agitation in her voice.

"Okay? Of course, he's okay. It's Christmas. Look at how lit his face is."

"Yeah, that's what everyone sees. But you know him. How he is in public. I just wonder—"

"If he is thinking about Vanno?"

"Yes!"

"Stop wondering. That's the furthest thing from his mind right now. He has you, and helloooo… it's Christmas. If his mind is on anything, it's whether he is getting that spaceship thingy." Ava was separating raw chicken cutlets and pulled out a hammer to tenderize them. "That's all it is, Dara. You are the best mom ever. And he is the best because of you."

"I'm sure you're right. Maybe it's me." Dara was about to leave the kitchen.

"Maybe it is you!" Ava yelled.

"What are you yelling for?" Dara snapped back.

"Seriously? You are just going to walk right on out and let me hammer these poor cutlets with a real steel hammer? Like really? Who are you right now?" Ava said with a slight laugh.

Dara immediately removed the hammer from Ava's hand, simultaneously reached into a drawer, and handed her a wooden hammer while taking the other one with her. "Thank you. I was looking for this."

"The hammer? Why?"

"Just in case you get out of line." Dara let out an insane sounding laugh and walked out of the kitchen.

Dara heard the spraying of the snow can and excitement in Jovan's voice as she walked out of the kitchen. She wanted to believe that Ava was right but was always worried about Jovan and wanted him to have what she never had.

"Mom, look! Mr. Lansdale showed me how to make a snowman on the tree with the spray," Jovan said exuberantly.

"Oh, wow! Look at that!" Dara said happily.

"See? Monique ain't the only creative one in this fam—"

BOOM! The sound immediately hushed everyone. It appeared to come from the front door, but none could say for sure. It was loud enough that Ava came running in from the kitchen.

"What was th—" she attempted to say, but Dara held her finger to her lip as if to say "quiet."

BOOM! BOOM! There was no question this time. Everyone knew it was the front door.

"FBI," said a husky female voice from the opposite side of the door.

Everyone in the room scrambled in a bit of a panic. Dara instantaneously nodded at Ava, giving her the go-ahead to remove Jovan from the room, while Malachi and Monique attempted to hide as many of the decorations as possible.

"Where we going?" Jovan asked Ava.

"Into the backroom," Ava whispered back. "Looks like some boring grownup talk is about to happen."

After more banging came from the front door, the voice said, "I can hear you in there! Don't make us break the thing down!"

Dara ran to the door and glanced through the peephole. She saw a woman with short black hair. The woman's back was to the door, spotlighting the rather large yellow letters *FBI*.

"Just a minute!" Dara yelled as she tried to give her friends time to clean up.

"That's all you have before we have a serious situation on our hands," the voice said.

"We aren't doing anything wrong," Malachi said softly to the group.

"It must have been Jacen," Monique responded. "He's been telling everyone about our jamboree, hoping for a great turnout."

Dara couldn't wait. Mrs. Harrieta hurried into the kitchen while Malachi and Monique stayed in the living room. Nervously, Dara said to the agent, "Okay. Sorry about that. Opening now."

There had been so much talk about the new laws, she wasn't sure what to expect. Many thoughts ran through her mind. *If I get arrested, what about Jovan? Will Lyanne take him? What about the others that show up later?* After Dara checked one last time to ensure Jovan was out of the room entirely, she opened the door. The woman turned around to see her face to face.

"Another minute out there, and my buns would literally be frozen. Can't be makin' a sista wait like that," the woman said.

Dara was speechless.

"Hey, kiddo! You all right? The little guy, is he in there?"

"Dayana, I am going to kill you," Dara said slowly in a stern voice. "Any idea the fear you just put me through, all of us through, over the past two minutes?"

"What? This? Come on! You knew it was me. I've been using that horrible fake voice for years."

"Yeah, but not with the FBI gear."

Dayana had a big giftwrapped box behind her that she picked up as she entered the apartment. "The little guy here? Is it safe?" she said as she peaked her head in.

"Yeah, he's back there," Monique said while shaking her head, rolling her eyes, and smirking.

"My buddy on the force gave me one of these," Dayana said, pointing to the jacket as Dara finally let her in. "It was a prop from a movie set. I don't think they really wear these."

"What's in the box?" Malachi asked.

"Just that Magnus Flash starship Jovan has been pleading for to no end," Dayana responded.

"Put it under the table that's next to the tree," Dara instructed, clearly showing some agitation to Dayana. "But make sure the tablecloth covers it."

"Like I'm going to just leave it out in the open," Dayana said sarcastically. "What's with you anyway? It's not like I haven't pulled similar stunts like that before."

"*Um*…I don't know. Maybe it's like, with HAL being in effect. I'm a bit on edge," Dara answered as she reset the snack table for the third time. "You didn't get stopped carrying this gift? It has Santa wrapping all over it."

"You do know that Jovan knows the gift don't come from Santa, right?" Monique asked Dayana.

"Of course, I do! But it was cute. I liked the dark red hat and the silver beard. It looked a little different from the super white beards and bright reds. Wish I had a Santa. Back to HAL. I saw a lot on the news about this new law in New Jersey and priests and pastors getting arrested, but I've been far too busy at work. Traveling from Staten Island and going into the city and then wherever takes its toll on a girl."

"Wait. You don't know about HAL?" Dara asked.

"No. Is he cute?"

"HAL is the new Holiday Autonomy Law being piloted in Jersey," Malachi interjected.

"Oh, that. At my job, they are saying it's just an official law allowing people to celebrate however they choose without offending people or something," Dayana answered nonchalantly as she finished putting the large gift under the table. "Dara, you can't see it, right?" Dayana said while checking from a few different angles.

"No, Day!" Dara said, tightening her lips subtly.

"You can't? Good. I wasn't sure if the white part of the tablecloth would show the the shad—"

"Not about that! *Ugh*. HAL! HAL! HAL!" Dara yelled.

"Whoa! Chill out, sista!" Dayana shot back.

"What is with all the shouting?" Ava whispered. "I'm trying to keep Jovan calm back there and...*oh*, Day, you're here. Did you bring the—"

"Yes, it's under the table."

"Oh, *duh*, I can see its shadow from here. We gotta do something 'bout that," Ava said.

Quickly Dayana took two steps toward the table "Let's hurry it up then before he sees it."

"Before who sees it?"

In a state of surprise, Dayana, Ava, and everyone else froze. They had not heard little Jovan enter the room.

"What is that thing under the table?"

"Table? What table?" Dayana asked nervously.

"The one you are standing next to, nitwit," Monique interjected.

"Just tell him," Malachi added.

"Tell him what?" Ava asked while offering beady eyes toward Malachi as if to say "shut up."

"What do you mean, tell him?" Dayana inquired. "Just like that—put it all on out there and tell him? Have you any Christmas spirit at all?"

"Sure do." Malachi adjusted his charcoal gray flat cap. "Growing up in the projects gives a man perspective. Mama didn't have much to offer, and because of that, there were many Christmases where the biggest things on my list just never came. I understood. But Mama never let me go without. I always appreciated everything she gave me. I am sure Jovan will as well. Right, sport?" Malachi rubbed the top of Jovan's head before nodding in Dayana and Ava's direction.

"Everyone quiet!" Dara cried. "I am not finished talking here. First off, Dayana, HAL isn't just some live and let live law. People are getting hit with fines in the amounts of hundreds for a first offense and an arrest for the second. And these arrests aren't for disturbing mosques or random people's homes, or schools, or even for decorating their own property!" Dara took a breath as everyone around her was immediately silenced and in awe. Her seraph Robin gave Dara a high five without her conscious self, knowing it as a show of support and admiration. "All right, Ava, I still need your help in the kitchen. Day, take this. It's a small list of what we need for tonight. Jovan, get your coat on and help Aunt Dayana. Oh, and, honey, if you are wondering what Aunt Ava and Dayana got you, it's socks. Malachi's right. You should know."

"*Huh?*" Dayana responded.

"Socks?" Jovan asked. "But I have socks."

"So much for your theory, baby," said Monique as she nudged Malachi. "Jovan, come on over here and let ol' Malachi explain to you the value in a good sock."

Malachi stared at his wife as if she was half-crazy.

"What do you mean, socks?" Ava whispered to Dara.

"He was going to guess."

"Well, it's not like you to lie to anyone, especially him."

"I didn't lie."

"You know full well we didn't get him socks," Dayana added softly.

"You're right. I also know full well that you will, just to show that I wasn't lying and to protect your surprise," Dara said as she handed Dayana a twenty-dollar bill. "Aisle three at the Srew Shop, being that you will be going there anyway. He likes white ones with the dark blue heel."

Dayana rolled her eyes but didn't say a word. She knew that Dara meant business, and after the stunt Dayana had just pulled on the group, she probably had it coming.

"Come on, kiddo," Dayana said to Jovan. "Let's get crackin'. We gotta be back in an hour."

Jovan hugged his mother and hurried toward the front door.

*　*　*

Later on that evening, Sarai and Bethany left their home to meet up with Mrs. McTenneb. Like they had done many times before, the mother and daughter duo had to evade the press and sometimes Secret Service-type agents just to get some private time together. Moving about in stealth was not new to them. However, meeting up with someone else, even someone as close to them as Mrs. McTenneb, was out of the ordinary.

They drove to the Candlehawk Café, a popular meeting spot for upperclass college students. Sarai ensured that both she and Bethany had their head's covered in black ski caps with wide matching scarves, plain-looking sunglasses, and long gray overcoats so as not to draw attention to themselves. From there she called for a taxi to take her to Mrs. McTenneb's, near Jersey City.

"Now, listen, munchkin," Sarai said affectionately to Bethany. "Stay close to me. I'm not sure exactly where we are going, except that Mrs. McT thinks we will love it."

"Okay, Mommy." Bethany grabbed her mother's arm in response as they got into the back of the taxi. "Mrs. McT is always fun."

Sarai was fairly edgy. Although she wanted more than anything for Bethany to be around different people, she was also starving for some good friendship. Most of the folks that she dealt with on a daily basis only knew of her or were kind to her because of who her husband was or who his family was. Sarai, on the other hand, came from a more meager and jaded upbringing.

As the taxi drove off, Sarai looked around at many of the college students gathered around laughing. For whatever reason, this brought her thoughts back to several years earlier—before Bethany had been born.

She was a clerk in one of those very same cafés where students hung out, living in Seattle. The customers there would often comment on her long red hair while using terms like striking, Hollywoodesque, and beautiful.

It was there when she met Alcee, as she and others called her husband. Sarai remembered how endearing he seemed at first. He was tall with dark brown hair and captivated her with a smile and ease of conversation. She recalled one day she was waiting on him while he was a patron in the café where she worked. He had file folders on the table and a tablet, which made her think he was working on some sort of business.

"Can I get you anything, sir?" she asked.

"Why, yes. Coffee, black please," he answered with a smile, returning back to his work. "Oh, and can I trouble you for an egg white on flat bread please?"

"Of course," she said, returning the smile.

That day had been the third day in a row she had seen him sitting by himself. It was not unusual to have regulars, but he was unfamiliar. She figured he was probably an out-of-towner on some sort of business trip. She intended to ask him what he did, but the place got so busy that another worker had to bring him his order. Sarai hoped to see him the next day, but he didn't show.

A few weeks went by, and she had pretty much forgotten all about him. One evening, the bell rang as the door opened to the café, and there he was. It was later this time. Normally he would come in very early in the morning. This happened to be closer to eight o'clock and not her normal shift.

Maybe he's been coming here each night and just wanted to avoid me. She was the only one working this late at night. He folded his long coat over a chair and began reading through his files and tablet.

With no one else in the building, she was a tad anxious. "Large black, egg white on flat bread?" she called over to the man.

The man politely nodded and smiled with his back facing the window at the corner table that he frequented most. As was the norm, he looked through his files some more.

Then it happened. While Sarai was preparing his meal, the man asked her a question.

"Would you wear these?"

Sarai had not been facing him, but the oddness of that question was enough to freak her out.

"Pardon me. Sarai, is it? These right here." He then pointed to a photo of zigzagged bright pink contact lenses.

Sarai, still startled by the question, slowly turned around, noticing the lenses. She involuntarily spewed out, *"Eww! Gross."* She then caught herself as she hoped to not offend the man.

He laughed and laughed some more.

She was fond of that laugh. It made her feel more at ease and comfortable around him. It felt warm and genuine.

He then held up another photo. "And these?" he asked. This time the photo was of a woman wearing green triangle sunglasses.

Scrunching up her face, Sarai shook her head *"Um...no way.* Third time a charm?"

He smirked but was less demonstrative while he was searching for something else to show her.

For some reason, Sarai was nervously anticipating what would be shown next. She actually liked this game, whatever it was. He did seem more serious this time, however, which piqued her curiosity. "Your coffee is going to be cold or distastefully nuked if you don't hurry it up," she said in an attempt to keep the conversation moving.

"All right," he said as if she hadn't just made a comment. "How about this one?"

"Oh, my!" she answered with her hand softly covering her lips. "That…is just hideous." Sarai couldn't contain herself, and she busted out in a loud laugh. She tried to apologize but just kept on laughing. "I can't say I like any of these. I'm so sorry." She then wiped the laughing tears from hear red cheeks.

"Well, I can't say that I blame you one bit," he answered. "One of my clients is modernizing—their terms not mine— current eyewear." He placed the third picture face up on the table as he was talking. Solid pewter brown goggles. "With all of the laser technology, they were looking to revive the market. Apparently, the first test subject failed." He smiled at Sarai.

"Oh," she said, "so these weren't your designs?"

"Now I am hurt," he laughed. "Actually, I'm not much of a designer. I am more of a, shall we say, financer."

"Like you give money to people who need it?"

"Well, almost. Companies sometimes pitch me their ideas to see if I am willing to invest in them. I rarely lean on my own judgment when those opportunities arise and appreciate folks like yourself, your opinion."

"*Ah,* the common rabble," she snickered while rolling her eyes.

"It's not like that, but I can understand why you would think that." He pointed toward the opposite chair. "I'll explain, if you'll join me for five minutes."

Her heart stopped. She was very attracted to him and enjoyed his company, but it was against her better judgment to just sit down with a stranger.

"I'm Alcee, by the way."

"I'm Sar-ai," she said slowly, realizing that he had recognized her nametag earlier. She looked around and said that there was still a lot of work to do.

"It's late, and I really shouldn't."

"Come on. No one is here. Besides, I'll even help you straighten up some."

"No, *um...* that won't be necessary, really." She looked around again, trying to convince herself that it was okay because it wasn't very busy. "Okay, you got me ... *um* ...I mean, I'll sit. Five minutes and then I absolutely have to get back to work."

"Can I negotiate ten?" he asked with eyebrows raised.

"Alcee, you said—"

"Are you drinking anything?" he asked.

"I don't usually," she said while getting a bit flustered.

"Well, this would be unusual, wouldn't it?"

"I shouldn't. It's during work hours, and Mel doesn't like us to drink when customers are here."

"Drink? There's no alcohol. And it's just silly ol' me."

"And you are down to four minutes, mister."

"What would you drink if you could?"

"Caramel Cinnablaze Latte, of course, *duh.*"

"Small?" he asked while slowly backing out from his seat.

"No way! Go big or go home!"

"Okay then. Wait here two minutes." Alcee then got up from his chair and went toward the counter.

"What are you doing?"

"You'll see."

"You're wasting your five minutes," Sarai answered, while checking her wrist as if she were looking at a watch but none was there.

"Perhaps, I am." Alcee put on an apron and went behind the register.

"Hey! You can't go back there, really." Sarai got up from her chair.

"I'm not going to rob the place. Even so, you have my tablet and my unlocked case in front of you which currently is housing my wallet." He clanked over to her. "Go ahead. You can check."

Indeed she did check as he grabbed a cup and apparently began making a latte.

"Do you know what you are doing?"

"Well, come on. How hard can it be?"

"You're kidding, right?"

"Sarai, would you mind bringing my wallet here?"

A strange man trusting her with his wallet certainly intrigued Sarai. She did as the man had asked.

He then handed her the latte and the removed a card from his wallet to scan for payment. "Go on drink. I bet it's dee-lish."

Sarai nervously looked around. "I am going to get into so much trouble for this." She then sipped the drink and suddenly rolled her eyes back in bliss. "This is utterly amazing. Oh, my goodness! How did you—"

"I'm a quick study," he glanced toward the large laminated card pasted on the countered with step by step instructions for latte basics.

The bell rang. Someone walked in. It was an older gentleman. No taller than five feet two inches around seventy years old, give or take a few years.

"Vanilla Bean Espresso, small please," he said in a somewhat high-pitched voice.

"*Um,*" Sarai responded while looking at Alcee and then toward his tablet as a reminder that he still had belongings out in the open. "I certainly can help with that. Will that be all?"

"How fresh are those croissants?"

"It's almost nine," Sarai responded.

"What she means, sir, is we normally finish baking our last batch sometime around six. However, we can give you one for half price. I assure you that they are quite good still," Alcee interjected as Sarai's jaw dropped nearly halfway to the floor in shock.

"Well, I have a van full of hungry cretes if ya catch my drift. We might be needin' them all for half price. Is that in the cards?" the old man asked.

"With the one espresso?" Alcee retorted.

"They parkin' the van now. Best wait till they all get in before we make any decisions, I think."

Sure enough, as he concluded speaking, his squad entered the café. A couple in their mid-thirties, an older woman, and two small children gathered behind the gentleman. Sarai figured this was a family vacationing someplace nearby.

The bell rang again and a very different group made up of teenagers came through the door. They wore red and black hooded sweatshirts, and each had a red bandana around their heads. Sarai counted three of them, but she thought it might be possible that more were outside.

"Five minutes are up it looks like," she said sarcastically just loud enough for only Alcee to hear. "And thank you for the coffee." She handed the old man the espresso.

"Let's call it overtime then," Alcee answered back. He reached for the croissants. "Sarai, you look like you could use some serious assistance. What a shtick. Right on cue, another bell ring and more customers. We should get crackin'."

Sarai was in awe of Alcee. He didn't work there and obviously could be doing other things. But she would have been tense handling all of these customers this late by herself, although she'd probably never admit it. She also knew that, if her boss came in, she would be in trouble but that was secondary for her now. She really did need the help. The café was usually considered dead at night as the competing chains usually dominated the evening business.

It was that night when she first felt feelings for Alcee. It wasn't just his looks or charm, but how he seemed to carry himself. It was something she hadn't been exposed to before.

Later that evening, as she set the alarm and closed the outer door behind her to lock up, she asked, "How did you know about half off for the bakery and how to make the latte, and for real, don't give me this garbage about the laminated cards. None of us use that ridiculous tutorial."

"Well, you got me," he responded. "I wonder if you'd believe me if I told you."

"What? Don't tell me? There's no way that you used to work here."

Alcee remained silent.

"Come on! Don't be like that! You have to tell me. Tell me!"

*   *   *

"Mom! Are you there? Wake up! We are here," yelled Bethany, shaking her mother gently.

Startled, Sarai looked around at first, wondering where she was. "What? *Huh*, are we there already?"

"Fifty dollars, miss," said the driver.

"Oh, *um*... yeah, sorry," Sarai answered as she began rummaging through her purse. "Fifty, for what? Like ten minutes?" she whispered during her search.

"It was thirty, miss. And you getting holiday discount," the driver said in a rather annoyed tone.

Sarai pulled out her Paychip, quickly thought against it and handed the driver cash instead.

"You're lucky that you got me. Some of the cabbies aren't taking cash anymore."

Sarai nodded and handed the man seventy dollars, grabbed Bethany's hand, and the two quickly got out and started walking.

The neighborhood was full of three-story brick townhouses. They were all in a row. It wasn't too different from the kind of place that Sarai had grown up in. But to Bethany, a middle class place such as this was quite far-off from what she was used to.

"Look, Mommy. There is Mrs. McTenneb."

"Where, honey?"

"Over there, by the light. I think she sees us."

The elder tutor, sure enough, had noticed her expected company and walked toward them.

"You made it," said Mrs. McTenneb after she squinted for a few seconds to ensure she was in the right company.

"We are so grateful to you for having us Mrs. McTenneb," Sarai responded.

"It's Irene tonight dear. Just Irene. It's a chilly night. Good thing you both bundled up. Heck, if I didn't know you both so well, I wouldn't have recognized you. Covered head to toe, I see."

Irene then pulled out a few winter masks meant to cover one's mouth and neck. She handed two of them to Sarai while putting one on herself.

"Put these on, dearies. The place is a few blocks away. Who knows what people are breathing out these days?"

"I really don't think these are necessary," Sarai said.

"Allow me to insist then, at least, for my own conscience."

"If you insist," Sarai answered. "Had I known how far we were to walk, I wouldn't have abandoned that taxi."

"Actually, I was surprised you took the taxi at all," Irene said, while starting to walk north. "But I do appreciate the discretion. Either way, it's better that we walk. You know," Irene then looked up, "the satellites and all, dear."

Sarai laughed softly while complying with the old lady's wishes. "This will keep you warm, honey. Stay close to Mommy."

Bethany took hold of her mother's coat as they walked with her tutor. She could see some stars in the night sky but between the sporadic, big gray clouds and seemingly eternal streetlights, most of the stars were not visible.

Several hot dog and pretzel wrappers blew in front of them. Bethany was always curious and quite observant. She was one to notice almost every detail. She could easily get lost in her own thoughts, as well, certainly not caring about whatever small talk would commence between her mother and teacher.

They made a right-hand turn onto a much narrower street, which happened to be dominated by parked cars on each side.

Bethany could see that this street was considerably different from where Mrs. McTenneb lived. A chill crawled up her spine as she smelled the burning of rubber. She noticed a tall man was walking toward them. The man had a long dark trench coat, a cane, and a matching top hat. For some odd reason, she was quite uncomfortable with this man who was approaching. She looked at her mother, whom she held on to a little tighter, and Mrs.

McTenneb, wondering why they didn't seem to be nervous and just carried on conversations about daily life.

The man got closer and looked Bethany directly in the eye. She turned her head away from him, and he harmlessly passed them by.

Two elderly ladies were behind the tall man and even they looked rather creepy to Bethany. Similar to the gentleman, the ladies looked Bethany in the eye, so she thought anyway, and passed them by just the same.

A few steps later, Bethany could hear the sounds of teenagers laughing and joking. The smell of the burning rubber was more powerful now. She also could hear bottles breaking. As they continued walking, Bethany could see the teens all gathered around a bonfire. She could feel their gazes fall upon her.

Bethany thought about her books and fireplace and wished she was at home.

With a firm grip on Sarai's coat, Bethany followed as they made a left-hand turn. As was the case with the previous couple of blocks, Bethany's attention was completely removed from the adult conversation and totally focused on the kind of street they were walking on.

This street was similar to the prior street; however, it was missing many streetlights and lamps, as if the bulbs had been broken. The darkness on the street was all Bethany needed to feel an even greater sense of worry. *How can Mom not be scared at all? I am.*

She heard a sound. Like the sound a squirrel makes when rustling through leaves or garbage. Because it was far too uneasy for Bethany to even try to decipher where the sound was coming from, she decided to close her eyes and imagine some other place; perhaps it would diminish her worry.

Her grip remained strong on her mother's coat and she played a game within herself to see how well she could determine their direction by feel rather than sight. Her imagination took her to fields of lilies, like she had often pictured in one of her favorite books. She did all she could to transport herself into some magical land of sunshine pouring heat on her face. However, the frozen tightness in her cheeks, regardless of the mask she was wearing, was evident that her concentration on sun-centered thoughts weren't helping very much.

"Excuse me!" Bethany suddenly heard as she felt herself crash into what felt like a massive wall.

"Bethany!" Sarai yelled. "You need to watch where you are going, honey. You almost barreled this poor gentleman over."

Bethany's eyes wouldn't move from the person she had just bumped into. He was a black man with a blue ski cap. His fiery stare caused quivers of dread. She felt glued into this moment forever. All thoughts were completed eroded by fear.

He looked at Sarai and Mrs. McTenneb and then lowered his head toward Bethany. "Sorry about that," he said. "Ever since they shut the lights down in this street, it's become harder to see at night."

"Oh, no, please accept our pardon," Mrs. McTenneb said.

"Well, then," said the man as he looked around to see if anyone else was around before whispering, "Have a Merry Christmas." He quickly moved over and went on his way.

Whoa! What happened? That wasn't so bad. Bethany wondered if she had been worrying over nothing.

"*Ah.* Yes, finally," Irene said. "Right over there on that corner behind that black railing, you see it?"

"Mrs. Mc...*um...* I mean, Irene, it doesn't look like much of a party. Actually I don't see any indication that anyone is there. Looks dead to me. You sure this is the right place?"

"Of course, deary, come, come, just come along."

They started to cross the street. No cars were in sight. Bethany understood what her mother was referring to. There wasn't a hint of anyone present. It looked like an abandoned storefront. As they got closer, Bethany hoped they would see some lights or something, but as they reached the railing, there still was no evidence of anything happening in the building.

"All righty, dearies, we are here," Irene said. "Right down these steps, and through that door."

Mrs. McTenneb took the first step down to what seemed like a cellar of sorts.

Sarai tentatively followed while holding onto Bethany's hand tightly.

Before going down the steps into the underground, Bethany noticed something that caused her another fright. The first man that had passed them a few blocks earlier with the top hat and long trench coat was on the adjacent corner (it was unmistakably him) with eyes frozen on them. *What if this is a trap? What if Mrs. McT is like the evil witch that sticks people into the gingerbread oven? I need to warn Mom.*

Mrs. McTenneb knocked on the door three times. No one answered. She knocked again, but just one time. Still there was no answer. Calmly, she knocked six more times.

The door immediately opened.

A young man was standing there. He wore wire-framed glasses with spikey styled hair arrayed in black and gold colors.

"*Um,* Irene is—" the man said before the old woman uncharacteristically rushed into him with a huge hug.

"Oh, Jacen!" she said. "It is so wonderful to see you. Hope you don't mind, but I brought some dear, dear folks of mine to the gala. You did say I could bring others correct?" She stopped herself to come up for air and awaited his response.

Jacen was alone in what looked like an empty gray walled foyer. "Well, of—" he attempted to respond.

"Where is everyone, dear?" Irene interrupted impatiently.

Jacen looked at Sarai and clearly seemed as confused as she did by Mrs. McTenneb's sudden outburst. He finally answered. "Yes, sorry. Of course…the more good company, the merrier. That's what this is all about, right? Why don't you all leave your coats and stuff with me?" He continued to stare at Sarai and Bethany. "Let me apologize for the stares. I'm not a creeper. Just not every day that I'm greeted by bank robbers on the run."

Is that why Mrs. McTenneb has been acting so strange? A bank robber? Sarai thought.

Jacen then laughed. "I'm kidding, of course. I'm Jacen," he said to Sarai as he put his hand out for a shake. "Why don't you guys go inside for fellowship and enjoy yourselves. There's plenty of hot punch, coffee, and hot chocolate for the little one."

"Thank you, Jacen," Sarai answered as she put her hand to meet his greeting. "I'm—"

"Oh, where are my manners?" Mrs. McTenneb interrupted again. "Jacen, this here is *Sarah*, and that there is *Umphany*. And she hates hot chocolate dear, unless it's white or dark." Irene looked back at Sarai. "Okay, dearies, let's go get warm."

Irene pushed her way through Jacen and toward a second door that she knew would lead to the gathering. Irene turned the knob after dropped her coat and hat on Jacen's arm. The door opened. Immediately a boisterous sound of laughter and holiday music leaked into the foyer. Sarai and Bethany were quite surprised. Irene wasted no time and ran into the group, mingling.

"I'm sorry," Jacen said. "Did she say Sarah?"

"Sarai!" she answered loudly to compensate for the noise.

Jacen couldn't really hear her as the shouting from the party drowned her out. He quickly motioned to them it was okay to enter into the room as she hung their attire up inside a rather cleverly hidden closet, which was behind the grated bar candle holder above an older unlit fire place.

Stepping into the room, Sarai couldn't help but notice a rather unattractive worn green carpet, which looked as if it had been peeled off of a beat up tennis ball. There were snack tables covered with cheap plastic covers, and everyone was wearing what the Crowmires would consider very middle-class attire. She was relieved. *Real people,* she thought to herself. *It's been such a long time.*

Sarai stood at the entryway for a moment, still holding Bethany's hand.

With cap, coat, and masks removed, Jacen couldn't help but admire Sarai's beautiful, long red hair. He then closed the door to continue keeping watch and greeting any new guests.

People in the room were quick to notice both Sarai and Bethany. Both were dressed in dark green turtlenecks, dark red slacks, black flats, with green socks that matched the tops.

Sarai's quick scan of the room led her to assume that there was roughly fifty or so folks at the party so far. It looked to her as if there were very modest-sized rooms where most were gathered. She could hear some of the murmurs throughout the current room already.

One young woman who could have passed as an elf working at the North Pole commented, "Aww! How cute! Twins! You both look like ya just walked off of a movie screen."

"Yes!" someone else said aloud. "Isn't that little girl from a magazine?"

"The lady looks familiar, too!" a man yelled.

Sarai felt uneasy, as if perhaps she'd made a miscalculation in bringing Bethany to such a gathering.

"Wait! Turn off the music," another woman in the background shouted. "Turn it off!"

The music stopped. The sudden laughter and smiles all over the room came to a halt. Everyone was fixed on the two newcomers. The only movement in the room came from the blinking lights on the Christmas tree and their reflection off of the wooden paneled walls.

"I know you. You're the senator's daughter or daughter-in-law or something," the same woman said.

Sarai could see this woman, who looked Puerto Rican to Sarai, was not very happy with their arrival.

"Aren't you?" the woman asked.

"I... *um...*" Sarai gathered her thoughts. "Yes, I am the daughter-in-law of Senator Crowmire, and this here is my—"

"Oh," the woman snapped. "She needs no introduction. Does she? Why this here is the little miss darling of New Jersey herself, in the flesh." The woman mocked some more.

This got under Sarai's skin, and she wanted to do nothing more than mash one of the pecan pies on the nearby snack table into this woman's face.

Jacen opened the door. "I've got it! I knew something was familiar when I saw that hair." He quickly lowered his voice as he realized that the room was no longer as celebratory as it had been before. "I am sure I speak for the room, but we are honored you came. Why are you here?" he asked Sarai.

Sarai looked at him with fire in her eyes, and then turned her attention to the woman interrogating her. "We came here because Mrs. McT ... Irene invited us."

"Yes, I know that," Jacen answered excitedly. "I mean, what I want to know and, well, I think the room wants to know is, why you are here? I mean, forgive me for this, but it's Christmas Eve and it's a Christmas party. Your father-in-law just pushed for a bill penned by the governor outlawing any public display of Christmas. I believe it's called HAL. Surely you had to know this could come up."

"Well, actually I," Sarai again attempted to collect her thoughts. Jacen was right; she should have been prepared for something like this. As she attempted to continue, an unexpected voice was heard from the end of the room.

"Sarai? Is that you?" said a woman's voice.

Sarai was confused for a second but once the crowd separated to let the woman through she no longer was.

"Sarai, it is you!" said Dara as she went to embrace Sarai as if they had been great, longlost friends. However she stopped herself once she saw how quiet the room was. It was pretty easy for her to determine what was happening. "What?" she said to the room. "Never seen a famous person before?" She scanned the room and was embarrassed that anyone would get this treatment from her friends. "This woman is my friend. Dare I say, one of my closest friends. So, if you want her gone—then I'm outy, too."

"No, it's absolutely cool," Jacen said and he backpedalled toward the entry way to continue manning his post. "We're honored, really, that you and your daughter chose to celebrate our Lord's birth with us."

"And what if she's not here to celebrate, *huh*?" said the Puerto Rican woman.

"Jamira," said Dara, "what are you nervous about? You worried she has a black ops team outside waiting to take you down for filling stocking stuffers or eating almandine pretzels?" Several in the room were brought to laughter. "I assure you. She is good peeps."

Dara pulled Sarai into the other room where, although it still had its clusters of people, was less crowded than the main room. "I'm so sorry about that, Sarai. I'm actually quite embarrassed."

"Dara," Sarai said with a visibly confused look on her face. "Like, Dara from the hospital. That Dara? When I had—" and then she looked at Bethany.

"You need to stop that. You know it's me," Dara answered.

"Do I? I mean, we clicked and all, but my phone must be dated because it hasn't rung since I left the hospital," Sarai answered sarcastically.

"Okay, okay, I deserve that. A lot happened to me right away, with Vanno, and looking for a place to live, and of course you are an empress. Didn't think you wanted a leech like me hanging around," Dara answered back.

"I get it. Really I do. But you need to accept friendship when it's offered to you. Believe it or not, it's a lot harder to come by for isolated rich folk, which is pretty much why we are here." Sarai opened a small plastic bottle of water that had been in one of the ice barrels near where they were standing. "And hey, I'm no empress either."

Sarai then saw a small boy move rather quickly toward Dara. At first, she didn't think anything of it, but then she realized how much time had passed since she and Dara had last spoken. The boy jumped into his mother's arms.

"This handsome boy is my dear Jovanny."

Sarai could not help but be in awe. She could see the resemblance, and it reminded her of her relationship with her daughter and how much had changed in their lives as well.

"Handsome doesn't do you justice, Mr. Jovan," Sarai said as she gently pinched his cheek.

Dara then put Jovan down and could tell he was curious about this unfamiliar face. "This is Mommy's good friend Sarai, from long ago."

Jovan stared at the woman and then looked at the people in the other room. "WH-why was that lady mean to you?" he asked Sarai.

Sarai smiled compassionately before giving her response. She adored the innocence she saw in the boy's eyes and the genuiness she heard in his voice. "Well, sometimes perhaps, people are afraid of what they don't understand."

"I'm not afraid of anything!" Jovan said as he did a straight jab followed by a left hook into the air. "Right, Mom?"

Sarai and Dara both chuckled at the same time.

"Bethany, honey," Sarai called to her daughter. "Come meet Dara and Jovan. Actually now that I think of it, you and Jovan share the same birthday. Dara and I gave birth to you both in the same place on the same day. Isn't that crazy?"

Bethany politely nodded in Dara's direction and then went over to Jovan with a smile that seemed to light up the room and put her hand out to shake it. "Hi! I'm Bethany."

In his attempt to respond, Jovan felt an intense amount of goose bumps all over his body. Heat radiated from this girl to him. Peering into her deep blue eyes captivated his very soul. And because he was so young, he could not understand what was happening and could only think of one response.

Run.

Jovan did an aboutface and ran as fast as he could through the small crowd and into the back room where he was staying and closed the door.

Bethany looked up, confused, at her mother.

"So much for not being afraid of anything," Sarai said while looking at Dara.

"Well, I think it's safe to say, at the very least, he has met his match," Dara said. "Don't worry, Bethany. It's nothing you did."

"I know. It's okay. I think he's funny." She followed up with a giggle.

"Forgive me for not mentioning it before, but, Bethany, you are an absolute doll," said Dara. "I cannot believe how big you are. I remember you as an infant, like it was yesterday."

"It's been forever in some ways and a flash in others," Sarai responded.

"How did you find out about us anyway, Sarai?"

"Mrs. Mc...*ugh* ...again why do I keep doing that? Irene, Irene McTenneb. She brought us." Sarai sounded unsure, as if she wasn't convinced Dara knew of her.

"Who?" Dara asked.

"That lady there," Bethany interjected as she pointed out her tutor to Dara. "She's my teacher."

"Your teacher? From school?" Dara asked.

"Nope," Bethany shook her head with arms crossed tightly. "I study at home."

"Like homeschooling?" Dara asked.

"Yes, sort of," Sarai responded. "With an Ivy League prep school professor," Sarai said with a modest head shake. "Not a ton of recess or many friends as you can imagine, I'm sure."

"I'm sure it's a rather incredible education and will be well worth it in the future, no?" Dara added in a comforting manner.

"That's just what my husband says. It's just so different from how I was raised. But even looking back at that, he is probably right. This will most likely work out best for her." Sarai's eyes suddenly welled up with tears. "Can I use your restroom?" Sarai asked as she was noticeably embarrassed to look like she was crying.

"Yes, of course," Dara said as she quickly handed Sarai a small box of tissues. "Down there, past the kitchen saloon doors, end of the hall, on your left."

"Thank you. Would you mind keeping an eye on—"
Sarai then noticed that Bethany was no longer in the vicinity. "Bethany? Honey?"

"Sarai, go do your thing. I'll get her," said Dara, who then began seeking out the little one.

The place was quite crowded with the overwhelming majority being adults. *Where could she have gone?* Dara checked under the dining table and the kitchen before entering the much larger room where most of the guests were mingling. As she went into the room, she bumped into Dayana and Ava.

"Where you off to, slugger?" Ava asked Dara.

"Have you seen a little girl?" Dara asked in a concerned tone.

"*Um,* her royal highness?" Dayana inquired.

"Enough, Day," Dara snapped. "The girl just wandered off."

"Oh, well, she's bound to be here somewhere," Ava said, while looking in some of the same spots Dara had already checked.

"She couldn't have gotten far. No way Jacen lets her leave alone," Dayana said. "What about the Secret Service peeps?"

"And if Jacen…" Dara responded.

"Oh, no way" Ava questioned. "You don't think?"

"Just go check with Jacen please?" Dara requested of the both of them.

Perhaps Bethany snuck off to find Jovan, Dara thought. *After all, she did think he was funny. And there are no other kids their age here.* Dara went toward the back room where Jovan had apparently gone to blow off some sort of steam.

"Jovanny," Dara said through the door. "It's Mommy."

"I told you not to call me that," he whined.

Dara knew that he preferred Jovan or Jo in public but couldn't help herself. *Bethany has to be in there with him.* Dara opened the door to find Jovan sitting on the edge of the bed.

"She's not here?" Dara asked.

"Who?"

"Bethany, of course. The little girl that you were afraid of a few minutes ago."

"I wasn't afraid, Mommy," Jovan responded stubbornly.

"Of course, you weren't," Dara said as she continued to check the closet and under the bed. "Where is she, Jo? This is no time for games. Sarai is worried. We can't find her."

"She's not here!" he answered back in an angry tone.

"Then come out and help us find her."

"Do I have to?" he pouted with head tilted to his right.

"Let's go, now!" his mother said in a stern voice.

Jovan stomped out of the room in front of Dara just as Sarai opened the door to come out of the bathroom.

"There you are, cutie!" Sarai said to Jovan, wiping her eyes and smiling. "Glad you decided to join us."

"Bethany's missing," he said nonchalantly. "Mom doesn't know where she is."

"What? Dara? You haven't found Bethany yet? You should have let—"

"Hey! Don't worry. She's here. There's no way she could have gotten out. It's a small place," Dara responded in an attempt to calm Sarai, albeit nervously.

"I know where she is," said Jovan, but his small voice trailed off quickly due to the loud Christmas music blasting and all of the talking and commotion.

"Sarai, my friends, Ava and Dayana, went to check with Jacen up front."

"What about Mrs. McTenneb?"

"Oh, I didn't think of that," Dara responded. "Is that her over there, with a glass of egg nog in each hand?"

"Mrs. McTenneb!" Sarai called out.

The older lady was dancing, waving her arms and laughing, careful not to spill her drinks.

"Irene!" Sarai shouted again, trying to get her attention.

Mrs. McTenneb had been chatting it up with Malachi, Monique, and others when she finally heard someone calling her name. She turned her head and saw it was a frantic-looking Sarai, attempting to flag her down.

"Coming deary!" she said while moving swiftly toward Sarai. "What is it, dear? You look like Reginald when he needs a snack. He gets all ghostly looking. You look like that, child."

"It's Bethany. I fear she's wandered off, or worse, been kidnapped."

"We checked with Jacen," Ava interrupted. "All clear. No sign of anyone coming or going since you both arrived."

Dara, Sarai, Ava, Dayana, and Irene stood in a semi-circle looking for little Bethany. They didn't want to alarm the room just yet. Because of who Sarai was, they felt it best not to call attention to the situation unless they absolutely had to. In their frightened state, however, they lost track of Jovan, as well. He was in the corner closest to the second room while his mother and friends were closer to the front door. Jovan was sure of Bethany's location.

He was both scared and mesmerized by her. Butterflies of excitement built up within his stomach, and the goose bumps returned once more. What he didn't know in his conscious mind was Dmna, his guardian seraph, had been guiding him toward Bethany's whereabouts and her seraph, Davin.

"There, you see the shadow under the table, like you did earlier?" Dmna whispered in her soft voice, while pawing at her whiskers. "Look at the red tablecloth. It's moving. Why does it move? Go check. Hurry."

Jovan obeyed and went over to the snack table. He lifted the red and white plastic tablecloth, and there she was.

"*He-he!*" she laughed. "I found presents."

"Found her!" Jovan announced to the noisy room where no one could hear him.

"Jovan-look!" Bethany called to him. "There's one for you!" She was doing her best to divert his attention.

He looked toward where his mother was and around the room, and unexcitedly said, "Yeah, I know…socks."

"*Uh*, no silly." Bethany laughed as she threw an unopened package of socks at his leg, also labeled for him, as she still remained nestled under the table. "Those are socks. But this—this box here does not in any way resemble socks."

Having his attention, she pointed to a rather large rectangular box neatly wrapped in Christmas wrapping paper.

"Jovan, this is a big gift with your name written clearly on it."

For a moment, Jovan forgot that Bethany's mother was looking for her and his focus had become glued to the mystery of this gift.

"Oh, snap!" he said. "It's for me. Really?"

"It says J-O-V-A-N right here! Look!" she answered back with a big grin on her face.

Jovan excitedly called over to his mother, and before he could decipher if she could hear him, he ran over to her. He tugged on her cardigan to get a response. "Mom, Mom, can I open my present? Please!"

"Jovan, not now. We need to find Bethany."

She turned her attention back toward the small crowd as he then tapped her annoyingly on the arm. "Mom, can I—"

"No, I said!"

He was desperate. What if this was the spaceship he'd always wanted? Or something else entirely that he wasn't expecting? He needed to come up with something clever to get her to agree to let him open his gift right then and there.

"Mom, what if I find Bethany? Then can I open it?"

Clearly bothered by being interrupted, Dara nonchalantly responded, "Sure, honey, you find her. Then you can open presents."

"Okay, found her." Again no one heard him.

This frustrated him, he was being ignored. "I FOUND HER!" he screamed.

This got the majority of the room's attention.

"What? Where?" Sarai eagerly asked.

"I'm right here, Mommy," Bethany yelled as she peeked her head out from beneath the snack table. "I found presents," she said innocently with a shrug and smile.

Everyone laughed at the adorable reaction. Even those who had no clue as to what had just happened couldn't help but adore her at that moment.

"What was I worried about?" Jamira was heard from the other side of the room.

Sarai ran over to give Bethany the tightest hug. Even though it had only been a few moments, Sarai had not experienced anything like this since having her daughter. "You had me so worried."

"I'm sorry, Mommy," Bethany said softly. "I saw presents and couldn't resist."

"You know," Sarai shrugged and couldn't keep from smiling, "it's not polite to look at other people's gifts without asking."

Bethany released the embrace halfway and put on a pouting frown, which brought out genuine laughter from the two of them.

"Should have known she'd be into the presents," Mrs. McTenneb said.

"Wish I woulda known she was coming," Dara said. "We could have had something here for her."

Sarai let Bethany go back to playing with Jovan, breathed a sigh of relief, and shook her head as she walked back toward Dara. "Trust me. There is no need for any more than she has.

And besides, don't look now, but I think she has finagled her way into opening a gift anyways."

Jovan was now under the table still awestruck by the size of the gift. He came from meager means, so to get a present of this size was eyeopening, to say the least.

Bethany joined him halfway under the table.

"You wanna open it with me?" he asked.

She giggled and nodded in response "Uh-huh."

Ava and Dayana were so enthusiastic; they could hardly wait to see the look on his face.

"Did Jester get this for you?" Bethany asked while grabbing the right side of the wrapped gift.

Jovan reached overhead and dropped the tablecloth down to give them a private moment. "Who's Jester?" he asked.

"You don't know Jester?"

"Come on, you guys! You gonna take all day?" Dayana shouted. "You have the rest of your lives to meander. Chop chop!"

Jovan tore into the gift. Once he was inside of the wrapping paper, there was more wrapping; this time it was brown paper. Another label was on it. It said, "Love Mommy, Aunt Ava, and Aunt Dayana." He ripped the tag off and showed it to Bethany. "Not Jester. See?"

The brand of the gift was now exposed. And his face lit up immediately.

Ava had lifted the tablecloth once she heard the wrapping ripping, so they could watch his reaction.

Jovan was stunned. The spaceship he had wanted so badly but never believed he would get was staring him right in the face.

"*Whoa*! Mom! Look! Look!" he yelled, momentarily forgetting his mother's name had been on the label.

"Let me see, baby," she said, trying her best to match his excitement.

He jumped out from under the table and couldn't help but yell over and over, "I got it! I got it!" Jovan ran to Ava and Dayana and hugged them tightly with each arm halfway around both waists. And, of course, he then ran to Dara and hugged her as well.

"Bethany, look!" he spun around barely able to contain himself.

She giggled and giggled some more.

"Do you know what this is?" he asked her, as if it was the most important artifact in history.

"*Uh, duh*...Who doesn't?" she reacted.

Just then, everything slowed down for Jovan for a moment. He had already been enamored by her, but now that he knew she was fluent in his newly revealed favorite toy, he was in total awe of her.

"Believe it or not, Jovan, I have one, too. And I have the Pirate Flanker Star Cruiser collection."

Jovan was officially captivated.

"Mommy! Can we go to Bethany's? She has Magnustar toys!" he yelled toward Dara.

"Not right now, honey," Dara said. "It's Christmas Eve."

Sarai laughed and added, "Perhaps one day over the next couple of weeks, okay? I'll talk it over with your mom."

Jovan high-fived Bethany as they both said, "Yes!"

For Jovan, this day, this moment was easily the happiest moment he could remember. It wasn't just a toy, or the intoxicating feeling of being around Bethany. It was those things and the closeness of his mother's friends, who were very much like family. And what he didn't know was that all of the seraphs gathered in celebration contributed to this amazing euphoria he was feeling.

"Okay, it's time, everyone!" the young man who had greeted them at the door said. He walked in from the foyer. "Monique, let's get everyone in the front room. It's time to fellowship among each other, celebrating the true meaning of Christmas: our Lord and Savior, Jesus Christ."

"Who's Jesus?" Bethany asked.

"You don't know Jesus?" Jovan asked.

*   *   *

"I still don't understand why she chose me, Lord," Roslyn said to Jaesu as she prepared for her coronation. "I don't see how I am qualified to stand in her majesty's stead."

"And it is that humility that made you such an easy choice for her. Your love for the vast beings on Gardenia has given her great confidence that you will take Gardenia toward greater heights than she ever hoped for," Jaesu answered.

"As usual, her majesty holds me in higher regard than I deserve. I am so very sad to see her go. She has been such a life source for us," Roslyn said while the final touches of her gown were being completed. She wasn't used to being the one fussed over and didn't quite know how to stand still and do nothing. Young souls brushed out her hair, fastened pearls around her neck, and slipped jeweled shoes on her feet.

"Indeed, I will also be saddened, Roslyn. Amana has been the dearest of friends to me. My last journey with her to the Endostream will surely be bittersweet. But for you, I have faith in the queen's choice to name you as her successor. I eagerly await the great things you will accomplish for Gardenia and the entire galaxy."

"Lord?" Roslyn inquired once more. "When I asked the queen what she relied on in her decision-making, she insisted that her relationship, trust, and guidance from you trumped everything. Will you be there for us when I become queen as well?"

With a smile that could melt an iceberg, Jaesu responded, "Of course. And although I would never overrule you or force my ways upon you, I will be there for you and your people whenever asked. I truly look forward to building greatness with you, young queen."

Many dignitaries from throughout the galaxy thronged the gardens and lawns outside of the royal palace. Majestic animals walked among them: great cats, wolves and horses. Everything looked beautiful. The trees were adorned in leaves of pink and white, colors that symbolized beauty and purity. The green grass shone as if it had been polished and the sky was a clear, singing blue.

Phan and Eleanora, in their disguises, had arrived with the delegation from Alpha. It might have been easy enough for them to blend in, even if they had not been incognito as there were so many beings, creatures, and courtesans of kings and queens in attendance. Amana was one of the most revered queens, not only of her day, but of all time.

The entire galaxy was gathered to hear Amana's final speech to the masses and to be introduced to the newly crowned and unknown Queen Roslyn of Merlot Forest. Many were ready to discuss the attire chosen by both queens, how they had behaved toward each other, whether Amana came across as happy or thoughtful, and whether or not Roslyn looked the part.

Orion and Grace were ensuring that security was tight around the perimeter of the planet. Since Orion's destruction of the previous asudem attack, to their knowledge, none had attempted to enter the Elevemada.

"Doesn't this seem a bit weird to you?" Grace asked Orion.

"What?"

"One of the most popular queens is passing on her crown to an unknown, and no one is even attempting an attack?"

"You know, Grace," Orion replied laughingly, "I have been known to be quite unstoppable."

"Anyway," Grace said, shaking her head. "It sure doesn't look like anything is imminent, but we should stay focused nonetheless. I just don't trust it."

"I hear ya, but there is nothing around, nothing at all. Our scouts haven't seen or heard anything," Orion said in response.

"What about the fact that Amana isn't taking you with her to Earth?" she asked. "Doesn't that concern you? I mean it's a bit risky having no protector. If Khrimson ever found out that she was leaving, especially leaving without you, he would send Soren to smash the Stream to keep her from ever getting to Earth alive."

"Soren? Wow! That's a name I have not heard in eons," Orion said.

"Well, he is good at what he does. I don't know. It's just weird. I can even smell the evil. Something is wrong," Grace said.

"Relax, kid," Orion responded. "Nothing to fret about. If we see an enemy, we will take him out. It's that simple. Don't get worked up. My emotions are already jagged with the queen leaving—and leaving me here to protect Gardenia and her new queen."

Grace nodded in response. Something didn't seem right, but maybe that was a part of her adjustment from life on Algolithar, a leftover paranoia from being a slave to the evil Phan. Perhaps she should listen to Orion, who'd been guarding the planet for so long. Besides, there weren't many that had such a powerful sidekick, so what was she worried about?

Queen Amana walked out onto the platform before a crowd of several hundred thousand. She did not have the loudest voice, but the owls around would feather her words with their wings, giving the effect of natural amplification so that the masses would hear her every word.

The crowd roared at her appearance. She wore a pale blue robe, her signature color, and had a crown on her head for the last time. The cats of Scepter were all with her, standing in a wide circle around her, both for protection and effect. Black stood closest. Amana grazed her hand over the cat's head, her slim fingers moving through the thick fur. Black felt both her strength and sorrow.

The queen moved to the front of the platform as Black stood directly behind her:

"My friends and fellow citizens of the Galaxy, it has been the greatest honor any being could have ever asked for to be queen of what I consider the most amazing world in the universe, my beloved Gardenia. This galaxy, in itself, is quite wonderful. To leave this behind is not a decision made in haste, but it is a choice I know deep down we are all meant to make at some point. I have wrestled with what I should say to you today. It has taken my entire existence from the beginning until now to reach this moment of choice. How can I put it simply?

"Have you ever asked yourselves 'Why am I here?' or 'Why was I created?' or 'What is the purpose of it all?' or 'How can I rid myself of this void?' I have often asked myself such questions. But usually the answers seemed to be far greater than my mind could comprehend. And like many before me, I accepted that I was created and did the best with that. All this time would have indeed been a waste had I not had the chance to know our great Lord Jaesu. To walk with him and know him has been magnificent—and I don't use that word lightly. To know his love, which encompasses compassion, honesty, patience, humor, no record of wrongdoing, and so much more is something I know Earth needs.

"At no time did Jaesu ever force his will upon me or manipulate politics in order for me to go in his preferred direction. He has allowed me to grow as a leader by encouraging me to make decisions and has loved me unconditionally, regardless of the result. That is a beautiful love. Our Great Father created us for a reason, a purpose. It wasn't in vain. It wasn't so he could have more servants because he already had millions of seraphs and angelic beings for that. He obviously wasn't lonely. But he desired to create beings with freewill. His greatest joy is to share all that he has, as the infinite resource, with us: all of us. That is why Evermore was created. It is a place of infinite abundance shared by the Great Father, our Lord Jaesu and the Blue Fire Spirit.

"We were not created just to exist. We are here to find out who we are by the consequences and circumstances of our choices and build upon that in order to achieve our fullest potential. But none of us can do that successfully alone.

"My peers and friends, I tell you this: I would not have been the ruler that I am today without Lord Jaesu. Do not take such a *relationship for granted. It is that reason that I choose Roslyn of Merlot Forest, the Lady of the Woods, to succeed me as queen. It is her unconditional love for this world and utter humility that is needed in a king or queen. I ask that you give her the same loyalty and respect that you have given and shown to me over these many, many great ages.*

"*As I introduce our next queen, I leave you with this: trust in Jaesu, be good to one another, and let no one ever take your crown.*

"*Black and the cats of Scepter, a special thank you for being my eyes and ears. And friends, I could not have done this without you. I trust that the new queen will be able to say the same. And with that said, may I introduce to you the new Queen of Gardenia—Lady Roslyn of Merlot Forest!*"

Roslyn, adorned in a flowing, pink gown edged with a ribbon of her trademark dark red, walked out escorted by Jaesu. The applause was strong yet considerate. Amana greeted her with an emotion-filled hug and smile. When the crowd quieted, Amana removed the crown from her own head and placed it upon Roslyn's. She then took two steps backward and went down on one knee as a sign of respect and loyalty for the new queen. The audience was mesmerized by this and joined her in bowing. Scepter did not move from the new queen's side. Roslyn turned toward Jaesu and bowed to him. As she rose, the crowd followed. Roslyn took this moment to address the galaxy and, more importantly, her own planet.

"*Gardenians, dignitaries, Queen Amana, and Lord Jaesu, I am honored to accept your support as queen of this wonderful world. Although I do not deem myself royalty, you all have my pledge to rule with the peace and joy that our beloved Queen Amana started ages ago. Your Majesty, you certainly see more in me than I could ever hope to see in myself. I admire your leadership and trust in your selection. You honor me, and I will do my best to live up to your trust.*

"Lord Jaesu, I welcome your counsel and guidance unconditionally. Help me to be the leader that I am called to be.

"And to my people: I love our world with the entirety of my heart. From the trees to the waters and from the creatures to, most importantly, all of you. We are truly blessed. The beauty of Gardenia is unmatched throughout the universe. I ask you to help me to lead and keep it so. No matter what our differences, and what obstacles we face, I firmly believe that, if we work together and love one another, then there is nothing we will not be able to accomplish.

"I want to thank our great protector Orion and Grace, his sidekick, for their continued defense and guardianship of our safety. It is your courage and strength, Orion and Grace, that allow us the peace to build a society that respects our differences and fits us together like pieces of a grand puzzle. It is easy for any of us to take our security for granted."

The audience started to applaud as Roslyn stepped back and offered a soft nod of respect toward the great protectors, who were able to carefully monitor events on the ground via hologram.

"There are many things that I want to share with you, but those can wait for now. Our greatest queen, Amana, is ready to ascend toward the Stream and into the morphing process to take that greatest journey to Earth."

Amana bowed to the crowds and gathered the cats from Scepter around her, hugging them all. This was it. It was time to go, and this was going to be harder than she had anticipated. Amana, upon releasing the lions, placed her hand on Queen Roslyn's head and spoke a blessing. She then held on to Jaesu's robe and began to glide up into the sky toward the mountains where the Stream was. To the naked eye, this process was immediate, but to those making the journey, time slowed down. The crowd rejoiced, jumping up and down and celebrating Amana's reign and choice. There were many tears. The trees and mountains bowed in respect to her as she faded away into the distance.

Roslyn looked to the sky. Once she saw Amana vanish, it finally hit her that she was queen. She had stepped in for Amana in the past, but this was different.

King Handel then raised his voice loudly for all to hear. "As our gaze is caught by our former glorious queen, our hopes and dreams now rest with the new sovereign, Queen Roslyn."

Many did not understand why such a mighty king would say something so humble. "That is certainly a noble and yet curious thing for King Handel to say. Quite out of character for him," someone from the crowd remarked.

Black, always observant, noticed small orange dots in the sky. "Your Majesty? Do you see that?" she whispered into the queen's ear.

"Yes, I do," Roslyn answered, "What …oh, no …GET DOWN! EVERYONE GET DOWN!"

The dots were quickly revealed as fireballs headed toward the planet's surface; it was like a meteor shower. The crowd was frozen in disbelief for a few precious seconds, and then fell into a panic. Souls and animals were running and flying in various directions, getting in one another's way. Some were roaring in anger. Then the fireballs hit. There was screaming and crying and the smell of scorched leaves. Trees, for the first time in the world's history, were introduced to fire and were burning. Explosions burst all around. Although the souls were not badly hurt by the fire, the grass, trees, and creatures were. Even the waters were becoming contaminated quickly.

Phan, noticing that the masses were in disarray, transposed himself into his normal form, knowing that no one would bother with him as long as the panic lasted. He shouted to Alina, Legatious, and Denacta. "Now is our time! It's time to go! Legatious, you and Denacta, as I have commanded, must find the Lighted Blade in the tall grass by the Royal Gardens. It is the strand of grass in the middle shining with blue fire. Alina, get the queen alone and destroy her. Take her crown and transpose yourself into her. This is it!" He looked up and saw a battle in the sky. He had stationed millions of Caultresses there.

Caultresses were asudem, not battle-hardened, but great archers with the ability to become invisible for a short time. That time had now ended. He knew that Orion could see them, and he would dispose of them quickly.

"It's time for me to destroy a legend," Phan whispered, as he shot into the sky with great quickness toward Orion.

Orion and Grace, both hit by the sneak attack, were doing everything they could to get back on course and eliminate the enemy. Grace, small but fast, had a unique ability to boomerang and bounce off her enemies, one to another. As she was taking out asudem, Grace yelled back at Orion, "Listen, the soultles won't affect *you*, but they will hurt the souls on the surface; do not let them get those off!"

"What in the world are soultles?" Orion shouted as he fought off the infestation of archers.

"You know how they are firing fireballs? Well, that's only the beginning. Soultles are iron meshes that can cause intense pain and induce temporary paralysis in souls. They can be lethal."

Grace was holding her own, and as usual Orion was dominating. At this rate, they would have this side of the globe cleared out within minutes. She then heard a voice in her ear. It was Amana's soft whisper, almost like a child's. "Don't forget about me, Grace."

Grace thought for a moment. "Oh, no! The Stream! Soren!" and raced toward where the Stream left the galaxy and headed toward the Milky Way.

"Where are you going?" Orion called out.

"The Stream! Queen Amana! I will be back as soon as she is safe." Grace moved as quickly as she could.

Orion knew she was right to go help the queen, and she was probably also right that he could handle these asudem on his own. They were much easier to fight than normal asudem. Several hundred thousand had been disposed of already. Orion would take a quick glance every now and then at the surface, only to see fires and flames everywhere. He was very angry, sad, and desperate to stop the damage in the sky so that he could get down to Gardenia and help. He thought about the new queen, Scepter, and a host of other things. He felt another archer climb on his back and he turned around to blast her.

BAAAM! Orion felt a detonation off of the side of his head. He was knocked into a daze hundreds of yards away from his post. He didn't even see what hit him. *WHAM!!* Another shot and he flipped over several times. Orion had never been tossed around like this before. He felt a huge iron grip around the back of his neck. "Notice anything familiar yet, old friend?"

That voice was familiar. It could only have been one person: Phan. *But how?* Orion thought.

"Now watch as my angels unbridle hell on your pathetic world."

With Grace gone and Orion no longer impeding the progress of the Caultresses, the archers loaded and shot out thousands of soultles toward the surface, as Grace had said they would.

Orion couldn't speak as Phan's grip jolted immense pain through his neck. He was forced to watch the fires and listen to the screams from the souls on Gardenia.

"You see?" Phan said. "You fools fell for everything. Now I will rule over you, and there is nothing you can do about it. And, powerful Orion, your carcass will be long feasted on by the ravens from Algolithar as they infest this land and destroy every living thing. There is no hope for you now." Phan laughed arrogantly and looked upon the remaining asudem, who were continuing their fire-and-soultles campaign.

Orion was shocked at Phan's power; he had never been this strong in the Elevemada before.

"Oh," Phan laughed, guessing his thoughts. "Don't tell me, you actually thought I was weak in this place? You are a dim one. We played you like a fiddle."

CHAPTER 11

Seven are One

Sarai lay awake. She was exhausted, weak, and cold to the point of shivering. It had been two days since Dara's party, and she couldn't help but relive those enjoyable moments over and over again. She could see and feel it vividly. As she relived it, she also could hear the children's laughter and conversations. There was a peace and joy between them that seemed timeless to her, as if Christmas were the greatest secret of the universe.

Having Bethany changed Sarai's entire life. Up until the birth of her child, she had been depressed, sad, and directionless. She still vividly recalled her own childhood, the days when she would get calls from local tavern owners to come get her mother at two and three in the morning. This had happened almost every night. Her father had hardly ever been around, always working. She didn't have many memories of him, just a deep feeling of longing. He had passed away years before, yet she wished, for a moment, that she could introduce him to his granddaughter.

Sarai had raised herself, in many respects, and whenever she looked back on her life, she had regrets. A wedding to a Crowmire man should not have been possible, yet it had happened. But the riches, fame, and luxuries were nothing. It was the gift of Bethany that was the true blessing. The everyday events that most took for granted—going to the store, shops, beaches, and the like with her daughter—were what really mattered. It wasn't about being able to buy whatever she wanted. In her youth, Sarai had believed that having money would make an enormous difference, that nothing could really hurt her if she were rich, but the more she was around Bethany, the more her attitude changed. Even with her husband hardly ever at home, she was happier than she had ever been, yet now she was vulnerable.

Sarai felt a lump in her throat as she reflected on a recent conversation she'd had with Phyllis.

"I find it disappointing that you would embarrass this family as you did, Sarai," Phyllis had said. "It's like you don't think your choices have any ramifications."

"How can you accuse me of something like that? I go to great lengths to ensure that I never put our family name or reputation in any sort of vulnerable state."

"*Our* family name? *Hmm* … and the great lengths you speak of are taking a taxi and paying with cash on your way to a Christmas party of all things?"

"How—"

"Oh, puh-leeze, Sarai …Do you honestly think anything gets past me? So naïve. And it's not your fault at all. I knew this from the start… if only my son had listened. I'm not even going to go there. Just explain how this could happen." Phyllis then handed Sarai a miniature tablet with pictures of Sarai and Bethany at the gathering on Christmas Eve. There were several pictures. None of them showed her in a compromising position, except for the Christmas decorations and themes in the background.

"Where did you get these?" Sarai asked.

"Great care you say? You don't think the paparazzi are everywhere watching our every move? Any idea how much we are going to have to pay for this to never see the light of day?"

Sarai paused for a moment. "Is this about money?"

Phyllis let out a sinister laugh while pouring a couple of drinks. "People in our position don't pay with money. I thought you would have figured that out by now. Money is far too trivial a thing. The folks we deal with expect to get paid with information, or favors, or legislative changes, perhaps an endorsement for president, that sort of thing. Did Mommy and Daddy not teach you that in the docks of Washington?"

Sarai never could quite fit in with the Crowmire family. Even though she had conformed to the way they lived, she always felt like an outsider. Sarai had grown up in Washington. Her family was lower middle class. Her father had worked the docks at night, while her mother worked part-time as a cashier in a fish-market.

Phyllis hadn't ever really been welcoming. She was too sophisticated to fight her son or treat her daughter-in-law badly, but that was not the same as being genuinely gracious—that was only something that Sarai had imagined in the first few minutes after they met. She had so wanted to be liked …to be seen as someone precious.

This recent conversation with her mother-in-law was
no different than many of the others from the past, but for
whatever reason, it haunted her more. She continued to ponder
it, remembering how Phyllis had made drinks at the living room
bar, bringing one over to her as a sort of a peace offering.

"We really shouldn't be fighting over this, Sarai. I am sorry
if you feel I was offending you," Phyllis said as Sarai accepted
the drink. "It's been a long couple of days for us. We see things
differently, that's all."

"Thank you," Sarai said. "I guess I still don't understand why
going to a harmless Christmas party would really put the family
in harm's way. After all, it wasn't a public gathering, and it shows
that we aren't above the people, you know, the voting public?
Wouldn't you want them to see us in that light?"

"You are so adorable sometimes, Sarai," Phyllis responded
while filling her own glass again. "Like the votes count anymore?
Doris Forsett has been voting for my husband for over thirty
years now. You think anything we do is going to change her
vote?"

"Well, I would think—"

"Doris has been deceased for forty years. When we need the
votes, we buy them. Not from the people but from the powerful.
And to answer your question regarding the party, it makes
us look bad because frankly, we are above it all. Not just the
commoners but the holiday itself. It's time that our country and
world embrace and accept the notion that we waste precious
time and resources on such events that ultimately divide us. That
is what we hope to achieve— true, perfect unity."

"Isn't it good for people to be different and unique and have
complimenting beliefs?"

"Ask those under the rubble of the World Trade Center, or those buried beneath today's storefronts in Baghdad or perhaps those on the streets of Pakistan where rapes and murders of the innocent are part of cultural acceptance." Phyllis stopped speaking for a moment and took a deep breath as if she was very torn by something.

"What's wrong, Mother? Are you sick?" Sarai asked in concern.

Phyllis, with an emotionless look on her face, responded, "I'll-I'll be fine. You may not see it right now, Sarai, but everything I do, I do for that beautiful daughter of yours. The world is a dangerous, perilous place, and we must do everything we can to pave the future for her."

"There's nothing more important to me in the whole world than her future."

"Then please learn to trust me," Phyllis answered in return. "My methods may come across to some like you as highhanded perhaps, but I assure you, our means are tried, true, and resilient."

"I do trust you, but I need that in return."

"What I trust is that you believe you are doing the right thing by Bethany and this family. But my perception is also that you are not ready for this position, which my son so recklessly placed you in. You have a long way to go yet before you earn my trust. I don't believe that you can handle being a duchess in the Crowmire family. If we are to talk trust, then answer me honestly, are you ready? Am I right?" Phyllis asked.

"I'm not sure what you are getting at. I love Alcee and have been devoted to him the entire way. I am a good wife and an even better mother," Sarai said, upset.

"What about a daughter?" Phyllis countered. "That's a part of your place in this family! Is it not? And do you consider yourself a good daughter in this family? If not for my son, do you honestly believe that you wouldn't still be some café slob whose entire life financial portfolio is determined by a minimum wage salary and some coins from a tip jar?"

"What does my past have to do with any of this? I have given up my life for this family and do my very best to be a good daughter to you and Mr. Crowmire. What more can I do to show you how honored I am to have been chosen to be a part of this family?"

"Nothing. There truly is nothing more I would need to see. But truth be told, because of that background, I don't see you as a fit for Alcee or this family."

"I can't believe I'm hearing this!" Sarai said as her emotions began to heat up. "This makes no sense coming from you. You and your husband have made a legacy of helping those who have struggled. How can you call Dara—or anyone—a peasant?!"

Phyllis erupted in laughter. "Oh, my dear. Now it's you who mustn't be serious. We use those public gestures to increase our power and support. I suppose you think that my friendship with Lyanne is legitimate as well?"

Sarai was very confused. "*Um*, yeah…"

"Rubbish, silly girl! She is a vehicle, like so many others I use to appear gracious. Have you not learned anything by being a part of this family?"

"What are you trying to say?"

"I'm not *trying* to say anything," Phyllis replied boldly. "Let's cut to the chase here. There are two types of people in this world: those who are elite and those who are born to live in the mud."

"That's ridiculous. All people deserve respect. Anyway, I believe our choices ultimately dictate our circumstances and destinies," Sarai answered. "My parents didn't have the most impressive purse strings. They could have never imagined me in the life I have now."

"And for good reason!" shouted Phyllis. "Because much like that friend of yours Dara, and that moocher Lyanne, you would be nothing more than a tramp, if it weren't for my son's irresponsible ways, shacking up with the first redhead he ran across on his travels."

Sarai had no response. A lump in her throat formed so fast she couldn't speak.

"Oh, yes, I know your secrets, the harlotry of your youth. My son was a fool to bring you home. You are a one-night stand and nothing more. He was meant for royalty, not for some no-name piece of dockworker peasant trash like you. I know you try your best. I know you do. But you were born beneath us, and beneath us is where you'll stay!"

That conversation happened earlier in the day, but as if it were a powerful magnet, Sarai felt it tugging at her, making her relive it again and again. She shivered as the memory persisted. Sarai, still exhausted to the point of feeling faint, could hear the echo of strange laughter. She remembered after the confrontation with Phyllis when she had been driving to run errands for her husband, the tears which had flooded her face. Thoughts like, *What if she is right? What if I am a harlot, unworthy of good things?* had crept into her mind and now had a stranglehold on her. Sarai again heard the laughter and remembered hearing a woman whisper, "He's meant for my sister, not you, feeble entity," and again the laughter and her car spinning out of control.

Earlier in the day—hadn't it been? This day? She heard Phyllis again, calling her a peasant and a harlot and then felt her own tears fall as she got in the car. Putting it out of her mind, planning the evening meal, a sudden sleepiness …then laughter …the car spinning …memories of her entire life flashed through her mind with great speed from the first to the last. It was as if they were all speaking to her at once.

Then everything stopped. The shivering, the cold, the damp feeling, the exhaustion… completely halted. She could move. She felt lighter and different. There was no breeze or heat, just quiet all around her.

Even though her eyes were still closed, she could feel that this was an unfamiliar place. She slowly opened her eyes and saw that she was in a room. The floors, walls, and ceiling were patterned in black-and-white checkerboard. It was dizzying. There were two locked doors in front of her, checkered in the same manner. There was also a door behind her, cracked open slightly. Each of the doors had a name written on the top. The language was familiar to Sarai, but still she could not read it. In between the doors was a small table, and sitting behind the table was a white skeleton with a black beanie wrapped around its cranium. There were no other people or decorations in the room. *Where am I?*

"Welcome to the Chamber of Choice, Sarai," said the skeleton in a surprisingly friendly voice. "I am Ul-Jalil, servant of the Grim Reaper. I await the key."

"*Um* …should I know what that is?" asked Sarai.

"Soon you shall," Ul-Jalil replied. "Each person works their entire life to forge their own key. The key will fit one of the two doors ahead."

"I don't understand," said Sarai. "Are you saying I'm dead?"

"No, not yet," Ul responded. "But you will be... once that door behind you closes."

"What? What about Bethany? My daughter? What happened? Where am I?"

"Your reaction is not uncommon, Sarai. Now that you are in the Chamber of Choice, you must resign yourself to the fact that you will never see your daughter again on Earth. Right now you are lying in a cold, muddy ditch on the side of the road because you lost control of your car. Help is on the scene now, but while you are breathing, you are comatose. By the time they get you to the hospital, you will likely be at the end—at least, at the end of your journey on Earth," Ul-Jalil explained.

As he expounded, everything became clearer to her. From memories of her home world of Seocia to the reasons she made her choice, to Jaesu, Owls and Seraphs, all the way through to her days on Earth. She even remembered her choice of seraph: Radak, the rhinoceros man. "Where is Jaesu? What happened to Radak?" she asked as it felt like a million questions were forming in her thoughts.

"Radak accompanied you the entire way. Over time, based on your decisions and influences, his own influence on you became smaller and smaller. By the time you were an adult, he was the size of a grain of sand and mostly unknown to you. As for the other questions, we will have to wait on those," Ul-Jalil answered.

Something was being created in the middle of the room directly in front of the skeleton. It was comprised of sounds and moments from her past. She could see a large key. Sarai then heard a click behind her, confirmation that the door had been shut, and if Ul-Jalil was correct, her life on Earth had officially ended.

"Well, that should just about do it," Ul-Jalil thought aloud.
"It looks like the next phase of your journey is about to begin.
Behind me are two doors. To my right and your left is the
doorway to Hadnessa and to my left and your right, the doorway
to the majestic Evermore—or, as you would say on the Earth: Hell
and Heaven, respectively." The key completed its formation and
presented itself to the skeleton. He, in turn, handed it to Sarai.

"What am I to do with this?" she asked.

"You know. Based on the choices you have made, your true
desires have shaped the key," Ul-Jalil answered. "Just position the
key into the lock and whichever one it opens, such is the place
which you have chosen to be your home, forever."

"It doesn't take a key to figure that out. I already know I want
Evermore!" she yelled.

"Yes, it would seem so. But our choices and actions are
greater than our words in many cases. Those are the true
decision makers in life," Ul-Jalil replied.

Sarai was now nervous. The shivers were returning and were
even more intense. She went over to the door that represented
Evermore. As she approached the door, memories came back to
her of how close she and Jaesu had once been. Times when they
had laughed and walked while discussing eternity were recalled.
She then remembered the times when she was younger and had
yearned to find him on Earth, remembering eventually giving up
that search, turning to the materialistic ways of Khrimson and
the world. Her love for Jaesu had still persisted, but she knew she
had become dispirited by life's difficulties, eager for any form of
comfort and warmth. Then in her shame—and maybe anger—
she had made an effort to forget about him.

She put the key in and it would not turn. This did not surprise her now. Still, she was broken-hearted. She whimpered as she removed the key and slowly walked toward the other door. Ul-Jalil had seen this many times before but even he, a being with a heart of stone, couldn't help but pity those sentenced to Hadnessa. She placed the key into the lock, slightly turned it, and felt a soft click. She knew the key fit but couldn't bring herself to turn it any further.

"Young one," the skeleton sighed, "just turn it. Stalling doesn't change the key's destination."

Sarai thought for a moment. She knew she didn't want it to be this way. She looked back at the door she had come through. "Is that door locked? Does it have a place for a key?" she asked with passionate desperation.

"That door does not have a lock for a key. It just closes," he responded.

To his surprise, Sarai yanked the key from the lock and ran toward the door that had closed behind her. She grabbed the knob in an attempt to open it.

"No!" Ul-Jalil shouted. "Sarai, you can't! You must not!"

She pulled open the door and was met with a huge wind fighting against her to close the door. There was no place for her to step out; it was entirely black. It was not possible for her to fight against this wind much longer. She screamed out as loud as she could, "JAESU! OH, LORD JAESU! PLEASE REMEMBER ME! I PLEAD! SAVE ME! PLEASE DO NOT ABANDON ME!"

Her strength gave out as the wind overcame her and the door slammed closed. The black-and-white squares rearranged themselves over and over at an extremely high speed. Ul attempted to grab onto one of the knobs to keep his own balance. They continued to move faster and faster until Sarai was eventually overwhelmed. She couldn't keep up. Her head was spinning. Everything went black.

*   *   *

By the time the EMTs got her transported to the nearby hospital, she had already passed away. She did not go without a fight. To their amazement, minutes after she had been pronounced dead, she fought to breathe once more and even barely speak before eventually dying again. Sarai had lost control of her vehicle while driving down a winding road. There were many questions, but nothing could bring back Sarai, Bethany's mother, Dara's friend, Alcee's wife, and a loyal member of the Crowmire family who perished at the tender age of twenty-seven.

*   *   *

The fires raging in Gardenia were ferocious. Never before had this planet felt such cruelty. Aside from the fiery archers and the soultles traps, newly crowned Queen Roslyn and the Scepter cats were also fending off raging attacks from Legatious, Denacta, and Alina, who were no longer in disguise. The three asudem were focused on finding the Lighted Blade and destroying it. Annihilating anything else in their path, although not a priority, offered immense gratification. Alina had an additional target in mind: the crown upon the queen's head. She wanted to take that for her own.

Alina had a unique power. Cold lightning could shoot out from her hands, seeking out fire wherever it was and freezing it. Once frozen, an object would explode due to the strange mixture of the fire and cold lightning. This was especially dangerous for those on Gardenia now, as flames and fires were everywhere as animals scurried for shelter any place they could find it.

"WHERE IS YOUR QUEEN? THE COWARDESS!" Alina shouted. "WHERE IS SHE?"

When no one answered, she quickly snagged a badger that had attempted to find shelter among other creatures, screaming again toward it, "WHERE IS THE QUEEN?"

The badger shook nervously and didn't know how to answer. Alina crushed its skull, and Gardenia saw something it had never seen before: death.

The trees screamed and mourned the badger instantly, as well as screaming in concert with their many fellow trees and plants that were burning and suffering in agonizing pain.

Pastel saw what happened to the badger and leaped forward toward Alina, attempting to claw her face off. But she was no match for the asudem princess. Alina caught the lioness and tossed her toward nearby jagged rocks.

Pastel would not stay down. She would have made another attack, but before she could move, Alina formed the lightning from her fingers into a lasso and began to strangle her.

Daffodil joined the fray and jumped on Alina in order to break her hold on Pastel. Once they were both on the ground, the cat tried to claw Alina's face, but the evil princess had anticipated that move, and with great speed jumped around the large cat and leaped vertically into the tree above.

She was now completely hidden from the cats. Alina believed she could win, even though there were two of them. What she didn't know was that behind her, lurking in the tree, was the lioness, Tree. The cat in hiding catapulted herself over the back of Alina's neck and snapped it forward, forcing them both to hit the ground hard. Alina, completely caught off guard, was both angered and dazed.

All four combatants slowly brought themselves to their feet.

Black was with Queen Roslyn watching this unfold. The timely battle between the asudem and the lionesses allowed them safe passage into the palace. The palace was impenetrable, meant to be a haven of refuge during times of war. Considering that Gardenia had never known war on its surface, no one knew how strong a fortress the palace would prove to be. Nevertheless, creatures, animals and souls alike began to flood into the palace for safety. Roslyn watched to ensure those in the area who could make it did. She called out encouragements and made sure the doors were wide open until the last little animals and young souls were inside. She was aided in this by her prodigious knowledge of the creatures of the forest. She knew which ones would be able to reach their dens and burrows easily and which wouldn't. She kept track of those who didn't show up, who were probably too terrified to move. She paid even closer attention to the battle almost directly in front of the palace. She knew, if the asudem could not be stopped, it was only a matter of time before all would be lost. Roslyn also knew the cats could only delay the asudem and an attack on the fortress temporarily. She looked around at the wounded piling in, the burnt trees and grass, the carcasses lying motionless in the field; they were like a heavy fist on her heart. Her home world was being destroyed before her eyes, and even though she was now queen, she was powerless. She felt *more* powerless being queen.

No, that's wrong. "Black, I have an urgent task for you," she called toward the big cat.

"Yes, Your Majesty?" Black was by her side at once.

"Go find Malvin the Owl. Get him to find a safe haven for the bucks, does, and other creatures unable to make it to the palace. Many of them will be hiding close by. His wisdom should be very useful. And then …" the queen paused for a second. "This will not be easy, but there is no other way, and we must move swiftly. Find the other two asudem who were with this one, ensure that no matter what, they do not get to the tall grasses surrounding the Lighted Blade."

"Your Majesty?" Black asked curiously. "Is a strand of some rogue grass worth it? Traditions and landmarks have their places, but I don't think for battle."

"It was once said that if the queen and the Blade were destroyed, then Gardenia would fall into darkness. Maybe that is true and maybe it isn't, but either way, I don't want to find out."

"And what about you, Your Majesty?" Black asked.

"Don't worry about me!" Roslyn responded sharply. "I know what I must do. We must move now!"

As always, Black did as she was commanded. Her devotion to discipline made her especially strong and allowed her to keep her head during crises. But she was used to protecting the queen, not abandoning her to danger.

Malvin had already made his way into the palace. Black immediately sought him out as the queen had commanded. Black could hear the owl as she entered into the palace's main chambers.

"MalBird," Black called to the owl.

Only Black called the owl by that name and only when it was serious. Malvin heard her and left the company of the refugees near the back chambers of the palace.

"Yes, Black?" Malvin answered nervously.

"Don't ask questions and follow me discreetly," the cat grumbled.

It was well-known that Malvin was afraid of his own shadow. This was another reason Black was so curious. She wouldn't dare disobey the queen, but a choice like this seemed reckless to one of Black's experience. She led the owl into a secret passage in the palace that would take them both to the roof. As the long-time right hand of the queen, Black knew the palace in and out, even more so than the new queen.

When they reached the rooftop, they were behind the Minabla. The Minabla was a massive tree formed out of marble. In the sunlight, it looked like water over diamonds and sparkled amazingly during the evenings. Black cautioned the owl to remain unseen behind the tree as she knew the battle between Alina and her fellow cats would still be going on. She did not want to give any indication to the enemy that a plan was in the works or that the queen was unprotected. The lioness couldn't help but notice what had happened in the battle. Alina was surrounded by the three Scepter members, but all looked weakened.

"Mighty cats!" Alina shouted. "You have proven your prowess. We should not be fighting. I am here for one thing and one thing alone—your queen. Hand her over to me and I will spare the rest of Gardenia."

The cats refused to answer her. To them, it would be a betrayal to even acknowledge such words.

"Oh, come now!" Alina continued. "You don't even know this queen, do you? Would such an attack have ever happened under the powerful Queen Amana? Face it! Hand your queen to me, and I will be doing Gardenia a service. And when I am done with her, I will take the crown and be the rightful Queen of Gardenia. Then there will be peace, as in the days of Amana. If you choose to help me now, I will not forget. But if you choose to stand against me, then once the inevitable happens, you will be skinned alive …slowly, for my amusement."

Pastel, Tree, and Daffodil looked at each other as if they might consider such a scurrilous act. Black saw this, and her impulse was to leap into battle herself. She was concerned as to why her sisters' countenances had changed. The ferocious scowl they normally displayed in any competition was absent. It was as if they were trying to talk themselves into the belief that maybe the asudem's rule would not be so bad.

Malvin whispered into Black's ear, "I don't know if you see anything, but it looks like there are bad things happening. I think it's wisest to wait this out in the palace."

"Not so fast," Black whispered sharply. "You see the mountain southeast of the palace and the battle? Well, we need to get over that quickly. You must get to Merlot Forest. The animals there will have no way of getting to shelter. Find them and get them to Scepter's den."

"*Umm.…* Yeah, but there seems to be a lot happening. Let's wait this out," Malvin urged.

"Look," Black replied, "you are going to die!" Black let that seep in for a moment. "Yes, that's right. And so am I. But others will be spared. The queen chose us specifically for this mission. You may not have the courage to do what you need to do, but she has deemed it so. Therefore, trust in your queen."

"But …she be a new queen, no?" Malvin asked nervously. "How can you trust a new queen?"

"Malbird!" Black whispered back. "I am told that queens see what we cannot and have wisdom far beyond our own understanding. To date, I have never seen that proven incorrect. Many of our friends will be slaughtered if we don't act. Gardenia is counting on you. This is far greater than any Owls and Seraphs tournament. Now, let's get going before we are noticed."

Malvin remained silent, gathering courage from what Black had explained. He was scared, but there was a part of him that felt proud to have been selected by the queen for such a mission. No one had ever selected him for anything. "But what about you, Black? What is your task?" he asked curiously.

"Oh …don't worry," Black said, as she could see with her own eyes the kind of power even one asudem was capable of. "I am chosen to do the impossible. Like I said, be ready to die."

As they began to slowly move away from the battle, Black hesitated slightly to see what her sisters would do. What she feared was impossible to accept.

"Still no answer, young felines?" Alina asked mockingly. "Perhaps it's that you cannot speak. I will make it simple. Bow before me! Kneel and acknowledge me as your queen, and we shall rule Gardenia and eventually the entire galaxy together."

The lionesses began to take a step in unison toward her. They then, in one motion, lowered themselves toward the ground. Black could not believe her eyes. Alina looked at the cats and waited for them to complete their bow. They eyed her; she had angered them as they had never been angered before. They roared and pounced, attempting to take her out of the battle in one shot. Alina, although surprised, responded instantly. With an easy flick of the wrist, she lightning-lassoed the three of them and began to strangle them using her immense asudem power. This frozen rope lightning was geared to numb the senses, dulling the mind and eventually the entire body until death. Their strength was being drained from them by the second. The harder they fought against her, the more strength was drained.

Black screamed, "NO!" without any thought that she was giving her location away.

Malvin, alert to the situation, wrapped his left wing around her mouth and, with all of his strength, flapped his right wing to fly toward the nearby mountain, carrying the large cat.

Black wasn't making it easy on him; she was struggling wildly. Seeing her sisters in danger brought out an instinct in her that even she didn't know she had.

Malvin was hideously nervous about his task. Flying through arrows of fire from the north and trying to remain unseen from the asudem fighting the lionesses, while trying to contain a grasp on Black and fly with one wing, would be enough to make any bird ready to fly to the nearest nest and crawl into an eggshell.

Malvin tried to keep Black from falling as they flew, and attempted to sing a chorus or two to calm their nerves. This only seemed to frustrate Black more. Reaching one of the mountain ledges nearly out of breath, Malvin dropped Black off safely.

"A song? Really? Seriously? Did you not see what is out there?"

Malvin had never seen Black like this before. They were further away from the battle, so they could be louder, but still, she usually was the voice of reason. No longer. She seemed to be in a panic. "*Um* ...I was being ...bold and following your orders, great cat." Malvin shook as he spoke. "Many lives depend on us, you said ...and I know they need us." He looked at Black as a child looks to a parent.

The lioness took a deep breath. "Malbird, you are right. I am scared we will never see Gardenia as it was, or our friends again. Since when did you become the bold one?"

"As Queen Amana used to say, 'The greater the level, the greater the devil,' right? I think we have that part figured out, no?" Malvin replied.

"And many more to come, I'm sure. Malbird, you are all right, kid. Get to that forest and get our people to safety. While I, on the other hand, must concoct the crazy of crazies. Now go!"

The owl took off right away toward Merlot Forest. Black had to come up with something. There was no way she would be able to withstand two asudem on her own.

* * *

Grace was near the edge of the galaxy's Endostream and believed that she had pinpointed Amana's location. The queen had morphed into the seed of a human infant. This process was quite delicate. Asudem often tried to bombard the Endostream from the outside in order to disrupt the process. Sometimes they were even able to destroy an entire seed so that it never made its way to Earth's system. Most times, the seeds got through unscathed. But when asudem targeted one in particular, they were usually successful in inflicting significant damage. Grace's ability to identify Amana's seed was crucial. She saw her counterpart, Soren, speeding toward Amana from a great distance.

Soren was her equal in stature and abilities. Like her, he had a knack for moving quickly and bouncing off objects at a high speed. Neither was very big, but both packed a powerful punch. She raced toward him. "Are you lost out here, brother?" she called to Soren.

Soren, arrayed in orange and charcoal gray, responded but did not take his eyes off Amana. It was very easy to lose sight of a seed going through the morphing process. "*Ah*, if it isn't the traitor. I believe it is you who is lost, sister."

"What makes you say such a thing, Soren? Can't a girl tour the galaxy from time to time?" she mocked.

"You must take me for a fool," he marveled. "We are both here for the same reason. You are here, I bet, to safely escort the queen, while I am here to destroy her. It is I who will succeed in my task, of course."

At that point, Grace had to make something happen in order to break his concentration. She picked up speed in an effort to knock him off course. Soren nonchalantly dodged her attempt and maintained his focus.

"Nice try, Pity. Perhaps you were more suited for chains. This is no place for you," Soren said, still intensely studying Amana's path.

Grace did not allow that to deter her. She studied the Stream to see if there was any pause in the flow of seeds. She didn't have to stay focused on Amana, she could use Soren's focus against him.

The Endostream was protected by the force of life. It had a covering more powerful than iron or any stone. It was invisible, however. Grace reasoned with herself that if she could find a break in the Stream, she could utilize her speed and ability to bounce and use the Endostream as a springboard. She had to be careful not to harm any of the seeds in the process, as that could have had dramatic ramifications on the souls making their journey to Earth.

She found what she was looking for about two hundred meters behind Amana's seed. This was going to be risky, because if she left to try bouncing off this spot, she would be giving Soren a free shot at Amana. But she had to take the risk. She didn't believe she could win a head-to-head battle with Soren.

She cannoned herself toward the Endostream. Carefully, she positioned herself to use it as a springboard. Soren saw her from the corner of his eye—sprinting away from him, which he found confusing—but he didn't take his eyes off Amana. He knew the moment was coming to annihilate her. He planned to crash into the Endostream head-on at the exact moment she passed. With Grace out of the picture, he was not going to get a better opportunity than now to wipe out the queen. Soren fired himself toward Amana's seed. He knew he wouldn't get to it head-on, but he could smash into it with enough force to do permanent damage and possibly kill the seed carrying her. He picked up speed and could clearly see the seed.

BAM! From the side, Grace smacked into Soren, sending the two of them away from the stream. Soren looked around, confused. He had completely lost sight of the seed. He was now battling against time, he knew the seed wasn't far from the end of the galaxy. Once out of the galaxy, the seeds were home free.

Soren space-swam toward the Endostream and tried to pick up where he'd left off, but to no avail. The queen was long gone.

He was seething with anger. He also knew that Khrimson did not accept failure graciously. Soren raced toward Grace and pummeled her across the black nothingness of space. He refused to let her go, smashing into her again and again with the force of a locomotive.

Grace was completely helpless and shell-shocked.

Soren charged toward the Endostream. Logic told him that
he could end both of them with one crash into the Stream and if
Amana was still in there then he, by chance, might succeed if he
crashed in front of Amana.

They gained incredible speed as they raced toward the
Stream.

Grace was dazed from his blows and, at first, could not resist.
Coming to her senses, she realized that she was in Soren's grasp
headed on a collision course with the Endostream. She ducked
her head and prayed that Amana was no longer there.

POW! The two collided full force into the Endostream's
strong covering. This sent a surging quake throughout the
stream. Neither could say for certain if Amana had made it out
of there in time, but they both knew that any seed near the crash
would be affected for the duration of their journey on Earth.

The crash immediately separated the two and shot them
thousands of miles apart in opposite directions.

Soren's attempt to destroy both of their lives had failed.
What he hadn't taken into account was their ability to bounce.
Crashing into an object did not hurt either one of them.

Grace looked around and saw no one near. She was confident
that she could find her way back to Gardenia. She hoped that
Amana had gotten through the Stream safely, but she couldn't
say for sure. She needed to get back to Orion, who could still be
fighting.

*　　*　　*

Legatious and Denacta were opposite the Royal Gardens,
making their way toward the tall grasses. Their plan was to burn
all of the grasses around the glowing blade of grass considered

the Lighted Blade, ensuring its destruction as well. Once the task was done, they were to meet up with Alina and overrun the remainder of Gardenia. This duo was very dangerous, as evidenced by the smoldering fires throughout every place they had walked on the planet so far. Beasts of the field had been burned alive, and once great trees were now nothing more than ashes. Both Legatious and Denacta had the ability to send fire from their hands as well as manipulate it, meaning that fire would have no effect on either one of them. Their bodies were made to take in fire and order it to do what they desired.

The scene was frantic. Souls and beasts tried their best to find avenues of escape. Even the waters, which normally barraged the shores, began to back down in fear.

"This has been far easier than I would have expected, Legatious," Denacta chuckled.

"Just stay focused on the Blade. That's all," Legatious ordered.

"A piece of grass? Seriously? We should be up there waging great battles against Orion, not gardening," Denacta scolded.

Legatious smacked his fellow knight in the back of the head. "Pay attention! You ever wonder why no one has ever invaded this planet? Doesn't it scare you? Or, at least, give you pause? We have gone further than anyone else ever has."

"No!" Denacta said. "This place is pathetic. With their bunnies, cats, deer, bear, foxes, trees—look at them now, all dead or in hiding. No one has invaded this place because of false legend, Orion and a queen who hid behind Jaesu—none of which are impeding us by any means."

Legatious pressed on. He saw hundreds of grassy rows that went on for miles and miles. "Look!"

"Look where?" Denacta asked.

"Over there! Where the light is shining in the grass!" He smacked him on the head again. "Didn't I tell you to pay attention?"

"Oh …look, it must be the Lighted Blade," Denacta said as if he were the one to point it out first.

Legatious rolled his eyes. "Let's go and get this over with." As he walked through the tall grass, he noticed Denacta wasn't moving. "What's wrong now?"

"Oh…nothing, I see no need to walk through hideous-looking grasses." Denacta then flung out both of his hands, shooting fire beams and destroyed every patch of grass remaining. Not one blade was left, except for the Lighted Blade. "See? My way is always better."

The asudem made their way toward the Blade. Denacta had expected it to burn up like the rest of the grass and was a bit uncertain as to why it hadn't. Legatious, on the other hand, had seen more battles and knew to expect the unexpected. He was on the lookout for a possible ambush while also wondering if the piece of grass standing was a fake. It seemed too easy.

Denacta fired again toward the lone standing grass, to no avail.

"I guess the first time wasn't good enough," Legatious mocked.

"Well, you try something, then," Denacta answered back.

"I am," Legatious responded. "I am walking there to investigate it and figure out how to destroy it."

Denacta was not very patient and badly wanted to destroy the blade of grass in order to get the credit. He again shot fire at it, but nothing happened. Everything around the standing grass was consumed by the fire, but not the Blade.

"Just be still, will ya?" Legatious said in annoyance. "We're coming up on it now. Be ready for anything. Birds, fish, traps— anything. Something this legendary isn't supposed to be easily destroyed."

"Boss, it's a piece of grass," Denacta said in return.

"Just a piece of grass?" Legatious looked at him sideways. "Behind you are about million pieces of grass burned to a crisp and before you stands one that is immune to fire. Just a piece of grass? I think not."

Legatious went up close to the blade, but still could not find the source of its light. He was puzzled. Denacta walked right up to it as well, attempting to yank it out of the ground.

"What are you doing?" whispered Legatious.

Denacta could not budge the grass, but he felt a vibration in his hands that caused him to step back.

"You wish to remove us, do you?" the grass spoke.

"Legatious …it's speaking," said a suddenly concerned Denacta.

"I told you to expect the unexpected," Legatious shot back at Denacta. Then he turned his attention to the Blade. "Why, yes …we would like to remove you and be on our way. Can you assist with that?" Legatious was not convinced that the Blade was speaking. He thought it was a trick.

"One is seven and seven are one, when six have gone, war has begun. Answer us this riddle, to show us your worth. Answer it wrong and be forever bound in Earth," the Blade said again in multiple voices.

"Riddles?" Denacta said with a smile. "Oh, I like riddles. Okay."

"I'm not quite following ya, grassy," said Legatious. "Is there a hint to go with that?"

"Whoever removes us is of us and must be the inception and the last BUT cannot be the beginning or the end. If this be you, then who are you?" the Blade asked.

"I was hoping for 'roses are red, violets are blue,' or something like that," Denacta responded.

Legatious rewarded him with another smack to the head. "I will speak here, idiot."

Denacta backed down and gave way to his partner.

"The answer is simple. I am Jaesu," Legatious answered.

A sinister laugh came from the Blade. "A wise answer and yet unwise. Lord Jaesu has commanded that he be not allowed to remove us. However, it is also blasphemy for you to say you are he if you are not. Should we destroy you now?"

"No, wait," Legatious backpedaled. "I was testing to make sure you could hear our answers. One more chance."

"Very well. We shall give you two more," the Blade answered.

"The Blue Fire Spirit," Legatious answered.

"Again wise and again unwise. And again... blasphemy," the Blade responded. "Need we remind you that one more false answer and you will be as the dust of the stars?"

Legatious was very cautious because he had seen no indication of trickery or a trap. He still wasn't convinced, but needed to find a way to destroy this riddle-filled fireproof weed. "What will happen to you if we answer incorrectly?" Legatious asked.

"A wise question. Now a wise answer. We will be locked in and irremovable," the Blade replied.

Legatious began to pace and Denacta looked around. It was dark now; only the flames of the burning trees gave any light. Legatious was unsure if they would get another shot at this and did not know how to proceed. He was lost. Denacta noticed something coming toward them.

"Look, someone approaches," he said.

A small being was alone, walking toward the two asudem. "Do you believe this, Denacta? Something must be off. Every living soul and creature is fleeing our presence, yet she walks right toward us."

"Should I burn her?" Denacta asked.

"Of course not. She is harmless and may know something we don't," Legatious answered.

The girl continued to walk toward them but was not stopping. It was as if she was drawn to something and oblivious to their presence.

"Little one, would you be so kind as to help us remove this piece of grass?" Legatious asked the girl.

She silently turned her head toward him and grinned softly, brazenly touching his cheek before continuing her walk. She stopped directly in front of the Blade and began to speak.

"Lighted Blade of the stone, Lighted Blade of the sea, Lighted Blade of the sky, Lighted Blade of the tree, Lighted Blade of the Scepter, Lighted Blade of the pawn, Lighted Blade of Blue Fire … Lighted Blade …I am …Dawn."

The Blade began to move around and spoke again. "We know that voice, master." The piece of grass plucked itself out from the ground and split into seven. All seven pieces began to spin round and round and then the seven became one. But as they reformed, the Blade was no longer grass but a fiery blue sword.

The sword faced the two asudem and screamed, "Blasphemers!"

Legatious and Denacta attempted to run, but the sword was too fast. It caught them and smote them within half a second. Immediately, the two asudem were piles of dust.

The sword reached down and, with the tip of its blade, flung the dust miles away into the Endostream and sent them forever into the sands of Earth where they would feel the pain of heat and drown in the sea and be walked on throughout eternity, as they had walked over innocent Gardenians. The sword returned to Dawn, the hilt sliding into her right hand. "We are ready, master," it spoke.

Dawn's appearance changed. She became slightly taller, more captivating, her hair like Dara's: long, spiky, and pink. Her eyes were as blue as Bethany's, and her mouth was laughing and proud at once. She felt a confidence she had never felt before. As the only remaining member of the Lighted Blade left on Gardenia, she was the only one with the authority to remove it. And it could only be removed in times of war. This was certainly one of those times.

From out of shadows walked Black, flanked by Crystalline, Waves, and Clouds. "Thank the Great Father that worked," she said to Dawn. "Wow! You really look like quite the warrior. You should see yourself."

Dawn walked over to a nearby pool to get a glimpse of herself in the firelight. She was not surprised at the difference. Her face was basically the same, and her thoughts were her own, but she felt different. A boldness had come over her that had never been there before. Her mind felt like it was growing by the second. "If it weren't for you, I don't know if I would have gotten here in time," she said to the head lioness.

Black had known all too well what the asudem were capable of and that there wasn't anything that could be done against them directly. She remembered Amana sharing with her the tales of the Lighted Blade from the book *Days of Old and Times of Battle*. Dawn also was aware of the Blade's legend, but was unaware of the asudem's plan.

"With those two out of the way, Malvin should have an easier time getting the beasts of the field to shelter," Black said. "The barrage of fire arrows and nets continue, however. If only there was a way to combat that! I imagine that Grace and Orion have their hands full, or else by now whatever force is unleashing such horrors on us would be destroyed."

"Follow me!" Dawn said as she took off through the air with great speed. The cats were left in the dust and lost sight of her right away. To her surprise, she moved at the speed of light and got to her destination in little time.

Dawn shot up to the peak of Scepter's mountain. She saw the arrows coming down and could actually focus her eyes, with vision like Jacen's, and could see the archers firing through Gardenia's atmosphere. She focused even closer in and perceived their eyes and behind them. There she saw Orion, unconscious, the great Phan standing over him. Grace was nowhere to be seen.

Dawn continued to focus on Phan, and her gaze became stronger; she could now read his thoughts. She saw that his plan was to destroy Orion and to have Alina take over as queen while she enslaved Gardenia.

That was all Dawn needed to see. Instinct took over as she raised the Lighted Blade above her head and stood on the peak of the mountain. She shouted as if she were Bethany, "In the name of Jaesu …magnetize!"

The arrows raining down upon Gardenia shifted direction and flew toward the sword. Every last one, whether it was a soultle or a flame, turned toward where Dawn stood.

She did not move. She stayed until every arrow had joined the Blade. The Blade absorbed each arrow and then returned it to where it had come from with a mighty wind. The archers, totally unprepared, were wiped out and dissolved by their own flame and net. All of the caultresses were eliminated completely.

Dawn knew something of importance was happening to her, but this wasn't the time to look for answers. She was concerned with whether Malvin and the animals had gotten to safety.

*　　*　　*

Alina had overpowered the cats. They'd fought hard, yet failed to become anything more than a mere distraction. But defeating them wasn't enough for her. She was forcing her will against theirs; vengefully, she desired to strip them of their dignity. She was breaking their collective spirits. Alina would not be satisfied until they fell upon their faces and worshipped her. The cats fought, but she was too strong. It was only a matter of time.

"STOP!"

Alina spun around. There, standing on the steps of the palace, was Queen Roslyn. She looked different than she had during the coronation. Her crown was still on her head, but she was wearing a gown more suited for combat. It was black, gray, and her trademark dark red. Green rose vines were wrapped around each arm, and her hands were large roses.

This piqued Alina's curiosity. "How nice of you to join us, Your Majesty," she mocked. "But you cannot be serious. Some deer herder from the woods is going to challenge me?"

"Leave them be! It is me you want," the queen replied.

"Why should I do that? I am winning."

"If you defeat me here and now, then you will have earned the crown. But if I defeat you, then you leave this place and only return upon pain of death," Roslyn answered.

Alina smiled and relinquished her grip on the lionesses, all of whom collapsed. They would be no help to Roslyn here. Alina turned viciously toward the queen. "You are a child. You know nothing of these battles. At least, your pets could entertain me for a while. You will be fodder for the same creatures you long to protect by the time I am through with you."

Roslyn did a three hundred sixty degree turn and unleashed a rose petal toward Alina. This petal flew like an arrow and wrapped itself over Alina's face, blinding her. The strong scent of the rose was soothing to the cats, acting as a subtle healer. They were still weakened and in extreme pain, but it was something. The petal was also extremely sticky. Alina was having a hard time removing it, although she soon would. Roslyn had to act quickly. From her palms shot out several thorns that pierced the petal and then Alina's face.

"*AGGGH!*" Alina screamed in pain as she ripped off the sticky petal. She could feel the air blow through the holes in her face. Wounds from battle did not heal if one was a seraph or asudem. Her once gorgeous face was now deformed and hideous.

Alina was in severe pain and embarrassed to be outwitted by a child, queen or not. "ENOUGH!" she shouted as she fired a soultle net at Roslyn. The queen could not evade it and was trapped, writhing in agony.

Alina put her ice grip on Roslyn to ensure she was completely paralyzed. "Little witch! How dare you deface my beauty! I will slaughter the beasts of this world and devour them myself before your eyes as you lie helpless like the slave that you are." Alina looked even more ferocious with the holes in her face. She looked at Roslyn and slowly removed the top of the soultle from her head and face. She wanted the crown. She spat on the queen and ripped the crown off from her head. "Now I am queen."

Roslyn's body was paralyzed, but her face could move. "Lord Jaesu," she whispered, "If you can hear, we need you. I ...tried to take it on ...without you. Forgive me. May my reign ...only continue by your will."

Suddenly, the Blue Fire Spirit came upon the queen, rendering the soultle powerless. Roslyn began to stand.

"This is impossible!" Alina shouted. She went to use her ice whip, but noticed something odd. Her hand and the crown that she had just taken were on the ground. She was without a hand. It had been completely severed from her body.

She saw a sword flying away from her and heard a new voice say, "Magnetize." The crown was lifted from the ground and went flying behind Alina. She turned and saw Dawn with the Lighted Blade firmly in hand. Malvin the Owl was on her shoulder with Black and the remaining Scepter cats behind her. Thousands of bucks and bears stood their ground behind them in defense of their queen.

"You are outnumbered, Alina!" said Dawn.

Alina was shocked at the turn of events. She couldn't get her hand back. She had lost the crown and realized that she had also met her match. It came upon her that Legatious and Denacta were defeated as well. She thought to herself, *Who is this warrior and how does she know my name?*

"I know your name because I have seen your master's plan and have seen you devise it in his mind. Needless to say, you will not be queen today. I am the servant of the Lord Jaesu and bow to one queen — Queen Roslyn. You can go now, as vengeance and violence are not the ways of this world. But rest assured, should you return, you shall meet your end."

Alina slowly backed away and ascended. In a cowardly manner, she went in the opposite direction from Phan so that she would not have to account for her defeat.

Alina turned around and asked Dawn, "Who are you? If I may ask?"

"I am one of the seven Lighted Blade members and its keeper. I am Dawn."

"Well, Dawn, I will return, and when I do, it shall be your end!" Alina said as she rose higher into the skies, "Oh, and, Your Majesty?" she said to the queen. "You may have a crown, but you will never be a real queen. Just like an owl. If he has wings but cannot use them, then he is no owl, just a pathetic life form."

With that, she used her other hand to ice-lightning Malvin's wings off of his body. He screamed and fell off Dawn's shoulder. Everyone ran toward Malvin.

Alina used the distraction to lasso up her missing hand. She then shot up and vanished from Gardenia, from Dawn and, more importantly, from Phan.

Chapter 12

Legacy

"Amen," was Reverend Jacobson's closing remark at Sarai Crowmire's funeral service. It was all that Bethany could remember. From the point when she was first told of her mother's sudden and tragic passing, through the condolences offered by friends, family, and strangers, everything was a blur.

Bethany was numb and in shock. To her grandmother's surprise, she hadn't even wept. It wasn't that she didn't care for her mother—Bethany and Sarai had shared a deep emotional bond. Still, she was unable to cry or display much of a reaction. Maybe it was because of the gentleman sitting to her left during the services: her father. Bethany loved her father, but he was rarely home and the two of them hadn't spent much time together. He worked hard, but to her, it seemed more like he was always trying to escape. Bethany was extremely perceptive for her age. It was not easy for anyone to pull the wool over her eyes.

The wake and funeral had come and gone quickly. There were literally hundreds of people who sent cards, flowers, and well wishes. Bethany felt quite uncomfortable; everyone was talking about her and what would happen to her.

It was the day after the funeral. Her grandparents lived in an older, luxurious estate called the Baaladine (pronounced bella-dean). It had been a part of her family's history for generations. The mansion was well-known in Montclair, New Jersey. Although Bethany enjoyed visiting her grandparents, like most young children, she preferred her own home. She hadn't been there since she received the news of her mother's accident, though.

The Baaladine had twenty-six rooms, many full of priceless antiques, others containing the newest gadgets and electronics, not to mention a huge pool and an attached recreational house within the backyard that spanned acres. There was a formal garden with statuaries, a tennis court, and a wide terrace where the adults could have cocktails. Bethany had plenty of toys and room to play, but this wasn't a playful time. She had no desire for fun. If anything, the statues and gargoyles throughout the estate, which she once had barely noticed, now seemed menacing.

Davin never left her side, not even for a second. He continuously mourned for Sarai and tried to comfort Bethany as much as he could. Although the child had not shed a tear, Davin could see how excruciating the pain was.

The house was flooded with family members; most were folks whom Bethany had no recollection of. She heard the whispers: "Has she cried yet?" and, "She's only seven; she couldn't possibly understand death."

If only. Bethany was feeling the horror of death more deeply than any adult ever could. Her wide-open child's mind was grappling with the immensity of it, trying to understand how her mother could not exist. It was a mystery too big for the human mind; her being a child had not stopped her from facing it. Only adults turned away.

It annoyed her to hear the grownups make such ridiculous assumptions. At this moment, they seemed to be blind and deaf, to be moving through the world like puppets. She was hurt, angry, sad, along with a host of other emotions that a child should not have to experience. Nothing could quell her pain or get her to speak much to anyone, although she would have spoken if she'd had even the faintest hope that anyone would understand.

Mom! She said in her mind, but Sarai didn't answer. Yet her mother was there, stuck in the past—speaking, hugging Bethany, alive as ever …in her past.

Bethany clung to the memories, but they confused her as well. How could someone just stop? Did that mean it would happen to her? The world was not what she had thought it was. Though she would never let anyone see, she was very, very afraid.

There was enough catering to feed an army and barely enough space to breathe. The family housekeeper, Nevada Cerventes, periodically checked on Bethany to see if she was okay. Bethany would give an expected head nod and pretend she was busy.

Nevada was in her early forties and had been a housekeeper for the Crowmires for over a decade. Her family had served the Crowmires for generations. She was a kind woman, but she had too much to do. Sarai had always taken care of Bethany.

"Any luck cheering up the muted princess, Davin?" said a female voice, filling the room with laughter. Davin could not see anything, but the voice was a familiar one to him.

"Come on out where I can see you, Anjelica!" he said sharply.

"Oh, such a pity …here I thought we could play Owls and Seraphs or Hide and Seek like the old days, my prince," said Anjelica, again laughing.

At that moment, a spirit being came out from beyond a statue of St. Augustine in the far right corner of the room. Anjelica was a powerful and formidable asudem knight. She wore a long, light blue gown with red rubies and golden jewels on the bodice and had long black hair. Slowly, she walked toward Bethany. Bethany could not see her or Davin, of course, but she would be affected by their conversations.

"You've come far enough, Anjelica. You have nothing to do with Bethany," said Davin.

"Oh, the mighty protector speaketh," mocked Anjelica. "Somehow I can't seem to feel my fear rising. I wonder why. *Hmmm.* I guess because I'm fearless and crazy. Wouldn't you agree, darling?"

"Anjelica," Davin responded, "we both know you don't want to battle me right now. So just keep your distance. Besides, why are you even here?"

"Perhaps you are right, my sweet," she answered, knowing that Davin was in the prime of his strength and could inflict some damage on her, though she was quite powerful herself. "Another time then?" she said with a sarcastic laugh. "And Davin, it's I that should be asking you why you are here. Besides, I hate hiding in my own house."

"Your house?" he asked, surprised.

"Oh, come now. Don't tell me that you didn't know that I've been roaming this estate for years," she replied. "The Crowmires and I have had quite a history. As sweet innocent—for now— Bethany will find out one day soon."

"THAT'S ENOUGH, WITCH!" Davin shouted in righteous anger. "You have no claim to Bethany. And until you do, I suggest you bridle that tongue before I give it a home far from here."

"I wouldn't dare trespass against the mighty Davin," Anjelica mocked again. "Bethany, it's okay not to listen to him. I never do. And keep holding back those tears, darling. Ya gotta prove you are strong enough to be a Crowmire."

This angered Davin more. As he reached out to grab hold of Anjelica, she vanished, laughing with a *ta-ta* echoing throughout the chamber.

She was gone for now, but Davin knew he would have a battle on his hands soon enough.

The second day after the burial mirrored the first from Bethany's viewpoint. More visitors and more time at her grandparent's mansion, more catered lunches and more flower arrangements along with maddening pats on the head from distant relatives. It was getting exhausting for the youngest Crowmire. She had hoped her dad would whisk her away from this drama, but it had not happened. Nor was she allowed to stay in her bedroom. Her grandmother had made sure she was up, dressed, and downstairs, so no one would think anything was more wrong than it was.

With no children her age around, Bethany took to listening in on the conversations around her. She was far too young to understand why something like eavesdropping would be frowned upon, and even if she had known, she would not have cared.

Nothing mattered now, except keeping a fragile hold on her emotions. Her mind was still wrestling with the permanence of death, the injustice and the terror of it.

Her father showed up now and then but mostly seemed to have found his own place to hide. Folks paid their respects to Phyllis and, if he was around, Josephus.

It was early afternoon, and the estate was already covered with masses of people. What Bethany found odd at this particular moment was that her grandmother was not in the front hall greeting guests as she had been for two days. She also wasn't in the kitchen making sure the servants were doing what they were supposed to. Instead, she had secluded herself in a small room at the back of the house that she sometimes used as an office. Bethany was in the next room, the library, and could barely make out what Phyllis was saying, but it must have been of some importance as she was speaking softly to a gentleman who was unfamiliar to Bethany. The granddaughter crept closer to the office door, trying to be unnoticed and yet hear what was so important.

"How is she, Miles?" Phyllis asked the taller man wearing a sleek charcoal-gray suit. He had on stylish glasses, which blended in nicely with his short brownish-gray hair. "Has she suffered any permanent damage?"

Nonchalantly, the man answered, "She is in stable condition, and aside from some slight brain trauma, I'd say she will be okay."

"Brain trauma?" Phyllis questioned in surprise, with her hand over her heart. "That doesn't mean that we—"

"No!" he replied, rolling his eyes. "Everything is under control and as planned."

"And this brain trauma nonsense?" Phyllis asked impatiently.

"Nothing for you to worry about," the man calmly said in a low tone.

"Miles, dear Miles, you of all people know and should appreciate how much I worry," Phyllis said while checking a nearby brown antique end table for any hint of dust.

"Mrs. Crowmire, I do. Of course, I do. I normally would not want to alarm you in the least, but if you need to know, then let me assure you that some scar tissue required, shall we say, some refurbishment. And of course, everything is as it should be," Miles said, while averting his eyes toward a younger lad entering the room, attempting to join the conversation.

"I trust you, Miles. You are without a doubt elite at what you do," Phyllis said, also turning her attention toward the lad. He was tall, with a mixture of brown and blond hair and held a striking resemblance to Miles. "And who might you be, young man? I don't believe we have been introduced."

"We have, many years ago, ma'am," he replied.

"You're not—" Phyllis responded with her eyes squinted which revealed her curiosity.

"Indeed, it is my oldest, Marcus," Miles interjected. "Several holiday gatherings ago, it has been."

"Well, I am sure your mother must be beating the girls off of you, Marcus. Miles, you didn't tell me what a handsome young man your son has become."

"And a highly regarded med student, if I am allowed to brag about him," Miles said while placing his arm around Marcus. "However, I believe his interest far transcends medicine, and although we disagree on topic at times, I couldn't be prouder."

"So another Dr. Morgansau in the works?" Phyllis asked as she glanced at the young man with a trivial smile and nod of approval. "What fascinates you beyond medicine, Marcus, if I may?"

The young man looked at his father before responding, as if he was awaiting permission.

"Go on, son," Miles said noticeably embarrassed at his son's lack of response and even more uncertain regarding what Marcus might say. "It's all right. Mrs. Crowmire is one of our closest confidants and clients."

"I like the unexplainable, Mrs. Crowmire," the young man said in a gentle but confident manner. "Those places where medicine and science haven't yet connected the dots, like the mind, are what keep me up at night. You asked what fascinates me. It's something like Carl Jung's thoughts on the ancestral archetypes and how much we give up on researching just because we can't comprehend something. Like this astronomy professor, who I consider brilliant, at a lecture once exclaimed how amazing it was to watch the creation of a galaxy."

At this point, Marcus became more animated with his hands and began to pace somewhat as if he were hosting a lecture. "He talked it up with such passion and excitement. He couldn't say for sure much about its origin but was certain it wasn't created by any sort of being because his eyes saw nothing and logically that was enough to disprove it. Now, don't get me wrong, I am not saying science is wrong, but there is enough unknown to warrant more discovery rather than make the same mistakes the old church made with Galileo. Okay, now that was a lot. I'm sorry. I tend to ramble."

Flashing a beautiful smile his way and a subtle laugh, Phyllis retorted, "I appreciate your honesty, even if it sounds a bit more religious than I would have hoped."

In a panic, Marcus attempted to respond. "Don't get me wrong, Mrs.—"

"Marcus, ease up," Phyllis answered while placing her hand on his shoulder. "I may not agree with your positions to a degree, but that does not mean that I should not respect them. Therefore, don't apologize for what you believe. One day, you will discover one of two things. Either you find something that none of us could have comprehended, or you just find that we all were right. Regardless of which, those are paths we all must face." She turned his shoulders so that he would face her courtyard window where many were gathered outside of it. "You see that young man who is almost your age? The one with the platinum hair?"

Both men could easily see the person she was referring to. He was easily the youngest person in the courtyard and although walking by himself, seemed to enjoy moving from conversation to conversation. He didn't stay in any one place for long and held a clear wineglass with water inside.

"That, my dears, is Jacen Alvarez. My daughter-in-law attended a party of his quite recently. He is what we used to call a 'holy roller.' Marcus, the two of you should chat it up one day."

"I'm no—"

"No apologies, remember?" Phyllis winked toward Marcus. "Boys, sadly, I believe my granddaughter is getting bored in her attempts to eavesdrop, so I must get back to working the crowds. Thank you both for coming, make yourselves at home, and in case I don't bump into either of you, let me say that our family is grateful for the relationship that we have with the best doctor, or should I say, pair of doctors, in the United States."

With that, Mrs. Crowmire kissed each one of them on both cheeks and moved toward the kitchen area. "Oh, and, Miles," Phyllis said as she continued her walk, "I expect to hear from you soon on our...patient."

Bethany slowly crept back down the stairs, knowing that her cover had been blown. Although she was unable to decipher much of the conversation, she couldn't help but continue to listen in on the men as they left.

Marcus looked on curiously and waited until Mrs. Crowmire had exited the room. "What did she mean by that?"

"Just a patient, son. Just a patient. Pretty soon, you will have the chance to take over for your old man in regards to such high-profile clients," Miles said while fidgeting with his wristwatch in a fairly nervous manner. "We should get going if you want to catch the Glynn Anders fight tonight."

"Dad, what's wrong? You seem a touch off."

"I have a patient on my mind. It's really nothing more than that."

"This same patient that Mrs. Crowmire cited?"

"No, no. The patient I alluded to earlier while we were coming over here."

"The one with child? What about her?" Marcus asked as he opened the front door as the two were leaving the mansion.

"I once asked her to consider..."

And with that, the door closed and the two men were gone from the home. Bethany could no longer hear them.

"Listening in on other people's conversation is exactly what I would do if I were in your shoes," said Jacen Alvarez, a community outreach worker.

"You scared me!" Bethany responded.

"Me? I couldn't scare a crow," Jacen said while attempting humor by mimicking a frog face.

"You're funny," giggled Bethany.

Jacen did what he could to bring a smile out of anyone he met. He knew what kind of medicine laughter was and felt it important to bring a moment of joy to folks during their hardest times. He got down on one knee to talk with Bethany on her level. "I saw Dara and Jovan at the service today. Did you?"

Bethany shook her head. Most of the family was heavily guarded with limited exposure to guests.

Jacen was seventeen years old and loved to help around the church. He had been accepted to college on a theology scholarship and was a good friend to most. He was allowed to attend the after procession due to his being a former student of Mrs. McTenneb.

"Mr. Jacen," Bethany asked nervously, rubbing her eyes, "can I ask you something?"

"Yes, Bethany, anything," he said.

"Is …is Mommy always gonna be in that box?"

Jacen knew exactly what Bethany was asking. He also knew that getting into a philosophical discussion with a seven-year-old who had just lost her mother wouldn't be prudent. "I can tell you this, Bethany; your momma is up in Heaven with Jesus, dancing with angels."

"Where is heaven? Who's Jesus? Why not Jester?" she said, tearing up.

"Heaven is a beautiful place that we, if we're fortunate, go to once our journey on this Earth is finished. One day, you will see your mom again. And you'll be able to dance with her."

Bethany was slightly comforted at the idea of Sarai dancing with angels, although she still didn't understand why her mother had to leave. Mommies were supposed to stay with their children. She had more questions for Jacen, but didn't get a chance to ask them.

"Hello. Nice to see you today …Jacen, is it? I didn't see you come in with all the commotion. Forgive me," said Phyllis.

"Oh, no worries, Mrs. Crowmire; I was checking in on Bethany here; my prayers and condolences to you once again. How are you holding up?" Jacen asked somberly.

"Bethany honey, would you get your father and grandfather out of the study and let them know our guests are piling up? Thank you, sweetie," Phyllis said.

She waited for Bethany to scurry along before she continued. "Don't take this the wrong way, Jacen, because I'm going to be direct. I'm not entirely sure what my daughter-in-law's wishes would be regarding Bethany's religious upbringing, but I would appreciate it if you kept this talk of Heaven and angels and Jesus to yourself when in the presence of my family. We pride ourselves on being well-educated. Using faith as a crutch is, quite frankly, not our style. Bethany is now to be raised as we all were in this family. Feeding her illusions of heavenly protection won't help her. I understand you have your beliefs and a job to do, but that is all it is as far as I'm concerned. There is no Heaven nor Hell or God or Devil—just people."

Jacen was not taken aback or surprised by her comments. Times had changed and such concepts had become more common than faith in an invisible being. "I understand, Mrs. Crowmire. I meant no harm." He nodded his head and was about to step toward the exit, but then he came back toward her. "So the way the moons revolve around Jupiter, or how Halley's Comet comes every eighty-something years like clockwork, or the beauty of the seasons, the depth of emotion, unique fingerprints and teeth, the complexities of our anatomy, the way DNA splits and rejoins—this is an accident with no meaning?" he asked, keeping his tone respectful.

"We are what we make of life. If we must have faith, it should be in our own selves; in a sense, we must be our own gods and light our own paths, dear," she said, as she gently placed her hand on his arm. "Now, if you'll excuse me." She smiled and walked toward the hall where the majority of guests were gathering.

The second day had come and gone.

*   *   *

On the third day, the house was like it would be on an average Saturday. No crowds or media gatherings, just the Crowmire family and housekeepers. Bethany could smell breakfast cooking and hear her grandmother and her father talking in the kitchen as she walked down the wide staircase, holding onto the polished bannister. She decided to stop where she was on the steps, sit down, and listen in.

"Mother, I don't quite understand why you are being so adamant about moving Bethany here so soon. She's been through enough," Bethany's father said.

"You'll see that I'm right, Alcee. You are never home. Unless you plan on giving up your aspirations to be a stay-at-home dad, which I would certainly forbid. Bethany is royalty as far as I'm concerned, and needs appropriate attention, while also feeling secure in who her father is and what he does, especially during times of adversity. I won't deny her advantages. After all, you will need her to be ready for the public eye as you enter a higher political arena.

"I have lived this life for very long time, my son, and I truly want what is best for you and my beautiful granddaughter, whom I cherish more than anything on this Earth," Phyllis said.

"What of her feelings on the matter. Perhaps she'd like it better at home?" Alcee asked.

"These things have a way of working out, my son. Do you still pal around with every friend you had when you were a little boy? I know you don't. I bet I remember more of your *BFFs'* names from your fifth birthday party than you," Phyllis countered. "Trust me; I have never led you astray."

"I just don't want her to go through any more pain than she has to."

"Better she puts everything behind her now. We have a long road ahead of us, and this most recent tragedy doesn't make things easier. My son, be strong. Do not allow these horrors to distract you," Phyllis said, making a point not to break eye contact.

"I hardly think that my daughter's well-being is unimportant," he said, rather angrily.

"Like it or not, this is the situation," Phyllis responded. "We all love her dearly, but your path is leading you to greater things. Not just for you, but for her. You will be able to make every dream come true for her, can't you see?"

At this point, Phyllis escorted her son into the east living room where no one could possibly hear what she had to say or how sternly she was to say it, including Bethany.

"Anton Leviticus Crowmire! You listen to me. We will not allow you to follow in your father's footsteps. The path we have set you on is far greater. Your father's charisma brilliantly camouflages his weakness. He and I both agree, however, that you have no political weakness or rival, save for the foolishness of womanizing from time to time.

"Your purpose is great. Look at the world today. People are lost and pathetic, a battalion of blind fools. They are so in love with their celebrities and luxuries that when the carpet slightly shifts below them, they won't even notice. When it's pulled out from under them, they won't be resourceful or manage to pull themselves up. No, they will jump on meds, drugs, riot, loot, and cry-cry-cry that their riches are gone, looking for someone to replenish their material novelties.

"Do not fear your destiny or for a moment believe that you are not above the people, the cultures, and the politics. You are," she continued, placing her hands on both of his shoulders and squeezing his once-broken collarbone. "You feel that pain?" she asked as Alcee tried to hide his red-faced grimace. "I want you to remember this. Here, my son, is a hard and painful truth: the American dream is dead, long dead. The old ways are over, and the future of this country, and even the world, lies at your feet. You may be state attorney general in the short term, but the path you will take is one of destiny.

"Remember, you are better than them all. You were born to rule over them. They are peasants. Stop hiding from your brilliance and passions. Embrace this. Everything your father and I have built is for you to be the king of this nation, of this world. Not some president that answers to squabbling deal-makers.

"Let this burn into your heart and never forget it. Be wise and strong. You know the world is crumbling. We will rebuild a new foundation and you, my son, and my granddaughter Bethany, will dominate history. The masses are paving the way to their own demise."

Phyllis took her hands off his shoulders. She kissed him on the cheek. "Now, go find your daughter and be a father to her while you have the chance."

* * *

Bethany, still sitting on the steps, was sadder than she had ever been before. She'd been devastated losing her mother but leaving her home where she had so many wonderful memories with her mother was too much to take.

Although she didn't quite understand everything her father and grandmother had discussed, she'd heard all that she needed to hear. She began to slowly walk up the stairs toward her room. Between sadness and anger, she had a massive lump building in her throat.

Davin tried hard to console her, but nothing worked. Even Anjelica, watching from a distance, felt it wise to keep that distance. The emotion spilling out of Bethany was powerful and quite uncommon for one so young.

But then again, so were the events she had recently been forced to endure.

* * *

Karita Ana Leese, who was pregnant and closer to giving birth than she would have liked, had been in and out of hospitals for several years. Now she rested in the new, high tech, Baaladine State University Hospital.

She contracted juvenile diabetes during her teen years and had already been battling epilepsy and a variety of abuses at home. For years, doctors told her it would not be possible for her to conceive and due to her troubling upbringing, her psychologists had been consistent in their thoughts that she might not be able to handle the stresses of raising a child, even if it were possible.

"You know, you might just be the most stubborn patient I've ever encountered," Dr. Morgansau said to Karita. "A forty-year-old woman who is eight months pregnant, severely anemic, who happens to have an egg basket of roadblocks that life has thrown at her, who is still pressing on."

"You are helping me, doctor," Karita answered, with a slight Danish accent. "Where would I be without your care? Not just now, but for the past several months."

"You say that now. But in reality, you fight me on doing what needs to be done," he responded.

"Doctor, I am fine. I'm hurting, but fine. And so far the baby is fine. I saw no reason to terminate the pregnancy," Karita answered in undeviating fashion. "I know you are probably thinking about what the book says on this, but part of choice is me having mine, and I still want to keep the baby, like when you first asked me some five months ago."

The doctor shook his head.

"Hey!" she said and started to straighten herself up in the hospital bed. "I want my life to matter. Do you know what it's like to always want a child? To go out to dinner night after night and see that all those couples with their cute babies, or always hear the great news when one of your social media friends has another one on the way and is posting pictures all over?" Karita paused as if to catch her breath a little. "Do you know what that's like, doc? I finally met a man that loves me after everything that I have been through, and I know a child would mean the world to him as well."

"I think you should relax," Miles replied. "I definitely understand your point. I want to save your life, and to be frank, I'm not convinced that you can survive delivery or any surgery. Not to mention, I can't see any reasonable way the baby can stay in there another month. This is precisely the reason why I was pushing for a termination several months ago. And now—"

"What are you saying?" Karita looked down as if she didn't want to hear the answer.

"I didn't want this. Trust me. I didn't," he said somberly. "We may have to deliver the baby soon. This week, possibly today or tomorrow…"

"Wait! I don't understand. The nurses said everything was—"

"I know they did. But the baby is having a hard time breathing right now, and if that doesn't get corrected, we are going to have to do something," Miles added.

"And?"

"And that's all we know, which is part of the problem," Miles sighed. "Karita, someone in your condition, especially after suffering this kind of accident, well, sometimes has to consider trade-offs. However, with you being at eight months, you are even in more harm's way right now. There are other obstacles to consider. The emotional stress from the car accident, your anemia, and the fact that your husband is even more banged up from the accident are all a part of this. I mean you can always try again if the fetus doesn't survive."

"Try again?" Karita replied, with clear frustration in her voice. "You know, a few months back you told me that my body would reject the pregnancy on its own if I didn't terminate. It hasn't happened. She's still alive and kicking."

"We're not God, Karita. We can't always say what will happen. We have to look at the medical reality and make decisions based on experience. As doctors, we have seen terrible outcomes; we have seen young women, such as you, die giving birth," the doctor said.

"Look, I'm not young; I'm forty-years-old and up until recently, I've been alone all of my life. To get pregnant now… what are the chances…like you said, and for the baby to fight through it all …I don't know. I now am starting to believe that this child must be a child of importance. A special child… one of destiny," she responded, and although to the doctor and nurses she sounded somewhat insane, she became more convinced of her words being true the more she said them.

"It is good that you feel that way. It is good to be strong. But I can only look at things medically and scientifically and…" The doctor stopped mid-sentence. He could see that Karita was starting to feel some strong discomfort.

"Gibberish," Karita responded, clearly struggling. "Believing in science sometimes proves in your ability to have faith. You weren't there …millions of years ago or whatever. Yet you believe some bunches of nothings gave birth to intelligence. I believe in something, too… Is it really that different?"

Miles always felt frustrated debating Karita, but he had a fondness for her. He truly cared for her well-being. She made him think and oftentimes go deeper than his comfort level would usually allow.

Karita's seraph protector was strong and in good health. He was a small brown and white bunny, Japper. He had been her conscience since birth. When things got tough, Japper always motivated her to stick it out and accept negativity from no one.

Japper was always cheering Karita on whenever she stood her ground. He grew especially formidable when she encountered Dr. Morgansau.

"Karita, I'm going to be blunt here, I don't think you and the baby can last another couple of weeks in your condition. We are going to have to perform a Caesarean and get working on you," Miles advised.

Karita did not put up a fight now. She could see that Dr. Morgansau was sincere in his desire to help both her and the unborn child. Just as important, Japper could now also see it, and shared that with Karita's unconscious.

Then another being walked in the room that was unbeknownst to any nurse, aide, doctor, or patient. It was Khrimson himself. He, of course, could transform into a fleshly form, but not this time. He was on a mission.

"Oh, doctor, doctor," Khrimson whispered into Miles' ear. "Can't you feel I'm burnin' burnin'?" Khrimson mocked the medical procedure of pretending to take his own temperature and laughed. He loved to toy with those most loyal to him. He enjoyed even more messing with those who would swear he never existed at all.

"Oh, hello, Japper. It's impossible to ignore your lewd aroma. Upholding my reputation as the father of lies and all, I must say, it is good to see you."

Japper was not impressed by Khrimson's overture. "You have no business with us. Don't you have a snake lady to charm someplace?" he shouted with his furry paws crossed.

Khrimson raised his chin as if Japper were beneath him and replied, "Yes, Medusa gets cranky this time of day. I dare say it is best to avoid her altogether." He then turned his attention to

Miles. "How long are you going to banter with this woman? It is unbecoming of you to allow yourself to be captivated by such a commoner." Khrimson attempted to irritate the doctor and force him to break off conversation with Karita.

Miles was sweating as he and his team prepped for Karita's Cesarean. He had gotten hot and anxious due to hearing Khrimson's taunts in his unconscious.

"This is quite useless," Khrimson said to himself. "As Francis used to say, 'I gotta do it my way.'"

Khrimson then transformed. This caught Japper's attention. The evil red knight of Algolithar changed himself into a being of the natural world but was unable to be viewed by the human naked eye because he had altered into a bacterium. Khrimson was moving fast, much too fast for Japper's eyes to keep up and far too small for the doctor or any of the nurses to notice. He entered into one of the pores in Karita's skin and began to poison some of the cells surrounding the child inside of her. The result of this caught everyone, including Miles by surprise.

"Nurse! She's crashing!" the doctor shouted.

But Karita was not Khrimson's target. Her child was. The asudem ruler persisted until he reached an entryway into the fetus and then began to spread an infection with the intention of causing certain death.

Nurses quickly gathered around Karita. The monitors had gone haywire. She wasn't in great shape to begin with, but this was unexpected. "I'm not picking up her white blood count or anything at all!" one nurse yelled out. "Heart rate is slowing dramatically!" another nurse shouted out.

Asudem came into the room in droves celebrating their leader's apparent victory. Japper was motionless. The demonic spirits waited for their master to transform into himself so that they could chant his praises.

Yet there was a peculiar breeze within the hospital that all could feel. The asudem were suddenly seized with fear. They began to tremble and then, in unison, paused. The ground shook. Every living being, both human and spirit, including asudem and seraphs, were frozen to a standstill.

The winds of time had stopped. Nothing moved. Not a car on the ground. Not a bird in the air. Everything stopped except for the mighty winged horse, who had landed on top of the hospital roof. His majestic wings could halt time in its place. As protector and servant of Jaesu, great authority had been given to Pegasus over the clocks of entire galaxies.

With everyone frozen in the hospital, Jaesu made his way within its walls toward Karita. She seemed lifeless and, for the moment, so did everyone else. He put his hand on Miles's shoulder and said to him, "My friend. How I've pondered our debates about the universe. We once walked for many eons. You used to connect the dots of faith and science so fluently, but now the flesh has clouded your judgment. May you find the third door so that we may walk together again. I bless you with brilliance now." Jaesu placed his own hand inside of the patient's body. He felt his way through and pulled out the bacteria Khrimson had disguised himself as.

"Khrimson, going over the line once more, I see. You were once glorious, and we enjoyed many cycles together as well. Those days are long gone. Your authority will soon come to a close." Jaesu then commanded the winds of the universe to carry Khrimson along with the clot he caused to his nearby lair on Saturn.

"My lord," Pegasus said, as he approached the room.

"I know, Pegasus," Jaesu said, as if he could read the horse's mind. He nodded and Pegasus beat his wings to command time to move again as seamlessly as if nothing had happened.

"Doctor, wait …we've got something!" one of the nurses shouted. All which had been chaotic had been restored to normal, and the doctor and his team could monitor Karita and the baby once more.

"Let's get this over with," Miles said.

Pegasus stood in the door, watching, as Jaesu would not leave Miles's side. "Doctor," Jaesu said into his ear, "Karita has the remnants of a bacterial infection. The tests and monitors won't show it."

Miles, a doctor known for doing things by the book, felt a shift in his thinking. For reasons beyond his understanding, he was suddenly certain that she had been suffering from a bacterial infection that hadn't shown up. He wouldn't be able to do anything meaningful for Karita until the baby had been delivered. This also had its risks as she had just completed her eighth month.

Karita was conscious now, but far from attentive. Jaesu continued on with the doctor, encouraging him, and coaching him. Although Miles couldn't see him, he felt an unknown energy flowing through him. "Talk to me, Karita, what are you feeling?" he urgently said upon noticing her newly awakened state.

"Like I just fell off a cliff," she said.

"Listen, once we take the baby out, we are going to have it tested and, at the same time, check you for infections, which may be what caused your blackout."

"I understand," she whispered, weak and in pain. "But I have one request."

"Now? Really?" The doctor shook his head. *What could she possibly be asking at this stage of the game?*

"No matter what happens, I want you to name the child. Please do me this honor!" Karita said, struggling to speak.

"*Um*...I...." Miles was uncomfortable with this task. He'd prefer having to commit to finding the cure for cancer by midnight or something.

"Please. It is important! The one who delivers the child should choose the name," Karita pleaded as she wheezed noticeably.

Miles didn't want her speaking much, so he nodded his head in agreement. But a name for a child was the very last thing on his mind.

Karita was cut open successfully. The child was lifted out and the cord cut. The baby seemed healthy from a distance.

"It's a girl!" The nurse smiled at Karita.

"Is she okay?" Karita gasped.

"She seems fine, but we need to examine her thoroughly," the nurse responded.

Jaesu placed his hand on the child and let out a joyful laugh. "There she is," he said.

Miles could only think of one name as he peered into her deep blue eyes, for a moment, forgetting how uncommon it is for a premature baby to open her eyes immediately after delivery. His own eyes welled up with tears. This was entirely out of character for him, but he couldn't help it. She was the most beautiful thing he'd ever seen.

"Doctor," Karita weakly whispered. "Would you?"

Still uncomfortable, he figured she could change the name later and probably would, but for the time being, he wanted to move on to getting both girls healthy. "I can only think of one name," he said.

"Okay?" Karita prompted.

"My son Marcus had always said growing up if he had a baby sister, he would have wanted us to name her Amana."

At that moment, Pegasus, Japper, and all angelic beings in the vicinity bowed their heads in respect to the infant and former Gardenian Queen. At the same time, all demonic presences, including the powerful asudem in the area, evacuated out of fear. Amana was known not to be taken lightly. Even in her infant stage, she commanded respect.

"Wow," one of the nurses responded. "Doctor that is a beautiful name, a very beautiful name."

"What is its meaning?"

Miles looked over to Karita and said, "In spite of everything you and the baby have been through, not just today but for these past few months, it's fitting." He smiled. "It means faithful."

CHAPTER 13

Generous Gifts

G race moved with all of her might and sped back toward
Gardenia. She couldn't be sure of Soren's whereabouts,
yet it didn't matter. All that mattered was the battle.
She had done her best to protect Amana as she entered Earth's
atmospheric belt. She had to have been born by now, Grace
figured.

She shook off such thoughts. Her focus had to be on the
current war raging over Gardenia. She reckoned it could still be
stopped, but great fear fell upon her as she saw the thousands of
archer knights who had surrounded the planet were no longer
there. *Where are they? Have they invaded already?*

Then, in the distance she saw two enormous titans in the
midst of battle: the lord of fear himself, Phan, and her friend and
the protector of Gardenia, Orion. The sight she saw was nothing
short of horrific. Orion was prostrate at Phan's feet.

"Oh, what a waste you have become, Orion," Phan said. "You could still be among the mighty ones."

"Kill me now," Orion softly muttered, clearly beaten. "It's better to be a waste with something to die for than a brilliant beast with nothing to live for."

This angered Phan even more, he took his boot to Orion's face and kicked him across the sky. He then chased quickly after the once-great seraph to continue the barrage. "You are a failure, Orion! A failure!" Phan screamed. He got on one knee and grabbed Orion by the head and said to him, "I can stop the pain. All you have to do is join me."

Orion's eyes widened. He couldn't believe what his ears had heard.

"Yes, you heard me right. Join me and we can destroy Khrimson together, and then Jaesu, and then we'll rule the universe."

"P-p-power ..." Orion was now barely able to speak, but could force out a few more words. "Power is the s-servant of vanity, whose master knows no end to appetites."

"You truly are worthless, Orion." Phan stood over him. "You have fought, not valiantly, but you, at least, deserve a warrior's death." Phan had become completely oblivious to what happened to his archers. His focus was squarely on Orion.

Orion closed his eyes, unable to go on. "Forgive me, Lord Jaesu," he whispered with the last of his strength.

The evil lord raised himself up over Orion. "Now you shall die, old adversary." Phan joined his hands together in an axe handle motion over his head and screamed, "Echoes of wickedness! I summon you for your powers. For tonight we conquer."

Instantaneously, thousands of black and violet spirits entered into his fists, making him larger and more powerful. He attempted to slam his conjoined fists in a punch on the fallen warrior, but heard a familiar voice from behind him.

"NO!" Grace shouted. "PHAN, STOP! PLEASE, I BEG YOU! STOP!"

Phan calmly turned to see his former slave. It was as if he were expecting her. "Ah, yes, Pity, returning to die at the hands of her real master. How fitting." He chuckled sinisterly.

Grace sped over to Orion's head and embraced it, demanding that he hold on. She could feel life within him, but it had been severely weakened.

"You can't do this, Phan! You can't," Grace said.

"A slave, a worthless slave, is going to lecture the mighty Phan on cans and cannots? Fool, you are not worthy of being in my presence. Do you not remember that I have the power to bring pain like no other?"

Grace knew. She had witnessed massive amounts of destruction done at his command throughout the universe. "What if I return to you?" she whispered. "Permanently, promising never to leave? Would you then spare his life?"

Phan was struck by her willingness to return to him as a slave and endure the further torment in order to spare Orion's life. For Phan, killing wasn't the biggest pleasure. Having power over someone was. Killing Orion could be done at any time, he reasoned. But having his prized slave to dominate with her promise to never escape was an offer too tempting to pass up. At that moment, Phan noticed that his archers were nowhere in sight. He would deal with that later. He was so consumed with his own arrogance and pride that nothing else concerned him.

"If you agree to bind yourself to me for eternity, even into the lakes of fire, should we be summoned there, to forever be my slave ... then, yes, I will spare him this once. But it must be now," Phan said, detaching the chain and collar from his waste for Grace to submit herself to.

She cried and kissed Orion on the head, giving him one last embrace. "I'm sorry, my friend," she whispered. "This is the only way." With that, she placed her neck into the iron collar and became one with the chain.

"*Ha-ha*," Phan laughed. "The slave returns to her master, one of my personal favorites," he snickered. "Have fun just floating in the skies for a while and reflecting on your own failure, Orion. It's time for me to finish conquering Gardenia."

"What?!" Grace shouted.

"Oh, my dear, we never agreed on anything regarding Gardenia. How ironic will it be for your newfound friends to see you by my side as I—well, as we—bring them to their knees," Phan answered. He was unaware of Alina's defeat and had figured, like Grace, that the archers had made their way to Gardenia at Alina's request. The thought of losing had never entered his mind.

"It doesn't matter now, anyway," Grace said with her head down.

"Oh, now, now, feeble servant, you should relish the chance to worship the mighty Phan forever," he said to her.

"It doesn't matter because ...because I ...forgive you, Phan."

Phan, completely caught off guard, said, "What did you say?"

"I forgive you... for the torture, beatings, insults, horrors, and nightmares. Yes, Phan, I forgive you," she said as she stared into his eyes.

"Don't say that," he said.

"What? That I forgive you?" she said, with more confidence as she noticed he struggled with the term. "Well, I do. You call me 'Pity,' yet that is what I feel for you."

"No one feels sorry for the great Phan!"

"No, Phan. I feel something more," she said. "I feel …love. For you, Phan."

At that moment, something started to happen within Phan. He did not know it or understand it and could only rail against it. "Spare me from this child's play."

"It's true," she said as she placed her hand on his cheek. "I have been forgiven for much, and it has changed me forevermore. Thus, nothing you do can separate you from my love. I speak the love and forgiveness of Jaesu upon you for all time."

Orion, with his eyes half-opened, could barely witness what was happening between Grace and Phan. He was powerless to help.

"What have you done?!" Phan shouted. He noticed particles of himself eroding.

"I've shared with you the one truth," Grace said, as one in a position of authority. "That Lord Jaesu's love is greater than all and he still has abundant love for you."

"No …no …stop!" Phan screamed as more of himself continued to erode. "Nook—" he let out a last gasp as a ball of light from within him erupted and annihilated him completely.

This lord of horror was destroyed and gone for good. All that remained was a grain of sand lit from inside, no greater in size than half a speck of dust.

The chains were gone as well. Grace was free forever. It was her sacrifice that saved Orion and her love that overcame Phan who had become pure evil and could not survive in love's presence.

Grace whispered, "Thank you, Jaesu," as she grabbed Orion and slowly dragged him across the sky toward Gardenia so she could get help.

*   *   *

The rings circling Saturn were hardly enough to seal in the chilling force of Khrimson's anger. He had scouted Amana's whereabouts precisely. His strategy was near perfect and accounted for every obstacle, save for one: Jaesu. Normally, Jaesu would not directly engage Khrimson physically unless Khrimson did the same to a human in the flesh. Khrimson had taken a chance and failed. This was not the first time he had been defeated in battle. He had won several thousand battles. He knew wins and losses were part of a greater strategic effort to eventually be hailed as the victor of the universe. He walked through the red sludge where Sardis waited outside of the Alpha painting portal.

"Look at her, Sardis," he said, referring to Alina. "She waits on her knees in the Alphan throne room. She desires another chance, mercy even; what do you fathom I should do?"

"Master, she is a mighty asset. Even now, her knowledge of dealing with Alphans and Gardenians supersedes most. She can run a covert operation better than any," the black horse replied.

"Yes, I am very well aware of that." Khrimson added, "I cannot foresee victory without her, especially with Phan gone."

Sardis was shocked to hear that his master was gone. "What do you mean gone, sire?" Sardis asked.

"Exactly as I said it. Are you unable to hear? He was defeated in the battle over Gardenia."

"Orion?" Sardis questioned.

"Interestingly, no," Khrimson said. "It is quite ironic that he toyed with the great warrior for quite some time. From what I understand, Orion was no match for Phan."

"Then, who? The blue beast from Dar? It would not be possible for any of their seraphs to touch Phan," Sardis said with certainty.

"Let this be a lesson to you, mighty warhorse. Underestimate no one. An old slave I believe once called Pity was his undoing," Khrimson replied, and could see the surprised on Sardis' face. "Yes, that is what happened! We are in a war now. Take nothing for granted. Assume nothing. Do what thou wilt, and yet it's time to leave nothing to chance. Kill at will."

Khrimson then started to walk toward the portal into Alpha. Alina was waiting for him. She had begged for mercy for what seemed like a lifetime on her knees without movement. She knew Khrimson's wrath would be swift. She saw his shadowy figure enter into the painting. Her nerves swelled like those of an earthling.

He arrived like a cool breeze. She could feel his presence at first without seeing him. But quickly, his impressive form was complete. His figure was like an iron silhouette before her.

"My lord," Alina said.

"I do not require you to speak," Khrimson responded. "I did not come to hear you but so that you could hear me."

She tried to speak again. Immediately, Khrimson cast his hand toward her lips and a tight web was sewn over them.

"Your arrogance should be strength, sneaky one, not weakness. And yet you can't even distract an inexperienced queen in order to bring me the Lighted Blade," Khrimson said, pacing back and forth.

Alina attempted to speak on her own behalf, but it was useless.

"Again, even with this, you fail to listen. For your talents, you are a disappointment. I could have trained a rat on Earth to accomplish the task set before you. And you knew Phan was battling Orion, didn't you? You fled in fear of his anger. Yet in doing so, you allowed him to be destroyed."

Khrimson continued, "Ah, yes, 'tis true that I do not embrace valor and honor and some of the customs Evermore bestows upon many of these worlds, but not understanding the art of war, not having respect for your opponent—well, that leads to quick failure …as you now know."

Alina bowed her head in submission. She could not speak, and if she could, she knew she had no good excuse. Her pride had been misplaced. She had been outsmarted by a new queen, an inexperienced warrior, and a bunch of cats.

"In short, I am going to win this war. And rule the universe. Perhaps then, you and I can have a different conversation. But for now, I have little …actually no use for you. You are banished from my court. You are an embarrassment to us all. And the beauty you once possessed apparently has been pierced by thorns," Khrimson added.

He picked her up with ease and brought her to the chamber where King Handel had been imprisoned. Without hesitation, he fired her down to where the king, now skin and bones, white-haired and blind, was lost and always wandering.

"Now a king unable to see can find comfort in the princess who deceived him and who is yet unable to speak," Khrimson said with his trademarked sinister laugh. "Alpha will tear itself apart while you two will probably do the same."

With that, he sealed the hidden library chamber and went toward the painting in the throne room. With a wave of his hand, the painting was no longer visible to anyone, although it stayed in place. He went through the portal toward Sardis in preparation for his greatest battle yet.

"Sardis, summon the scales and bring your remaining three brothers to Algolithar. It is time the world revisited the prophetic fears of the apocalyptic Four Horsemen."

* * *

On Gardenia, word of victory had spread worldwide. But even with Alina defeated and Phan destroyed, it was a time of mourning throughout the land. Between the fires that had consumed trees and the death of Massa the badger and others, not to mention the toll of warfare, Gardenians had experienced something they had never expected.

Queen Roslyn toured the planet, walked gingerly, taking in the damage and horror her people and land had experienced. Dawn was with her, along with Black, Grace, and Jaesu. Orion was resting in Scepter Falls, regaining his strength. Pegasus, also on Gardenia with Jaesu and the queen, had brought Michaelio with him to keep watch over the outer world until Orion was strong enough to take over his post.

"I can't believe it, Lord," the queen said to Jaesu. "This horror that has befallen my people I… feel within every part of me. It's not something I have ever dealt with."

"You are feeling what it is like to be queen, Your Majesty," Jaesu responded. "What happened here has never happened before. How you react and the decisions you make will determine how others handle such matters as we move forward."

"What will I do, Lord?" she asked.

"I will certainly guide you, but I cannot choose for you," Jaesu answered.

"Black, what would Queen Amana do?" Roslyn asked Amana's once most trusted assistant.

"Your Majesty, I suppose, she would have felt as you do, and like any true queen, sought guidance from Lord Jaesu."

Roslyn continued to walk and studied the loss throughout the land. She knew this was her charge, and she still trusted Amana's choice and Jaesu's approval more than she ever could trust her own ability. "Look at this. How could they emanate with such revulsion?" she asked aloud.

"Your Majesty, if I may?" asked Dawn. Roslyn nodded. "We were not trained for battle, yet even through the shock and turmoil, facing some of universe's most dangerous warriors, we stand victorious. A message was clearly sent throughout the worlds that Queen Roslyn and Gardenia are indeed resilient. Yes, the losses we endured and the evil that came against us were great, but we stood in the face of firm annihilation and by the hand of our Lord Jaesu, and the strategic leadership of his servant—you, my queen—we see the suns rise to start another day."

"Dawn's right, my queen," Black exclaimed. "Things sometimes aren't what they seem. How long will they be scratching their heads on Algolithar? Will they ever believe that it was Grace who defeated Phan, one of the most powerful beings in the universe? There is something grander here."

"Your Majesty," Jaesu added, "remember: you are queen now and your word is law. Ponder that for a moment. And Grace, when you fought Phan, you did so in protection of Orion. Why?"

"I value him more than I value myself," she responded.

"And yet when Phan was defeated, did you not take the speck of bright dust that represented who he once was? Why?"

"I guess I wanted to remember that he wasn't always the monster he died as. It was a symbolic hope, I think," she answered.

"And when you forgave Phan, did you know what his reaction would be?" Jaesu asked.

"No, I didn't, but I knew it to be the right thing to do at the time. I felt it in my very being," she replied.

"How did you know, Grace? That it was the right thing to do, I mean?" Jaesu continued.

"It was a kind of faith, I guess. I can't explain it," she answered again.

"Faith, yes… you see, Your Majesty, Grace defended a friend, conquered a warrior, and lived to tell of it by faith, hope, and love. These are often overlooked in favor of weapons of fire and stone, but Grace chose to embrace the greatest power of them all, love and forgiveness. At no time should we lose sight of that," said Jaesu as he placed his hand on the queen's shoulder.

"Black, may I ask you something?" The queen looked over to the large cat. "Queen Amana, do you feel alone without her by your side?"

"Well, Your Majesty, she and I spent many cycles together. So, of course, I do. But I anticipate that you and I will have a similar bond in time. You are both different in some ways and the same in others," Black answered.

"I appreciate your candor, Black. In my heart, I know that Amana still will play a great part in bringing about the Great Father's will. I'm not sure exactly what it is, but I believe she would be best served with a comforter that she trusts," Roslyn said.

"You mean a protector?" Black asked.

"No, great cat," Pegasus broke in. "That is a role I shall assume by the generosity of Lord Jaesu."

"Wait. You? You are Jaesu's seraph. How can you be Amana's protector?" asked Grace.

"Queen Amana chose to take the journey to be there for Jovan and Bethany, her friends. She chose to leave her personal protector, Orion, behind for Gardenia's safety. As she is always thinking of others rather than herself, she shall receive even greater things, unasked for, in return," Jaesu answered.

"So where do I factor in?" asked Black.

"I would like for you to go with Pegasus to Earth, not as Amana's protector, but as her friend, one who comforts her. It will only be for a short time as I will summon you back when the time is needed for you to return," said the queen.

"But what about Scepter and the kingdom?"

"If this is something you are willing to do, then Dawn will lead Scepter until you return," said Roslyn.

"Black, if we are to go, we should go now," Pegasus added. "It won't be long before the asudem realize that Amana is unprotected."

"Is it normal for a mighty lioness to walk with a human on Earth?" Black asked.

"Pegasus can go over that with you on the way," Roslyn answered with a slight laugh while playfully petting the cat's black fur. "You are among the highest blessings Gardenia has ever known. You are to play an important part in what lies ahead. Be ready to take up your place upon your return here." She kissed Black on the forehead. "Be blessed, trusted and faithful servant."

Black bowed her head toward the queen and Lord Jaesu. She embraced her sisters and chided Dawn, in fun, to lead Scepter with greatness. She climbed upon the majestic horse, ready to travel to the former Gardenian Queen.

"Pegasus," Jaesu called. "Thank you for doing this. May goodness follow you always," he whispered to him, "Be ready for days of sudden destruction when this mission is completed."

The horse bowed his head and leaped under the power of his mystical wings. All were amazed at the site of Pegasus and Black flying off toward space. The winged horse's exit from a planet was a legendary sight to behold.

Dawn took Scepter and began to scout the remaining places in Gardenia. Grace flew toward Orion to check on him. This gave Jaesu and Roslyn some time to discuss her reign and other events.

"That was noble, what you did," Jaesu said to the queen. "It could not be easy to let go of such a valuable leader at a time such as this."

"I felt it was the right thing to do," she said in response.

"For Amana, yes. But you also felt that Black was missing her strongly, and you put her feelings ahead of the circumstances," Jaesu added. "Not a very common choice."

"I want to do right by my people. I keep replaying over and over in my mind how everything happened," she said.

"Don't allow yourself to fall into that trap. Remembering such events is powerful, but only to prevent them from happening again. It is unwise for anyone, queen or not, to allow tragic events to dictate their future steps," Jaesu replied. "I keep saying this as a reminder: you are queen. And Gardenia was made to follow its queen. I can safely say that you are indeed the right queen for this moment in history."

"And Jovan, Bethany, Amana, Da-"

"I am with them," said Jaesu as he knelt down to check on the plants and grass. "Not a millisecond passes, nor a tear, nor a laugh, a hurt, a joy, a smile, a fright, a dream, nor any substance or circumstance connected to their lives passes my gaze. As I am here with you, I am there with them. Your eyes may see me and their eyes may not, but the soul always knows. My love grows for them with each passing moment that they are away from this place. And yes, I long for them to reap the rewards and treasures and joys of the Great Father and Evermore."

Grateful for his guidance and comfort, Queen Roslyn turned toward the forests that were still standing and commanded them to follow her lead. She had piled up so many emotions from the moment of her coronation through having fought and won a war. Far from the deer herder she always saw herself as!

She cracked open and released the emotion in song. A glorious sound came from her. She sang the following over and over:

> Blessed are you, O Lord,
> Blessed are you, O Lord,
> Blessed are you, O Lord,
> Greater than all riches.

This burst from her heart as the traumatic events inflicted on her planet consumed her. As she sang, the winds followed suit as if they were playing many harps. The leaves on the trees also followed along and then the animals did so. The oceans raged in praises, and the birds joined in beautiful harmony. Even the rocks cried out in thanks and joy.

This was not Jaesu's command, but it touched him immensely. The more the planet put forth song toward him, the more it began to heal itself. Burnt trees became whole, even down to the last fallen leaf. The scars of war began to heal, and the vibrancy of the land returned. And when it returned there was a hint of dark red among the edges of the plant life to symbolize their allegiance to the new queen by bearing the rose of Roslyn colors.

Then it happened. An enormous sound of rejoicing from all things, living and not, was heard in the capital city of Gardenia. The praise that had brought life back to the recently war-torn planet had found its way toward the slain badger and the wounded Malvin, along with hosts of others. Love and life and breath engulfed them as the badger arose, alive and well, and all were healed. Gardenia was whole once more.

As Jaesu ascended toward Evermore, Queen Roslyn stood facing the three suns on the queen's stone. The stone was an oval in the ground overlooking the oceans. It was there she let out her loudest vocalization toward Jaesu and the Great Father and the Blue Fire Spirit. Song flowed from her lips like the songs of angels. The anointing placed upon her as queen spread throughout the planet. Even the three suns slightly bowed toward her and outlined her in rose red flame for a moment. This was not done in worship but out of respect for her majesty, for the queen of love and conscience, who would serve the Lord Jaesu and the people of Gardenia for as long as her reign would last.

*   *   *

Jovan and Bethany were together in the park. Bethany wore a black nightgown, which seemed strange to Jovan. He also found it odd that she was in the park without any supervision. He had often gone there after school because it was close to the school, but Bethany was schooled from home and should not have been here alone.

"Do you know what it's like to walk along these thin branches, Jovan?" Bethany asked as she attempted to do so.

"Bethany, don't! You'll fall," Jovan answered.

"And you'd care? Just like my mother, you will leave me when I already have no one."

"That's not true!"

"Oh, Jovan, you will never understand, will you? I am not like you. I'm above you, don't you see? You are just a poor boy. I am royalty."

"Whatever that means," Jovan answered, clearly not following what she was saying.

"It's all I can say. It doesn't matter anymore, Jovan. I'm sorry. It's too hard."

With that, she spread her arms open wide and fell back off the tree with no attempt to break her fall. As she was about to hit the ground and come to her demise, Jovan awoke.

He had been dreaming. He woke up trembling in a sweat. It had indeed been several weeks since he had first met Bethany. From that moment, she was never far from his heart. Each day after school, he would run to that same park with half of him hoping to find her and the other half hoping that his dream was only a dream. Bethany was clearly in some sort of pain in Jovan's dream. And although he was very happy to be with her, witnessing her agony was excruciating for him.

Each night when he went to sleep, he was visited by exactly the same dream. This went on for a couple of weeks. No matter what he did, nothing altered the outcome of the dream. Each of these days he also ran to the park to see if she was there. She never was. It was becoming apparent to him that if he were to see her again, he couldn't leave it up to chance, but had to seek her out himself.

Jovan's thoughts on Bethany at this point were driven by compassion. Losing her mother was something Jovan would hope to never experience, nor could he comprehend.

When he could sleep, Bethany's face was often the last in his thoughts and the first when he would awake. The closeness he felt to her was far beyond what he could understand.

On Saturdays, Dara would take Jovan to go to the park where his older cousin Zach would play soccer in a local kids' league and watch him play.

This one particular Saturday, Jovan had wanted to take on a risky journey. He had done his research through both the web and friends at school. After hearing on the news that Bethany and her father were staying at the Baaladine Estate, he searched far and wide for an address. He wasn't sure if it was the right one, but it didn't concern him. All that concerned him were the nightmares and getting to Bethany.

The address he received turned out not to be very far from the park where his cousin played.

"Mom," Jovan said "will you take me somewhere this morning?"

Dara was making blueberry pancakes as was the norm before they went to watch Zach. "You mean, after the game?"

"Well, maybe before?" Jovan asked.

"Before? I don't think we will make it to the game on time, sweetie. We are running late as it is."

"I mostly run on the side field during the game anyway, and don't get to see Zach before it's over. Maybe we can be late this once?" asked Jovan.

"But we are the only ones that watch him on the Jersey field. It means so much to him that we are there. Maybe another time."

Dara could see that Jovan was very disappointed. He sat at the kitchen table with his head down. He normally would tear the pancakes apart because he enjoyed them so much. But as she gave him his customary three stack, he just seemed to pick at it and had little interest at all.

"What's wrong, honey?" Dara asked.

"Nothing, not hungry," Jovan said with his head down.

"Jo, you are always hungry, especially for pancakes. You were just clamoring for them fifteen minutes ago. Is it this place you want to go to?"

"I don't understand why we can't go quick. We won't be long, I promise."

"Just where is it that you want to go exactly?"

"Promise you won't get mad?"

"Why would I get mad?"

"Promise?"

"I'm not going to promise anything. Just tell me."

Then Jovan out of nervousness just blurted everything out as fast as he could.

Dara was moved. She wasn't sure how pleased she was about Jovan getting addresses from fellow classmates, but the fact that he was so passionate about seeing Bethany did something to Dara.

"Where is the card you got her?" Dara asked.

"It's in my room," Jovan replied.

"Can I see it?"

"No! It's for Bethany."

"Just how do you know this is the right address?"

"Rob says it is. He knows a boy on threadbeetle who has connections."

"Connections. I see. How old is this friend of Rob's? Seven? Eight?"

Jovan brought his shoulders back as if he was quite confident in his response. "Nope. He's twelve. So there!"

This caused Dara to laugh. "What if we go, and it's the wrong house?"

"Then we go back to the game. The address isn't far, he told me."

"May I see that, at least?" she asked.

Jovan reached into the left front pocket of his jeans and handed his mother the folded piece of paper with the address on it. Interestingly, he began to eat his pancakes as his mother opened the paper.

"Nine Angel Food Cake Court?" Dara asked mockingly. "Come on, Jovan. This can't be real."

"It is! It really is. I checked!"

"You checked?" she asked, lowering her dark pink colored glasses to her nose while staring back at him in disbelief. "I find that hard to believe." Dara then picked up her tablet to look up the address herself.

Sure enough, the address was correct. *It must be newer or some sort of special address.* Nonetheless, although it may have come across to her as a bit stalkerish, Dara figured it would be harmless to pay a visit just to drop off a card.

*   *   *

They drove toward the park. Once they reached the area, the directions mandated they turn north for several blocks. As they continued further, the road became slightly narrower and switched from 216th Street to Eveness Alley, which led to a rather large cul-de-sac made of what seemed like hundreds of evergreen trees.

As they approached the corner, Jovan said, "Let me get out here."

"No, Jo, why would you get out here? There are no houses. I think it's a bad address."

"This is it. Rob's friend said when we get to the trees, to get out and walk toward the black light things. You see? Over there."

Dara didn't notice them at first, but once Jovan pointed them out, she could see two black light posts each next to gray pillars and a driveway under an arch, which was created by the trees.

"Okay. You can get out, but just go to the end of the driveway. If there is a mailbox, you can leave the card there. Mommy will be right here waiting."

"But, Mom, I want to see her."

"I know, sweetie. Another time maybe. This place creeps me out a bit, and the driveway seems to go into dark places."

Jovan, although not entirely happy, got out of the car and walked further up toward the light posts. The butterflies were rapidly building in his stomach, letting him know that Bethany was near. He was also nervous because the driveway looked strange and cold to him. He got to the edge of the driveway by a gray pillar. He saw a mailbox as his mother said he would.

"Excuse me, young master, may I help you find something?" a voice came from inside the shadows of the driveway.

Jovan studied the area ahead, deep within the driveway under the arch, and then looked around and saw no one.

"Young master, over here." A man slowly became visible from where Jovan had originally heard the voice. He was walking toward Jovan from out of the shadows. He was dressed in all black and wore a hat that resembled a policeman's.

"*Uh...*" Jovan was trying to think of a response, but his brain froze because the man had caught him off guard. "Is... *um...*is this Bethany's house?"

"Well, I must say, that would all depend on which Bethany you are looking for," the man said as he continued to walk closer.

Jovan could now make out that the man was Caucasian with whitish-gray facial hair. "She's seven, like me, and she's small like me."

"So you are looking for Bethany White then?" the man asked.

"*Um...* no, I don't think so. I think her last name is Cr—"

"Perhaps you are wishing for Bethany Black then?"

"No, I said her name—"

"Bethany Blue is often treacherous to be around, I might add."

Jovan was confused and just stared at the man.

"Bethany Stepany? Ring a bell?" The man stared curiously back at Jovan.

"Crowmire!" Jovan yelled.

"*Ah.* That's a good name, isn't it? Do you have a good name, young master?"

"I do. Yes. My name is—"

"Before you answer, may I ask, do you always talk with strangers?" the man questioned as he took notice of the car down the block, which he determined to most likely be awaiting Jovan.

Jovan paused and took a step back, tempted to run away.

The man also could see Jovan's dilemma written on his face. "Allow me to ease your worry, young master. My name is Jennings Hoyt. Indeed, I assist the Lady Crowmire, and the estate grounds. You may, however, call me Mr. Hoyt, young sir."

"You can call me Jovan, but not Jovanny. My mother calls me that, but I don't really like it."

"Very well. I guess we are acquaintances now, so to speak. What is your business with young Bethany?"

"She's my friend. We were going to play one day. She has space toys, you know?"

"Ah, of course. Yes, I see," Jennings responded but quickly became distracted by a sound coming from his ear piece as he gently placed his right hand over it, to ensure he heard it correctly. "Perhaps another time then? She is unable to have visitors at the moment."

"Oh," Jo said, trying hard not to look disappointed. He reached into the inside of is jacket and pulled out the light blue envelope. "Well, please give this to her." He then handed the card to Jennings. "And tell her how sad we are about Sarai. She was a nice lady."

Jennings closed his eyes slowly and let out a sigh. "Yes, indeed, she was something wonderful."

Jovan turned to walk away. "Thank you," he said somberly as he completed his turn to walk back toward Dara, who was now standing outside of the car to get a better glimpse of what was happening.

"Young master? Are you familiar with *The Little Engine That Could?*"

Jovan turned back quickly. "Why, yes sir. My mother reads it to me."

"There's a good lesson in that, you know," Jennings said as he straightened his hat. "I will see that your generous and thoughtful card makes it to Lady Bethany. Good day, sir."

*   *   *

On the following Saturday, Jovan convinced his mother to take him back. Once again he bumped into Jennings, and this time, he handed him a folded two-page letter to give to Bethany because, once again, she was unable to receive company.

The next Saturday, Dara again drove Jovan to the Crowmire estate. Again, Jovan saw Jennings who seemed amused by his persistence. Jovan, this time, didn't have a card or a two-page letter, but simply handed him a note which had one line on it. It was folded so that Jennings could not see it initially.

Jovan, then, as he had done the previous two weeks, got back in the car with his mother, and they drove back toward the fields where his cousin was playing soccer.

During the games, Jovan would normally run around on the small track that was close enough to the soccer field for Dara to keep an eye on him from the stands. He would sometimes play announcer and pretend to race himself as he was the only young kid on the sidelines. This day was no different.

He mimicked the stretches that he had seen his cousin do before the games. It was cold enough for a jacket, but still not too cold to keep him from wanting to play outside.

"Here goes Jovan," he said out loud as no one appeared to be around him, "the fastest runner in the galaxy."

"Why are you talking to yourself?" a voice came from behind him. "There's no one else here."

Jovan was startled and embarrassed. He thought he was alone. He anxiously turned around to see who was talking, and to his horror and delight, it was Bethany.

"H-H-Hi," he said. "How did you know I was here?"

"Well, your letter last week said you would be here. So Jennings and I thought that you might be here today also." She then pointed toward the limousine in the street, which had Jennings stationed outside of it.

"Well, thank you for coming. I missed you." Jovan really hadn't the faintest idea as to what he was saying; words were just flowing out beyond his control.

"Well, I just had to come after reading the note."

"The note? Not the card or letter?"

"Thank you for those. But nope. I liked the note."

"Why?" Jovan asked.

Bethany looked around and whispered to him. "I felt them, too."

"Goose bumps?" Jovan yelled.

"*Shhh*...not so loud," Bethany said in a low tone. "People will think us mad. Yes, goose bumps. At the party."

"Wow. You know I'm really sorry about your mom."

"Me, too. And thank you. What are you doing here? Running?"

"Yeah, I like to race myself while the game is going on."

"How do you race yourself?"

"I time the speed each week and keep running until I beat it," Jovan answered.

"Just you? Anyone else?" she asked.

As this conversation was happening, Jovan and Bethany both could feel the warmth of summer on their flesh, yet it was still winter. They both felt as if they were in the right place at the right moment and yet, could probably never put those exact feelings into words.

Davin, Bethany's seraph, and Dmna, Jovan's white tiger twin seraph, were also talking. They were both very close friends and encouraged Jovan and Bethany through their very presence to want to be close.

"That was pretty easy, wouldn't ya say?" Dmna said to Davin.

"Easy? Getting them together? Easier, I would say, but not easy. Watching her tears over Sarai is gut-wrenching, as humans would call it."

"Yes, and even then, death sometimes opens a pathway to our greater destinies," she responded. "Yet, it brings many questions and pain."

Just then, the two seraphs noticed something slithering in the grass toward Jovan and Bethany, who had walked a few steps away toward the entryway of the track.

"What do you desire, slithering creature?" Davin asked.

The creature showed its head above the grass, and it was a snake. He maneuvered himself in the children's direction once more.

Dmna then jumped in front of it with a growl.

"Okay, okay, point taken. Testy tessssssty," the snake responded. "Can't a fella get some eggs?"

Davin stared at the snake some more and studied his black skin, while also noticing a rattling tail. "And since when does a rattlesnake find his way into these parts and look for eggs of all things?"

The snake breathed out subtle smoke from his mouth in annoyance.

This alarmed both Davin and Dmna. "If I were you, I'd hold quite still, slowly turn around, and go back to where you came from," Dmna said in a double voice.

"Ah, yesss, but sssssseeeee you aren't me," the snake answered. "Otherwise, you'd have noticed the army of asudem steadfastly approaching your position."

"Asudem?" Davin and Dmna said in unison.

"There are no asudem here."

"And now there are!" the snake responded.

At that moment, hidden in the shadows of the grass, were many small asudem who were unseen. They immediately leaped toward the eyes of both Davin and Dmna.

The white tiger attempted to knock the little nuisances away from her eyes. When she succeeded, they would cleverly hide within her black stripes, looking like miniature shadows, attacking in her ears, under her paws and pulling on her belly.

Davin was being attacked from within his cape. The evil shadows pulled the inside of his cape in order to strangle him. Although seraphs didn't breathe as humans did, they could still be distracted by battles. In this case, all the mini-shadows wanted to do was minimize the ability Davin and Dmna had to protect the children.

With the two mighty seraphs occupied with the irritating skirmish, the snake was free to take on his target. No seraphs to interfere, parents watching the soccer games were too far to make any real time impact, the snake quickly moved toward Bethany and Jovan.

He looked back nervously to ensure the seraphs were no longer attentive to him as they continued to fight off the shadows.

Quietly, the snake crept within the grass, focusing around Jovan's ankle for starters. He coiled his tail in excitement and snapped toward the children.

A split second before he could reach his target, a sight of great horror appeared before him. A human-looking foot in what appeared to be a sandal came crashing down directly in front of Jovan completely blocking the snake from reaching his target.

"Ambiandis, no," a man's calm voice was heard. Not by the children, but the snake certainly did hear it. He froze in reverence. The mini-shadows also heard it and fled in fear.

Davin and Dmna collapsed in exhaustion.

"*Uh, uh* L-L-ord," the snake stuttered. "W-what can I-I help y-you with?"

"Why do you call me Lord? Is not your lord, the Red Knight, Khrimson?"

"Who... *um*... me? I'm just a snake. I was at the nearby zoo, and somehow I got here. Just let me be, and I'll be on my way."

"AMBIANDIS!" the voice sternly. "Your tricks don't deceive me. I order you out of Xlumi!"

The serpent's eyes glowed red in anger. "Leave me be!"

"Spirit of the shadow, I command you to retreat from this body and return from whence you came. Never return here."

At that second, a red and black shadowy mist came out from the snake, the mist had red, then yellow eyes, and darted off world within a nanosecond.

The snake called Xlumi shook his head and looked around in completed confusion. "Um… where am I?"

He looked around some more and none of the surroundings looked familiar to him at all. He then looked in the direction of the being that had commanded Ambiandis to leave. "Sir, do you know what has happened to me? I feel a sense of freedom, but I am lost. I don't know where I am."

"Xlumi, you were possessed by a shadow knight called Ambiandis. He had complete control over you, and if he wasn't checked, these two children would have been no more."

The snake was startled. *How could I have allowed this?*

"You did not. He forced control upon you against your will, without your knowledge. That is the way of Khrimson."

Xlumi raised his head up and looked at the being. The being wore a long gown as if it had been made from ivory tusks, but the robe itself flowed like a river. He couldn't help but notice sparkling rows of clear gold woven throughout the robe. He could not see his face, but he felt a presence that had only been told to him through legend. Xlumi slowly bowed his head and asked, "Are you not the Lord Jaesu, Son of the Great Father of Evermore?"

"I am," Jaesu said, while gently placing his hand on the side of the snake's face.

"And you have come here? For these children? All the way from Evermore?"

"Yes," Jaesu said. "But not just for them."

Xlumi looked at Jaesu in wonder.

"Xlumi, many of your kind don't know me," Jaesu said.

"Well, Lord, no disrespect intended, but the whole rumor of heels crushing our heads gets around."

Jaesu smiled compassionately at the snake. "Could you suppose that is meant for just one serpent?"

Xlumi raised his head and basked in the light from Jaesu's face. "I could suppose. It's reserved for Khrimson."

"Rightly, you have said," Jaesu answered.

"Why else have you come then?" Xlumi asked.

"Well, although many of your kind have not known me, your mother was one of the few who sought me out and always prayed to me for you and your purpose."

"I see, well, what took you so long then? It's not like she prayed those prayers yesterday. She died in the zoo shortly after I was born. And now I am in a new zoo. Well, actually now, I'm lost."

"I have come at the time appointed for your purpose. And what a just one it is."

"Can I refuse?"

"You can," Jaesu answered.

"Will you smite me?"

"No."

"Punish me?"

"No."

"Chastise or insult me?"

"No."

"Force me to do it anyway?"

"No. All of those things are the ways of Khrimson. You have witnessed this firsthand, under the spell of Ambiandis."

Xlumi looked at him curiously again. "Well, then why would I do this thing, purpose, you have appointed for me?"

"Because deep down, it is truly your greatest desire. I am here to reveal that path to you."

Xlumi's spirit within him jumped slightly for the first time since he was very young. His insides trembled. "Unity among my species?"

"Not just yours. But all. And a bridge from all species to mankind."

"A bridge? Like in the legends of the Adam's day?" Xlumi asked excitedly.

"The same."

"But how——"

"Tell them of me."

"But many know of you. They know you are of the humans, which many of us fear."

"I am for all. There are no limits or bounds to my love and sacrifice."

"The third door is r-real?" Xlumi gulped.

"Yes." Jaesu smiled.

"Well, then let me ask you this," Xlumi asked in a doubting tone, "if you are for all, how are you just here for these children who are just talking, and even me, why me? What about the beggar woman, or the buck whose antlers are being ripped from his head while he is yet alive simply for man's pleasure, or the wars of man? Aren't you better off in those places?"

A tear fell from Jaesu's eye, and although the snake could not see his face, he could feel the tear as if it were a massive vibration from a thunderstorm. Jaesu then waved his hand over the snake's eyes and tongue. "Now, for this moment, you may use your actual eyes to see clearly, as if they were mine."

Xlumi, in immediate amazement, saw hundreds, thousands, and millions of Blue Fire Spirits.

Then the glimpse stopped.

"Please, let me see more, just a little longer."

"In due time, my friend, more will be revealed to you."

"That spirit was everywhere it seemed. Even for a split moment, it felt like unexplainable power. With such power, you could conquer all evil before it happens."

"I have and I will."

"I don't understand, Lord."

"Like many worlds created by the Great Father of Evermore, this world has a king. Its ruler is man. Man is charged with the governance of Earth. Therefore, his freewill and desires are its king. And in this day and age, many worship and serve themselves and their own perceived desires. I do not interfere in the matters of freewill."

"But why not? If you know what is best?"

"Because those are the ways of Khrimson. The power you saw is that of true love. I offer my love and hope and freedom freely, not by force. Man must choose from his own heart who and what he truly loves. But again more shall be revealed to you in due time. It is time for you take on your purpose. Are you ready?"

"Ready? It's not every day that the Lord Jaesu delivers me from the wicked one and offers me a ticket toward my heart's truest desire, so in that case, I am ready. But I can't help but feel anxious about the task, I mean, what is it that I can do? I am just a zoo snake, unfamiliar with the wild."

"My vision doesn't see what you are by your own limitations or circumstances, but who you are by what you were meant to be. So start with one. One tree, or fellow snake, or bird ... wherever you go, tell them of me, of this encounter and your faith will grow stronger." Jaesu then turned his attention toward a sewer entrance and raised his hand pointing to it. "There. Begin your journey in there. Many of those trapped within the depths of Earth are destined to be freed and part of its magnificence. Begin there and be encouraged that the journey will take you to many places."

"Okay, one more question, Lord. This bridge you speak of. Man has slaughtered many beasts over the ages for trivial pleasures. Is there a human building a bridge toward our kind from their side?"

Jaesu remained silent but for a moment thought of Amana. And just his thoughts alone put the snake's apprehension on the subject to rest.

"Over there you say?" Xlumi looked inquisitively at the sewer hole. "But wouldn't it be—Lord? Lord, where'd you go?"

Jaesu vanished from sight.

The snake let out a sigh and slowly slithered toward the sewer Jaesu had revealed to him. The closer he got to the sewer, the more he could hear voices growing louder and louder. They were from the mini-shadows, who he could both hear and see from where he was in the grass.

"Xlumi, Jaesu did not command you, did he? He said you wouldn't be punished. He knows nothing of the battles. Go back to the zoo, your home, where you belong. There's nothing for you down in the grimy hole."

Xlumi paused.

"We could lead you back to the zoo. Safely we will." They were attempting to encourage him off of his newfound path.

Xlumi looked ahead toward the sewer and then back toward the zoo, and once again at the sewer.

Jovan and Bethany were completely oblivious to all that had gone on around them.

"How about you race me?" Bethany asked.

"Race you? You're a girl. It wouldn't be fair," Jovan responded.

Bethany smirked. "You are in big trouble, mister." She took a few steps to the starting line. "Are you ready or what?"

Jovan had never raced a girl before. He actually didn't usually race anyone but himself. Truth be told, he was quite nervous.

"Set?" Jovan said as he lined up next to Bethany.

The two of them stared into each other's eyes and couldn't help but be happy. Bethany even let out her slight trademark giggle before doing her best to focus on the challenge.

"GO!" they said in harmony, and the race began.

The track was a half-mile long. Both runners took off with great speed. To their eyes, the park was empty, and it was them racing alone. But what they couldn't have known was that thousands and thousands of seraphs and angels were gathering quickly as if the soul mates were racing inside of a massive coliseum. The Jovan versus Bethany rivalry, when it came to racing, was well-known throughout both Evermore and the Elevemada system. And now it was quite the treat for the spirits positioned on Earth.

The crowds roared. Some were rooting for Jovan and some for Bethany. It was neck and neck. Every time one would pull ahead, the other would catch up.

For a split second, Jovan thought about slowing down just enough for Bethany to take the lead and win, thinking that it would make her feel better.

"Don't you dare slow down!" Bethany shouted as if she could read his mind.

That was all Jovan needed to hear, assuring him that she was every bit as fast as him, if not faster, regardless of her gender.

They were more than halfway home and neither one would give an inch. Jovan was trying his best for a win, but he would have settled for a close loss if it meant keeping his friendship with Bethany. Bethany felt the same. This moment was the happiest she had been since the Christmas Eve party where she first met Jovan and before she lost her mother. She felt that for some reason this was where she was supposed to be. Bethany couldn't imagine herself anywhere else at this moment.

She looked at the upcoming finish line and at Jovan. He was still step for step with her. She had to win, but in her heart, Bethany felt that she already had.

"Come on!" Jovan barked with a newfound confidence. "You are better than this! Keep up!"

*   *   *

"Yes," Phyllis answered a phone call through her pearl blue-toothed earrings. "She's safe, and okay? At the park with that Jovan kid, I suspect?" She looked at Josephus and nodded while still listening intently to the person calling her at the estate. "No, Jennings shouldn't be punished for bringing her against my wishes. He's her servant, if she wanted him to take her, then— well, it doesn't matter. They will be home soon enough. And what of the mother, Dara? Remember, she is the real prize here."

Phyllis smiled subtly upon hearing the response. "Excellent. Just keep an eye on her for the day. We will use Bethany's friendship with …this boy and my connections to Lyanne for leverage."

Josephus shook his head in amazement. "Is there anything you won't manipulate?" he said as he toasted his morning coffee with his wife's champagne glass.

"No, no need to keep watch on Bethany."

Phyllis continued her phone conversation. "She's in good hands with Jennings overseeing her. Let's just watch Dara. Everything has gone according to our plan, and I've got big plans for her." Phyllis sipped her customary weekend morning beverage. "Yes, as always, you never disappoint. Yes, and you, too…deary."

Phyllis kissed Josephus on the cheek and whispered, "You know what you signed up for."

*　*　*

Bethany and Jovan's race was a dead heat. Both were going at it as hard as they could. Jovan felt as if this was as fast as he had ever run. Bethany had brought something out in him that, at his young age, he never knew existed within him. And for Bethany, she felt a security and a trust around Jovan not known before. She had run many races in track leagues and was a local champ for Ivy prep students.

At the finish line awaiting them, laughing and rooting them on, was Jaesu.

With one step until the race concluded, Jovan and Bethany gave each other a quick glance and then put their heads down, intensely focused on the win.

The race ended. The crowds erupted, and the two children laughed feverishly.

It was close. No one in the crowd could decipher who won. Only Jaesu could determine the true victor.

"So close," Jovan said.

"You're right, Jovan. So close," Bethany responded as she placed her hand on his shoulder, trying to catch her breath.

Regardless of the wars and battles raging throughout the Earth or the galaxies, or the sickness, hatred, rebellion, and pain, it was this moment that was most important. The innocence and joy that only childhood friends could bring to the universe made the winner irrelevant.

They both had won this round.

"You are fast!" Jovan said to Bethany.

"You are, too!" she responded, still trying to catch her breath but still showing her glowing smile.

Jovan noticed a unique three-dotted birthmark in the form of an upside down triangle under Bethany's left ear. He went to gently touch it.

"Don't you dare!" she responded with a serious look and then a laugh. "Daddy says that's my sign from the golden eagles."

Jovan raised his eyebrows, not knowing how to respond to that.

"Want Jennings to take you home?" Bethany asked.

"No, thank you. Mom is over there, and I'm gonna watch the end of Zach's game," Jovan said, but he didn't want to conversation to end. "Jennings is nice. But he talks funny."

"Um...okay," Bethany giggled. "He's from England, silly. He thinks we talk very funny." Bethany, also not wanting the conversation to end, added a question of her own. "Who's Zach?"

"He's my older cousin. You see the one over there in the white and blue uniform, with the big afro? Yep, that's my best cousin."

Jovan walked Bethany halfway toward the limo, which was about as far as he could go while also remaining within Dara's sight.

"Maybe I could come with you next week to watch your cousin play?" Bethany asked.

"Yeah, okay," Jovan said, not knowing what to say while butterflies were exploding inside him.

The crowds of seraphs and angelic spirits who gathered for the race had followed them closely, still attempting to determine a winner. They had asked Jaesu to provide a ruling.

He turned to them, smiled, and then walked with the two Gardenians, placing his arms around them both.

"Do you feel that?" Jovan asked Bethany, just as Jaesu touched each of their shoulders.

"Goose bumps!" she responded, "I love this kind."

"Yes, me, too. Goose bumps."

THE END

"Before I formed you in the womb, I knew you."
Jeremiah 1:5

About the Author

John is an accomplished musician, songwriter, and has an affinity for Political Science, Psychology, and Biblical studies. He has two musical releases titled Political Novacane, and Choose This Day. He currently resides in Pennsylvania where usually he is guarded by a calico lioness; Evie. The Lighted Blade is John's debut novel.